Adam Foulds was born in 1974 and lives in South London. He is a graduate of the Creative Writing MA at the University of East Anglia and his poetry has appeared in a number of literary magazines. *The Truth about These Strange Times* is his first novel.

By Adam Foulds

The Truth about These Strange Times
The Broken Word (poetry)

The Truth about These Strange Times

ADAM FOULDS

To Felix,

with thanks & best wishes,

Adam Foulds

12th June 2008

PHOENIX

A PHOENIX PAPERBACK

First published in Great Britain in 2007
by Weidenfeld & Nicolson
This paperback edition published in 2008
by Phoenix,
an imprint of Orion Books Ltd,
Orion House, 5 Upper St Martin's Lane,
London WC2H 9EA

An Hachette Livre UK company

1 3 5 7 9 10 8 6 4 2

A CIP catalogue record for this book
is available from the British Library.

ISBN 978-0-7538-2409-2

Printed in Great Britain by Clays Ltd, St Ives plc

The Orion Publishing Group's policy is to use papers that
are natural, renewable and recyclable products and made
from wood grown in sustainable forests. The logging and
manufacturing processes are expected to conform to the
environmental regulations of the country of origin.

www.orionbooks.co.uk

To Jenny

'Come, come, what kind of nonsense is that?' said M'sieur Pierre, squirming in his chair. 'Only in fairy tales do people escape from prison. As for your remarks about my physique, kindly keep them to yourself.'

Invitation to a Beheading
VLADIMIR NABOKOV

PART I

Burnley, How Howard Met Saul

'The fact is,' Mr Cox dragged a four-link paper clip chain a few inches across the pine of his desk with a stocky forefinger, 'we think that you are, essentially, failing.'

'Oh.' Howard rocked his upper-body bulk back slightly to absorb the news, or at least to appear to absorb what wasn't really news any more, this being his third disciplinary visit to Mr Cox's office. Maybe if he really thought about it he would feel ashamed but at that moment the sensation of caring eluded him.

Mr Cox leaned forward smoothing his moustache with two short digits, splaying them as the fingertips slid to the sides in a vaguely obscene V. These hypnotic fingers were then redeployed for counting. 'A, you're not punctual; you don't turn up for shifts, and when you are here your work's completely half-hearted. You're just not a worker, Howard.'

'I see.' Howard looked over Mr Cox's head at the poster of the ponytailed smiling woman made of equal parts Lycra and contoured brown flesh. There was an unpleasant widening silence with Mr Cox's bald head in the middle of it. Howard suggested: 'Is it because I'm fat?'

'No, it isn't. Not really.' Mr Cox slumped back into his swivel chair and dropped his arms down over its sides in a demonstration of exhausted patience. 'You're not wrong, however' (Mr Cox made three separate facial expressions on that last word, all of them sarcastic), 'that your physical appearance isn't ideal for a gym, for a fitness and leisure environment, the only premiere facility of its kind in the Burnley area. It is not in all honesty the sort of image Falcon's wishes to project to our clientele but we'll not be prejudiced about it . . .'

Howard watched the striping reflections of the fluorescent lights slide about on Mr Cox's bald head, a narrow, knuckly head, and thought how nice it would be to give it a slap, not because he was angry at him – although the conversation was embarrassing, painful – but just because it would be so much fun. A good, resounding, open-handed, hard spank on his head.

'What we're trying to create here is an aspirational environment, somewhere which makes people want to train, a place which reflects that part of themselves they like and want to build on.'

'But can they no just look at me and think, *God, I don't want to look like that big Scots lummox who collects the towels. I shall certainly stay off this kids for another ten minutes?*'

'Do you expect me to answer that?' Mr Cox sort of hung his face contemptuously at Howard. His expression showed four of his front teeth.

Howard was confused. Why wouldn't he answer that? He pushed his glasses up his nose thinking, *I'd better be careful, God knows I need this money.* 'No, Mr Cox.'

'Your personal appearance isn't your strongest feature, we've established that, and while your tasks may be limited to laundry and refuse, you are still a representative of this company. An ambassador.' That was just what the nuns at primary school used to say, 'An ambassador for St Xavier's,' before taking them out to be madly bored at the shipbuilding museum. 'I don't expect you to look like any of the personal trainers, but you could at least look like you wash your uniform once in a while. I mean, Christ alive, you do work in the laundry.'

Mr Cox's voice was raised now and Howard knew he had to retreat, assume the bad-dog cringe. He dropped his head and looked at the big red hands that lay in his lap.

'I'm sorry, Howard, but I don't want to be having this little chat either. I've got a business to run. So, because I don't want us to waste any more time like this, I'm going to make this an official warning.' Howard looked up, mouth open. 'It's a simple three-strikes-and-you're-out formula and you can count this as strike one. There are lots of other buggers round here who'd be very happy to have your job so don't push it.'

Howard looked down again at his hands, six foot three of postural apology. 'I mean, how old are you now, Howard?' Mr Cox asked him.

'Twenty-eight.'

'You're twenty-eight,' he repeated, with dire implication. 'It's time to get a life, son.' Howard nodded. 'Ay. I'm sorry, Mr Cox. I've had a lot on my mind mind. I've—'

'I'm not bothered about all that, Howard.' Mr Cox's voice was gentle in victory. 'Just be on time and smarten yourself up a bit.'

Stepping out of Mr Cox's office Howard felt a slap on his back, a macho-friendly, not really friendly at all whack which was hard enough to sting and knocked his glasses half an inch down his nose. Howard knew it could only be, inevitably, the last person he wanted to see after his 'little chat'.

'Y'aright, big man? In trouble again?' Hassan grinned at him.

Howard shunted the bridge of his glasses with his right middle finger. 'Not really. Not trouble. The man's just told me to be, you know, more punctual an' that.'

'Oh, ay. Did you tell him to buy you an alarm clock for Christmas?'

Maybe one of the reasons Hassan obviously didn't like Howard was because Howard never found his jokes funny, found them hard to identify as jokes in the first place and therefore never laughed when Hassan wanted him to. Howard opened his mouth and breathed out through an ambiguous smile.

'Yeah, and tell him to get you some weights as well, you fat bastard.'

Hassan was short and square-chested with thick, hairy, fascinatingly unpleasant legs, which Howard found himself looking at whilst Hassan trained between clients in the main gym. Hassan always watched himself in the wall mirrors as he lifted weights, even afterwards just walking about and towelling his neck. If Howard had had to describe Hassan he would have got stuck on the fact that he bore a weird but compelling resemblance to Howard's waist-high fridge. The likeness was so strong that Howard had tried, one night of too many lonely beers, to draw Hassan's face on its door with a felt-tip. Hassan's face, however, turned out to be hard to draw, being just a plain brown rectangle with heavy eyebrows as the only distinguishing characteristic. Howard's drawing bore no resemblance to the man and he had tried to rub it off immediately. There was still a greasy blue ink stain on Howard's fridge which he somehow held Hassan responsible for, adding to his dislike. Howard also now obscurely disliked his fridge and kept meaning to stick something over the dirty blur which had never been Hassan but somehow very much was him in its general power to lower Howard's mood when he reached for milk for his tea or for cold baked beans.

'You're a big lad, Howie. If you turned all that lard into muscle you'd be a 'cking monster. But you won't,' Hassan sprang back and uncurled a slow-motion roundhouse kick to Howard's belly, ''cause you're a lazy fucking smoker.'

'Are you finished now, pal?'

'Och ay the noo, yes, I am. Go and pick up them sweaty towels, laundry man.' Howard walked away, muttering 'Prick' under his breath as he went.

'What were that? You want some, big boy?'

Howard went to find Andy at the bar. The gym was decorated for Christmas, the narrow, noisy corridor alongside the squash courts hung with tinsel and springy foil bells. Falcon's had also commissioned its own Christmas graphics and bandy-legged elves in vests with heavily muscled torsos and violently red cheeks expressive of cardiovascular health and good cheer grinned down, flexing, from the walls. They added to the unpleasantness of this corridor. Howard hated the walloping percussions of the squash courts, the grunts of men flung about in their game, the squeaks of expensive trainers. He always took this passage at some speed.

In the bar, underneath a motivational poster depicting a hard-bodied man in T-shirt and shorts, appropriately and not unattractively sweat-stained, mid sit-up, his face contorted with a manful effort which suggested he was probably on his tenth set of fifteen, sat four pregnant women drinking fruit juice. Above their wet heads the poster said, Burn It! It must be Tuesday, Howard realised, because that was aquacise for mums-to-be. He liked seeing the pregnant ladies about the place, dazed and smiling glassily above their swollen bodies, easing themselves on chairs, or sailing past, calm ships. He liked their no-nonsense look: hair scraped back, no make-up on. They looked kind. The class for water babies was nice as well, each infant dwarfed by its flotation devices, wriggling and bubbling in the pool led around by a mum. Walking past the pregnant ladies, Howard smelt chlorine and soap, flowery shampoos. Andy nodded at him from the bar as he handed a frothy fruit cocktail to an old lady in tracksuit and glasses.

'You'll never guess what I did with Beautiful this morning,' Andy began as Howard subsided onto a stool. 'Move your big arms,' Andy told him, making swift circles on the counter with a cloth. 'She was in this morning looking like a bloody supermodel, sunglasses on 'er head in the middle of December, this short little skirt under a long coat and blouse and boots and obviously just out of the shower. I mean, God.' He mimed banging his head against the bar very hard twice. 'And I'm thinking, All right, Andy, why not just say something? Because she's ruining me life, in a way, coming here every other day looking like that. So she buys the strawberry and kiwi number she always gets and says, "Oh, I'm sorry, I've got no cash. Can I pay with a card?"' Howard found Andy's impression of a very attractive woman's voice a bit disturbing. 'And I can't speak and just nod like an idiot. Anyway, she hands it over and I do the card and everything and I'm handing it back to her and I'm definitely about to say something only my brain short-circuits and instead of saying something I— Oh my God, it's embarrassing.' Andy looked straight up at the ceiling as if to drain the memory from his head. 'I don't know why I did it unless it's because I always call her Princess and Beautiful in my mind but what I do is, instead of speaking, I sort of bow and kiss her card and receipt as I hand it to her.' Howard buried his face in his hands in sympathy. 'I mean, what the bloody hell were that? She looked at me like, well, like you would if someone had just turned all weird and medieval on you, and I thought if I say anything I'm only going to make it worse so I just pretend it's all perfectly normal even though I can feel I'm completely sweating and my face must be wah-wah-wah like a bloody traffic light and that only goes to make me spots look worse.'

Howard shook his head, peeping through fingers spread on his face. Andy shrugged. 'It's not like she's interested anyway. You've seen that car her boyfriend picks her up in. Still, she won't forget me, I reckon.'

'Oh ay, son. She'll remember you no problem.'

'Here,' Andy sidestepped to the fridge, 'd'you want a Coke? I'll tell you if Mr Cock is coming and hide it. Here, go on.' He levered the cap from a bottle and set it smoking in front of Howard.

'Thanks, pal.' Howard swallowed a flurry of sweet bubbles and burped immediately.

'Ooh, you filthy haggis.'

'Soft Sassenach.'

'Caber-tossing pig.'

'English wee card-kisser, you.' Howard made a kissy mouth. 'Mwa, mwa, mwa, mwa, mwa.'

'Bloody foreign Scottish— Oh Christ, it's Cocky. Quick.'

Mr Cox approached with quick scissory steps and tapped Howard on the shoulder, three hard, demeaning taps. Through clenched teeth he said, 'Towels. Now.'

On his way to his trolley Howard stepped out of the fire exit – checking quickly over his shoulder, leaning on the wide metal emergency handle, and disappearing suddenly through as if sucked out of an aeroplane door – to smoke a cigarette. He sat down on the cold step and lit up, narrowing his eyes against the dense white light that crowded down from the sky. The cold air ached against his front teeth. He smoked and between drags held his cigarette in his mouth and wedged his hands up into his armpits for warmth. Off-white sky and bitter wind; Lancashire was no different to Glasgow apart from the longer days. A few weeds struggled in the grim weather and Howard's eye was drawn to their little shaking movements. Nor was there much else to look at: wind-scraped puddles and Biffa bins. Shabby plants, unlovely, rusty with fungus, seemed still to thrive around a hot-water drain, one even still hung with tiny yellow flowers. On the roof above them a pigeon, huddled into itself for warmth, shifted on raw-looking toes. By the end of his smoke, despite his efforts, Howard's hands were gloved with numbness. Still, good to take a wee break, take your time. That Cocky should give himself a second to breathe.

Howard had just retrieved his trolley from the cupboard when he heard a familiar voice. ''Ello, love.' It was Mrs Dawson, an arthritic old lady who liked him for some reason and always stopped to chat. He turned around to greet her and immediately thought, *Something's wrong,* then, *No trousers!* Mrs Dawson stood there smiling in blouse and cardigan and large mushroom pants and nothing else.

'How are you, love?' she asked.

A sweat of embarrassment grew out of Howard's scalp. Her legs were veined and mottled and gathered like cloth at the knees, right there underneath her smiling face. Howard worked hard to master his expression and speak.

'I'm tip-top, Mrs Dawson. And yoursel'?'

'Oh, you know, I'm grand. Eeh,' she put a hand to her face, the other on her hip, teapot style, 'I've forgotten what I wanted to say . . .'

Inside his head Howard's voice screamed, *You've forgotten your trousers!* With Mrs Dawson standing in front of him tapping her chin, trying to remember, he wondered if this might not actually be the ideal moment to raise gently the lack of lower-half clothing but couldn't find the courage.

'Oh, well, couldn't have been that important. Yes, I'm just after using one of them walking machines and watching the telly with the headset – there was this thing on about a woman whose husband was one of them transvestites and likes to dress up, you know, as a lady, and he were sitting there, bold as anything next to his wife, in a big Laura Ashley number.' Mrs Dawson held Howard's thick, freckled forearm and laughed up into his face. *If she steps any closer her legs will touch me and somebody's going to walk past any minute,* Howard thought, unreasonably, as he'd never known anyone's legs to touch him during the course of normal conversation. He grinned tensely down at her. 'Well, I thought, if you don't mind your hubby dressed up like that why should anyone—' She broke off. 'I've remembered what I wanted to ask you. Are you any good with watches, clever chap like you, because mine's stopped.' She slipped it from her wrist, an elasticated strap bulging around her hand. 'You couldn't look at it, love. Gosh, it's hot in here. I'm just going to sit down a moment.' And she slumped backwards against the wall and slid down, her bare, wrinkled legs collapsing under her.

'Oh Jesus, Mrs Dawson?' Howard squatted down beside her. She kept her eyes on him but her neck muscles had gone and her head lolled, rolling. She moved her mouth to speak and Howard saw her upper dentures sliding from her gums. Howard had had basic first aid training along with all the other bullshit when he first started working for Falcon's but of course couldn't remember any of it. They had taken turns at giving the kiss of life to a freakishly breathing mannequin but Mrs Dawson was breathing, leaving him no obvious way to help her. And there was the recovery position. But then again weren't you supposed not to move them? 'Hold my arm,' he said, 'hold my arm.' It was the only thing he could think of and he clamped her hand to his forearm, holding it there himself because she had no grip.

She made a noise as she looked at him, a vowel that slowly surged out of her throat. 'Ngaaaa.'

Howard cried down the quiet corridor, 'Help! Somebody, please!'

Hassan was the first person there. 'What the fuck've you done?' he asked, squatting down on his heels.

'I haven't done anything; she just fell down.' Howard's imploring voice was high. Hassan fitted his fingers into Mrs Dawson's throat to take her pulse.

'Why are you doing that?' Howard begged. 'She's still conscious. She needs an ambulance. We're going to get an ambulance for you, Mrs Dawson.'

'It's a heart attack,' Hassan said.

Mrs Dawson wasn't making the vowel any more. She blew through her lips still looking at Howard. Howard thought of something and without hesitation or disgust reached a finger into her mouth and removed the floating denture. Hassan seemed impressed by that, crediting Howard enough now to get up and call the ambulance. 'If it turns out you did something,' he warned before he sprinted off.

Howard talked to Mrs Dawson quietly for the next ten minutes, promising to fix her watch, commenting on the awful weather, a bad time to be wandering about without your trewies on, cajoling her to stay awake, be patient, not worry, until two ambulance men in green jumpsuits arrived with a stretcher. Mr Cox stood by stroking his moustache nervously as they lifted her up. Mrs Dawson's eyes kept returning to Howard throughout and one of the paramedics, noticing this, said, 'You'd better come with us. Looks like you're keeping her awake.'

Howard blushed at the attention of the other staff, gathered there to cordon off the area. His skin prickled under their eyes, the least visible man in the gym now everybody's focus. He could tell that Mr Cox and Hassan weren't happy with his central role in this drama. He kept his eyes on the stretcher. 'It's all right, Mrs Dawson, you'll be fine.' He'd get the sack after this, definitely.

They exited through the fire door – Mr Cox was keen they shouldn't be seen out front – and walked past the shivering weeds, just the four of them now, towards the waiting ambulance.

Les stood amid the beautiful furnishings of his hallway, the curved wood and gilt mirror and thick cream carpeting, stood in his socks with a hand pressed to his forehead and stared at the phone, that puncture in the security of home through which all of his peace of mind now made a screaming exit like breathable air from a damaged fuselage. This was a bad time, Jesus Christ, for this to be happening, couldn't be a worse time. Years of nothing and suddenly this. He looked at the phone pad and the dark cross-hatchings he had etched around the floral ideogram printed on the page. Triangulated spikes ran along the top of the doodle. Underneath there were spirals and a fish. But he had time, maybe – what had the nurse said, weeks, maybe months, even years? Which, all right fine, months was what they needed in this most crucial time of preparation. And things were going so well. He said 'Fuck' looking down, hand still to his head, slamming into the consonant like kicking a wall – "ck!', the way you swear at home when you don't want people to hear you. Then he looked up, rolling his head in maybe an overdramatic way, to see his wife there, leaning into his space with concern. She was taller than him, still beautiful although her long back now had a gooseneck curve to it which he occasionally wondered if he had caused by her focusing her attention always down to him. That curve became more pronounced when she was tense, was visible now inside her fine cardigan. She stood with one arm crossed under her breasts, the other holding her necklace out to one side with a fingertip, a gesture that had developed once as flirtatious and had dried now into something else, a habit. Her blue eyes were wide, showing flecked whites all around the irises. Les said nothing, resisting.

'What is it?' she asked, more like released, translating her posture into words. Why did she have to appear immediately and not give him even just a moment? Round every corner the blue eyes, the high, expensive hair, the face more familiar than his own. Always having to account for himself. If it weren't for Saul he'd spend more time out of the house than he already did.

'Nothing,' he said. He watched her mouth open. 'Nothing. My mother. She's ill.'

'Seriously?'

'Do you mean am I or is it serious?'

'Les.'

'She's seriously ill.'

Saul now appeared in the doorway, inquisitive head wavering on its stalk of neck. He leaned against the jamb and put one wrinkle-socked foot on the other.

'Go back to that table, young man. Nobody said you'd finished.'

'Dad, I'm holding seventy-five in my head. I have to wait ten minutes before I write them down.'

'I said go back to that table.'

Howard shrugged on his coat and stepped outside to smoke a cigarette, narrowing his eyes at low sunshine and the blowing air. Cold drips fell from the roof onto the step next to him. They stretched in the air as they fell, looked long, light shining through them. Shrivelled snow still stayed on the square of lawn, or what you might take for lawn as long as you couldn't see it or whilst it was still winter and could appear legitimately dead. The air was a little freer and softer than it had been. Howard in his light coat realised he wasn't holding his ribs tense with his arms against his sides even though he could feel the wind bending back the prow of his hair. He reached with his spare hand to feel his bald spot, a recent discovery which was interesting to touch, smooth and cold. Tilting his head back, the fingers of his right hand bearing the cigarette to his lips, those of the left feeling the disc of skin at its edges where hair grew sidelong out and away from it, he looked at the sky and saw in its whiteness cracks of blue which right now were letting through the sun. Slow as an ocean liner the season was beginning to turn. Beyond the gardens and house tops prickly with aerials, away beyond the estate the snow on the hills had shrunk, splats of white-grey on khaki with spidery legs still clean and blue in clefts where streams ran down. Howard felt it for a moment, the season itself, a strong hand pressed gently to his chest. Then his eyes watered with looking at the distance. Instead he looked at next door's wristy, leafless tree, at the laundry snapping on the line a few doors up. Then nearer movement: the ginger cat Howard had named Ginger looked at him steadily from behind a pockmarked crust of snow. It bobbed its head once, still looking, then turned and cringed and dragged itself under the back fence with a surprisingly loud rasping sound of cat against wood. Howard heard a voice then and turned to see his neighbour come shuddering out into the light, head dropped, moaning to himself. Howard tucked himself out of sight in his doorway. The man stood and swayed, still drunk from the night before probably, and the fringes on his stupid cowboy coat fluttered. The light treated him rawly. His chin was sharp and stubbled, his eyes retreating into his face. The collar of his jacket was dark with grease from long hair that stuck together in strappy lengths and hung down his dirty neck. Howard found him frightening to look at, the man who kept him awake with country and western music until three in the morning, wailing with it, not even in time to the music, just crying out, a man completely lost to himself. Howard had no idea how he survived. The man turned and Howard shut his door.

Back inside, Howard made himself an instant coffee, hooking shut the door of the Hassan-fridge with his foot, then went upstairs to talk to his mother.

The smell in the room wasn't really hers any more. He'd kept buying the plug-in air freshener that she liked but the other smells were gone leaving only that clean chemical odour that was meant to make you think of mountains. Despite the fact that he hadn't changed anything in there, not moved the plants and photographs and knick-knacks, remade the bed, or even cleaned really, she was fading from the room. Dust had silvered the carpet during the six months of Howard's failure to clean. His footprints left darker smudges on the pile. The wardrobe was where she remained most strongly present, there and somehow in the bronze cross over the bed although that obviously belonged to Christ. It was to the wardrobe that he talked. Inside hung her dresses, a green winter coat. Her tops were folded on its shelves, her underwear hidden in its drawers. Empty shoes stood patiently, open-mouthed under the dresses. On a top shelf was the felt hat that always made him smile – she'd always looked so silly in it with its Robin Hood pointy brim and feather. He knocked gently once on the door then kept his hand pressed to it. 'Hi, Ma.' The wardrobe was chest height to him, about the same height she had been. The dark wood had fine patterns of darker grain that seemed to speed up and swirl around the knots and marked it here and there in a personal way. 'The weather's turning. I was just outside for a fag and it's starting to melt and everything. Ginger was out there, the wee feller you didn't like me feeding.' He took a sip of coffee, eyes resting on the Blackpool ornament on the window sill, a china post with a rubber ring and starfish which if it had been in proportion would have been about two feet tall. Howard's mother had a weakness for fancy goods, a Catholic tendency to meaningful clutter, and most corners of the place, most available surfaces in fact, held a dimpled child or smiling dog or a cat in an outfit. Two ballerinas kept dainty poses on his mother's bedside tables, the faint light of dust clinging to them. Behind them prayer cards picturing the Virgin and the skewered Sacred Heart leaned against the wallpaper. 'I'll get to dusting in here soon, Ma. You know it's just I'm so busy with work and Mrs Dawson and everything.' Between the Blackpool ornament and a goose wearing a bonnet stood a photograph of him aged ten still in the brown cardboard frame he'd brought it home from school in. His face looked slightly off to one side, averted from the gaze of the camera. His bulky body was tightly contained by his grey St Xavier's jumper with the scarlet cross over his heart. His soft white neck overlapped his whiter collar under which the lumpy knot of his tie was half hidden. Brass-wool hair brushed into waves. Pink mouth open and eyes without glasses shut tight against the flash although it looked just as much as though he had shut them to receive the thick spattering of freckles across his nose and cheeks. This image, being the one he saw most often as he preferred to avoid the unfriendliness of mirrors and was in this room with the photo every day, was more or less what he thought he looked like. Howard thought he resembled a giant version of that squirming, blinking child, which, naturally enough, wasn't entirely untrue. The goose in the bonnet next to the photograph must have been as old as he was. He remembered it looming invitingly above a raging radiator of sharp metal pleats in the first place he could remember, the flat in Glasgow with its bubbly wallpaper, chipped skirting boards, his father's dark legs and shirtless forearms, a balcony with big children playing below. Terrifying and exciting were their screams and running. Howard moved and sat down on the end of the bed in the wrinkled depression he had left the last time and faced the wardrobe saying nothing for a couple of minutes. His mind went quiet. He licked the side of his mug where drips of coffee had formed a sticky stain, licking carefully to make it completely clean. 'Ay, Ma, right y'are. I'll just go downstairs now,' he said eventually. 'I'll leave you to it.'

He walked down into the living room and subsided groaning onto the couch with a practised single move that included sweeping up the remote and flicking on the television. Just a few minutes more before going out to face the world. Things were so much easier at home without other people squeezing him with their looks, dismissing him, ordering him about. Howard preferred to be invisible, beyond notice, which was easy, mostly, being menial. A newsreader's square head appeared on the screen. What the hell time was it? Christ, he'd be late for work.

'Evening, Howard. How are we today?'

'Oh, ay, not too bad.' Howard looked at the nurse's clean parting as she bent over her pile of forms, eyelashes beating. 'And yourself?'

'Oh, you know. Busy.' Her biro made small sticky sounds as she rapidly filled in shaded boxes. The sound, her quick hand, made Howard want to sit and watch her as she worked. The sensual quietness of women working: his mother cooking, patting mutton mince and onion into pie crust at the kitchen table; the nice art teacher at St Xavier's who would add guiding touches to his work, one hand on his shoulder, her pencil light and perfect. 'Your aunt's not any better, I'm afraid.'

'I know,' Howard sighed, crossing his arms with his hands flat against his breasts. 'My aunt,' he improvised, 'she were bad off and on for a while, you know.' His face contracted with panic, though, when he thought of the medical files the nurse must have seen. Mrs Dawson's collapse might have been completely out of the blue.

'It's good that you come and visit. I'm sure it makes a difference to her.'

She looked up at him, full-faced, near. Soft white hairs on her cheek were caught by her desk light and glowed in a slightly holy way. Pretty! A hand shot up to Howard's face and found something to do adjusting his glasses.

'Ay, well, I'd best be getting in there then.'

'I'll see you later, Howard.' She bent back over her work.

Howard walked the grey linoleum corridor, the floor squeaking under his trainers, to the room in which Mrs Dawson lay.

She was still the same, afloat on her bed, tube fed, a monitor bleeping out the rhythm of her recovering heart. She looked so light and old now that Howard imagined she'd levitate up towards the fluorescent lights if he unhooked her from the machines. Her cheekbones stood out; the crooked bones in her hands were sharp. She was dwindling painfully into focus.

'Hello, Mrs D,' he said as he sat down, touching her wrist lightly with one meaty finger.

'How are you today? I see, I see. Nice nurses looking after you. Nice weather today. Warming up a bit.' Howard noticed a smell and wondered if he should call a nurse. He bent forward to sniff the air over the old woman and traced the reek back to his own hands soiled with the sweat of the towels he had collected at the gym. He must have forgotten to wash them again. Despite the smell, he preferred collecting those training towels rather than the wet ones in the changing rooms where he was surrounded by alarming, brisk, completely naked men, a very odd sensation when you're fully dressed and can't help looking at all the knobs and bums just because it's the last thing you want to do. The pong of his hands lowered his mood by a notch or two as he remembered. 'I'm still in a bit of trouble at work, Mrs D. On my second strike with Co—with Mr Cox. I don't tell my ma about it really because I don't want her to worry even though I know she knows anyway.' The door opened, pushed by the round back of a lady called Doris whose mother was hooked up on the other side of the room and who always seemed to be carrying heavy shopping bags. The other lady in the room never seemed to be visited at all except by that awful Protestant lady who read the Bible to her.

Doris pulled in a tartan trolley behind her. 'Hello,' she said, then mouthed, 'How is she?'

'She's not too bad. Sometimes it sounds like her heart gets quicker when I'm talking.'

'Oh, that's good. My mother's the same.' Doris removed a quilted coat and hung it on a hook by the door, touching her hair into shape afterwards. 'I'll leave you to it, then,' she said and settled herself by her mother. In a few moments she was under way, starting, as she always did, in tears.

Howard turned back to Mrs Dawson, recommencing audibly with, 'So, Auntie,' then dropping his voice to continue, 'you see the thing is I need this job, you know, with the rent and everything which is getting difficult, and when Ma's money has run out I just don't know even if anyway I have the job.' Howard pushed his glasses up his nose then squeezed his knees, rocking, thinking. 'Not that you want to hear about all this, like this will wake you up, which you're going to do very

soon anyway, hearing about Mr Cox and the rent man. I saw
Ginger in the garden again today hiding behind the snow like
I couldn't see him. I bet he spends all night by the fire after
that hot as anything. Next door come out looking the worse
for it, not that I care. Kept me up into the wee hours with
Hank Williams. I mean, a cowboy round here. That cat –
little eyes looking at me like, "Oo, there's the big man now?"'
Howard paused again and tuned into Doris reading the paper
to her mother, the story of a missing student, 'a superbright
stunna' who'd gone missing from her home in Canterbury the
week before. She must be worse than him with his tales of the
rent man for making someone glad they were out of it. He
looked at Mrs Dawson and thought, *Come back.* He sat still
and looked at her for a while. Her hair was still growing;
it made a larger cloud now around her head. Read them
horoscopes, he thought; that way they'll want to come back
for their future. Or stories: find out what happens. A spray of
gurgling acid in his stomach reminded Howard that he was
hungry. He could get chips on the way back then telly then
bed as long as the cowboys weren't wailing. 'I best be off for
me tea, Auntie,' he said. 'Next time I'm back I want to see you
wide awake. I'm off now, Doris, bye.' Doris looked round and
said goodbye to him with her face as she kept on reading, the
way you do while you're talking to someone on the phone.

March 8th

In the stillness he sits and looks at her, alone among the sleeping women. At first it is hard to look, the day's agitations bubble up through him, his head is cloudy with thoughts of the landlord's visit. A nice, windswept, family sort of man wearing a brown anorak over his suit, balding with a torn scrap of hair fluttering from his forehead, he was firm and not unfriendly when he spelt out clearly what would happen: bailiffs will come to remove items to the value of the rent in arrears. Howard nodded, 'The rent I haven't paid yet,' trying to guess the value of the TV, the fridge, the beds.

'That's right. It's mounted up, Howard. I'm going to send you a letter, okay, so, spelling it all out, okay, so, and I want you to read it carefully so you understand exactly, okay?' Afterwards Howard couldn't face telling his mother that it was going to go, their clean house in England free of his father, that it would be taken away by strangers bit by bit. If he'd known about benefits that might help, but that was taboo to his mother. Howard had never seen the inside of a dole office. After Ridgemont he knew never to trust the authorities. The thought made him sick with horror. He had meant to tell Mrs Dawson about it but now sat there looking at her waiting for his thoughts to quieten down.

He thought of the gym, the sight of Andy silent and shamed and suffering as Beautiful approached the bar for a drink. He thought of Mr Cox stalking past as he was again standing still staring at the TV screens in the gym, five channels all without sound but still hypnotic. Least he didn't stand there like Hassan, scowling at the rhythmical buttocks of the exercising women. He thought that he missed his bus so often that he really should start thinking of the next bus as his bus. He thought of the empty house, frail as an eggshell, and the wardrobe alone there. He thought again of the landlord and the bailiffs. He wondered if the cowboy would be keeping him up tonight. He wondered if they still had the 99p Mariner's Pie in the corner shop because they didn't always.

And then after ten minutes of watching her breathe, hearing the regular beep of the heart monitor, it was all gone and what was left was the clear water of being there and looking. She had outlasted it. Was still there. Her skin had a silver shine and looked so thin, kind of worn out and crispy, looking breakable on her arms. Her eyelids were tenderest with like leaf skeletons of red veins. The knuckles of her left hand were twisted with arthritis. It rested, tagged around the wrist, a delicate claw on the bed sheets. He hadn't dared to put on her the watch he had taken to be repaired while she slept, not wanting to do any damage. It lay now on the table beside the bed. He realised he didn't really know what her right hand looked like, always sitting on this side of her body. Lines converged towards her mouth, fine pleats and wrinkles like the grain of the wardrobe around the knots. Her mouth had sunken − they must never have replaced the wandering false teeth. The dark lips looked dry. A few hairs strayed out from the knob of her chin. Her ears were shiny and yellow.

Looking. Somewhere inside that body Mrs Dawson slept, hid, had crept down out of the way. Hidden like crystals in a cave. So unlike his mother's quick, convulsive exit, this leaving the world in stages, leaving a feeding body like something to step over. And leaving hope, hope for ages, that kept your heart squeezed thinking it might be all right again, that nobody was going to die, that she was going to come back. 'Mrs Dawson,' he whispered, 'can you hear me, darlin'?' And her immortal soul, where was that? Howard didn't have to ask. He definitely felt it there in the room, roosting like a bird up in the corner behind his shoulder. So why wouldn't it fly back in? What on earth was there to stop it flying back in?

March 12th

Howard looked at Mr Cox across the desk. Mr Cox leaned forward, elbows on pale pine the cleaners had sprayed and wiped at the beginning of the day, hands up, palms pressed together in an explanatory posture. Keeping the heels of his hands together, he clapped to begin.

'So I suppose you can guess why I've called you in.'

'Not really.'

'Howard, please don't make this any more difficult than it has to be.' Howard didn't see that this was going to be difficult for Mr Cox. He thought it might be rather enjoyable for Mr Cox. He considered slapping his bald head again, this time with lethal power. The muscles in his throat were very tight as he chewed back unexpected tears and mashed his sweaty hands together in his lap.

'You want to give me a raise?' Howard felt his mouth trembling. He felt ugly with rage and stupid that all that Mr Cox thought about him was true.

'Howard, please.'

Stupid to let this go on longer than it had to. 'Shall I just get going then?' Howard asked, making to rise, his hands on the arms of his chair.

Mr Cox sighed, dropped his hands and fell back into his revolving chair, which emitted a cartilagey creaking sound. 'Might as well.'

Howard followed through on his altered posture and got up. 'Right, bye then,' he said lamely. Outside the door he thought, *Fucker! Waiting till the end of my shift to sack me.*

Howard was making for the door when he thought to go

and tell Andy, whom he found alone, sitting behind the bar with only the top half of his face visible, watching the sports channel they pumped into there all day.

'Well, you won't be seeing my ugly face around here any more,' he called.

'You what? Did he finally do it? That Cocky's a bastard.'

'Ay, well. I had it coming a wee bit maybe.'

Andy laughed, a single slingshot from the diaphragm that knocked his head back. His laugh always seemed uncontrollable and left him looking sheepish, swallowing. 'Ay, you might have done,' he said. 'Here, why don't you take my number so we can meet up in the real world some time maybe.' Howard's heart, still sour from his meeting with Mr Cox, now fluttered with pleasure. Howard liked Andy, found he alone made the job more than just about bearable, but he had never seen him outside of Falcon's. He never saw anyone, being happier out of the way at home, watching telly with his mother upstairs. Or visiting only Mrs Dawson now. His hand actually trembled as he wrote down Andy's number on the back of a Falcon's card and he had to restart it on another several times he was so flustered at the thought of this friend. When he'd finally got it down Andy said, 'Now all you have to do is learn how to use the phone.'

The bus ride home was awful. Waiting in the shelter, rain blew sideways onto Howard out of the night. The large hard spaces of the dual carriageway were painful in a lonely, empty, public way. And now home was doomed. Safety was doomed and Howard had nothing to do but wait and think of the bailiffs arriving at his door. Out of a window streaked with shuddering drops, Howard looked at the yellow lights of other people's safe front rooms. At one stop, an old man took at least five minutes to get on the bus, struggling up with sticks and a trolley. When he got home, Howard decided he'd buy a big meal at the chippie, cod and peas and everything, large chips. Food was so lovely and warm, so friendly, a home in the night and bad weather.

Alf, the chip shop man, somehow spotted that something was wrong. 'What's a matter you? Face like your dog dead.'

'I lost my job.'

'So. That's okay. I give you a job. Work here. My cousin who works here is gone, back to Portugal to his father farm again. He not like Burnley. I been working myself down into the ground on my own this week and you never even notice. Sometimes I think you only love me for my chips.'

Alf was small, jerky, marionettish, very mobile on his slippered feet – checked carpet slippers Howard would have never guessed at from the other side of the counter – Portuguese, with waxy yellow skin, wide, puffy sockets around lashless eyes, a shiny broken nose and deep-fried black hair. That he was a boxing enthusiast Howard already knew from the photographs along the tiled walls. Among the pictures of dinners you could have was Muhammad Ali young and hand-some, leaning over his fists towards the camera; two fighters Howard couldn't identify, one receiving a mighty punch on the left cheek, eyes closed, face crumpled, sparks of sweat metallic in the camera flash, but looking oddly peaceful as though resting his head on that giant fist to go to sleep. There was a faded colour photo of Henry Cooper, grey haired, in a neat tracksuit, a smiling elder statesman of the sport. Also there was an old black and white photo of a Portuguese fea-therweight with tiny legs emerging from enormous silk shorts, heavy eyebrows, a lacquered quiff, lover-boy eyes and gloveless hands held in bandaged half-fists. 'This one,' Alf explained, 'is one of the greatest fighters, quick like bang what happen but also clever, sly man, and fights all day like a dog, but nobody knows him because who wants to know about fea-therweights? He could make like,' Alf danced in front of Howard, jabbing air, 'bang, bang, bang, you sleep like a big baby.'

Howard had a thought. 'It's not you is it, Alf?'

'No, not me. I spar him one time. He beat the shit out of me real quick.'

Howard was immensely happy to have landed this job at the chip shop, a place he knew and liked, learning a trade which maybe could become his own. He pictured himself as the round, red-faced, smiling owner of a chip shop, spraying vinegar into an expert paper cone of chips, angling sleek battered sausages into the ticking oil, exchanging pleasantries with his devoted customers.

It was the exact opposite place, he realised, to Falcon's gym. While bodies there had been spare, tightening, self-punishing, rich and vain, expensive healthy bodies, those in the chip shop were spreading and softening although there were some dog-skinny little working blokes who looked unable to put on weight no matter how many jumbo saveloys they ate. Likewise the young lads in baseball caps with the fat sisters. There was less conversation than in the gym also, less hanging about, although people were friendly enough. Alf talked to the people waiting in the chip shop, chirruping away in his funny English to men who held five-pound notes in paint-spattered hands that looked so worked they seemed hardly able to close them. Meanwhile Howard discovered his life's true forte: skulking in the corner with a mop or a cloth in his hand.

Also, Howard would never have to buy himself dinner again. And he could have chicken, saveloys, fish, pies, anything. The variety was endless.

Alf's real name was the comical Alfonso. Howard learned this when he first heard Alf's wife call him from the home behind the shop, a dark, Catholic gloom that none of the customers would have imagined, a whole world through a trap door. She shuffled forward on Howard's first day to meet him, pudgy hands clasped in front of her, black clothes, cylindrical, ankleless legs, a gold cross wriggling on her enormous chest. 'Hello, hello,' she said quietly, nodding, before turning to speak in rapid Portuguese to Alfonso. She hadn't raised her eyes to Howard at all, as though looking directly at his big, freckly, profane face might be too much for her nerves.

Howard wanted to explain that it was familiar to him too, the Catholic darkness, the twitching candles, the atmosphere in churches of a huge holy cupboard, the books, beads, whispers and bells. Mrs Alfonso, Theresa, wouldn't think it possible that he had grown up with the same circling nuns. She didn't even seem to speak English. She receded back into the flat still clutching her hands in front of her, apparently imploring to be left alone.

'She wears black all the time,' Alf whispered, lips beaky behind a shielding hand. 'Sometimes I look at her and think I'm dead already.' He shrugged, turning a pickled cucumber jar so that its label faced outwards. 'She is a good woman, though. Keeps the nice house. Maybe we send for her sister for you. You get on well. She's blind. Eh?' Alf sprang towards him, fluttering punches into his personal space. 'Eh? Eh?' He stopped, again apparently as calmly contemplative as he had been thinking of his wife's finer qualities, then said, 'One thing I forget to tell you today – never do this.' Alf pretended to plunge his hand into the heating oil and writhed around on buckling legs as if electrocuted.

Howard laughed, a high, nervous snort. 'I'll try not,' he said breathily, pushing his glasses back up his nose.

Howard loved the new job. The only problem, as he explained to Mrs Dawson but not his mother, whom he was too scared to tell (even though he knew she knew), was that the job paid even less than the gym, even after you subtracted money for dinners and there'd now be no way to keep the bailiffs from the door.

At six in the morning there was a thunder of knocking. Howard, his head soggy with dreams, ran downstairs in his vest and gaping boxer shorts, his heels thumping painfully on the thin carpet of the stairs, his breasts jogging, his chest full of panic and one hand he had been sleeping on stiff-fingered, buzzing with pins and needles. At the bottom he found that the noise, thank God, the noise was coming from next door. Howard could hear the cowboy on the other side of the wall protesting, 'There's nowt to take, ya fuckers! Go back! Go back!' Howard peeked through the net curtains. Two big men in bomber jackets continued to beat at the door. They didn't look like they were going to take no for an answer. 'No, no, no' was presumably the last thing they heard before they busted through your door into your living room. Howard flinched away and hurried back upstairs when he saw one of them winding up for a first kick at the door. He padded into his mother's room to tell her and found he had a knick-knack in his hand, a little metal Eiffel Tower which he must have picked up from the windowsill downstairs. He dropped it onto the bedside table next to one of the dusty ballerinas and sat down to explain to the wardrobe, hearing now a racket of voices inside next door.

Mrs Dawson in the room of vanished ladies. Glacial light, medical air, surfaces disinfected. He watched the pulse at her temple, a faintly throbbing blue tree of vein under the white skin. Blood her damaged heart still sent round, a heart that surgeons had sliced and sewn, now getting stronger maybe. Maybe her soul was shifting on its perch, wobbling, ready to take flight and resume its life inside her. Howard leaned forward, hands pressed together, willing it to happen. But if nobody else was coming to see her, if he was the only one, why should she come back; what was there for her soul to do?

The Tuesday of Howard's second week at the Sea Breeze Fish Bar was quiet with a long lull between lunch time and evening customers. Slow time the pickled eggs seemed to understand, resting silently on each other in clear vinegar the light slanted through, casting a haemorrhoidal shadow on the counter. Alf was bored, restless, stirring the batter and picking up the spoon to watch its long, creamy pour and the furrows it made in the surface. He stopped. 'Maybe I teach you to fight,' he said, 'make you a winner.'

'You're all right there,' Howard reassured him. 'It's four o'clock already. I'll make some chips now, I reckon.' Howard scooped up a netful and set them seething in the oil, white foam roiling on the surface.

'Don't be a big baby,' Alf said. 'Look at you. Hands like sledgehammers. First we start you off middleweight then we build you up. Come on, on your feet. Come on, you fat poof.' Alf was on his toes now, bouncing on the balls of his feet, swerving his torso from the waist, shooting out little punches in time with breaths puffed out of his flattened nostrils. Howard thought he looked like a mad little fellow. 'Come on, fat boy, fight me. Dance aroun' a bit.'

'Aw, Alf. I don't want to. I'm no good at sport and that.'

Alf didn't stop lunging and striking the air, his comb-over now coming loose in flapping liquorice strips. 'Don't be stupid. Man your size you can knock down a car.'

'But I don't want to.'

'Move it! Move it!'

So Howard started moving halfheartedly, holding his hands cocked in front of him, trying to demonstrate with his posture how ridiculous it all was.

But Alf was having none of it. 'That's it! You good!'

And Howard started moving more quickly, moving very oddly it must be said, out of time with himself, his knees jerking upward as he stepped in little leprechaun leaps.

'Very nice. Now come and punch me, big haggis boy.'

'I'm no gonna hit you, Alf.'

'You are because your mamma does it with everybody.'

'I don't want to.'

'Hit my ugly face, you big bastard.'

'I'm not going to.'

'Okay. I punch you.' Howard hid terrified behind his arms as Alf stuttered forward and poked a punch into the softness of his belly then mimed a ferocious barrage of punches all over him then skipped back to the counter smiling, his small feet flicking back beneath him.

'All right, you wee freak. You want it?' Howard said, already out of breath but on his mettle now. He jogged towards Alf and felt his ankle give way as his whole weight slalomed over one foot and he lashed out an arm to grab the counter and hit the handle of the fryer and saw with gorgeous clarity happening very quickly and at the same time with a serene and liquid slowness – it was just the most riveting sight – a cloud of golden oil rise into the air with half-cooked chips twirling like propeller blades inside it.

Howard was sure that he was dead. There was soft whiteness all around him, a sunny window with the light somehow detached, a floating rectangle of beams. Howard himself floated, warm and peaceful. There were whispers. Above him was a shape, a fine line of doorway which he wondered if maybe he was supposed to go through. The whispering came from a particular place, a dark woman shape. Ma! He found that you still needed to turn your head to look at things. He tried to say 'Ma' and heard his voice make a distant, cattle-like noise which maybe was him singing. His mother jolted backwards and stopped her whispering. Howard heard the dry, jittery sound of rosary beads. She lifted her beads to kiss them. A blurred cross swung. He'd been forgiven! Finally! For all of it! Howard felt his face breaking up to cry. His mother said, 'Good, you wake up. Everythin' okay. Alfonso don't come here. He is workin'. You don't sue him.'

Howard didn't understand, floated thinking for a while, then understood. He bleated again then rolled his head away. 'I thought . . . I thought you were . . .'

Theresa got to her feet and bustled beside him. She opened his glasses and fitted them down on his nose with small soapy hands. Howard felt lost as the real world hardened in front of him. A hospital room came into view as the punchline of an elaborate practical joke. The threshold above him turned out to be a curtain rail. Unexpectedly, Theresa placed a hand on top of his head to soothe him. 'It's okay. You okay. Nothing bad.'

'But what . . .' Howard pushed his tongue around inside his mouth to moisten it for speech. 'But what happened?'

'What happen? You don't remember? Look.' She gently angled his head and pointed at his hugely bandaged left arm. Another joke. What happened? he asked, bandaged like a mummy.

'Aw,' he said.

'Oil burned you. This is hospital.'

'Hospital.' Howard remembered Mrs Dawson asleep in her hospital bed and had a thought which fired him with panic. 'How long?' he yapped. 'How long have I been asleep?'

'One night. It's okay. Alfonso say it's your fault. You were fighting and you fell over. So you don't sue him, please.'

'I'm not going to sue him.' Who did she think he was? Like he was going to go and hire a lawyer. Anyway it was his fault. But this was beside the point. What the hell was under his bandages? How burned was he?

Theresa seemed comforted to have discharged her duty and avoided legal ruin for the Sea Breeze Fish Bar. She patted Howard's pyjamaed shoulder. 'You a brave man. When you come out, I make you a nice cake. I got to go now.' She hefted herself delicately out of the chair onto the tiny pained feet of a little fat woman.

'Ay, right y'are. Would you get me a nurse on your way out.'

'Yes. I get one.' Theresa signed off perkily, 'All the best,' which somehow reminded Howard to be surprised that she spoke English at all. Howard watched her round black shape receding down the white room. There were other men lying in other beds. As Howard turned again he realised that his pants felt large and padded. They crinkled under him. Maybe they were incontinence pants, a big nappy. Maybe they were full. Maybe he'd shat himself in the ambulance or even on the floor of the chip shop. More panic and humiliation. A nurse approached quickly and directly on those super-quiet white shoes nurses seem to have. He was sweating with shame by the time she arrived. 'Good afternoon, Mr MacNamee. How are you?'

'I'm . . . I . . .' Howard was confused. He seemed to remember this nurse from a dim puddle of memory in the middle of the night but he could have been imagining things. What was worse was that he definitely seemed to remember her doing something to his bum.

'You're still weak after the operations so try and relax.'

'What operations? What happened to me, to my arm?' Howard pronounced 'arm' with two syllables – *arrum* – so the nurse had to make him repeat the question.

'What happened to your arm? It was burned, quite badly in one area, so we had to do a couple of little skin grafts, taking skin from your left buttock, two pieces about so big.' She made a ring of her thumb and forefinger.

'Skin from my arse, my buttock?'

'That's right.'

'Onto my arm?'

'That's right, yes.'

Howard let his straining head fall back onto the pillow. 'I see.' Bum skin on his arm! He hoped this joke might now finally be over.

Howard had two more nights in hospital, meals provided, with one brief visit from a frightening bum-skin specialist with muscular apples in his cheeks, black hair in three chunks (side, top, side) and a way of breathing powerfully through his nose when he smiled in a way Howard thought that he probably thought was reassuring. He was given painkillers, shiny, sweetie-coloured capsules which most certainly took away the pain, leaving Howard flat on his bed smiling peacefully, a bandaged Buddha, looking up wonderingly at the curtain rail which wavered as if through water.

The nights were unpleasant. Howard was upset by the snores and grunts and farts and whimpers of the strange men sharing his ward. One man on both nights was helpless in his dreams, thrashing quietly, making little wet not-quite-word sounds. Howard tried putting on the hospital headphones, stethoscope-shaped and made from medical-coloured plastic, but he found that they poked painfully far into his ears then blasted music so loudly that he tore them off in a panic that he'd woken everybody up. The last person in that bed must have been deaf. Not only that, but the music which had been unleashed with such terrifying force towards his brain was, of all things, a Johnny Cash song with lolloping bass and shuddery guitar beloved of the cowboy next door. He thought of him and what he had left, maybe, drunk in his empty house, or evicted now and drunk on the street. He thought of the approaching bailiffs, his mother's house unprotected in the night. Howard sweated into his pyjamas, unravelling in the dark.

On the third day Howard awoke lens-clear for no good reason, healthy, almost enjoying the bustle of breakfast trolleys wheeled to patients, and clutching one bright coin of an idea: Mrs Dawson was very likely in the same hospital. Which hospital he was in was not a question which had occurred to Howard to ask, as was typical of him. He took the world as it came, events looming and diminishing in dramatic chiaroscuro. He hardly saw the coming of one nor the passing of another. A neighbouring bed confirmed that he was indeed in St Thomas's and Howard swung himself out of bed – bringing his legs down fast and levering up his body, causing unforeseen pain to his fulcrumatic bottom – then had to stand and wait for a moment as the effervescence of low blood pressure cleared from his head. He put on his grey hospital dressing gown and set out to find her.

Walking the corridors, Howard thought with pleasure about how their lives, his and Mrs Dawson's, had drawn together, how much more legitimately connected he was to his 'aunt', now another patient in bed wear and slippers in the same institution, enjoying the peculiar liberty of being allowed to roam dressed like that, a rightful resident.

It was when he sat down next to Mrs Dawson in his usual place, having exchanged a few chirpy words with the nurse about that very fact of his being there as a fellow patient, and he was about to start the story of his comical adventure that he realised how sad he was that he had been burned and how much he really wanted her to wake up this time and sympathise and say 'Brave wee soldier' because his own ma sure as hell couldn't. He thought of seeing his ma the other day and how he had sung her name even if it was only Theresa, because who was to say what had really happened? He hung his head and tried to gather his short breaths to speak, chewing his lips against his teeth the way he always did when he was trying not to cry, the technique he'd used ever since the earliest days of his mother and father and all of that. It was no use. He put his hand frankly around Mrs Dawson's forearm, which was light as a chicken bone, and cried stupid tears down the sides of his nose.

A few hours later he was discharged.

Despite having sent his wife to keep watch and petition Howard to give up any unlikely plans of legal action as soon as he regained bewildered consciousness, Alfonso did all right by Howard. He invited him around for tea one morning before the shop opened and Theresa produced the promised cake, a dark, sugar-dusted circle of baked custard which Howard ate half of and decided made the early rising worthwhile. They drank tea from proper dainty cups and saucers with flowers painted on them which Howard found hard to hold by the handle and too hot to hold by the fine, conductive china and so settled on holding by the saucer and tipping towards his mouth. Their living room was dark and indescribably foreign with large pieces of carved wooden furniture taking up most of the space. Photographs of moustached male relatives in tight shirts stood on the surfaces. The milk jug was protected by a lace cover weighted at its edge with tinkling beads. They didn't speak too much as they sipped and forked. Howard had enough to do not breaking anything and Alfonso had become a formal little stranger in the presence of his wife. The real Alf only twinkled out at Howard when he thought she wasn't looking. Afterwards, Alf gave Howard three weeks' wages in advance and told him that the job was his whenever he had recovered. Howard needed to get back in the ring, Alf said. 'You can't work in a chip shop if you're afraid from oil.'

So Howard found himself with three weeks of nothing to do but heal and note the intricate warm swarming sensations under his dressings. He peeked under the bandages on his arm to see two patches of coarse skin (bum skin!) set as if melting onto raw flesh, cracked with rivulets of wet plasma, white ridges, sticky gauze, grains of dry blood, stuck hairs. Well, he wasn't going to scratch at that no matter how itchy it got, but when it became too unbearable he squeezed the bandage for relief. He watched hours of television, smoked fags in the convalescent, early-spring garden and spent the rest of the time by Mrs Dawson's bed. He could walk from there to his own check-ups with the nurse.

He laid siege to Mrs Dawson, forcing her with the force of his loudest thoughts to wake up and resume being Mrs Dawson, sitting there howling at her in his head. Then his rage would slacken and he'd be left looking numbly into the crater left by a person, by a person gone inside, probably forever. He was there when Doris arrived and sat down and burst into tears by her mother and he was there when she left.

He acknowledged the greeting of the Bible-reading lady, who was now up to tedious Leviticus with the unvisited lady, who one day all of a sudden, then never again, was visited by a couple in motorcycle leathers, huge and creaking in their outfits like they were visitors from the future, the man straightening his ponytail as they sat down. They left behind them useless fruit. He was there when the nurses made him stand outside as they had to wash the ladies and change pans and drips. And the rest of the time he was alone with Mrs Dawson.

Wake up. Wake up! Wake up. Wake up. Wake up. Wake up. Wake up. Wake up. Wake up. Wake up. Wake up. Wake up. Wake up. Wake up.

The room was so familiar it was invisible to him, a whiteness with Mrs Dawson's body anchored at the centre of the world. He'd heard her heart monitor beeping for so many hours that he didn't hear it any more, sitting staring until finally he saw something, a change that was almost intangibly subtle. But it was something, something happening in her face. He was staring at it at the time, the papery eyelids, the pouched skin, its drape over her bones, and suddenly something changed, went, like water sinking into sand. The moment spread out from her face, filling the room. His heart gripped his blood. He stared. The moment he realised that the monitor was now making one long beep and his heart gripped again was the moment the nurses rushed in, one ushering him out by his good arm, the other drawing the curtain quickly. In the corridor speeding towards them was a man he'd never seen before pushing a trolley of equipment.

Les felt so sick he didn't dare move for fear of the slightest emetic motion. He stood trapped in space. His wife had her long fingers to her face. Saul stood there neatly combed, tightly dressed, very grandsonish, holding flowers. Les held his arms out as though to steady himself on invisible rails and said to his wife, 'Take him back to the car. Take him back to the car now.' He was careful to move only his mouth, exert only his voice. She obeyed, grasping Saul by the upper arm and leading him back down the long corridor to the car park where minutes earlier they had got out of the car into a different world.

The nurse appeared with a large, bandaged, red-haired man, and said something incomprehensible about family being together and please could they wait there; they were doing the best they could. She vanished again and Les, now alone, looked up at Howard and his large, moist face looked back down at him. Howard jabbed at his glasses with his middle finger and stared at the floor. His mouth worked to make words before he had a sentence to say, then he produced: 'I come here. I've been visiting.' 'The nurse said "nephew",' Les said. 'Yes. I'm not,' said Howard. 'I know you're not,' Les said. 'I'm her son.' Howard looked quickly at the small man in the lemon jumper with his hands cocked in the air. His body flashed with a sheet lightning of fear. The nurse reappeared, her face grave, slightly stricken but professional and in control. Howard felt weightless. Les's hands were floating up towards his head. She said quietly to both of them, 'I'm afraid she's gone. It was very peaceful, as you know,' indicating Howard with a shy half-turn towards him. 'Usually we advise people at this time to take a moment and go and say goodbye.' Les and Howard looked at each other, Howard trying to shrink down inside himself and hide. Les nodded and took a step forward and found that, yes, moving did make him want to be sick. 'Toilet,' he said to the nurse and jogged away. The nurse met him outside when he had finished and led him quietly up the corridor to where his dead mother lay.

The figure that was so familiar to Howard, the thing Howard now knew best in the world, was coldly strange to Les. She was recognisable, but she had changed so much. So old, her skin fractured with the weight of age, and herself so light, pale and gone. There was no one there. A leaf. A husk. He'd failed to make it to see her, his own mother, and this strange man all this time visiting her. What kind of a man could Les be to prioritise out his own dying mother, no matter what had gone before between them? He looked at the still, dead shape that was his mother and felt nothing for her but disgust at himself.

Slowly he became aware that things were still going on. The clock on the wall. Saul in the car. The nurse seemed to be expecting him to make some sort of act of farewell and he realised that if he obliged he would be able to leave. He stepped closer to the bed and frightened himself by touching her collarbone with his fingertips. 'Bye, then,' he said and left the room.

Howard was stuck by the nurses' station, unsure whether to run away or not, unable to make a decision, overwhelmed by it all – Mrs D's soul taken flight, never coming back. He squeezed his arm until a solid pain appeared. Les returned with the nurse. The small man stood and listened in a businesslike manner as she explained what needed to happen in terms of death certificate, releasing the body, and so on. Howard heard her use the word 'undertaker-wise'. She handed Mrs Dawson's son some pieces of paper. He folded them crisply with one thumbnail. Howard thought he looked like an important man. He nodded as the nurse spoke. Howard was relieved that he had turned up, otherwise, who knows, he might have had to go through again all the terrors he went through when his own mother died. Mrs Dawson's son produced a silver pen and clicked it with his thumb when there was a form to sign. Afterwards he turned to Howard and said, 'Can I give you a lift anywhere or are you all right?'

'Uh,' said Howard, staggering slightly.

'Can I give you a lift? I understand you've been visiting my mother very regularly.'

'Yes.'

'Right, well, follow me,' Les instructed him, and Howard followed the man's quick steps to the car park and a very Falcon's-gym-member-type silver car which already contained an elegant lady passenger and a small boy buckled in the back. When the man got in, Howard followed, opening the back door and lowering himself onto slithery leather upholstery. The mood in the car was too tense and unhappy to respond to Howard's presence. The small boy looked at him with the mutest of questioning looks. 'This is . . . I'm sorry I don't know your name,' the man said and Howard supplied it. 'He has been visiting my mother for some time. We're giving him a lift. Actually, Howard, it occurs to me that we will need to set up here for a few days so perhaps you could direct me to a hotel?' The woman turned round to look now, wide, blood-flecked, questioning eyes meeting Howard's.

'Ay, no problem,' Howard mumbled, his voice squeezed small from his throat. The boy wriggled round inside his seat belt and silently extended a hand to be shaken. Howard took the small, light-boned shape in his own big paw and the man started the car.

Ignition was barely audible, more a rising confidence that you could drive. 'Saul,' the man said to the boy, 'your grand-mother has just died. My mother.' He paused, working his tongue inside his mouth, swallowing. 'Today is a significant day, therefore, one that you should remember.'

They drove off in silence, the car easing the world around to behind them, Howard directing and misdirecting them until they found a chain hotel on a roundabout that Howard remembered from his bus route. They parked and got out, Howard posting his bulk up through the gap of the car door.

The lady then put a hand on Howard's shoulder and spoke in a low-toned voice, one that would not disturb anyone's inner experience of grief, and asked if he would come in to join them for a drink. They were nearly eye to eye, Howard noticed, making her much taller than her husband.

The man, Mr Dawson, put one hand on top of the boy's head. 'What did you see?' he asked.

The boy stood still, head forward, eyelids fluttering against the breeze, and said in a flat, rehearsed, high voice, 'We passed six traffic lights. Red, red, green, amber, red, green. Five species of birds: carrion crows, house sparrows, magpies, star-lings, wood pigeons. Possibly one black-headed gull in the distance. Twenty-three traffic cones at an intersection. Buses numbered seventeen, eighty-seven, one-one-seven. An ambu-lance. Two lorries with TIR stickers.'

His father said, 'Good. But wasn't there another category? Didn't we say dogs as well?'

'Yes, we did.'

'Well then?'

'Yes, but I didn't see any dogs.'

His father ruffled the boy's head and swayed him affectionately. 'Come on, champ. Let's go in. I'm freezing.'

The hotel bar, peachily wallpapered, softly lit, the air smoothly textured with muzak, contained no one but the group Howard now found himself in, the barman – a sharp-chinned boy of about nineteen with keenly gelled hair above the strained gaze of traineeship – and a group of six loud, fleshy girls knocking back drinks in the opening stages of a hen night. At least Howard assumed it was a hen night because the central girl – clearly marked out with waggling deely-boppers on her head and an L-plate slung in front of her cleavage – hid under the table what could only have been a dildo (unless it was a torch) when they walked in, an action which caused the girls to glance over at them then ricochet around on their seats with hysterical laughter. It was a good job he'd seen the dildo because otherwise he would have been sure they were laughing at him, as groups of girls could. Mr Dawson chose a table at the other end of the bar and beckoned the barman over with a curling finger. The girls poured themselves another round of shots from a cocktail shaker then flung back their heads to drink; it looked more like biting their drinks off. The barman arrived with alacrity, holding his pad at chest height with pen poised. He even, unnecessarily, touched the tip of his pen to the tip of his tongue and pretended there wasn't a bad taste.

'Tonic water and an orange juice, please,' Mr Dawson said, then raised his eyebrows at his wife.

'I'll have a G and T,' she said. 'And you?' She turned to Howard.

'Oh, ah, ah, ah, ah, ah, just a beer, please.'

When the barman had gone, the wife said to Howard, again low-toned and in the melody of polite conversation as though the day's death was no reason to fail in such niceties, 'I'm sorry I haven't properly introduced myself. I'm Barbara Dawson-Smith. My husband, Les, you've met. This is Saul.'

'Hello, yes, hello,' Howard managed. The pause that followed Howard realised he needed to fill by introducing himself, despite their learning his name in the car. 'I'm Howard,' he said. 'MacNamee. Howard MacNamee. I knew Mrs Dawson-Smith.'

'Mrs Dawson,' Barbara Dawson-Smith smilingly corrected. Howard noticed that, like her husband's, her accent was southern.

'I knew Mrs Dawson from the gym where I worked where she went. She was a very nice lady. We used to chat a bit and then, you know, I visited her when she was sick. I just said she was me aunt because it seemed the easiest, you know, thing.'

Les Dawson-Smith helped unload the drinks from the barman's tray but did it suddenly and without even eye-contact warning so that the tray unbalanced and the orange juice, caught quickly by the barman, sloshed over and spilt a few drops onto the carpet. Les looked at him with jaw clenched, defying him not to accept full responsibility. 'It's all right, sir,' the barman said. 'I'll just get you another one.'

Barbara looked at Les and Les looked back, still clenched, his expression saying, 'And?' They're tense with the upset, Howard thought. Everybody's tense.

There were shrieks from the other end of the bar. Howard looked over to see one girl refitting her breasts inside her top, spooning them with her fingers like dessert into cups.

'Why are they shouting?' Saul asked.

'They're having a party,' his mother explained.

The barman returned with orange juice to set in front of Saul, waiting patiently until the boy realised he had to stop spinning the beer mat in front of him.

'Yes, I know,' said Saul once he had his drink. 'But don't they know you don't need to shout to have a good time.'

'No, they don't.' His father sipped tonic. 'They're ignorant.'

Saul seemed to accept this, taking a moment to look at them as if to memorise the appearance of ignorant people.

'You remembered all those things in the car, Saul,' Howard said. In his Glaswegian accent he heard his mother say 'soul' on that last word. 'How did you do that?'

Les answered him. 'That's what he does. His brain is more highly trained than yours or mine, courtesy of us. I wish I'd been given his opportunities at that age, then maybe I'd be about to have his success.'

Howard wanted to ask more but a beer-burp surprised him and he had to nod, puffing out his cheeks.

The way Mrs Dawson had gone, just sunk out of sight. He would never forget that.

'Look,' Les said, turning his glass on its coaster and leaning forward. Neat hands, a fringe of dark hairs at the wrist, a nice, thin watch. Hands that looked confidently in contact with the world, unlike Howard's, always knocking things off and tearing them, soiling. 'Look, I don't know what to say. I know what you're thinking and maybe you're right to be thinking it. You've been visiting my mother all this time and here I am turning up only on the day ... the day she dies, so you're wondering where I've been all this time.'

Howard shook his head slowly, trying to dissuade the man, all his attention on that small, pained, dark-eyed face.

'But what you don't understand and why should you is my commitments in London which are many and serious.' Howard nodded, commitments in London being presumably the most serious kind possible. 'And also Saul here, who needs a great deal of training and is in the most important period of preparation in his life, in all our lives, so if you want an answer to the question Why didn't this horrendous man visit his mother all this time? the answer is he would have done, he would have done, he would but he wasn't able to for various stated reasons and other reasons, Howard, which no one could expect you to know.'

'It's all right,' Howard said as tears wetted the man's face, a face which betrayed no change in expression so that the tears appeared a kind of smarting and only the smallest trembling could be seen in the man's mouth. 'You're all right,' Howard said, reaching into his pocket and handing the man a crumpled tissue already perforated with blows of Howard's nose, which the man refused, wiping his cheeks.

April 9th

From where she sat quietly in her chair, her thighs parallel under the grey fabric of her skirt, Barbara watched Saul staring at the machines. Quite still, concentrating, he was trying to learn them, probably, a still boy beyond the empty chairs. She straightened the novel she wasn't reading along the arm of her chair and looked up to see Howard arrive, searching from side to side but not seeing her, gently flapping the sides of his coat to cool down.

Howard stood for a moment on the thick carpet of the hotel drinks lounge, thinking that he'd arrived too early and there was nobody there. Barbara, tucked in the gloom, almost called to him but didn't; it felt like it would have been too great a disarrangement of her throat. He checked the watch strapped tightly into the creamy fat of his wrist. No, he was on time. When he looked up again he saw Saul. The boy was frowning at the changing lights of a fruit machine.

In deference to the quiet of the place, Howard tiptoed towards Saul, or rather took careful lurching steps, pausing with each foot flat until Saul turned to him and said, 'Oh, hello.'

'Hello.'

'It's not worth playing this machine, I don't think.'

'Oh.'

'There are nine things: cherries, strawberries, grapes, apples, bars, pound signs, dollar signs, a joker and a coin, okay, and three wheels. So to get all three the same is one over nine times one over nine times one over nine.'

'Aha.'

'That's one in seven hundred and twenty-nine. That's not worth it.' Howard nodded sagely, as a comprehending adult. 'They say you can't win on them things.'

'No,' Saul agreed. 'Well, you can, it's just not really likely. We could win on this one, though.' He pointed to another machine just alongside.

'Could we?'

'Maybe. It's questions. General knowledge. Have you got a pound?'

Knowledge? A pound? 'A pound?'

'Yes. So we can play it.'

'Ah. Ah, well.' Faced with the boy's calm and quite reasonable intent, Howard felt he had to at least feel in his pocket. Unfortunately in amongst the grit and shreds he found a warm pound coin. 'Seems I do.'

'Thank you.'

Howard now walked right up to him, produced the coin and dropped it into Saul's hand. They turned to the machine together. QUIZMASTER 4000, the screen said. 10 CORRECT ANSWERS WINS £100! *That would be all right,* Howard thought. And the boy beside him, resting one foot on the other, obviously knew a lot more than he did.

The coin dropped as into a pond, disturbing the surface of the screen. All sorts of things flashed across it. When it was still, Saul looked up at Howard.

'Which category first? Sport? World history? The movies? Geography . . .?'

'Not geography.'

'Okay. Science?

'Ah . . .'

'Fine, science.'

Howard, horse-like, shifted on his feet as the question appeared.

'Oh, oh, I don't know.' Saul hesitated, then pressed a large button with four fingers before Howard had finished reading the options. 'Phew. We got it. Next category, sport. You'll be good at that,' Saul told him. All grown-up men knew about sport.

'Oh, ay,' Howard agreed hopefully, imagining the gush of a hundred pounds into the drawer.

'Which team won the 1999 FA Cup Final? Everton. Manchester United. Wimbledon. Arsenal.'

'Oh, ah, ah . . .' Didn't Manchester United always win? But then didn't Arsenal always win as well? 'Manchester United,' he said quickly.

Saul hit the button. CORRECT! flashed on the screen. 'Come on,' Howard said, raising a fist.

Saul tried to match his enthusiasm. 'Great,' he said, without moving. 'Next question. World history.'

'Over to you, wee man. I've done my expert area.'

'Philip IV of Spain belonged to which royal family – the Bourbons, the Stuarts, the Habsburgs, the Romanovs? I don't know that. I don't know.'

'Bourbon? Was he made of biscuit, do you know? Did he have a creamy filling?'

Saul laughed and Barbara, at her distance, felt a little stun of anger. But why? It was envy, that was why. Saul's little body had jerked with the sudden free movement of laughter. But she didn't say anything; she kept on watching, kept still in her corner.

'This is serious, though. I don't know the answer.'

'Just put custard cream or whatever.'

Saul smiled; frowned. 'We have a one in four chance, twenty-five per cent probability.'

'Go for it, then.'

Saul pressed a button. SORRY! flashed on the screen. MAYBE NEXT TIME! His shoulders dropped. 'I'm sorry,' he said. 'General knowledge isn't my strongest subject. It isn't even really a subject. I mean I don't study it.' Saul turned a pinched, apologetic face to Howard.

'Don't worry, wee man. You can always have another go. It's made so you don't win, otherwise it would have to give people a hundred pounds all the time.'

'Have you got another pound?'

'No.' Probably he didn't – the last one was a fluke – but this time he didn't check. He hated the way the machine was all friendly and interested in you when you had put your money in and now, when it had your money, it was like you'd never existed. So insincere.

'Why don't we sit down,' Saul said.

'Why not, eh?' Howard glanced again at his watch.

Saul pulled out a chair at an empty table and sat. Howard sat in the chair opposite, picked up a laminated menu and started bending it aimlessly. He looked at Saul, who had one leg crossed over the other, his hands in his lap forming a delicate shape, fingertips pressed lightly together. He looked like a chat-show host or like in a fairy-tale, magicky film, a wise little creature that Howard was consulting. 'So,' Howard said.

'Yes,' Saul replied. 'What do you do for a living?'

'What, my job?'

'Yes. What is it?'

'Yes, so, I work in a fish and chip shop.'

'Really?' The boy's eyes were wide.

'Yes.'

'Isn't that very unhealthy?'

'Looks like it.' Howard raised his arm, pulled back the sleeve to show Saul the bandage.

'I burned it.'

'Can I see?'

'No. It wouldn't be nice.'

'With boiling oil?'

'Aha. Got on my arm.'

'They used it in medieval castles to pour over the walls onto attackers.'

'Well, that'll keep them away. I fainted,' he said proudly.

'Really? I fainted once. I'd been sitting down for ages and ages and I was hungry and then I got up and tried to run and answer the door and I passed out. It was because of low blood pressure combined with low blood sugar. Strange sensation, isn't it, when it happens?'

'Ay. You know lots of things, don't you?'

'I have to. I have to memorise things. And I study.'

'Do you know how to say it in Scottish, say, "I know a lot"?'

'No. They speak English in Scotland.'

'Most of the time. Say, "Ah ken muckle."'

Saul laughed again. 'You just made that up.'

'No, I didnae. Swear to God. Ah ken muckle.'

'Ah ken muckle.'

'Bingo. You're a natural.'

'Bingo!'

'No, that's not Scottish.'

Saul smiled, wiped a hand across closed eyes. 'I know. Bingo! Maybe it's Latin. I bing!'

'Who knows?'

'Someone does. Latin teachers.'

Les was late and hurrying. After a shower, his humid skin was starting to sweat and he could feel his hair lying in flat, glossy ribbons across his head. He'd forgotten that he'd asked Howard to come over to the hotel. Forgotten! He rushed into the lounge to find the strange man sitting alone with his son. How was this happening? First his mother – well, that was something else – and now Saul. Les was disgusted at his neglect. He was so attentive, so hard-working. There was no reason for this slackness in his affairs. Howard and Saul sat upright in their seats as he approached.

'You two all right together, are you?'

Saul nodded silently. Howard had to answer. 'Yes. Fine. Yes.'

'Really? Everything's okay?'

Howard couldn't understand why the man was acting so angry. 'Everything's okay,' he tried to calm him, 'we were just talking about ... bingo.'

'They're fine.' Barbara's voice from out of her corner. They all looked round. 'They're really fine. Really.'

'You're here?' Les demanded, squinting to find her. 'I thought you were having a spa treatment.'

'I'm not. I'm here.'

'Are you? Where?'

'Yes, Mum,' Saul demanded. 'Where are you?'

'I'm near the window.' She stood up, smokily dark and silvered down one side by the window's light. 'Really, they are fine together,' she said again with emphasis.

Les considered. 'Howard,' he said, 'can I have a quick word?'

'Sure.' Howard followed him over towards the shuttered bar.

Les didn't like leaning his head back to meet Howard's gaze so asked his questions of his Adam's apple. 'You work near here, don't you?'

'Ay, I do.'

'And live?'

'Here.'

'Alone?'

Howard almost answered incorrectly. 'Yes, yes, alone. My mother ... well, she died.'

'Oh.' Les did look up at Howard now. Howard stoically withstood his gaze. 'I'm sorry.'

Howard shrugged. 'Ay. Well. You know how it is.'

Les pursed his lips, made a brave, sincere face and nodded. Then he changed gear. 'Now, ah, now, I'm sorry to have to ask this, I mean just with you being around my family ...'

'Ay, nice lad.'

'Yes, he's special. Very special. You haven't been in trouble have you? Haven't been arrested or anything? No skeletons?'

Howard's heart leaped like a salmon. He coughed and

thumped his chest hard. 'No, no, of course not.'

Les kept looking at him then decided, resumed his expression of sincere shared grief.

'That's good. That's good. I've just got to ask.'

'Of course, I know what you're worrying – I could be anyone. But I'm not. Really, I'm not.'

'Good. I really am, am,' Les's voice thickened, 'grateful actually for what you did for my mother. I didn't know that your own ...'

'There you go,' Howard said quietly. 'There you go.'

'Shall we sit down?'

'Sure.'

Barbara was at Saul's table when they returned. 'These two have been having a lovely conversation,' she informed Les. 'Saul's been very friendly and grown-up. It's made me quite proud,' she said, squeezing Saul by the forearm. Saul, embarrassed, tutted and looked at the floor.

'He's embarrassed,' Les said to Howard, his eyes small and humid with pride. 'He's not used to making new friends.'

April 11th

Barbara switched on the little hotel-room kettle and looked at Les lying on the floral bed, hands knitted behind his head, dressed in his new black suit and tie – entirely dressed, in fact, except for the polished black shoes which waited on the carpet. His small socked feet pointed at the ceiling. His lips were pushed forward in his thinking face. The kettle rumbled, misting the mirror, rumbled violently, and clicked. Barbara poured water onto a tea bag then flapped a sachet of sweetener before opening it, resorting to her teeth to do so rather than risking a rose-coloured nail. You made all the effort to ornament yourself appropriately, to assume the elegance of your station, and these things would so easily be snapped off, the world abrade your finesse away, revealing underneath ... well, the woman she wasn't. Working carefully with fingers fanned she squeezed the tea bag against the side of the cup with a teaspoon and dumped it into the airily plastic-lined little bin. She shook milk from a single-serving carton and fluttered a few drops onto the dressing table. She was tense, naturally. She needed a tissue.

'Was it tea or coffee you wanted?' Les didn't reply.

Barbara repeated the question. 'Mm?' he asked.

Of course it was bound to be a horrendous day. Just bloody well get through it, Barbara; nothing else you can do.

'Was it tea or coffee you wanted?' She leant forward on the upholstered stool and squeezed the end of his foot, which made him flinch and say 'Ow!' like she'd actually hurt him. Cruel in his abstraction, he was, always alone in his projects and worry. Part of his strength, his dynamism, of course, but he made her so outside, knocking on the door which her husband refused to answer. Understandable today. But it wasn't just today. 'Coffee,' he said, changing his position on the bed.

Biting open a sachet of coffee, she worried about him. He'd detached a hand now and was feeling his forehead. All the tension in that light, lean body. She'd had no idea how this business with his mother would affect him but she certainly hadn't expected this. After years of the rarest mention of awful Jean Dawson he was a desperate child again, prostrate with guilt. Probably it was the sight of the dead body lying there alone in some God-awful National Health hospital. She didn't know but he hadn't said a word about it, which was usually a bad sign. She couldn't even bear to imagine it with her own mother. And of course he was stressed anyway with work and Saul, trying to do everything as usual while Ted is away for weeks on end in his Tuscan villa. And, as she had recently read, it's not the bosses who get the heart attacks but the people who are second in command, under the bosses and above everyone else, bearing the brunt of everything, stress from both sides. And clearly there was heart trouble in the family. She thought of her ferocious, go-getting Les like one of those sculptures on stately homes made to look like they're holding up the building, only he was cracking under the pressure. She stirred milk into the coffee then dared do no more than set it on the bedside table by his head. He said nothing.

It seemed to her that this sense of guilt was coming out partly in gratitude to this man, Howard, who'd been visiting Jean Dawson ever since she'd got ill. He was a nice enough big lug of a fellow but not someone Les would under normal circumstances even condescend to speak to, and here he was hanging on his every word, checking every detail of the funeral arrangements with him. It turned out the chap's own mother died just six months ago so in a way he'd got the requisite experience. Which maybe, come to think of it, was why he was visiting Jean Dawson every day, something to do with his own mother. But who knows finally what goes on in other people's minds. Not a lot seemed to happen in his. Les had checked him out the other day – a security assessment he had called it – and he had been reassured. Apparently he was safe. He certainly seemed safe, fine to have around, quiet and gentle, and good for Saul, acting as a buffer between him and his father, stopping Les's tension getting to the boy and upsetting him. Les would want that, not trusting his influence on the boy's performance in his current state. Meanwhile Saul had actually been perkier – this was practically a holiday for him away from all his exercises. He'd been sleeping through the night, apparently. Strange, he too seemed to like this Howard and was lighter, more childish in his company. What nonsense were they talking yesterday? Saul was telling Howard about memorising pi to however many decimal points he was up to at the moment and Howard was saying in his nice soft accent, 'I can memorise pie: apple pie, steak and kidney pie, tomato pie.' 'There's no such thing as tomato pie.' 'All right. Mud pie.' And Saul had laughed. It was lovely to see him laugh. He looked surprised out of himself, mouth open, face floating, and bubbles of laugh escaping. Les said it would enhance his performance to relax into a more creative state of mind, good for the neural connections to form. Les couldn't do it himself, said all he could give was tense goal-orientation. He feared limiting the boy's achievement. But he was happy deploying the stranger. Yesterday, the three of them together, Les had been excited. 'Explain to Howard about exercising with the matrix.' And Saul was also excited, rapid in speech and gesture, as he explained to Howard, who listened politely to all of it, betraying no obvious sign of understanding or not.

Barbara was herself glad of him, she realised. A buffer also between herself and Les, a distraction, a subject of con- versation.

She finished her tea and looked at herself in the dressing

table mirror, her face assuming its habitual mirror expression with chin down, eyes wide, nostrils flaring as she breathed in. She experimentally tightened her cheeks with the flats of her hands. But could she face the rigmarole of a face lift? Not necessary quite yet. And her looks had served their turn, brought her the life she had, the comfort. She got out and put on her new black hat, adjusting its bit of veil. That was what today was about: there was a dead woman to cremate. A body. Les's mother. End of another life. Nothing you could say. She turned her head slowly and looked out of the window at the roundabout. The different, tedious cars curving around that circle of mangy civic grass glinted in the sunlight, windscreens flashing one after the other. The day was bright. There was one stiff meringue of spring cloud unmoving in the sky. Les had got up behind her and was bent over, lacing his shoes. 'Right,' he said. 'Let's get the boy and go.'

Howard stood in his anorak cleaning his glasses with the end of his tie. When he put them on again he saw his mother's room empty of everything except the cross, the photograph and the wardrobe. There was a dark rectangle of carpet where the bed had been. There was dust in the corners. The room seemed large. He had pleaded for the wardrobe, bargaining away all the ornaments, assuring the men they were worth at least three pounds each and therefore when you added them all together were a lot of money. It was like something from the weirdest, most frightening dream, watching this couple of hard men walking out of the house with handfuls of figurines: ballerinas and cats and smiling children and mice in suits. He dragged a line in the dust in the carpet with the pointy toe of his good shoes. The carpet was thicker in the corners, rising in plump little hills. You could see the angle at which the wardrobe canted forwards. He went outside into the spring sunshine, the air glittering and clean as his polished glasses, to smoke and wait for the Dawson-Smiths in their car.

*

It seemed to Howard a poor way to go. The crematorium was a low modern building with a vaguely ecclesiastical roof that pitched steeply up into two points at the corners. Inside, there were seats like pews, a plain, conference-style lectern with built-in electric light, a mechanical bier with a coffin containing Mrs Dawson set before a thin mechanical curtain which, struck by direct sunlight from windows behind, shone a fierce orange. Unfortunately for Howard, the sun also shone directly onto the back of his head. His neck felt damp and loamy inside his anorak. The light struck the side of his face so that the skin next to his left eye was vividly reflected in the lens of his glasses. The image was grotesquely detailed, the skin rough and pitted as elephant hide. Also, his burn under his bandage was intensely uncomfortable, busy as the snow on a broken TV screen. It was like he could feel individual nerves in their suffering. So there were too many sensations. He couldn't attend, couldn't concentrate on the vicar's dribbling sermon about mourning, Jean's passing over, of course, but, more than that, celebrating her life and what she meant to each of us. Saul was sitting next to Howard, very still, head at an attentive angle, his feet swinging gently under him. In the opposite pew sat Saul's father, hunched and dark. Next to him, his mother was erect, her hat properly directed towards the vicar. The other people there were friends of Mrs Dawson he'd never seen before, a few old women who sat together in a clump of hats and scent and tweed coats. A workman for the crematorium loitered behind them in the doorway.

It was a strange way to go. The sun shone. The vicar droned. Falcon's had sent a wreath. Nobody knew anybody. Death was shabby, lonely, ordinary. Only Les seemed really caught up in it, switching posture, jerking in his seat like a kite snapping into place in a strong wind. Which reminded Howard again that it was Mrs Dawson over there in that box. In the same room. He took his glasses off and blurred the scene.

They sang two hymns. They said a prayer. The curtains buzzed apart and to gentle organ music Mrs Dawson's body slid away to be burnt down to ashes and put in a jar. The curtains closed behind. Les Dawson-Smith made noises. Saul stared with fascination. Sniffles were heard among Mrs Dawson's friends. Then that was it. Shuffling departures. Dispersal into the brilliant sun and a small, tranquillising gravelled garden. The vicar loitered sympathetically, hands clasped behind his stout back. Les shook him firmly by the hand. Saul hovered around Howard away from his parents and hung his head. Mrs Dawson-Smith now said a few words to the vicar. Howard suddenly thought he'd have to leave in a minute. And go back to what? The fear gripped him of falling into the hands of the social services, the SS his mother had called them, and ending up in one of the estates with all the killer dogs, the drugs, the lads keen for trouble with the Pakis, men like his dad hanging around. And all alone! Les was in front of him suddenly, shaking his hand. 'I can't thank you enough, Howard. I don't know what to say. I don't ... Thank you, Howard.' Saul had tucked himself behind Howard and now tugged on his coat. In one hand he held two kinds of leaves he had pulled off of bushes in the garden. The other hand he held up to Howard to shake. Howard took it, realising the end, remembering Mrs Dawson lying tiny on her bed, the moment, water sinking into sand, and the big *No!* the big *Come back!* sounded in his head. Howard tried to speak but found himself overcome. He made the thin metallic sound, like squealing brakes, he made when starting to cry. He looked again and Mrs Dawson-Smith was standing next to him, touching his arm with concern, those wide eyes fastened on his face. Les was losing it as well. Emotions gusted about the little garden. 'What is it, Howard?' she asked. Les mustered himself enough to say, 'If there's anything we can do.' 'No, no, you can't.' 'You were close to Jean,' Barbara said. 'This must be hard.' 'Ay. No. It's not that.' Howard gulped air for words.

'It's my house.' 'You just come and sit down and tell me all about it,' Barbara said, and led him to a small memorial bench under an ornamental tree. Howard slowed down, breathed.

'I have a house,' he began.

'Yes,' she encouraged.

'I did have a house. With my mother.'

'Who died.'

'Yes. How did—'

'Les mentioned.'

'And so now well I haven't had the rent for quite a while now . . .'

'I see. So you're going to lose your place.'

'Yes. I am. Going to lose it.'

'I see.' Barbara looked across at Les standing in his black suit, soothing himself by stroking his forehead with two fingers. And there was Saul, near his father, watching Barbara and Howard. The boy was so interested in Howard, and didn't Howard make him laugh? She remembered the moment of Saul's laughter in the hotel bar. Well then surely there was an answer, a really striking answer to all this. Plus Les so obviously wanted to do something for the man.

'I imagine,' she said in warm, patrician terms, 'that you might like to start again somewhere. I mean an opportunity, a change.' She pulled Les towards them, almost magnetically, by holding out her hand and smiling.

'I suppose,' Howard said, thinking of himself inside his small, disintegrating home, 'I'd like to get out.'

'Darling,' she said to Les, her mind now shining with images of a happier Saul, a solution, 'I've had a good idea. Howard needs to move out of his house . . .'

'Really?'

'Yes.' Barbara saw suspicion in Les's eye, and quashed it. 'His contract's up. There are new tenants. So couldn't he come back to London with us, just for a while? Saul could carry on showing him his work.' She looked up now deferentially at

Les, inviting him to make the decision, and he plucked his cuffs, nodding. 'Yes. It's good. It's a good idea. At least for a while. Get you on your feet.' What were these people saying? They couldn't possibly mean it. There was too much emotion, too much confusion. What would these people decide, left together in a funeral garden? 'What do you think?' Les asked Saul. The boy looked at Howard, looked at his leaves. 'I could show him my computer,' he said.

PART 2

London, How Howard
Might Meet Irina

At the end of his second week with the Dawson-Smiths, Howard accidentally had the cleaner fired, which was unfortunate because by then he liked her a lot. Her name was Varya; she was Russian, wore a soft grey jumper, and arrived as calming relief from the state of nervous tension caused by living with the Dawson-Smiths.

After the long drive south from the funeral with Saul accumulating his statistics out of the window and Howard beside him, his fat cut by the seat belt, the two parents in the front seats not saying anything or saying things that couldn't be heard in the back, after the countryside flattened and paled and houses ganged up and took over in the evening darkness, after they'd parked and Howard had no idea at all where he was, only that he was hours and hours from home, Howard entered the thick atmosphere of an unfamiliar house full of hard little things he knew he'd break if he touched. He stood enormously in the hall while Barbara burbled, Saul stood patiently, and Les ran to switch off the burglar alarm and put on the lights. They snapped on one by one. Howard felt close to epilepsy. His glimpsed views through large rooms into other rooms beyond left zigzags of plush interior in his head. He gripped the handle of his one large suitcase. Saul, the kind boy, took him by the other hand and led him up several flights of steps – there were thirty-six altogether, Saul informed him – to a guest room with a skylight and a sloping ceiling, florally wallpapered, against which Howard immediately hit his head. 'You can put your clothes in here.' Saul opened a wardrobe of jangling wire hangers. 'And there is a bathroom next door where you can brush your teeth and everything.' 'Oh, terrific.' Howard was very grateful for that privacy. Sharing a bathroom with them would have been, he suddenly realised, nearly impossible. 'Thank you, wee man.' Saul stopped and looked at him. 'In Scotland "wee" means small, doesn't it? Like *petit* in French.' 'That's right. It doesn't mean, you know—' Saul cut him off. 'Urine. Yes, I thought so.'

Saul and Howard descended together. Les and Barbara, who had been talking in the hall, stopped. They looked up at Howard and he saw in their eyes a kind of tense sincerity in which was visible their fear at the decision they had taken but a definite determination for it to work. Not more scared than he was, that was for sure. He smiled desperately while his hands looked for something to do, grasping each other behind his back then into his pockets then by his sides then one up on the wall then a two-handed adjustment of his glasses.

What was he doing there, in their home? There was an answer, obviously, but right then he couldn't remember it. The house seemed huge. In his room, to which he quickly fled to unpack and 'settle himself in', he couldn't even hear their voices downstairs. He opened the fat, noisy latches of his mother's suitcase and hung his wrinkled clothes in the wardrobe then put up a photograph of his mother, her Sacred Heart and rosary, along with the one ornament of hers that he had kept – the lifebelt souvenir from Blackpool. The school photograph of himself he put in a drawer. At the bottom of his suitcase he came to the one dress of his mother's that he'd brought with him, not a nice dress but one he clearly remembered her wearing – actually it must have been that same time in Blackpool. Red and gold paisley on a white background. A summer dress. He touched the fabric with his fingertips. He thought that although this wardrobe was nothing like her maybe if he hung the dress in it, well, she'd be there in a way. So he did. And looked at it and thought about it, then leaned his forehead against its unfamiliar resonance and whispered to her where he was and how everything was fine, trying to believe it through his tiredness, clinging to the tilted surface of this new place. The days ahead were unimaginable. And what about when they found out who he was and what he'd done, what then?

At dinner their questions started. Les wanted to know all about his jobs. Between mouthfuls of something vegetably rendered tasteless with fear, Howard answered him.

'I've had a few jobs, you know how it is. I worked in a garage for a bit. And a barber's. And a supermarket. Then a warehouse. Then a gym, where I met your mother.' Les nodded gravely. 'And I've worked in a chip shop with a little fellow named Alf who used to be a boxer. That was just right now where I burned my arm.'

'I see. But I imagine you'd like to move into something better, something where you can start at the bottom and work up.'

'Oh, yes. That sounds an ideal kind of thing.'

'Well, after what you did for my mother, I'll be pleased to put you up for a bit while you find yourself a position down here. There's no point staying up north, I think. Nothing doing. That's why I left myself.'

'Oh, you're right. It's dead quiet. Nothing at all.'

'So, you can be our guest for a wee while.' Les did his version of a Scottish accent, smiling at his own good humour. 'It might be good to have another ambitious person in the house. As you know, this is an important time for Saul here,' he placed a clean hand on the boy's head, 'so we want things nice and calm.'

'Of course. In the car Saul said something about a world championships.'

'He's told you? Two months and counting. And serious chances, high hopes.'

'It's amazing. All the things he can remember just from seeing them once. He must get through his school books in no time. I wish I could've done that.'

'So do I, friend. And that's nothing.' Les leaned forward again, moving his wine glass to one side. 'What if I told you that this boy has learned a number that is a thousand digits long.'

'What, like three thousand?'

'No, not a thousand. A number made up of a thousand numbers.'

Howard forgot himself and slapped the table. 'No way!'

'Or that he could memorise a shuffled pack of cards in one minute.'

'I don't believe it.'

'You will, Howard, when you see it. That's the kind of talent we're talking about. This boy has unimaginable success ahead of him. So,' he skipped his fingers across the surface of the table in time to his conclusion, 'everything nice and calm and focused.'

'I understand. I'll start looking for a job tomorrow. Why not, you know. And, you know, I'll pay for my food and everything.'

Les grimaced, waving a dismissive hand. 'You're my guest, Howard. I thought I'd already told you that.'

'I've had a thought myself,' Barbara interrupted. Six male eyes turned to her. She held the back of her neck as she continued. 'I thought maybe, well, just for the now, the garden. You know, there's lots that needs doing.' She turned encouragingly to Howard. 'You've gardened before, haven't you?'

He lied again, mostly to help her out. 'Aha, a wee bit, yes.'

'Well then.' She smiled. 'As I say, it needs doing. I can give you instructions. You can be our gardener for a bit.'

Howard turned for confirmation to Les, who turned back to him shrugging, hands held up in a gesture of mock defeat.

When the clouds let down a pattering rain, Howard stood in the shed watching the drops strike its dusty glass, feeling ruddy and large and full of air, an outdoors man briefly taking shelter. He kept the door open and lit a cigarette. The rain deepened the quiet of the garden; through the trees it made a gracious sound.

Everything about working in the garden was good. Barbara told him what he needed to do and he got on with it, happy to take orders, happy to have things to do. At his own sweet pace he could mow the lawn and weed between the waxy crocuses, so purple in the sun, the long-stemmed cups of the tulips, and the little crowds of daffs blowing their golden noses. It was already well weeded, the garden, so it wasn't hard to find the little dowdy interlopers full of big plans and tug them gently, gently out of the soil so that their roots didn't break. Although once or twice he wasn't sure if he'd pulled out some legitimate, intended plant. He'd be mulching soon, whatever that was exactly, once he'd gone to buy some mulch with Barbara.

He could smoke whenever he liked now and he loved being outside among the first drowsy insects and other creatures – a robin that watched him turning the earth then hunted where he'd been, nervy squirrels that raced in the branches and rippled away over the lawn when he approached. There was a neighbourhood cat as well that reminded him of Ginger, although only really by virtue of being a cat. This one was black and white and sleek and inquisitive, and allowed Howard to pet it a little, slitting its eyes and angling its warm head into the pleasure. Howard liked all animals without exception, he thought. There was a spider swaying on its web right there by the shed window, brown as a rat and fat on its prey, and Howard felt well disposed towards it. 'Hello, Spider,' he whispered. 'Hello, Spider.' He wondered if there were any more and looked at the slumped tools, a tangle of teeth and useful blades. That was another job he could do – sorting the shed out.

There was just a whole different kind of time you lived in the garden, the kind you usually only got to glimpse in your

69

fag breaks, wide and free, the time of things growing and cats exploring and rain showers (which now had passed) and the day's light growing and fading, the day's warmth. This southern spring seemed gentler than the northern one and sort of kind, motherly.

Yes, Howard was all for this gardening business. Apart from anything else it didn't seem that hard. He could learn it as a job, training himself up in the Dawson-Smiths' garden then starting on other people's, or maybe work in a park. Hyde Park, Regent's Park, London was full of them. And shopping centres always had things growing. He pictured himself full of health in a checked shirt, seeds in his pockets and earth in the cracks of his hands, knowing the names of all the plants, bending over some green shoot that curled up towards him like a hopeful child.

Howard stepped out of the shed into a garden of rain-deepened colours, breezy sunlight and wet glimmerings among the plants. Birds restated their songs. Saul walked towards him across the lawn with hands in his pockets and head bent, forehead first. He looked very small in the distance in his school uniform and remained small when he arrived by Howard's side. 'Hello, Howard,' he said without looking up. His forehead was wrinkled against the light.

'Hello, wee man. Are y'aright?' Howard asked the thoughtful boy.

'Yes,' Saul sighed. 'It's just I haven't practised the flute for ages and Simon Clifford is coming later.'

The boy played the flute! Really there was no end to him. 'Does Simon Clifford teach you the flute?'

'No. I learn the flute at school. I've got a class tomorrow. Simon teaches me memory. He's from Canada.'

'Oh. I just found a big old spider in the shed. Do you want to see?'

'No,' Saul said. 'Well, I would but I haven't got time. I haven't even been on the rowing machine yet.' He turned and walked slowly back to the house like a weary convalescent returning up the path to the sanatorium.

Barbara appeared at the French doors that gave onto the garden and ushered him in.

That boy worked unbelievably hard. Howard had never seen anything like it. At Ridgemont you worked hard at avoiding trouble with the other lads and the wardens; you were tired a lot of the time, but it was a useless effort to be invisible in full view. Your energy frittered away each day, bitten down like fingernails, until you went to bed exhausted and hoped there'd be no bother after that. But Saul was always learning, always making progress. There was a rota, a timetable, for every day of his life, and Howard was now himself part of it. There were set times for conversation and relaxation. This wasn't one of them.

Les zizzed around the house like an insect when he was at home. Howard kept waiting for him to mention Mrs Dawson and what had happened but he never did. She remained in Howard's mind, though. Alone in his room he thought of her, remembered her so slightly, so delicately leaving the world, following his own mother to wherever they went. He sat in his room and spoke to his mother while he changed the dressing on his arm – the wound smaller now, almost healed, but tender. He said, 'You wouldn't believe this place, Ma, really,' thinking of their own flat when he was Saul's age in Glasgow, a cage in which his father exploded. The comparison of families smeared his mind with shame. He touched his arm too hard and flinched. Thank God after Ridgemont his mother had taken him south to their own place. *Just us two souls together.* Until that came apart and he woke up here among these strangers. Barbara blankly kind, Les in motion, Saul anxiously working. It was Varya who calmed him. Not at first, of course, and not when he got her fired.

He was descending the stairs on his way to the garden the first time they met. He heard noises from one of the rooms and found that worrying because Barbara's car wasn't in the drive. 'Barbara?' he asked the empty hallway. Before he had time to think about burglars and get scared he opened the door of the living room to find a blonde girl in an apron dusting the table. 'Hello?' She didn't answer him. 'Hello?' he tried again. He went and stood in her line of vision but still she didn't acknowledge him. She moved to the mantelshelf and dusted the photographs, a silver cigarette case, a little statue of a kingfisher. She turned towards Howard now, still without making eye contact or saying a word. 'Oh!' he said when she plucked his glasses from his face, polished the lenses with her yellow cloth, then set them back on his nose and came into focus still apparently ignoring him. She went on polishing the mantel without saying a word but Howard could see that the side of her mouth was crooked with a smile.

Howard and Varya stood in the garden together and smoked. 'How often do you come here?' Howard asked.

Varya laughed. 'And what is nice girl like you doing in place like this? I come two times in one week. It's a big house.'

'It is that,' Howard agreed.

'I am Varya,' she said.

'Var . . .'

'Ee-a. Var-ee-a.'

'Var-ee-a.'

'That is right.'

'Pleased to meet you.'

She smiled. 'You welcome.'

Varya fell silent. Between bits of talk and laughter, Varya fell deeply into silence. And they looked at the garden, the shivering leaves, or up at the sky when a plane scraped over-head. It was her foreignness, maybe, but to Howard she seemed very far away when she wasn't speaking. It was hyp-notic, a marine silence of unguessable depth. It made Howard feel lucky to be standing next to her, next to a woman, a young woman with that serious, lyrical distance all around her. And then when she snapped out of it she was very friendly.

'So you live here?' she asked him.

'Yes.'

'You family?'

'No.'

'No. I don't think so. The hair.' She flicked up the side of his red hair with her hand. Howard flinched.

'No, I ... It's complicated. I do the garden.'

'So, you like me. You work for them. They pay you good?'

'No. Not really. I mean, I live here.'

Her eyes widened. 'You live? Here?'

'Yes, but ... I knew Les's mother.'

'Oh.' She paused. 'I don't see him much. I don't like him.'

She sank away again into silence. Howard looked at her sidelong. She was pretty in a not very pretty way. Narrow, grey eyes. A dimpled chin. A mouth as wide as it was deep. And a dominating nose comprised of four distinct planes: a bent diamond. Smoke wandered from her nostrils. Pale hair streamed from her forehead in the breeze. She seemed quite happy standing there next to Howard. She didn't move away.

Another bush had come into flower in the garden. All over it hung small, four-petalled white flowers with trailing stamens, fine as an insect's legs. Howard tilted one up to look into its eye, then carried on with his work. Howard painstakingly tied many climbing shoots with bits of twine to a trellis along the fence, an activity he found soothing, like doing up his shoelaces a hundred times. He finished all the weeding. He scattered scraps of his lunch to the hungry birds. After a companionable trip to the garden centre with Barbara, where he got to play the big man, carrying heavy sacks on his shoulders, he finally discovered what mulch is: just lots of bits of old bark to keep the weeds out. It rattled dryly as he spread it around the growing plants. On the one solidly rainy day he sorted out the shed, cleaning and lining up the tools by size while the roof drummed and the window streamed. He pruned some straggly bushes having been shown how to by Barbara, finding the forks in the growth and cutting through scabby, brown rind and creamy pith. He fed the lawn and imagined the grass as millions of tiny, grateful, underground mouths. His beneficence was wonderful. A loving god, he helped life to flourish in the garden. But gradually he started running out of jobs, started taking as much time as he could with the ones he had. He found the broom a great aid for this. At the very least he could always be found pensively sweeping.

Three times he stood and smoked with Varya. He gave her a guided tour of the garden. 'From Amsterdam,' she said, pointing at the tulips. 'You know, Amsterdam,' she continued. She held her cigarette in her mouth and staggered, acting woozy. She was very funny, always joking. About different plants she kept assuring him, 'We have this in Russia. In Russia spring is many, many flowers on trees.' 'Oh, it sounds beautiful,' Howard replied. He adopted broken English himself when he was speaking to her, assuming she'd understand better if he spoke the language as badly as she did. 'In Glasgow spring,' he said, 'is many, many rain.'

He explained his bandages to her, telling the story with gestures (' . . . it all went whoosh') and falling over. She sniggered but was then appropriately frightened, widening those grey eyes and opening her mouth. She examined the bandages and pitied his wound.

Saul worked without anyone's pity, or only Howard's and that he never uttered out loud. Saul worked, urged on with the tense festiveness of Les's encouragement and Barbara's smiling pride. He worked for hours at the table then emerged pale and heavy-lidded to walk around the garden with Howard for ten minutes before dinner. Saul didn't like to talk much about the work he was doing; by then he'd had enough of it. But he was very interested in Howard and where he came from. He asked him if people drove the same sorts of cars in Scotland. He asked him who his friends were; Howard discovered with pleasure and relief that he could answer with Andy's name and Alf's. Saul asked him about his parents and Howard said that they were ordinary folk and turned the conversation back to the memory championships. Howard wanted to see what it was the wee prodigy actually did.

Saul was so inquisitive, so light and quick and intelligent, that Howard enjoyed just looking at him as he might at a squirrel or some other clever animal. He was beautiful in his movements even if his head seemed to weigh so much and he didn't attack the world with his father's certainty because of his delicacy. There was a kind of envelope of clarity around him, visible in the bright air between his thin fingers for example, that made huge Howard happy to be near him. It reminded Howard of being a little boy, the way it felt like a friendship was starting between them just because they liked standing next to each other.

Howard repeated the request to see some of Saul's memory work when they went back inside and that evening Les compèred a demonstration. His head reddening with 'fun' – a kind of dry, almost angry rushing – he asked Howard to shuffle two packs of cards, which he did very badly with much apology. Saul then carefully scrutinised them – his face compressed, his lips moving – handed them back and recited while Howard read the cards in disbelief. How did it all go into that small head? 'It's a trick, isn't it? Show me how you do it, show me,' he pleaded. 'Ah,' said Les, tapping the side of his nose with his finger. 'Actually, anyone can do it with enough training. Maybe even you.' 'No way!' Howard objected. 'Maybe Saul will train you. And now ... pi!' Les announced. 'To a thousand digits.'

Saul stood up. 'Pi,' he began, 'is the constant ratio between the circumference of a perfect circle and its diameter.' He started to recite the number in a high-pitched monotone. 'Its

75

value to a thousand decimal places is three point one four one five nine two six five three five zero six two eight six two zero eight nine nine five three five nine four zero eight one two eight six six five nine three three four four six one one three three nine three six zero seven two six seven eight nine two five nine zero three six zero zero nine two one eight six one one seven three eight three zero one one nine four nine one two zero five three nine two one seven one seven six seven five seven seven eight nine six zero nine one ...' And on and on until suddenly the fit was off; Saul faltered. The voice that sounded more like a possession than his own voice stopped. Marooned in the middle of the carpet, he looked panic-stricken at Les. Les remained calm. Firmly and gently he said, 'It's there. Just relax. You can find it.' Saul looked up at the ceiling, then said, 'Oh, oh,' and carried on, the voice starting again, emitting numbers one by one. 'Two six four three three eight three two seven nine three four two one one seven zero six seven nine ...' All the way to the thousandth digit, which Barbara applauded with her long-fingered hands held high over her head.

These people were geniuses, no doubt about it, and never calm, never just watching telly and vegging out. Howard really missed telly. Without it, he couldn't switch off and hang his tired mind in the wash of colours and friendliness. He thought of all the comedy shows he was missing, major new adverts he wouldn't even know about, all the gardening shows he could be learning from. Not having telly kept Howard inside himself at all times and this wasn't good. What with Saul's questions, all the tumult in his life, the questions provoked by every scrap of difference between his old life and the lives of these strangers, he was starting to have memories.

April 26th

Howard came inside to find Varya and show her a ladybird he had tickling the large pads of his cupped hands. He thought it an insect that Varya should see; it was very English somehow: an oddity, pottering about, Royal Mail red and smart. Concentrating on taking care of the small life in his big paws, he searched slowly round the house, only too quietly – when he eventually found Varya in the living room she didn't hear him or turn round. Instead, he saw the strangest thing. Varya picked up a small silver cigarette case and dropped it into the front pocket of her apron. 'Varya,' he said and she turned round quickly. She seemed startled but didn't look guilty. Maybe she was just moving it or it needed special cleaning. 'Hyoward,' she said. 'Varya, I've got something to show you.' He came close to her and slowly opened his hands into a bowl showing the ladybird heading up the ridges of his fingers towards the light.

'It's very nice. Little bug.'

'It's a ladybird. We call it a ladybird.'

'Lady Bird. That's nice name. Careful.' Howard turned his hand to keep it upright. 'But I am busy now. Please. I have to finish.'

Howard returned to the garden, mission accomplished, and blew against the ladybird, which crouched, reluctant to leave him. He blew harder until it flipped up its red shell and purred away on its fragile wings.

He went back inside again and this time saw Varya doing something definitely wrong. He saw her bending over in the hall and that same silver cigarette case slipped, quick as a fish, into her bag. He backed away into the kitchen, his brain flooding with fear. *Why had he had to see it?* he thought. If he hadn't nothing would be wrong. But then hang on, no, he could still make it better. It was simple. All he had to do was put it back. Wait till she was somewhere else, filch it from her bag and make sure everything was how it had been.

Howard stood behind the kitchen door, breathing through his mouth, waiting for his moment until it came. Varya disappeared into the downstairs toilet. Howard emerged, ears singing, and bent down over her canvas bag, his neck thick and throbbing, his hands odorous with sweat. He felt inside, found the cold cigarette case and was standing up when he heard Barbara say his name twice either side of a revelation.

'Howard? Howard!'

'No, no, Barbara, it's not. This . . . I'm not.'

'What have you got in your hand?'

Howard seemed to need to look down to remember. 'Nothing. It's not . . .'

'Howard, we trusted you!' Instant tears enlarged Barbara's eyes.

To the accompaniment of her flush, Varya re-entered the room and paled. She gave Howard a look that felt like a blow. 'Varya, really, I didn't . . .'

'What is problem?' she demanded. She seemed more angry than frightened. 'When I clean I move this. Maybe Hyoward is put it back.'

'Ay, that's right, Barbara, I'm put it back.'

'I don't believe you.' Barbara stared at them with brimming eyes. 'I don't believe either of you. Neither of you are going anywhere until Les gets back.'

Saul opened the door to his father and saw the image of the man that lived so forcefully inside his mind, work-weary and with loosened tie. That was always how he came home from work. His briefcase and car keys and silver watch still connected him to the world of adult importance but now his energies, after a drink, would come streaming towards Saul, forcing him to work. Saul was glad this one evening to be able to deflect them towards the thrilling drama in the living room.

'Dad, Mum wants you. It's important.'

Les found his wife with eyes hard and pale mouth and Howard and Varya seated in sour silence in the living room. Howard worked his face, practically chattering like a monkey with fear, while the Russian girl's small eyes were narrowed with contempt.

In front of the two employees and holding the cigarette case in her hand, Barbara, in a confidential whisper that reminded Howard of being helplessly under discussion while teachers or policemen or guards talked, explained what she had found to Les, a man she knew was used to employees and sacking people. He shook his head. 'This has got to be some sort of bloody joke,' he said. Howard looked up at him, the small, quick man who clapped his hands once and commenced. 'Right. I'm not going to waste time. I've got better things to be doing. What happened?'

Varya stayed leaning back in her chair as she spoke, hands in the pocket of her apron. 'I cleaned, move something. Hyoward move it back. No big drama.'

'Is that right, Howard?'

Howard held the side of his glasses with a trembling hand. 'Aha, yes it is. That's what happened. Yes.'

'Okay, Howard. So why were you found removing the cigarette case from Varya's bag? Had she moved it into her bag? This was my father's cigarette case, by the way. I want you both to know that. It is a very precious object to me.'

'Not in bag,' Varya interjected. 'Next to it. Next to bag.'

'Aha. That's right,' Howard confirmed.

Les turned rhetorically to Barbara, shaking his head with weary disgust. 'But that's not what you saw, is it, darling?' It occurred to Howard he had never heard Les call Barbara 'darling' before. 'You saw Howard removing the cigarette case from Varya's bag, didn't you?'

Barbara tugged at her necklace. 'He had one strap in his hand,' she said very quietly.

Had he? Howard didn't remember that. But Barbara's general accusation was true so that couldn't be a lie.

Les turned again to Howard, turned on him his full, angry attention. Howard quaked. This was hopeless. He couldn't lie. It felt like Les could see right into him, see right through his skin to the frightened rabbit of his heart. 'Howard,' Les barked, setting off bombs inside Howard's chest. Howard looked at Varya, who was hard and unflinching, her face a mask of defiance, 'Howard, don't look at her. Look at me.' Les crouched down beside Howard's chair. Howard could feel the force of his intent, could smell his tepid breath, could see each hair as it curved back from Les's hairline.

'Howard,' Les's voice was quiet now, 'that doesn't really make sense to me. I mean, if Varya moves a cigarette case why would she move it right next to her bag? I mean, I could understand it if it were on the wrong table upstairs or things were put back in the wrong order ...'

This was taking so long and Howard felt so lonely. The wait for Les to return had been endless, an endless tightening of the situation around him. And now he was at the centre of this thing, responsible for it all, when all he'd tried to do was help. The only way out now was to hurt Varya: nakedly and in full view to grass on her. His attempts at lies would not stand up to Les's scrutiny. Such a small man, Howard could have knocked him across the room with a slap. He could pick up the poker and make everyone nice and quiet. But you can't do that. You kick against authority and it surrounds and destroys you. Besides, they were his friends. Les and Barbara were so kind, so good to him. He owed them so much that he had to do what they wanted. *Why me?* he thought. *Why me?*

Les's quiet, persistent voice burrowed into his ear. 'So, the natural assumption that I am making, Howard, is that you were retrieving something she had stolen because you're a good and loyal man whom I have welcomed as a guest into my home.'

Howard gibbered bits of words.

'Please, Howard. This has taken far too long already. All you have to do is say "Yes" or "No". Had Varya stolen the picture?'

'She moved it. I don't know.'

'Had she stolen it? Had she? Had she stolen the cigarette case?'

Close to tears, with his mouth open and his hands twitching in his lap, Howard nodded twice. The second nod made it definite.

'Right. Good. Varya, get out. You're fired.' Varya's tears started now. 'Thank you, Howard. It was a noble attempt to protect a fellow worker, but it's good to know that you're on our side after all.'

Varya pleaded: 'Please. I steal because poor. Need money is only why. Only. Please.' Each word hit Howard like a thrown pebble. Les ignored her.

'I'm sorry,' Howard mumbled. 'I'm sorry.'

She started cursing now in rapid Russian, words that hissed and writhed from her lips. Howard looked at his knees. Saul appeared in the doorway just in time to see Varya tear off her apron and fling it onto the freshly hoovered carpet before grabbing her bag and banging out of the house.

April 30th

In the quiet of the garden, while bees wound their way in lazy spirals to the small flowers in the grass and a breeze stirred the new growth, Howard's head was loud with thoughts. Hidden from view of the house by the trunk of a large tree, he smoked and considered Varya's departure. He saw again and again the moments when he could have said something different or said nothing at all and just slipped off to hide in the shed. But each time the little doors slammed shut and what had happened closed around him until he saw himself trapped, bent in a posture of servile cunning and treachery while tears trembled from the end of Varya's sharp chin. He heard her repeating, 'Please, I have no money, please.' The interrogation had been like being in court again. Isolated, trapped, crushed. If only he hadn't tried to put it back (but then *he* would have been suspected); if only he had said something to Varya (without upsetting her?); if only he had said something else to Barbara (lies?). If, if, if. He exhaled smoke he could taste but not see into the bright air. It never tasted quite so good when you couldn't see it and he turned and rubbed his cigarette out against the tree trunk then cursed the ashy mess he'd made, rubbing at it with his fingers.

'Hello, Howard.'

He turned and found that rubbing the tree had produced, like an awful genie, Les.

'Yes, hello.'

Les held his hands behind his back, rocked up on his toes. 'What are you doing there?' His receding hair, bulked into a small quiff, was pulsingly alive in the wind.

'Just, ah, cleaning.' Howard's tongue failed him typically. There was ant, you see, an ant.'

'Oh, right.' Les nodded, worryingly pensive. 'I'll leave you to it, then. I just didn't know where you were. I'm off to work.'

Howard rushed to reassure him. 'I was just here, out here.'

'So I see.' Les turned back towards the house. 'Don't kill them all, by the way.'

Blood surged into Howard's head so quickly his lips buzzed. 'What?' he called.

'Ants.' Les smiled. 'They're not all bad.'

When he heard the back door shut, Howard moaned and pressed his forehead into the biting roughness of the bark. He ground his skull against the tree for a moment in an effort to relax. Everywhere he could be seen was the new thought in his head. Any guilt was immediately obvious. He just would not be able to conceal the fact that he now had pretty much nothing to do. It would be plain as the plants he'd burnt the other day by watering at noon. (Who knew that water could burn plants?) Barbara had been upset by that. She'd touched the crackling frills of burn with long, regretful fingers and sweat had poured down between Howard's breasts. He was starting to accumulate mistakes; the syndrome was familiar. He would not be able to make any more if he was going to stay, if he was not going to have to leave, which is what always happened when his mistakes multiplied. And now it was obvious that Les thought he was skiving. Hadn't he just caught him hidden behind a tree with one arm as long as the other? Maybe if he could do the cleaning as well now that Varya was gone . . . Yes, Howard realised, that might save him. He made straight for the house to find Barbara, his round face puckered to whistle.

He found her standing by a window with her hands in her cardigan pockets. Now, if there was ever a person not doing anything . . . She turned quickly.

'Sorry . . .' he struggled to fetch out a name to call her, 'sorry, Miss, I just wanted a word.'

'Certainly, Howard.' She spread a smile over her features like a pristine table cloth. 'I was just noticing these pots could do with a water.'

'Uch, I know.' Howard stepped forward and prodded the crummy dry earth with thick fingers. He found himself near to her, inside her bubble. She was close when she said, 'Oh, you've got something on your forehead.'

'What?' He rubbed at it. Ash. What? Oh, the tree. 'It's just a bit of ash,' he explained.

'You haven't just come from church, have you?' She smiled.

'No, no, I havenae.' He dismissed the suggestion quickly, frowning.

'I'm sorry. You might have done, mightn't you?'

Mightn't you? Posh people really did speak another language. 'I'm sorry?'

'The Sacred Heart in your room. There's a Catholic church just up the road from here, you know.'

'Yes. No. Is there?' This conversation was sliding sideways, listing uncomfortably into heavy waters. He must try to get back to what he wanted to say. 'I don't really anyways.'

'I'm sorry.' She smiled again. 'It's none of my business, really. I don't mean to pry.' It was funny how sometimes you could hear a London accent in her voice and how it disappeared.

'Yes. No.' He shut his eyes tight and waved his hand in front of his face to erase the conversation so far then started again, still with his eyes closed. 'I just wanted to say maybe I could do some cleaning for you, you know, now . . .' He opened his eyes. Barbara was still right there. She blinked slowly to indicate that she understood the reference to the unmentionable event. 'And there's no so much to do in the garden. I could sort of do it as well, see.'

'What a good idea,' she replied. 'I was wondering what we could do with you.'

So his time *had* been running out.

'Well, I'll do everything you tell me,' he protested.

Barbara laughed. 'What an offer. It's just ordinary cleaning. I'll write you a list.'

'Oh, yes.' Relief, finally. Conversations with the Dawson-Smiths always seemed to veer between embarrassment and fear, ending, finally, at least so far, in safety. 'Yes, as I say,' he announced in the tone of a reliable factotum, 'I'd be very happy to do it.'

'Well, go and wash your hands. I'll get you an extra large pinny and you can get started.'

Cleaning proved to be the most frightening activity anyone had ever devised It involved vigorous force in a small space. It involved handling every most precious, expensive and breakable object in the house, often applying violent friction to those objects. It involved accidentally whacking the legs of chairs and tables with the vacuum cleaner, which howled on impact like an injured animal. It meant dusting pictures askew and not being able to get them straight again. It meant almost bouncing mirrors off the wall as you got distracted by the bouncing reflection of your own red face. It meant, simply, very nearly destroying everything in the house and getting very sweaty in the process. Howard hated cleaning and felt the evil of his fate lurking inside every smashable wee thing just waiting to break out.

May 6th

Saul backed away in fright when Howard tried to repeat Varya's funny joke and polished the boy's startled face with a yellow duster. With a look of annoyance and by carefully checking his face for damage, Saul let Howard know of his enormity. 'Sorry, wee man,' Howard explained, 'I thought you needed polishing up.' Saul scowled, but Howard was not abashed. He would draw the boy out of himself, wake him out of his dream of work. They were both trapped in this house, Howard had decided, working away for the two grown-ups. They should at least have some fun while they were there. Shining in Howard's mind's eye was the present he had bought that waited in the shed. 'Why don't we go for a walk in the garden to recover,' he suggested. 'I've got something to show you.' Saul said nothing but with his pet-like loyalty followed when Howard exited through the French windows.

'It's a ball,' said Saul.

'So it is.' Howard grinned. Howard held aloft on his fingertips a plastic ball he'd bought at the sweet shop in the parade a few long roads away. It had cost exactly one pound fifty and was decorated with aerosol blotches of glittery pink and blue. When tapped it made tight, echoey noises that suggested a great willingness to bounce and float.

'What do you want me to do with it?' Saul asked nervously.

'I don't know. Catch it maybe,' Howard suggested. The ball made a wincing sound as Howard bounced it once on the patio. He looked at Saul, who had taken a pace back. He hadn't even loosened his school tie, let alone removed it. 'Why don't you stand over there and I'll throw it to you.'

Saul sighed and scratched his nose. His skin was pale, his hair cinnamon-coloured in the light.

'Go on. Get back.' Howard marshalled him away with a strictly pointing finger. Saul moaned and took reluctant backward steps out onto the grass. Howard nodded encouragement.

'Ready?' Howard called.

'Ready,' he admitted.

'Good man. Here it comes.'

Howard threw the ball and Saul, shifting into line, lunging at the last moment, caught it.

'What now?' he asked.

'I don't know. Throw it back?'

'All right.' Saul launched the ball with a single desperate shove towards Howard, who stooped to catch it by his knees.

'Why don't you come onto the patio so the light isn't in your eyes,' Howard advised. Saul's face was pinched against the sun that came over the house. He nodded and trotted over.

'I'm ready.'

Howard threw the ball again, this time hefting it one-handed from his shoulder like an airy shot put. Saul caught it with two hands directly over his head. The ball rang with sudden arrest. 'I know,' he said, holding it there. 'You've got to throw it with one bounce on the patio.' He hurled it down and up it popped to Howard's side, who tapped it up once with his healing forearm and caught it.

'Look out!' Howard called and threw it down himself with great force. It bounced up loudly as if frightened then drifted wobbling quickly into Saul's arms, who had to hug it under his chin to keep hold. He threw it back, each time more vigorously, each of them enjoying the yelp of the ball up from the stones, Saul taking pleasure in the dreamy, weightless flight that meant he could pluck it tamely from the air. 'I know what,' he breathed, holding the ball like a natural, footballer-style, against his hip with a resting arm. 'You can't catch it. You just have to smack it back.' Howard nodded, puffing, adjusting his glasses with a trembling hand.

Saul smacked the ball. It jerked up at an angle. Howard swatted it so hard his palm tingled. Saul watched it, wide-eyed, side-stepping, and banged it back. Howard waited, aligned, and struck again. They played until their hands were red with the impacts against the ball's tight skin, Saul's hair was sweated up into a crest at the fringe, and Howard's heart flopped and struggled inside his chest. Howard begged finally to be excused, holding up a defeated hand as he doubled over. He sat down on the step by the window and dragged the needed pints of air into his chest. Saul held the ball and started laughing. 'Come on, come on,' he cajoled. He dribbled the ball like a basketball player, an inexpert one, slapping the ball flat-handed, and edged towards Howard. He grabbed the ball and held it over Howard's head. 'Come on, I'll do it,' he warned. As Howard looked up he saw that the boy's eyes were wild. With his flaring hair and now loosened tie he looked properly naughty.

'Just one . . .' Howard struggled to speak.

'Too late,' Saul cried and bounced the ball off Howard's defenceless head. Howard ducked and the ball ricocheted from his bald spot. He felt and found funny the spank of plastic skin against his own. He started laughing and coughing as Saul ran out onto the grass to fetch back the ball which Howard now knew had been a brilliant gift. Saul was running up again to launch the ball at Howard's damp, red head when there was a loud knocking at the window behind. Howard staggered light-headed to his feet. Les stood murkily on the other side of the glass, half-masked by reflected sky, with a strange man standing next to him. He wore glasses and had the mild, wide-mouthed face of a browsing animal. 'Oh no, it's Simon Clifford,' Saul said. 'I forgot I had him as well tonight.' So that was the tutor who came to train Saul. Even though both Howard and Saul were turned guiltily to face them, Les knocked again sharply against the glass.

Howard did not want to leave his room for dinner that evening. He sat in his room pulling at the lacy scabs at the edge of his burn that lifted up like little hinges. The centre of the wound was smooth now, white and opaque, resembling molten plastic. He stood up as the time approached and paced, muttering, knowing he'd made his next mistake. He avoided the staring wardrobe and paced. Finally he just walked out of his door and downstairs as though absent-mindedly doing nothing at all. The family were seated in silence, or at least Howard's entrance created a silence, which he then broke with a rambling, mendacious apology about his watch having stopped. Les listened without looking up, stroking his right eyebrow with his forefinger. When Howard had settled, feeling his mouth still talking, into his chair, Barbara disappeared and returned with dishes of broccoli, knobby little potatoes and grilled fish fillets. Howard didn't really understand why anyone would eat broccoli out of choice and the other items he knew had that pale, healthy flavour (that is to say, very little flavour) which saddened his appetite. He helped himself without enthusiasm when the others had done so. Under cover of his fringe, Saul shot him a glance. Les apparently noticed this. He cleared his throat and started talking.

'There are different kinds of exercise,' Les began, 'some of which are conducive to learning and others which aren't.'

'I see what you mean,' Howard quickly assured him, hoping to agree the conversation to a rapid conclusion.

'Do you?' Les regarded Howard with curiosity. 'Rowing, swift walking, measured, rhythmical, cardiovascular exercise is good for building endurance and circulating blood to the brain.'

'Yes, I see that.'

'Aping around with a ball, however ...'

'... is not, no.' Howard quickly completed, irrelevantly

amused by the phrase 'aping around'. His gaze flicked across to Saul to see if he was smirking. He wasn't.

'No, it isn't,' Les insisted as though Howard had said otherwise.

'We appreciate the gift that you bought,' Barbara interjected as she lifted to her mouth a white triangle of fish. Les visibly ignored her, leaving a small pause. Her chewing slowed. Les exhaled slowly through his nose.

Suddenly Howard remembered what he ought to say. 'I'm very sorry,' he said. 'I didn't mean no harm by it. I thought, you know, for the boy ...'

Les relented slightly; his shoulders dropped slightly. 'I know you're sorry, Howard.'

'It was a nice thought,' Barbara assured him, her gaze downcast.

'But inappropriate,' Les continued. 'We have a competition that is now just two months away. July ninth through eleventh. Two months! The world championships! And our boy here,' Saul shielded his eyes with his hand and pushed broccoli across his plate with his fork, 'has a serious chance of winning. The junior world champion! That's what's up for grabs here.'

'It's amazing, I know. I'm really sorry.' Howard looked over at Saul hunched over his plate. The boy balanced his fork on the fulcrum of his fingertip. He kept the other hand hiding his face and said nothing at all.

May 8th

Howard had been discovered by Barbara doing nothing at the kitchen table. He tried to leave but she insisted that he should stay to keep her company while she prepared the dinner. Howard worried that she was lonely and would try to talk to him. He hid by pretending to read. The Mensa magazine was not very good for pictures so he was forced unwillingly into uncomfortable densities of print. He'd given up an article about science teaching and another one about whether or not Anne Frank would have made a good Mensa member – she would have been very good, apparently – and now found himself running his eye down the long list of meetings and events. To his surprise he discovered that these clever people were very fond of pub lunches. *And why shouldn't they be?* he reflected. They can't just sit around all day doing Rubik's cubes. By the time Les walked through the door and jabbed his wife's cheek with a kiss, Howard knew that Vera's sixtieth would have been celebrated in Colchester three days previously. He wondered what the party had been like. Had they all recited pi together?

'I've got some news for you, Howard,' Les told him, loosening his tie.

Howard struggled to get his tongue moving. 'Ga,' he said.

Les then left the room and Howard got up anxiously and followed. Les looked around surprised but allowed it anyway. Howard was a man, after all, who must have been in changing rooms before. Howard followed Les into his bedroom and the small man began to undress.

'What it is,' Les began, shucking off his shoes, 'is an

opportunity for you that has opened up.' Les lifted his tie as a noose over his head and popped open his shirt. Les may have been small, Howard discovered, but he was not short of hair. Howard couldn't look away from his host's black pelt, the thick line of hair seaming his centre. 'You can come and work for me at Holland's Supplies.'

Nipples! Howard was thinking, *nipples!* as Les's chest muscles pouted with the movement of his arms. 'Right,' he answered. 'And, ah, ah, what is it you do, exactly?'

'It's office supplies. We're one of London's largest,' Les said with pride, standing only in his pants. 'For you it would be warehouse work.'

'Oh, I see.'

'A bit physical, you know.'

'Ay, yes.' Howard did know. He'd worked in a warehouse before and didn't much like the idea of going back.

'Good work for a big man like yourself.' Les pulled down over his head a clean linen shirt. 'And a decent salary. It'll get you back on your feet.'

'Oh ay, thanks definitely.' Howard excused himself by pointing at the door and leaving sideways. Dusty gloom and weights to lift – no more gardening! Howard walked back towards that boring magazine heavy-hearted and knew that he was being punished for the ball. He couldn't even talk to Saul for another half-hour until he'd finished his work with this Simon Clifford, who was Saul's memory coach. A coach – like it was a real sport. He was frighteningly clever and obviously not normal, Simon Clifford, but actually almost nice. He was foreign, a Canadian. Earlier that evening he'd told Howard off for smoking in the garden where Saul could see him.

'You shouldn't smoke anyway, you know.'

Howard looked at Simon Clifford's large and detailed Adam's apple. 'Ay. So I've been told.' A million rules in this house. Even strangers were invited in to tell Howard what to do.

'Ah,' Simon sighed, placing his hands on his hips. His dark hair was parted well to one side, a thick lid to cover his clever head. 'I envy you working in the garden.'

'Oh yes. It's very nice. I have to clean now as well, though. I'm thinking, you know, turn professional at it, at the gardening, that is. Why not?'

'It's your own timetable. Organic activity.'

Howard put his cigarette out against his heel. Simon Clifford was not going away. And it seemed to be up to Howard to keep the talk going. 'And what do you do? Is it teaching only?'

'No, no. I work in a shop also. A bookshop.'

'Really?' He almost added, 'Is that all?' He'd expected something grand and scientific, maybe, or being a professor. 'And why did you move here?'

'Oh.' Simon shook his head and looked at the ground. 'I followed a girl over here and then she wandered away.'

'Oh, that's beautiful. I mean, and sad. I'm sorry to hear that. Girls are nice,' Howard went on, thinking of Varya.

'She was an exchange student, an English girl. Natalie.' Simon uttered her name in his slow way and it floated out onto the spring air expressing somehow a complete and destroying girl. Natalie.

'She sounds nice.'

'She was. She was nice. But now, well, I have memory pursuits to keep me busy.'

'And your job.'

'And my job.' Simon laughed to himself and confessed, 'My job, you have to wear a uniform, not a uniform properly but you have to wear black and white and black shoes. I have these black lace-up shoes that I wear. And I get back to my flat in the evenings. I'm on my own. And sometimes I look down and see I've still got my shoes on three, four hours later.' He shook his head. 'I'm just sitting there on my own couch in my shoes. Do you understand what I'm saying?'

Howard did. 'Oh yes. I'm with you there, pal. It used to be the same way for me. Before I came here.' Howard felt when he said that a fullness in his chest which was a wave of gratitude pushing through all his fear and discomfort at being with these people because at least he was with people.

That gratitude had gone now he'd been sentenced by Les to Howard's ordinary kind of shitty job, and working directly for the man himself. He was trapped by these people. He went upstairs to tell his mother.

He sat mashing his hands together between his knees as he spoke to the wardrobe.

'. . . it's a punishment is what it is. For mucking about with the ball. Or for the stupid business with Varya. No money at all she had. But they won't say that's what they're doing. Little prick. I'm sorry, Ma, I don't. I mean Jesus I'm grateful but now I have to do everything they say. I'm never on my own for five minutes together.' Howard thought of Varya in her grey jumper, her soft, slanted eyes. 'You would have liked her, Ma, you would. Lovely lassie. Very tidy. Normal, you know, like us, in a way. No money and that. And I never get to watch TV. Least I'm not their poor kid, sweating with his brain all night long.'

'Who are you talking to?'

'Oh Jesus, please. You scared me.' Howard put a hand on his chest and looked at the smiling face in the opened door. He glanced back at the wardrobe; it looked somehow shocked and defenceless, exposed. Could Saul tell?

Saul was smiling at having made Howard jump. 'So, just tell me. Who were you talking to?'

Howard looked at the boy, the other prisoner in the house. 'Can I tell you the answer to that, wee man? Can I really tell you the answer to that one?'

'What do you mean?' Saul's smile had faded. He was confused. He sensed something happening. 'You were just talking to yourself, weren't you? Because you're a headcase.'

'Not exactly.'

'What do you mean?'

'Well, shut the door if you're coming in.'

Saul pushed the door behind him until it clicked then slid down it so that he was sitting on the carpet. 'So go on then? Tell me.'

Howard thought better of it. 'No, doesn't matter.' He shook his head.

'No, come on, you've got to tell me now. Tell me.'

Howard looked again at Saul. The boy was bright. They were in private and nearly friends, in a peculiar way. But it wasn't really that consideration that made Howard speak. Howard was alone, alone with his life and his mother, and now someone he'd half-invited was asking directly. It didn't really matter who it was. Howard wanted to speak. 'I talk,' Howard cleared his throat to steady his voice, 'I talk to my ma sometimes. You know, just to talk to her.'

'Your mother?'

'Ay.'

'But how can you? When I showed you mine you told me you don't have a mobile phone.'

'That's true.' Howard sighed through his teeth, finding courage. 'She's dead, my ma, so I don't really need one.'

'She's dead?'

'What did I just say?'

'Keep your shirt on. I'm very sorry to hear that. Please accept my ... Really dead? Like Grandma.'

'Like Grandma.' For a moment, Howard felt an impulse to share it all, to get up and show Saul his mother's dress in the wardrobe, but that would have been too much: he checked himself. They sat silently. Saul skated his hands back and forth over the carpet by his sides.

'Your dad hasn't said much about Grandma since we got back,' Howard said. 'Hasn't said anything at all, to be scientific about it.'

'That's true. There was a rift,' Saul explained, using the word his parents had. 'I heard them talking about it once.'

'A rift?' Such a grown-up little fellow. 'That can be bad.'

'I don't know why. I think it was when my dad had business difficulties. He feels guilty now, of course, but you can't turn the clock back.'

Howard nodded. The boy made sense. A good choice to confide in. 'That's what you think,' he said without thinking.

'But you can't.'

'Have you tried?'

'What are you talking about?'

'I don't know.' Howard felt the back of his neck. 'Just talking.'

'Hm. It's nice talking, isn't it?'

Howard agreed. 'There're worse ways to pass the time.'

'So do you think your mum can hear you?'

'Don't know.'

'Like a ghost or something?'

'Maybe. A spirit. I hope so. Bit lonely otherwise.'

'But you're with us now.'

'Uch, so I've noticed.'

May 9th

Les thought it would be inappropriate for Howard to arrive in the boss's car and gave Howard instructions for using public transport. So Howard found himself walking towards the station through the grey-blue of the morning as cars eased out of driveways in front of him. As he got nearer the station he found that he was walking behind a suited man headed in the same direction. And then another. And then a tall one with head held stiffly cocked to one side strode past him. Howard sped up but then so did the man. It seemed important to him that he should walk more quickly and Howard dropped out of the race. As roads converged there were more, women with hastily arranged hair, briefcases, and percussive shoes. Like sand grains in an egg timer they all sank towards the station doors. Howard, caught in the same swirl, felt spectatorial and unserious in his own soft clothes, going to a job he still didn't quite believe in because he'd never seen.

Howard's lunch was set down in front of him with a click and with it descended peace. He leaned and inhaled greasy steam while the waitress returned with a mug of tea and a plate of bread and butter. 'There you go, sweetheart.' She walked back to the counter and her friend, who was calmly closing the gaps between cake slices in the display cabinet. Howard liked the waitresses here. They were all foreign ladies, motherly types, with round shoulders and honest, fat ankles. Over their black dresses they wore white aprons which tied with enormous bows at the back, big butterfly wings that flapped as they walked. It tended to be quiet as well, this café, and nobody from Holland's went there. It was almost ten minutes up the high street away from the warehouse and Howard had to paddle hard to get there and back in time. But the effort was worthwhile when it procured him this relief. His two eggs were edged with lacy burn and were fried nice and rubbery. With care he bisected each yolk and watched the gold liquid slide down around the nearest chips. He squeezed a wavy line of sauce around the edge of the plate and criss-crossed the pile of food. He'd found this place on the second day, when he'd spent his lunchtime walking madly anywhere away eating a Mars bar and smoking simultaneously. He'd ducked in to try and calm down with a mug of coffee which, combined with the Mars bar, had made him feel fizzingly intense. He more or less adjusted his glasses right off his face a couple of times before noticing that the room he was in was large, quiet and full of nice food.

By now things were calmer. He had started to think that

everyone didn't hate him, that maybe people in London were just different.

Ron, who had had to train Howard, was short and shaven-headed, with a roll of nape and a neck thicker than his head, giving him a blunt triangular shape. The back of the hand he'd used to shake Howard's – one hard downward tug, like flushing a toilet – was webby with tattoo. He spoke in a croaking whisper almost too quietly to hear in the noisy loading bay as forklifts passed and well-spoken vehicles loudly declared, 'Warning: vehicle reversing.' Howard therefore missed the instruction to put on gloves and sliced two fingers on the plastic strapping of the first crate he lifted. Ron, saying nothing, pointed to the first aid box on the wall and turned away.

His other workmates included a completely uncom-municative skinny lad in a holey T-shirt and greasy jeans who might not have been a person at all. He might have been a purely rhythmical thing made up of loading, unloading, the Walkman music that pumped into his ears and the gum that was pounded in his jaws. Between times he smoked and skulked and drummed his fingers on his thigh. He was Cro-atian, Howard learned from Big Mick, and never spoke to anyone. Big Mick was not big. The name dated from when a Little Mick, very tiny and now departed, also worked at Holland's. Big Mick laboured silently and without fuss in clean, blue overalls. In tea breaks, he read the paper thoroughly, even down to the horoscopes. Before going back out to the loading bay, he carefully combed his hair. Lester, a black man, cursed most things under his breath, wore a woolly hat even when it was hot, and kept wandering off to talk to people on his mobile phone. Only Gary seemed vaguely friendly at first. He had a convex face with soft furnishings of sideburns, moustache and goatee. There was a hint of early man about him. At rest, he looked as though he'd just been released from a glass case in a museum and stood bewildered by his new freedom. His hands were large. He would seem melancholy and withdrawn until his face split with a smeary, yellow smile, as it did the first time he shook Howard's hand. Howard had wanted to pat his head in gratitude.

They were a terrifying bunch to start in amongst, particularly when Howard arrived haggard from the unpredictable horrors of his first Tube journey. But now Howard was starting to see something else in these hard, quick, London men. There was no softness there but a kind of sly glinting that came off them sometimes and felt like friendliness. Gary led the way in this, showing Howard's acceptance by greeting him each morning with the cry, 'Donald, where's yer troosers?' to which Howard still hadn't thought of a response. Each morning he shook his head indulgently and looked as though he were about to say something until the moment had passed.

Apart from the weird, heart-thumpy subterfuge of occasionally having to pretend not to know Les, travel was the thing Howard found hardest about his job. Getting the Tube was in itself exhausting, even before humping crates and unpacking boxes for seven hours. The journey in wasn't so bad because the Dawson-Smiths lived so far out in suburbia that the carriages were half empty and he could sit down and rest while beyond his knees the train filled, stop by stop, with swaying bodies. Going home was a very different activity. That involved fighting his way on, seeing his fatness tutted at by all around him as he bulged and slithered into a gap by the door. The light in the carriages was mercilessly bright and cold and, crushed in amongst people so close, Howard found himself in a world of unpleasant detail, of greasy pores and sprouting hairs and piercings, of grey five o'clock shadow and women's tired faces scummy with make-up. Howard knew that if these normal people looked like this, he must look horrifying. He knew also that he often smelt bad. His odours caused faces to crinkle and turn away. With no regard to decency women's bodies were crushed against him in the busiest stations; even worse, so were men's. People were packed coitally close and meanwhile everyone pretended they were alone. Once, when Howard had been exhausted and anxiety had worked like yeast to grow his thoughts, he had seen himself in his mind's eye swelling and swelling, his fat inflating until it filled every corner of the bucking carriage and all his fellow commuters were pressed into him, embedded in his voluminous flesh.

The whole thing was so vile that Howard would have thought all these commuters were having him on if they hadn't looked so bored and depressed as they piled on and off. The Tube made everybody somehow excessively ordinary and sterile and grey, although once Howard had had another odd vision and thought of travelling to the next world – the people in his carriage had seemed world-weary and abstract as souls.

Howard had grown used to it by the second week. He'd realised the etiquette was the same as that of a public toilet. You said nothing, you avoided eye contact. People who did have conversations provided furtive entertainment for the other travellers. A threat of violence seemed to underlie the no-eye-contact rule. London was overtly hostile; people looked murderously at you if you got in their way. All you could do was keep your head down and pick up your speed to keep pace with the pushing crowd as you climbed stairs, breasted ticket barriers, fought along the street. Eventually your gears sort of meshed with the larger machine and you started to turn in time with the city. Any deviation, however, and you were flung off again to the sides. Howard was daily amazed by the stoicism of the commuters, each of them engaged in an endless, tedious, heroic, unrelenting, exhausting fight just to live salaried lives with a few weeks' holiday a year.

Howard tried to think without resentment of little Les gliding to work in his car. As keen as Les was on keeping their connection a secret, Howard was keener. He was happy to merge with the crowd. The fear of their relationship being discovered churned quietly in Howard. It would not be at all appreciated by his new workmates. Ron had evinced something like anger when Howard had named the suburb in which he was living. 'What the hell are they paying you?' Ron asked. 'Nothing much,' Howard answered before adding with unusual inspiration, 'It's just, you know, over a Chinese.'

As for the work itself, well, office supplies weren't the most interesting things to handle but it could have been worse. Howard had done similar things in the storeroom of a supermarket, where you were in and out of refrigeration lockers, your sweat freezing stiff in your hair. It didn't inspire Howard, though, as gardening and the Sea Breeze Fish Bar had, with visions of a working future. The facilities were okay – the usual fluorescent hutch for warehousemen and drivers with safety regulations pinned up, tabloids, stained mugs, tea bags, a fridge for milk, a large tin of instant coffee with a sticky spoon dropped inside. Les's office was in the front half of the building so he was easy to avoid. The work was hard on your arms a bit as well as your back, and at lunch time Howard often raised chips rolled up in white bread with hands that trembled weakly. The money was good, more than he'd ever earned up north, and he was paid every Friday in cash. He missed the garden, of course, but at least he was out of the way and doing a proper job. Standing behind the retracted metal doors, waiting as a vehicle reversed, gloved, his arms heavy at his sides, waiting to unload thirty or more crates, Howard felt in no way like a charity case. No, he worked and he earned. He was in the machine.

But where was Varya whose downfall he'd wrought? He thought of her soon after receiving his first brown envelope of twenty-pound notes and odd change. He thought of her money running desperately short.

Howard's meal reached its calm climax when he swabbed the last traces of egg yolk and sauce from his plate with the last of the bread. He lit a cigarette with half a mug of tea still to drink. Ten minutes of peace to follow the ten flurried, wonderful minutes of eating. Then he paid, exited back into the raw, busy street and started his quick walk back to work. Jittery pigeons flounced away from his step as he passed the *Big Issue* seller, a youngish man with long shadows down from cheekbones to bearded chin who no longer asked people to buy but stood there swaying slightly on his feet. Once Howard had seen him struck by some internal pain event, at least that's what it looked like as the man straightened up and closed his eyes to bear it.

Traffic and faces. Gritty blasts of exhaust. People to sidestep and walk around. Litter to dodge over. Howard saw as he hurried back the grey-suited figure of Les taking the glass front door back into the building. Les saw Howard and gave him a clipped salute, a quick token of confederacy which caused in Howard a panicky blush. He made to wave back then thought of what he was doing and redeployed his hand to touch nonchalantly his bald spot.

Les closed the door of his office and resumed his seat. He produced from a paper bag a hot bacon roll. He opened the roll to pull any excess fat from the bacon and dab off the grease with a plasticky napkin. The flung fat hit the side of the bin like a satisfying expectoration. He closed the roll again, licked his fingers, shuffled them in the napkin. Then he slid a disk into the computer then took a bite of the roll and leaned back to chew, sighing through his nose.

His office was square with the desk placed at its centre. It was glazed on two sides and a film-noirish parting of the slats of his blinds gave him a proprietary view of the girls receiving the orders from the call centre and of Lynette at the reception desk, vacant, coiffed, personable, not exactly pretty. Les was the London regional manager and the building was his domain. The eponymous Ted Holland rarely visited. His image, however, was ubiquitous. Every catalogue cover had that white surf of hair breaking over a tanned, genial, you-couldn't-find-it-cheaper-if-you-tried face. The calendar that hung over Les's filing cabinets also showed Ted, this time smiling open-mouthed like a cartoon character, outside the front of the building making a magician's sudden gesture as though he'd conjured the whole thing into being at that very moment just out of sheer exuberance and the desire to offer businesses the best supply deals in the country. Ted conjured, Ted impressed, Ted charmed and imposed and holidayed at length. Les worked. That was pretty much how Les saw the situation.

Les worked. Les liaised with the factories. 'Liaised' was the term he used for the tedious haggling over prices, for chasing orders, for mutual threats of cancelled business over product returns. Les liaised also with the major clients, but then it was referred to as account management. That was more haggling, more threats and chased invoices. Les kept an eye on payroll, who was the same person as the finance department, a plump and very competent Indian lady called Sunita. There was a part-timer in finance as well, a thirtyish man called Jeff with long fingers and hair that curled down beyond the collar of his one light grey suit who let everybody know that he was doing something a lot more interesting (Les pretended he couldn't remember what) with the rest of his time. Les made routine patrols of the warehouse and loading bay. Les kept immaculate stock figures. Les, as far as Les was concerned, was Holland's Office Supplies whatever Ted might think.

Of course it was frustrating or worse (abject, humiliating) to be working for someone else. Les had taken the job after the far more demeaning, destroying, unbearable period when his own business had, in Ted's casual and pornographic phrase, 'gone tits up'. Nordic Furniture had been an import business which had also involved dealing with factories; that had helped Les secure the job at Holland's. It had been, finally, just one factory's late supply of what turned out to be faulty goods (chair legs of unequal length, the awful, humiliating, slapstick stupidity of it!) that had wiped out Les's business. With nowhere left to borrow money, refused even by his own mother, with the good stock unshiftable in rented warehouse space as stores closed their accounts, there was nothing left but liquidation. Tired, adult men came and interviewed him at length, calculated his debts and made public Les's unambiguously total failure.

Les swallowed a sweet, meaty mouthful and clicked his way into the chess game he'd saved unfinished. Les liked chess, liked particularly the look of its diagrams, the notation with its cleanliness and authority. The look was intellectual and historical, like Saul's sheets of flute music. He loved also the heroes of the game in their suits and ties, dark-browed Eastern Europeans with forbidding names who smoked cigarettes and thought. Very masculine, real intellectuals. Les was himself no good at the game. After the championships he would work on it together with Saul. His programme allowed him to take back moves and ask the computer to reveal the optimum move. By move six the computer was usually playing itself. But Les enjoyed watching as the machine calculated its way through to the check mate, the pieces sliding back and forth and locking into a final diagram of victory. Playing with it at lunch time, twenty minutes out of the tedium of the working day, reminded him of what it was all about, of the elite, elegant life he tried to live outside this place which would be Saul's life entirely.

On one side of his desk Les had the family shrine: three silver-framed photographs of, accompanied or otherwise, his miraculous son. The photograph his eye fell on most regularly, that he looked at for luck or relief, was of Saul at Barbara's cousin's wedding. Saul wore miniature evening dress complete with scarlet cummerbund and bow tie. His expression was intelligently mischievous, his mouth curled in the slightest smile. If Les looked at it for long enough, Saul's expression could make him laugh out loud.

The phone rang. Les got up to tap on the glass. Lynette looked up. Les waved his roll at her. She shrugged, indicating her helplessness. Les cursed, chewed at double speed, then picked up the phone. Lynette's voice introduced the call, twittering up a minor scale with the words, 'Les, your wife on the phone for you.' Then the descending, 'Putting you through.' Les turned in his chair away from the windows.

'Hello?'

'Oh, hello, love, it's me.'

'Yes?'

'Yes.' Barbara paused. 'Is this a bad time? I thought you took your break about now.'

'I do. I've got a sandwich on the go. It's fine. How are things back at the ranch?'

'Oh,' Barbara answered, 'quiet. Well, Howard's with you. Saul's at school. How should they be?'

'Sounds about right. Did you call Simon?'

'Yes, I did.'

'Good.'

There was a long pause. Les chewed and swallowed.

'What's in your sandwich?'

'Bacon.'

'Les. Fat?'

'In the bin. I'm the same weight I was fifteen years ago.'

'Yes. Busy all the time, burning it off.'

There was another pause.

'Well, I don't have any other news.'

'Didn't sound like you had any news.'

'It'll be Mediterranean chicken breasts tonight.'

'Sounds good. Look, I ought to get on.'

'Of course. I'll see you later. Bye.'

Now that Howard was also working at Holland's, Barbara was again quite alone in the house. She missed Howard, having become used to his drifting, bovine figure in the garden occasionally emitting pretty blue clouds of smoke like any honest workman. With Howard and his comforting atmosphere of small tasks accomplished gone, Barbara felt more solitary than she had before he'd come. Laundry, shopping, her jobs were quickly done. There was so much space around them in which she became intermittent to herself. She breathed shallowly and looked out from herself. There were gaps when absolutely nothing was happening. She would sit down. A clock ticked. Outside the trees moved according to the wind. Then she would come to with a sharp inhalation as if out of a sleep. But it wasn't sleep. She was gone for a while and then the world resumed. It was almost a habit, this vanishing. She remembered being a little girl and sitting halfway up the stairs, the small crockery of her forehead becoming vivid to her as she rested it between two bannisters. She would listen to the traffic outside and look at the light on the wallpaper and float absolutely on the surface of things. Or she would sink away inside, reaching a silent bottom before pushing back up to the top. Either way it was a silence that she felt as one thing, a presence, larger than herself, there. It was just there.

Barbara moved through rooms, haunting her own house, haunting her life. She thought about all the people she knew, Les and Saul and her mother and so on, until there was nothing more to think about them. Often she felt generic: the wife. Oh, how her mother would disapprove. And rightly, perhaps. But it wasn't terrible. She felt appropriate, sometimes exquisitely so. Then a magazine glossiness covered everything she saw and she could say, almost religiously, *beautiful home*. She had a nun's soul, maybe, or she just didn't want to have to do with the smaller, necessary things. It was the larger something she was waiting for. Les told her that it was Saul's success. She awaited success.

There were two and a half hours to go before she had to pick up Saul. She sat down for a while and stood up again.

*

After dinner Howard made a request he hadn't made before. Through the long hours at Holland's beautiful Varya was often in Howard's thoughts. Two pay packets had given him a pile of notes in a drawer upstairs. It was time for him to make it all good. He raised his chin nervously high and quavered, 'I was wondering possibly if maybe if it's okay for me to make a phone ... use the phone ... call.'

'Of course,' Barbara responded when the sentence appeared finally to have ended.

'Thank you,' he said. 'It's a private call,' he elaborated awkwardly.

'Well.' Barbara smiled. 'You can use the phone upstairs in the study.'

'Uch, no,' he said, anxious not to arouse suspicion. 'Down here is fine.'

There was a pause.

'Well, I'll go then.' Howard rose hugely from his seat and lurched out half on tiptoe, closing the door carefully behind him. Les spread his hands and smiled at Howard's amusing character. Saul also smiled.

Howard moved quickly to the phone in the hall and spent several frantic minutes searching through Barbara's address book, which was, unhelpfully, of the pop-up kind requiring popping, closing, changing letter, popping. Howard was sure he was making an obvious noise and grew clumsier with fear. Finally, having popped his way through the entire alphabet and started again, he saw under C what he guessed was Varya's number. She was listed as 'cleaner'. He punched the number in quickly and twined his fingers into the phone cord.

A voice, a woman's, answered. 'Hello?'

'Ah, yes,' Howard whispered. 'Varya? Is that Varya?'

The voice was slow to respond. 'Who is this?'

'This is Howard, from the Dawson-Smiths. Please don't hang up. Is that Varya?'

'Yes, this is Varya.'

'Yes,' Howard was at a loss for how to continue, 'this is Howard.'

'Hyoward. I remember you. What you want?'

That was the cue Howard had rehearsed in his mind. He stuttered, 'Sorry, please, first. I just wanted ... I wanted ... I wondered are you all right? I just thought if you were having problems with money, I could ...'

Varya was silent before crooning a single note of appreciation. 'Aw, you are kind man, Hyoward. But it's okay. I have other cleaning.'

'Oh,' Howard said, realising that he now had nothing else to say. 'Oh, that's good.'

'Yes, is okay.'

'Okay.'

'Hyoward.'

'Aha, yes?'

'You are alright man. If you come here I give you food.'

Howard's throat closed and his tongue struggled. 'Gles,' he managed to say.

'I am busy now. Call me again in few days.'

'Okay, then,' he said quickly, 'bye,' and put the phone down. He wiped the sudden sweat from his forehead and grinned to himself before his face fell in fright.

Saul was tired but far from sleep. He stood for the fourth night in a row at his window waiting for his brain to tire, defocus, stop working, give him a rest. He looked out at the dirty orange sky crossed by flashing planes. He watched the large bushes lumbering in the wind, the small leaves flick in the light of the street lamp. He stood inside the curtain and felt secret and disobedient, smelling the dusty, mineral smell of cold glass. His school friends would be asleep. He remembered each one of them and counted them in their beds. He knew also each of their birthdays, having learned them as a feat to impress them, and it had worked, briefly, until they'd stopped asking. He looked at the leaves very quick against the light, the dark houses set back. The street was lonely. The night was a different time that he knew about; different animals were awake. His head was light as an eggshell and hot. The crotch of his pyjamas was spotted with urine that was still warm. He held his crotch with a tight hand and stood with one bare foot on the other. A passing car, its headlights producing intersecting parabolas on the dark tarmac, made him fall guiltily back from the window, almost out from under the curtain. When it was gone he crept back. His eyes ached. His mouth didn't taste clean any more. He stood just wishing the sharp edges of his brain would go so that he could sleep.

Saul thought about Howard, who was awake elsewhere in the house. He would have liked to have gone and talked to him. Because he was an amazing clue, this stranger, a man unlike any he'd been allowed to meet. There was a different horizon behind him, a different life, a freedom and a readiness to do things which seemed very manly. Howard did what he wanted and had no one holding him back. He changed cities and jobs just like that. He was like a person in a story. Saul wanted to know all about how it was done. But he had come at the wrong time; Saul couldn't concentrate, or rather could only concentrate on his preparation even though Howard was really the one lesson he wanted to be learning. He wanted to run to the big man right then and ask him what he was thinking and be awake with him in the adult dark.

May 29th

Saul and Howard were left alone together after dinner. One thing Howard would not have expected about Les and Barbara was that they were devoted watchers of a particular soap opera. Otherwise they didn't seem to watch television at all. News reporters' voices could be heard late at night sometimes, but the television was kept in a cupboard and its little doors were always shut. That cupboard stood there blankly, pretending it was just another piece of furniture, that they didn't even have a television. Saul never watched anything, was forbidden to, probably, and Howard, despite increasing need, didn't dare to open those doors himself. When the programme was on, Les and Barbara left together to watch it in sheepish quiet, obviously ashamed at being so frivolous and common. Howard thought of them sitting in stiff silence as though on church pews watching the inhabitants of that famous pretend street going through their three-times-weekly turmoil. Les had said in parting, 'Saul, why don't you explain the matrix to Howard?' Thus work and the hour's relaxation could be combined.

Howard blinked and nodded as Saul took him through the intricacies of the system. He didn't really understand a word – something to do with numbers becoming letters becoming words becoming a table that you could fit in anything you could think of. Work had been hard and there had been a delay on the line coming home. The carriage had stood for ten minutes at an uncomfortable angle in the middle of a tunnel. Howard's sweaty hand cramped around the slippery bulb at the end of a strap. The lucky seated ones could sleep or read their papers and sigh, checking their watches. Howard

111

looked out at the filth-furred pipes, easier to bear than all the faces around him. Now, after food, Howard felt sludgy inside, subject to small avalanches of sleep. Repeated soft collapses made him blink and swallow and pull himself upright again.

'So, if you look,' Saul explained, showing Howard in a book a table of unrelated short words ('dad' Howard saw, and 'mash'), 'the numbers turn into letters, turn into words, and that's where you start from. So what's seventeen?' 'I dunno.' It was comfortable sitting at the table with Saul talking to him. Howard felt tended and warm. He watched the boy's serious face with its knitting eyebrows and compressed lips. 'Look,' Saul said, pointing at something, 'so you can multiply up to the big matrix which has room for ten thousand. Why don't we start you on a small list.'

'Fine. What do you want me to remember?'

'What do you want to remember?'

'I'm not so good with faces,' Howard admitted.

Saul looked almost hurt. 'It can't do faces.'

'Oh, okay. Names, then.'

'Names. Good, I'll write a list.' With deft small fingers Saul wrote smoothly in blue fountain pen:

Alastair	Laura
Mary	Stephen
James	Taylor
Ben	John
Josh	Henry
Gary	Simon

He was embarrassed and felt obvious when he wrote Laura, the name of a girl at school. It was so blatant on the page. It practically flashed on and off. Meanwhile all Howard was wondering at was the neatness of Saul's writing, the sure pen in his thin fingers. 'Right,' Saul started.

Howard objected, 'But I know all those names.'

'Yes, but it's the list,' Saul explained.

'Oh, I see. What about Maxim?' That was a fairly new one on Howard. It had turned out to be the name of the silent Croatian at work. Howard smiled; Maxim had worked for half the day with parcel tape stuck to him, flapping from his shoulder. The boys at work were always secretly sticking things to each other. Often it was Howard, who was also the star of a new game, Hide the Haggis, which just involved hiding Howard's gloves or any of his possessions behind boxes.

'If you like,' Saul said patiently, 'we can add Maxim to the list.'

'Uch, no, I can't be bothered to learn it right now, Sauly-boy. Can we do something else?'

'But just try.'

'I'm too tired. I'll fall asleep on your head,' Howard offered.

Saul sank back into his chair before rebounding brightly. 'Mind charts! We need different coloured pens for that. I'll get them.' He got up and ran to his bag, then returned bearing before him a wide plastic wallet of felt-tips.

'This is for organising information,' Saul commenced.

'Hip, hip,' Howard answered. Saul looked at him satirically. 'You've got to say "hooray",' Howard persisted.

'Hooray. You start in the middle with the main subject, the key word, then you go out to things that come from it then smaller ones that come from them.'

'I havenae the faintest idea of what you're talking about, wee man.' Saul kept his attention by sliding a blank sheet of paper in front of him; also, the idea of using the coloured pens appealed to Howard. 'Okay, wee man, where do we start?'

Saul liked being called 'wee man'. The intimate sensation of playing together made him feel fluttery and warm towards his grown-up friend. 'Well,' he began in a teacherly drawl, 'we need a subject first. What's a good one? Education.'

'Uch, yes. I could do with one of those,' Howard quipped.

'So you put it in the middle of the paper and draw a circle round it.'

'What, just the word "education"?'

'Alright, "my education".'

'*My* education?'

'Yes,' Saul patiently confirmed. 'Do it in red.'

'Do you always come top in school, like by miles and miles and miles and miles?'

Saul looked uncomfortable. 'Almost,' he admitted.

'Well, it can't be almost. Do you or no?'

'No. There's another boy who always beats me. But don't tell Dad; he doesn't know.'

'Really? How can you not? I mean, you know everything.'

'I just don't. Please can we just do what we're doing. You need to write.'

Howard took the pen and started writing in chunky capitals, naming the letters out loud as he went. 'E, D, U, C, what's next?'

'Don't pretend,' Saul replied, thankfully falling for it. 'A, T, I, O, N. You're not doing this properly.'

'I am. You told me to write the words. I've written them.'

'Now, coming out of that, you draw lines and other circles with related topics in them.' Quickly, Saul started a chart of his own on another piece of paper, grabbing different coloured pens to add spokes that ended in bubbles around the words 'school', 'teacher', 'Simon Clifford'. 'Now, you've got to do your things, from your education.'

'Okay, boss.' Quietly, schoolboyishly, breathing through his nose and trying to be neat, Howard wrote, 'St Xavier's' and 'Telferscot Secondary' in purple, then, glancing at Saul's, he chose another colour for 'teachers'. 'Now what?'

'Did you go to any other schools or university?' Saul asked.

Howard was silent, thinking briefly of the unmentionable place where he'd learned a good deal that Saul would never know. He could write the name down – Saul wouldn't recognise it – but then he'd have to explain it. Better not to own up to it. 'No, I didnae.' Howard set his glasses back on the bridge of his nose, then took the sky-blue pen from the packet. After a moment with the pen whispering behind a concealing forearm, Howard showed Saul a decorated bubble. 'Look, that's one of my teachers. He had hair that went straight up.'

'Howard, that's not proper.'

'And look.' Howard drew again. 'What's that?' Howard showed Saul a tiny outline, roughly rectangular.

'I don't know.'

'It's a piece of chalk.'

Howard was warming up now. He reached across with a lime-green pen and scratched lines up from Saul's central bubble. 'Your education's got green hair,' he said.

'Don't.' Saul covered his paper with spread hands.

'And now,' Howard retrieved the blue pen and started dotting between Saul's fingers anywhere he could reach, 'it's started to rain. Awful drear day on your sheet, Sauly-boy.'

'Right.' Saul grabbed a pen and struck at Howard's page. 'It's a big storm on your page with lightning and everything.' Saul drew wild black zigzags down the page.

'Oh dear, look,' Howard cooed. 'It's started raining on the back of you hand as well.' Saul looked up, his eyes wide in delighted outrage. He took his pen to Howard's freckled paw. Their voices grew louder as they tried to catch each other's hands while protecting their own. Howard finally grabbed Saul by the wrist and held his hand still, away from Saul's squirming body, as he drew leisurely squiggles on his palm and Saul protested, 'Mercy, mercy.' The door opened sharply and Barbara stood there, her long figure swaying apparently with horror. She emitted a long, pleading, whispered 'Boys' and checked over her shoulder to see if Les had heard anything.

Saul whitened and sat back in his seat. Without acknowledging his mother, he said to Howard, 'I told you to put the top back on that one.'

Howard thought to hide his hand under the table and was about to start apologising when Barbara was called away, Les's voice from the other room announcing, 'It's starting again.' Barbara whispered an urgent 'Please' then closed the door carefully behind her.

Saul and Howard exchanged glances. Howard said, 'I'm sorry I got you into trouble with your ma there.'

Saul answered, 'We were both bad. This better come off.' He rubbed at the ink. They mingled their multicoloured hands as they tidied away, calming slowly as every last pen received its top and was slid back into the wallet. Saul glazed over again with studious precision, with good behaviour.

June 9th

The guards were trying to surround a man at the exit. He had a shallow, grey face of broken teeth, a flattened nose, eyes chemically dull. He tried evading them on his light, thin legs but the guards kept meeting him, palms upraised, apologising as they obstructed him. He staggered and raised an arm the hand of which was hidden by his dirty sleeve so that only shiny fingernails could be seen holding a can. Howard looked away, invisibled himself, as the man found enough composure to start shouting. Hidden among the other commuters who all stoically refused to notice, Howard passed through the clacking ticket barriers just as two policemen with belts of equipment and chests massive inside black jumpers arrived to deal with the situation. Howard stepped out into an unfamiliar part of London with only Varya's remembered instructions as a guide.

Howard bought beer in a corner shop where a small grey television showed him himself standing nervously at the counter, a fat man still in his work clothes with no chance of achieving attractiveness. His wide pale face was bleached by the camera to a moon wearing flashing glasses. When he tilted his head his bald spot showed as a radiant crater in the grey shape of his hair. The man at the counter, an African with a high-cheeked face that shone like wet rubber, disturbed his contemplation by handing Howard his change. Howard went out. He knew by smell that he was passing a fried chicken shop. He looked up to see indeed a white-tiled interior with unsmiling black youths in pristine leisurewear eating wings and fries. Two Muslim men passed. They had long grey beards

117

but no moustaches and walked with clerkly stiffness, piously ignoring the place in which they walked. Suited commuters walked at twice their speed, streaming home. A grocery shop sold fruit and vegetables some of which Howard had never seen before, one of them looking just like a pile of inedible logs. This grocery shop had been mentioned by Varya so he knew he was on the right road. Turning a couple of corners he found himself approaching the estate, three tower blocks set behind lawns. He looked up at them looming overhead. He saw laundry and satellite dishes and looked up right to the aerials at the top and saw small pink clouds moving swiftly over. Six pigeons spluttered out from a balcony, sliding out of place, and Howard almost tried to step into the air to keep his balance. The pigeons reminded him, the travelling clouds, the towers' height, of his home when he was small. That unnerved him enough to stop him worrying about meeting lovely Varya in her soft, grey jumper. He hurried in. The first block was the right one – DeVere Tower – and he got into the urinous, dented metal lift in which he was reflected as an agitated pink blur up to the eighth floor. Corridors with numbers and arrows eventually produced the right number on a door behind a metal grille. He rang the bell and waited, alarmed at the sound of several voices inside. He squeezed his wound and wondered why he was there. He hated strangeness, strangers, strange food. He felt his hands and armpits, the crease between his buttocks, begin to sweat.

She opened the door, shorter than in memory, wearing slippers, smiling. Howard was somehow almost startled by how she materialised in front of him, wearing precisely the face she had in his memory, the same angled nose, small eyes and pale, wooden-looking hair. 'Hyoward, you come,' she said in welcome, and pushed the metal grille forward for him to enter. He stepped into a small hallway of sombre yellow light which tilted as his forehead met the lampshade. 'I take your coat,' she instructed, squinting in sudden brightness as he tried to stop the light swinging. He unzipped and handed her his warm anorak to reveal the red shirt he'd put on that morning specially. It had been a gift from his mother several Christmases ago. It fitted him well. The collar buttoned down smartly. 'You look nice,' said Varya, 'like a nice, lovely bus.'

'It was a present,' Howard replied, as if apologising.

Varya hung his coat on a hook, struggling over the projecting soft mass of other coats so that Howard moved to help her just as she succeeded. Other voices could be heard from another room, voices which, frighteningly, they now walked towards. They turned out to belong to three people and yet others on an enormous television screen, a programme showing people redecorating a house. A large man surged towards Howard and shook his hand. 'Hello,' he said, 'I am Misha.' His hair was a dark cumulus which could be seen persisting in smoky trails down the sides of his neck. He wore a loose T-shirt. His arms also were loose (and hairy) and his handshake had been fast. His smiling face was now very close to Howard's, nodding. Howard, wondering what relation this man was to Varya, remembered to give his name. 'Delighted to meet you!' Misha exploded and Howard averted his face from the blast. Below he glimpsed large feet in swimming-pool flip-flops, just one green plastic loop over big toes that looked like thumbs. Misha's smothering greeting then gave way to a more courtly introduction from a woman (Misha's girlfriend?) who had unfashionably set hair, a deep woollen bosom that twinkled with sequins, large blotches of make-up, and elliptical, secretaryish glasses. A secretary was exactly what she looked like: one from an old sitcom. She introduced herself and Howard shook her soft, weightless hand. Her name was Helena or Eleanor or Yelena, Howard wasn't sure which; her telling him coincided with an eruption about lilac paint on the telly. 'I'm Howard, Howard.' He nodded, half-bowed. 'I'm very pleased to make your acquaintance,' she pronounced. The third person in the room was not introduced to Howard and did not even move. He was an old man in vest and cardigan and large boot-shaped slippers. He had chemically bright black hair. A dense air of deafness surounded him as he watched the huge, booming television with highly arched, disdainful nostrils and pale, unshifting eyes. The room was smoky, which was good news for Howard. Beyond his own mazy nervousness Howard could see that this was a relaxed wee place. Open windows let in shouts from the dusk below. Varya, Misha and Yelena exchanged quick Russian words (funny, squishy words they were) then turned unified smiles towards Howard. Misha clapped him on the shoulder, moved in close, expressing their new brotherliness, and said, 'Now we have drink because you arrive.'

'I brought beer,' Howard offered.

'We can save that for later when we thirsty,' Misha said.

'Come, come.' Varya made a beckoning gesture (not one curling finger but her whole hand) that Howard felt a little helplessly in his chest. Howard followed with Misha walking behind him, his flip-flops slapping up against the soles of his feet. Howard entered a kitchen where pots simmered and the oven whirred. 'Please to sit,' Varya invited. Howard was directed to one of the four chairs around an old garden table while Yelena mooned in. The two ladies stood and smiled while Misha collected chiming glasses from a cupboard. Holding two in one hand he poured clear spirit from a narrow bottle and offered the foremost to Howard. When everyone was similarly equipped, Misha spread his arms and made an aria of the word, 'Welcome!' He raised his glass to his chin; his eyes were naughty. 'Down the khatch,' he instructed. The glasses were clinked and Misha led the way tossing back his drink. Howard copied the action and afterwards hung his head, bearing down on the fire-cloud that raged around his lungs. Eventually he looked up to find Varya and Yelena with empty glasses smiling demurely. He wormed a finger under his spectacles to wipe his eyes. 'Very nice,' he said juicily. His mouth, lush with saliva, tasted freshly varnished. Misha looked at him eagerly.

'Tonight,' Varya announced, 'we have very Russian food, almost like is funny. Soup and everything.' She made an inclusive flourish with one hand above her head.

'Sounds delicious.' Howard's hunger had been rendered instantly acute by the drink; his stomach burned sharply. Misha now occupied a seat next to him, descending onto it bottle in hand by swinging one leg over its back. 'Please, I pour again,' he insisted, shaking his head as Howard tried to cover his glass. Howard gave up. 'Thank you. It's lovely. What is it?' Misha laughed vigorously at Howard's extraordinary witticism. He turned in his hilarity to Yelena, seating herself, who smiled also and explained, 'It's vodka.' 'What you think?' laughed Misha and refilled Howard's glass.

'Oh.' Howard talked through the laughter: 'I'm from Scotland. We drink whisky there.' Howard's father had been a whisky man.

Misha's face broadened in wonder. 'From Scotland? Is very beautiful. Mountains.' He whistled, modelling a dramatic horizon with his free hand as another man might model a woman's shape, and Yelena nodded her appreciation. Howard, whose memories of Scotland were less of mountains and more of estates like the one he sat in now, accepted the compliment to his nation. 'Ay, it's a fine place.'

'Walter Scott is from Scotland!' Misha exclaimed. 'Rob Roy! And Conan Doyle. Is true!' he assured him.

'Uch yes.' Howard took it on trust.

Misha raised his glass. 'To Scotland! Better than England.' Howard's glass had been refilled and he joined the toast. The liquor this time found a clear, scorched path down his gullet.

'So, what do you do?' Misha asked, his round, friendly features very vivid after the second drink.

'I tell you already,' Varya called over her shoulder, busy with some pans. 'He is a gardener.'

'I'm not actually,' Howard cut in apologetically before proceeding to explain about the warehouse and office furniture and stationery. He found himself unusually talkative. The words just bubbled out of him for a minute or two. 'I've done a lot of jobs,' he told them, describing the gym and Alf's chip shop and the burn on his arm that was almost healed (he didn't mention the sore patches on his bum) through lips that felt fast and partly numb. Yelena insisted on seeing his wound. Howard wondered if she might be a nurse or even a doctor but her reaction of shrivelling back in disgust at the sight of it suggested not. Howard asked Misha, 'What is it you do?'

'I am windows cleaner,' he answered. He produced from his jeans pocket a business card which was bare but for a mobile phone number and the legend,

MISHA
***

YOUR WINDOWS CLEANER

'Oh, I did a bit of that mysel' when I was a kid,' Howard remembered.

'Yes, is not too bad. I can do it when I like.'

'Cold wrists,' Howard pointed out sadly.

'But cash in khand,' Misha countered. 'No questions, thank you mister. So, is all right.' He tilted his head philosophically. 'And you do it too?'

'Ay, that's right.'

Misha slapped the table. 'So you can work with me. We be partners!' Misha's face was full of joy at their bright future together.

'Ah, but I explained I've already got a job.'

'Yes, rubbish one in warehouse. I want nice Scottish man in tartan skirt up a ladder. Good on a windy day.' Misha laughed for a long time and Howard did somewhat as well. The kitchen was warm and friendly. With the two tumblers of vodka inside him, faces bent kindly into his field of vision. Misha was offering him a cigarette, he noticed, and he accepted.

'And what do you do?' Howard asked the woman whose chest glittered.

'I am secretary,' she answered, 'for a Russian person.'

'Uch, that's nice,' said Howard, who was delighted that this woman who looked so much like a secretary with her glasses, neat hands and upswept hair should turn out to be one. Sometimes the world was wonderfully sensibly arranged.

Varya had diffused into kitchen noise and motion beyond the table. She came into focus again when she set a bowl of purple soup in front of Howard. 'Beetroot soup.' She spoke near his ear.

'Oh. Lovely,' Howard hazarded, inhaling with frightened curiosity its sweet fumes. *Purple soup!*

'Is very nice, very traditional.' Varya returned with bowls for her other guests.

'And how is your job, Varya? Are you okay?' Howard asked.

She waved a hand over her head to dispel his concern. 'Not too bad.' There was an eruption of Russian, probably soup-related, between Misha and Yelena, which Varya waited to subside before continuing. 'It is an agency. There are always more places to clean. Offices not so good.'

'That's good,' he said, not expecting his sentiment to sound nonsensical after her last phrase. He stubbed out his cigarette before noticing that Misha was keeping his lit in his left hand whilst he attacked his soup with his right.

Varya set on the table a sliced loaf in its plastic bag then sat down finally herself. Smiles were exchanged and Howard had no choice but to taste his soup. He found it sweet and very pleasant actually and worked his spoon rapidly to and fro. When he'd done scooping at the last magenta traces at the bottom of his bowl he felt strangely swollen with the differently hot liquids – vodka and soup – now filling his stomach.

He ate a slice of bread, thinking of it as a sponge that might mop some of it up. He had another to help the process. The bowls were lifted away. Varya's hand passed so closely by his face that he could smell washing-up liquid on her fingers. Howard relit what remained of his cigarette.

'Very nice!' shouted Misha.

'Yes, lovely,' added Howard, whose compliment overlapped with Yelena's.

'We have another drink.' Misha returned to business, filling glasses as Varya's round, cloth-wrapped behind was for a moment wonderfully, alarmingly prominent as she bent to the oven. Howard looked quickly away and took refuge in sipping his drink, which tasted of tepid paint stripper, until Misha corrected him. 'No, no, no, no, no. You have to take it all down all at once or is no good.' Howard obeyed as best he could and managed to wrangle it down in several swallows. He then exhaled a flammable breath and regathered himself around a deep drag on his cigarette. The place wasn't just a break from the policed good manners of the Dawson-Smiths, it was wild. Howard now slumped to one side of his seat and the room slumped with him. A round of applause alerted him that something was happening. Thankfully it was food. 'Potato pancakes,' Varya said as Howard studied his plate, 'with sour cream and pork.'

'Varya, it looks top notch,' Howard said as he contemplated a dream come true: meat and potatoes. And just in time – Howard set to, eager to build a dam against the high tide of alcohol that was carrying him off. Softness of potato, fried, hot, with cold cream, a knuckly piece of pork that came away on his fork in frayed, salty scraps. Very kindly his entire world contracted to the space of Howard's mouth and the operations at his plate. He went safely unnoticed as Russian conversation went on around him, reducing his portion to a pearly bone and the faintest residue of oil and cream. He accepted another drink, confident that sobriety was on its way and knocked it back, encouraged by Misha. He had been wrong: sobriety would quickly become a state that could barely be imagined.

From this point on he had much less idea what he was saying. Two other men somehow appeared in the room both carrying bottles. The food had all gone and now there were only glasses and cigarettes on the table. Howard greeted the new arrivals with much friendliness but failed to grasp their names. One, the tall one, he understood to be called Doglatch, while the shorter fellow in the tracksuit top was apparently called Pobble. Howard thought that was a splendid name. Now unambiguously and totally drunk, Howard found himself without social fear. Usually, just recalling the far-from-homeness of his situation would have made him shudder. But wherever he went here – people were leaving the kitchen now, himself, at times, included – people greeted him with joy. After one passage of movement, Howard found himself on the sofa next to the old man with the imperious face and crowwing hair. On the television people were going down a rope slide in jumpsuits. Howard fell to studying the old man's hand which rested lightly on the pattern of the sofa. If Howard kept very still he could see the veins pumping under the fine, foxed skin. For a few seconds Howard's chest filled unbearably with the thought of Mrs Dawson but then he heard a guitar being played in the kitchen and he launched himself off to have a look.

Pobble had his arm around Misha's waist. Misha had his arm around little Pobble's shoulder. Both of them stood crooning something squishy and melancholy as Doglatch calmly fetched chords from the guitar and Yelena looked on with shining eyes. Misha saw Howard come in and pulled him tight to his side, into his friendly male odour. Howard swelled the final chord with a random but passionate note. Misha clapped his hands. 'Another drink!'

'Oh, please. Just a beer for me,' Howard pleaded.

'Okay,' Misha conceded. 'One beer for thirst and then one vodka.'

Misha, the nicest man Howard had ever met, whether or not he was Varya's boyfriend, hurried away on his slappy shoes and returned with a full glass of Howard's beer. Howard bowed deeply in gratitude and drank. The beer was fine and bitingly cold. It tasted airy and very innocent after the vodka. Howard tossed it down with relish thinking that this now would sober him up. Pobble was speaking to him, he realised. He turned and looked down into emotional brown eyes. 'Eighty thousand each day,' he said. 'Shift is twelve hours. All these blue crates come from supermarkets and I and one other Russian man wash them. They stink of fish. But eighty thousand in one day! Half-hour for lunch. English people don't want to do this job. So much work. My arms ... they are dreaming.'

What an amazing thing to say! Howard knew exactly what he meant. His arms were dreaming, floating from him, fending off hours of labour, pulling and lifting in their sleep.

'That's just terrible.'

Pobble shrugged. 'Work, work. Maybe I can soon to drive the truck. That would be better.'

'Aha.' Pobble drifted away, leaving Howard unmoored. He sat back in his old seat, his place from dinner which seemed to have its own intense gravity. The chair sucked him back down and the room looked mind-blowingly similar to how it did then − it brought it all flooding back.

Varya appeared in the room. Had she been out of it? Howard wanted to talk to her, his old workmate. 'Varya!' he greeted her. She came and sat by him and started talking. Her narrow eyes were very nice. She was very funny. She wasn't being funny now but you could tell she was. She sat in a womanly way, loosely folded arms resting on crossed legs. Howard thought he heard her say, 'Do you have a girlfriend?' Amazed, frightened, enthralled, he checked by repeating the question. 'No, do *you* have a girlfriend?' Varya repeated, laughing.

Howard's heart felt like a fat man trying to get out of a chair. 'No,' he answered very definitely.

'That's good,' Varya said. 'I know someone very nice for you.'

Howard was handed from above out of the swirl of other people another vodka.

'Oh, yes?' Howard asked. Gravity was now pouring him very heavily down onto the table top. His eyes struggled to keep hold of Varya's face.

'She is a girl who wants to come and live here.'

'It's not you, is it?' Howard said. The words sounded in his ears as *Snow noo, ni?* Yelena's multicoloured face appeared over a plate of sweet pastries. 'Take one.' She proffered the plate to Howard, so he took one and in it went. 'More,' she said. 'Take.' He took another and decided to eat this one more slowly but the first bite so undermined its structural integrity that he had to stuff it in fast with all ten fingers to stop it falling everywhere. He sucked powdered sugar from his fingers. Afterwards, Varya was still there smiling but now showing him a photograph of a girl. The girl was not unlike Varya, with the same sour, Slavic prettiness, only this girl's hair was dark and permed. She wore a jersey dress of black and white horizontal stripes with shoulder pads. Her narrow waist was defined by a broad vinyl belt. Her eyes looked through many strands of fringe. Next to her was a lightning ball of flash reflected in a glass picture frame.

'She is very nice girl but she needs help to come,' Varya said.

'Uch, that's sad. She looks very nice,' Howard agreed, very eager to please.

'Yes, she is very nice.' Varya continued talking for a moment and Howard looked at her mouth, struck by the strangeness of what she was doing with those wriggling lips and lifting tongue and thought, *Words.* Then he heard, 'Can you sign a paper for her?'

'Sure, darlin'. I'd do anything ...' Then Howard paused, remembering to worry. 'What for? For her to come and stay here?'

'Yes. Like me. To live here.'

'Okay, then,' Howard decided.

'Oh!' Varya clapped her hands. 'You are wonderful man!' She leapt up and kissed him resoundingly on his greasy forehead. Howard shuddered in fright, thinking he felt her breasts against his shoulder. Then, rather surprisingly, Yelena kissed him too.

'Can I have another cake?' he asked in confusion.

'Please, more, take more.' Yelena thrust them at him with desperate hospitality. Varya vanished, appeared, set before Howard a pen and the form, pointing with a red thumbnail to where he should sign. He ran his eye vaguely up the form to check before he did so, but it didn't really come into focus. He half-thought he saw the word 'fiancé' as he wrote his name with as much benign majesty as he could. He was kissed again. He felt vastly magnanimous and filled his mouth with cake. He then went to the toilet, where the pinkness of his urine startled and terrified him until he remembered the beetroot soup. In the mirror his big pale, drained and strangely sober-looking face was decorated with lipstick on the forehead and sugar on his chin. He emerged to be greeted by Misha, who embraced him wonderfully hard, slapping loudly the fine Scotsman's back before dancing away to fetch him another drink.

June 10th

Howard, pried open by light from the windows, began what was to be a catastrophic day in great pain. A mash of leaky red colour, brightening and fading, kept time with a violent new pulse located just behind his left eye. He stood up and discovered that, outside of this centre, everything ran at angles and was impossible to put in its place or fend off with clumsy hands. It was early, very early, he didn't know when – primitive morning, blue and cold, everything asleep. His internal organs felt to be sliding down the back wall of himself. When they reached the bottom something threw them back up to continue sliding.

He stumbled to the bathroom, vomited, rinsed his mouth, spat remnants, peed, found the kitchen, where he discovered Pobble silently asleep on a chair, like a pet in its basket. When he sniffed a glass to drink from, the sticky smell of vodka almost sent him back to the bathroom. He stood recovering, swallowing his rising throat, before drinking four glasses of tap water that set the alcohol afloat in his bloodstream again. Very drunk, he staggered back to the sofa and buried his face in the corner under the armrest – tiny, kindly fabric world, moonscape of bobbles in grainy half-light, a world familiar from hiding as a child. Slowly, too tired to fear even the consequences of not getting home, he fell back asleep.

Or he drifted at least until six o'clock, when Varya got up. He became aware of her passing and repassing the door of the room he was in. With tremendous effort he gathered himself upright to say good morning to her but she had passed again in the other direction by the time he'd done so. He found her in the kitchen. He expressed absolute apology with his crushed-shut eyes, his whisper, his stoop, his frail hands feeling at the air. He was full of sin but Varya didn't seem to mind. She was all bright business, getting herself ready for work. Her first job of the day was cleaning in an office, she explained, and she was already late. 'Good bye, Hyoward, and thank you,' she whispered to avoid waking Pobble. 'You are very kind man for Irina. I will call you. Next time maybe you have less vodka. Good bye.' And she picked up a bag Howard suddenly recognised from that last awful day at the Dawson-Smiths and was gone.

Irina?

He waited a moment after the front door had shut, checked that Pobble was still dormant, and grabbed a potato pancake left on a plate on the side. He ate it bestially and rinsed the grease from his fingers and face. His stomach seemed to settle slightly with the new arrival and burned quietly. Ten minutes later, past snores from the other rooms, he made his own way out and, picturing consequences of this very large mistake, headed towards a fortifying pre-work fry-up.

The Tube journey did not help. Rocking carriages, lights that made his eyes ache, screaming brakes, tunnels, stairs. Afterwards he took refuge in his café, where the large waitresses in priestly black brought him a necessary plate of eggs, bacon, beans, mushrooms, tomatoes, sausage and a fat-spotted hockey puck of black pudding. When all that had been before him had been rapidly relocated inside him, he fell asleep in his chair, feeling fat, warm and happy. He woke up, paid, and dashed to Holland's Office Supplies just in time to be warned by Lester standing at the door, 'Yarrin farrit dis mornin.'

'What? What's going on?' Howard's temples throbbed. His breakfast felt very various and undigested inside him.

'Doan know but da lickle man aks for you arreddy.'

Howard looked into the gloomy space of the warehouse to have this confirmed. Coming towards him through the sour suspension of his hangover was Les wearing a pink shirt and a narrow grey tie sharp as a sting. Howard had the wit to say, 'Good morning, Mr Dawson-Smith.' But Les ignored his ingenuity and summoned him to his office. Ron and Big Mick watched closely as Les and Howard retreated through the shelves towards the door.

In the office, Les leaned his snooker-ball buttocks against the edge of his desk, folded his arms and demanded, 'Well?'

Howard fought even to stand. He made noises which eventually gave way to, 'I stayed at Ron's.'

'At Ron's?' Les's expression was, understandably, of squinting incredulity.

'Yes, that's right. I stayed at Ron's. It was very late, you know, after the film ...'

'Which film?'

'The one we saw, and I didn't want to wake anybody up so I thought I'd better stay.' Howard took a moment to be impressed by his own plausibility. He alerted Les to it also: 'I told you I was going to see a film last night.'

Les's small face shook away the details. His smallness was momentarily hateful to Howard. He wasn't usually bothered by people's shapes but Les now made him shudder, as light and painful as a hornet heading straight at him. 'So, you stay overnight at someone else's place without even having the courtesy to call and let us know you won't be coming back.' He counted on his fingers, a device which became obsolete by the third finger. 'We don't know whether to set the burglar alarm, whether anything's happened to you, whether you're on the bloody moon. It's not on, Howard.'

The situation reminded Howard of others he'd been in. The words came naturally. 'I'm sorry, I really am, really, really sorry. I just, I didn't want to wake you. I didn't realise. And I thought,' Howard found a line he could take, 'I wouldn't want to disturb Saul, you know, during his preparation.'

'Saul was disturbed enough by your absence,' Les told him.

Howard looked at his boss's hairline, soft and human, to avoid his hard eyes.

'Really?' Howard asked.

'Yes, really.'

'What ... how?'

Les dropped his gaze. 'I wouldn't even have known if I hadn't got up so early this morning. I don't think he wanted either of us to know.'

'What are you talking about, Les?'

Les looked up at Howard momentarily, then looked away. 'He's obviously become attached to you, Howard. And that means you've got to be a bit bloody responsible while you're in my house.'

Howard was terrified at what he had done. 'But how did I disturb him?'

'No, no, no. What it was was ... Like I said I wouldn't have known. I found him coming downstairs this morning. It seems with you not there, Saul had slept in your bed.'

Les said nothing more about it at home. The atmosphere when all were assembled for food was, even while Howard sat there mauled again and again by shame, not recriminatory but stiff. Peace carefully preserved, a unified moral front, was expressed by the upright spines of Les and Barbara. No particular attention was paid to Howard – Les had said all he thought needed saying at work – but Saul kept stealing glances. Howard responded with cringing smiles. But Saul's eyes were not happy. Maybe he was angry.

After dinner, Saul collected three well-worn packs of cards to work on with Les and Howard made his excuses and headed upstairs to face his mother. His hangover had thinned to a fine covering film but he was still exhausted from lack of sleep. As he climbed he heard Saul starting to work, the first chirps of information he'd swallowed being expelled. When he reached his room, Howard laid a hand on the wardrobe but found himself too tired really to speak. He mumbled, 'I'm sorry,' and climbed into bed.

He was woken out of a sleep that was seabed deep by a hand that had reached down and grabbed his pyjama sleeve. A high voice said '... if we're collecting them we've got to don't put them they do ...' then broke into wordless noises, lonely animal whimpers and rapid breaths. Howard found the button on his bedside light and illuminated Saul standing next to him wearing only his pyjama bottoms, his navel soft in the smooth dough of his belly, his ribcage throbbing, his eyes unseeing. He said, 'Please, please start,' then, 'I don't, it's not ...' shaking his fingers as if to rid himself of something stuck to them.

'Saul,' Howard croaked, 'wee man, you're having a nightmare, Saul.' But at the repetition of his name the boy reeled back then crumpled to the floor, crying. Howard swung himself out of bed and provoked screams, real screams. Saul stood up and rocked back and forth for a step he wouldn't take. 'No, no, no, no.' 'Saul, wee man, it's Howard your friend.' Emotions boiled in Saul's face but his eyes were flat. He grabbed from the side and threw Howard's Sacred Heart, which whirred in a frisbee spin and lightly struck the wardrobe. The moment was so precisely demonic that Howard for a moment wasn't sure if he was dreaming. Then he thought of immediate reasons to be scared – here he was in the middle of the night with a half-dressed Saul in his room screaming. It was certainly real. Horrible to watch – the desperation, the terror working in him, making him stutter and weep. Howard was approaching the collapsed boy to try and calm him just as Barbara entered the room. She frightened Howard by coming in quickly and seizing Saul's twisting arms, just physically overwhelming him, pressing him down on the floor. Howard could see too much of her body in her nightdress, could see the vague shade of pubic hair. This was not right, was intimate and violent and so strange. Her bare feet, getting a grip, were brutal. Howard added his pleading voice to the noise. 'I never,' he began. Saul tried to lie on his side on the floor, sobbing, 'We have to, we have to.' 'It's all right, Howard,' Barbara shouted. 'He gets this, this is normal, before competitions. Saul!' she said sharply. 'Saul!' Saul seethed, curving on the floor. Barbara yanked him upright and dragged him out of the door. The two apparitions seemed sucked out of the room leaving Howard again alone.

June 12th

Les returned from work feeling light in his body and sensual as a cat, for no reason. Just the sunshine, the fullness of the day, the health of his body. In a good mood, Les had no worries at all. He wasn't susceptible to them, not like Barbara. Les could seize the day. He found his son's beautiful, domed head bent in study and stooped to kiss it. Howard was not yet back from Holland's. The house felt peaceful and entirely his. He noticed for the first time in a while the quality of his furniture. Trophies and photographs gleamed. The stairs responded to his weight with a familiar voice as he climbed, creaks he knew as well as words. He found his wife busy in a cupboard in the master bedroom. There was light behind her. She turned. She had that elegant, tall shape, that stillness which had always attracted him. It told him somehow that she was not quite available and that maddened him. Barbara was always half hidden, bright and ready as she was, always disappearing around a corner of herself. She had it still, that girlish thing, that endless dancing away, not noticing him, that made him crave. 'You're early,' she said. 'I wanted to see you,' he answered, and stepped towards her loosening his tie, knowing he had that look in his eye that she well knew.

Barbara was thankful to be given him again, and sighed encouragingly for him, although his small sharp thrusting was not comfortable and all the edges of the experience remained hard and clear.

She wanted to keep hold of him afterwards and laze in bed, face to face, at eyelash-counting distance, blurring together, lacing their limbs. Just whispering was a pleasure; it seemed lately they had hardly spoken to each other at anything other than the public volume of work colleagues. Barbara hesitated, though, knowing it would be difficult to keep hold of him while she got through what she had to say. She hated breaking up his good moods.

'Wowie-zowie,' he said. 'You're very good at that, you know.'

'You liked that?'

'I liked. I liked. Wife, mother, chef, love goddess.'

'And that's with no practice.'

'I'm glad to hear it.'

Barbara rubbed his left earlobe between her thumb and forefinger. 'Les,' she said.

'Is that my name? I'd forgotten in the excitement.'

'You know Saul had one of his nightmares the other night.' There, it was started; she had said it. And felt his neck muscles harden.

'Of course I know.'

'Well.' Her larynx tightened. She had to swallow. 'I'm worried about him. This time, I mean, I'm worried about him. You understand.'

'Not really. What do you mean this time?' He jerked his ear out of her hand. Barbara pulled up the duvet and covered her breasts.

'I mean more than before is what I mean.'

'He was like this two years ago. He'll be fine.'

'Two years ago he was nine, darling. It's not the same.'

Les sat up and reached for his underwear on the floor. He hooked his feet through the holes and stood up, sheathing his buttocks with one quick action. 'He'll be fine. He *is* fine.'

'Don't go.' Barbara caught hold of his wrist.

'I've got to go,' he said. 'I've got to go and make sure our son isn't cracking up.'

'Les.' She pulled his arm and he sat down on the edge of the bed. 'Just talk to me for a moment.' You had to hang on to Les. If you didn't you'd see him through his dust.

'I am talking to you. Who isn't talking?'

'You know what I mean. You're not letting up on him at all. You know what I think?' Barbara's heart beat very hard. She dreaded to broach the subject. It meant recalling also the bankruptcy, the time when she'd taken charge of Les and kept him going, which now he resented. He'd been absolutely in charge since then, and she'd gladly relinquished herself to him. It was now an unmentionable time. She wasn't mentioning it, she reminded herself. But she had to name something else, something maybe even worse. 'I think it's because of your mother.'

Les laughed, not in an amused way, but as the strongest possible denial. 'You've been watching too much daytime talk shows. White-trash psychology.'

'If you say so. You just seem so driven since then.'

'I was driven before then, darling. Well, wasn't I?'

'You were,' she admitted.

'I don't think I've got any more intense. The world memory championships are coming up. That's got more intense.' He always named the competition in full. It was too important, too noble a contest, to abbreviate. Les sighed through his nose, dropped his head. 'What can I say? He's stressed. Of course he's stressed. He *should* be stressed. But it's not as if we're going to pull out of the competition, is it? We'll get through it. We have to keep pushing him and looking after him at the same time.'

'And Howard? You think that helps?'

Les stared at a point on the duvet cover, scratched at it, then spoke. 'Yes, I think it does, actually. It's good, it's a good attachment.'

'Always so positive.'

'Do you think this is helping?' he snapped. 'Do you think this is what we need?' Les held Barbara's bare foot, held it tight around the arch. 'It'll all be fine. Just try not to worry so much. Your worry leaks out and affects Saul. So just bloody well keep quiet and let's just do what we're doing and not lose our nerve and fuck it up.' He walked out to the bathroom.

June 15th

Rain pelted the French windows. Beyond them the garden was a molten green gloom. Simon Clifford leaned close to Saul. His breath smelt of extra-strong mints. 'To be a champion,' he said, 'you need to know who your enemies are. So who are they, Saul?'

'Vikram Chandrasinghe,' Saul offered. 'Linda Chang.'

'They are both strong competitors. Some serious neurons there. But who is your number-one enemy?'

Simon Clifford's face expressed nothing as it waited. 'Well,' Saul attempted, 'if I could compete with the under-eighteens then it would be Jamie Lever.' Saul thought of mentioning Betty Zorin, the queen of memory systems and products, whose round face smiled up at him from the back of a book right now. Saul wondered how Simon would react to the naming of his hero. Meanwhile Simon's camelish face, with eyes closed, moved from side to side in a slow negative.

'No, Saul. Your number-one enemy is yourself.'

'Not Vikram.'

Simon Clifford's face tilted. Saul imagined it was because a sniper's bullet had hit him from behind. The rainy windows were reflected in his glasses. 'Is that sarcasm I'm hearing?' Saul fitted his hands under his thighs. 'No.' Each of Simon's lenses looked like pond water under a microscope, cellular shapes crawling down their surfaces.

'No, because sarcasm would not be appropriate with the championships a matter of days – count them, Saul – *days* away.'

Saul felt the time dwindling even more perceptibly as Simon spoke in his drawling, precise accent. He hastened to learn in time. 'It's myself.'

'It's yourself because your limitations are internal and can be conquered by will alone. You have to want to fight yourself, compete against yourself, break down all the little walls inside yourself to get to the treasure.'

Saul's voice emerged as a whine. 'I'm trying.'

'I know you are, Saul. But it's a paradoxical effort,' Simon theorised, looking over Saul's head as a gust of wind thickened the rainfall for a moment. 'You have to relinquish stress, to work through, not work. It's Zen. You need to stop worrying about aiming and then you will hit the target.'

Saul's mouth was open. He looked helpless and almost angry. 'I'm trying,' he insisted.

Visibly Simon Clifford relinquished the attempt to impart to Saul the higher reaches of competitive philosophy and retracted it for personal meditation. His posture lost its airy dignity as he turned again to the boy. 'And you're doing a damn good job, Saul, damn good. There are a few things we need to tighten up on, though, aren't there? And one of them is the poem event. I have a new one for you today. I want you to start by reading it out loud.'

'But I can't do that in the competition.'

'I know you can't. There you read it out loud in your head.'

Saul hung his shoulders in annoyance. 'Then it's not out loud, is it? Did you write it?'

'I did. It's nothing. Just for our purposes. It is unrhymed according to championship requirements because rhyme is mnemonic, as you know.' He fished a sheet of paper from one of several clear plastic wallets. 'So, here it is. You have fifteen minutes to commit it in its entirety to memory as precisely as you can, punctuation, capitalisations, everything.'

Saul took the paper and read out Simon's poem.

SCIENCE is an angel
that dwells in hearts
and minds of men
who peer through optic instruments
at the whirling cosmos
or at our kaleidoscopic DNA
that shows us what we are
and what we'll be.
MEDICINE she brings us,
drugs and scans and surgery,
as well as computers
more powerful than Charles Babbidge
did dare dream.
We have weapons, spaceships,
crops that feed us all.
And the last of Her gifts
makes Her disappear:
the truth that angels exist nowhere
but in the wondrous minds of men.

Simon walked to the window and looked out at the garden while Saul began learning the poem. He stood there frighteningly still and calm for the full fifteen minutes, engaged in some mental process of his own, then suddenly reactivated to remove the page from Saul's possession. 'You have half an hour,' he said, and left the room.

Saul had half an hour before he had to recall the poem. He was alone. He stood up. He checked the words were embedded in his brain.

He went to the window and saw the garden furniture coldly glazed with rain.

He stepped back.

He jogged the length of the room. He approached an armchair, put his hands on its armrest and jumped so he wavered briefly up to an angle of forty-five degrees.

He said, 'Drugs and scans and surgeree, drugs and scans and surgeree.' He sat.

He bit his nails.

He felt his eyes well up for no reason. He had the power to make that happen at any moment: all he had to do was say, preferably out loud, like Monica did at school, 'Saul, you're going to cry. Stop crying. Why are you crying?' Saul wiped his cheeks.

He pressed his eyes with his thumbs for the entertaining red-brown patterns.

Then he just sat and waited, hearing Simon Clifford talking to his father.

Meaning no one in particular he got up and cried, 'Number one enemy, haya!' and kicked the sofa. He would like to be able to do karate to save Laura from something.

He sat down again and this time really did nothing, put his hands in his pockets and switched off, waiting for Simon to come and call him back to work.

His skin hurt for some reason.

He wanted to cry again but this time the challenge was to stop himself. By breathing carefully he remained dry and fine until the door opened.

He wanted to run out.

'Okay, ready to go.' That was Simon's ritual phrase and Saul returned to the table and wrote out the poem.

Les opened the door a little way and inserted his smiling face into the room.

'How are we doing?'

Simon Clifford ran his eye down Saul's version of the poem. 'Well, sport here has reproduced my masterpiece perfectly. Top score! This is an improvement, Saul.'

Les's smile widened and he trotted into the room, high-fiving his son then pincering his shoulders in a massage the way a trainer does a boxer.

'Within the time, as well. Barbara's getting something ready,' Les promised. 'So that's a nice reward.'

'Splendid,' Simon said, and Saul shrugged his father's hands from his back.

June 21st

Halfway up the road Howard stopped to eat his snacks. He had found that a couple of Scotch eggs on the way home blanketed his gut against after-dinner hunger pangs when Barbara's small sharp foods passed though him without touching the sides. He'd been generally hungrier since that night at Varya's. Misha must be her boyfriend. He had to be. Varya wouldn't not have a boyfriend. Like wanting Howard, that was just something that wouldn't occur. She was far too beautiful.

He fed himself the sweet pulp of meat and egg from fingers that still smelt of the warehouse.

Burping quietly as he came through the door, he was met by Barbara, who said, with a frightening studied indifference, 'I've just had Varya on the phone.'

'Varya?' Howard repeated, aware of a crumb itching on his chin.

'Yes, Varya. You remember, she used to work here. I've just spoken to her. She said she needed to talk to you about Irina.'

'Irina?'

'Don't those names mean anything to you?'

'Irina, Irina.' Howard sought the answer in the carpet at his feet.

'I'm sure she said Irina.'

Realisation jerked Howard's head up. 'Oh my God, Irina. That was the name on the form.'

'So you do know her?'

'Do you have Varya's number? I mean can I use the telephone, please – I'll be quick.'

'Go ahead. It's in the book. As long as it all makes sense to you. I'll leave you to sort it out.'

Howard tried to paste together his bits of drunken memory. He'd signed a form, he knew that. These bloody foreign Russian whatevers . . .

He grabbed up the phone and slapped open the pop-up address book. He was going to give Varya a piece of his mind and tell her to stop the whole thing and never call him again. Lovely Varya, that was. Was there no one out there who wasn't against him?

He called. Varya's flat was rowdy in his ear. He held the receiver out to check how much noise was escaping into the air.

'Varya, it's me. Howard. What have you done? What have I done? What did I sign? Quick. I need to know.'

She laughed at his worry but assured him she wouldn't call him there again if it bothered him.

Howard repeated the question: 'What did I sign? What was it?'

'You know what it was.'

'No, I don't know. I really, really don't.'

Misha came onto the line and insisted that Howard meet him in a pub in Dalston. He gave the day and time. Howard was not given time to refuse. He hung up the phone feeling only more tightly ensnared, picturing thick seaweed wrapped round his legs. He suffered a clear memory. He was standing by his mother in the sea. He remembered the white of her legs in the water. He was small with a white belly, and hot. The waves as they lapsed dragged ticklish sand grains from under his feet. The world pulled sideways and down. He resisted reaching for Ma's hand and held himself all by himself tensely vertical against this complicated undermining, even as his mother danced back out of the wave, laughing. His father was somewhere away behind them. The memory just appeared, detailed and whole. It was unsettling.

There were too many memories. And Howard knew now that they would not stop coming back. That night he dreamt that Saul, poor exhausted Saul, came to him and showed him the stump where his left hand had been severed. The stump was raw, the wound apparently fresh, but bloodless and very smooth and pink. A glazed, agonising wound. Howard did not know what to say. What could he say? How could he make anything better when he was the one to blame?

June 23rd

Misha waited alone at a table. He rose when he saw Howard approaching and, as if timed to do so, the lights of a fruit machine began to flutter and spin. Howard took long angry strides but Misha grabbed his hand, bent forward from the waist and seized it before it was raised, then used it to pull furious Howard into an unrefusable hug.

'Welcome, welcome. I buy you a drink. Not vodka today.' He laughed and made a peculiar gesture of holding his mouth open and flicking his cheek.

Howard, wishing to argue, found himself vehemently agreeing. 'No. No vodka for me today, pal.'

'What you like?' Misha's dark-featured face was genially expressive, like a dog's. 'Not vodka,' Howard repeated and discovered in the silence that followed that he had to provide an answer. 'Just a Coke for me.'

Misha regarded him warily, as if he were being joked with. 'No? Not beer? Not wine, anything?'

'What did I just say?'

'Okay. Coke. I buy it.' And Misha walked away to the bar shaking his head in wonderment.

Howard sat down, annoyed with himself at not having made an impression with his anger. He looked at Misha, who lay forward over the bar to order the drinks, the soft bottom of his belly showing where his T-shirt hung down. The barman seemed to be a friend of his. The pub was quiet. A dog-eared beer mat in front of Howard showed a smiling man in armour. Howard had always liked armour, liked thinking about it as a child, the safe, interlocking plates, the crunching metal as they

147

walked, the spiked, hefty mace – no one would have a chance against that. He looked up. Across the patterned carpet sat a lone drinker. In silence he poured into himself in one movement most of a pint, watching Howard with steady pink eyes. This was no time for Howard to think about his father.

Misha returned. 'I buy you fizzy.' He handed Howard his drink. 'For me, great British beer.' He drank encouragingly, his upper lip reaching through foam as he pulled in a mouthful. Howard sipped a drink made awkward by turning ice.

'So,' said Misha, folding his arms and cocking his head at Howard.

'So?' Howard replied, angrily.

'So,' Misha replied.

'So, what the bloody hell is going on? I mean, to come straight out with it and be quite honest I'm really not happy with this entire situation.'

'But I am very happy. We are all so pleased for your help.' Misha tucked down his chin and raised his glass in honour of Howard.

'But I am no happy,' Howard said, pointing to himself. 'I have been tricked. It's skulduggery is what it is. You got me drunk and made me sign papers to get married to some foreign lassie.'

'But we didn't trick you. We didn't get you drunk.'

'But I did, though. I got very, very drunk.'

'But we didn't trick you to do this. We always drink like this. And we explain everything and you agree. Oh my God, you think we are cheating you? This is not the people we are, I tell you that.' Misha struck his breast with the flat of his hand.

Howard rolled his eyes rhetorically and caught a dizzy glimpse of the pink-eyed man still staring at him. Outside clouds had shifted and a strong shaft of light transpierced the brown gloom of the pub. It lit the menacing drinker's hair very specifically. Howard hid his face a moment in his freezing drink.

'You did trick me,' he repeated.

'No.' This time Misha struck the table. 'I am alright man. You agreed.'

'Is it too late to change back?'

'No, but please you can help us. I know you are a nice man who can help us.'

'How do you know that?'

'Varya said you call her, you are worried she is poor. And Irina is poor.'

'But I could get into trouble.'

'No, you cannot. I make it for you. Look, I show you. We go back to flat and I show you.'

The first thing Misha actually showed Howard when they got back to the flat, which brought back unsteadying, drunken memories, was not how his marriage to Irina could be easily effected, but, suddenly distracted, a pile of his own artwork. He pulled large pages from a drawer in the bedroom and placed them on the bed. Howard was more shaken by the fact that this was the bed in which Misha and Varya slept. Women's clothes over the back of a chair and a bedside photograph of a laughing Varya seated high on Misha's shoulders made that clear.

The pages were mostly blank with abstract dots and dashes of coloured felt-tip, occasionally spiralling together to make maybe a planet or an eye.

'Did you do these?' Howard asked.

'Yes, yes.' Misha smiled proudly. 'But really I would like to make films.'

'They're very nice.' Howard lifted another page with horizontal dashes which were maybe the sea or grass. 'I'm not that big on modern art,' he said as though he was a little bit big on it, 'but they're very nice.' At Ridgemont there had been two boys who could draw, one who did the most amazingly realistic cars that gleamed in the sunshine, and one who did good graffiti but also beautiful faces when he wanted to. He was always getting into trouble for tagging the place and Howard remembered that definitely the best day at Ridgemont (apart from leaving day) was the one when they'd woken up to discover, amazingly, thrillingly, that he'd escaped, his tag mocking them all from high on the perimeter wall. He was back within three weeks but back a legend, a hero. He told them all what he'd done outside, mostly fucking, apparently, and not boys either.

Drawing was one of those secret talents, like playing the piano or kung fu, that Howard wished he would someday just discover he had.

'Yes, yes. Not just windows cleaner. Now, you like some food? I see you do.' Misha slapped him on the back. 'I make something then we talk about Irina.'

'Okay,' Howard agreed, trying to keep his voice disgruntled. 'But I need to call home this time first.'

Misha cooked well, preparing pork steaks and fried eggs, carrying a tray through to the papery old man, whose name was Adam and who was still in front of the television. Howard ate with pleasure while Misha made many positive statements about him – they were a real feature of his conversation: 'You are a good man.' 'Yes, but you're not stupid.' 'You are a strong one – and with courage!' And halfway through the meal Varya returned. Howard stood up and she kissed him on both cheeks. She wasn't hungry, she said, but she ate a little from Misha's plate and made a pot of coffee.

After dinner, Varya cleared the table, cigarettes were lit and Misha produced a file of documents so extraordinary that Howard's breath became heavy and tangled and he held the side of the table as he struggled to think.

'Open it. Read,' Misha encouraged.

Howard opened the folder. It was full of different envelopes. 'What, anything?'

'Yes, yes. Read.'

The first thing Howard pulled out was a greetings card. He opened it. It read,

Darling Howard.
I am so happy to write to you again. I miss you always.
*   I love you, Irina x.*

'What is …'
'Try another one,' Misha smiled.
Howard pulled out a letter. The paper was pink and decorated with linked daisies. It read,

Darling Howard,
*   this time I do not use the computer. For a nice change! I*
want to say you how happy I am to meet a man like you and
fall in love with him. Every day I think about you. Always
my friends ask me why I am smiling and I say love. I show
my grandmother your words on the computer and she says I
am a lucky girl.

Howard opened another. 'I cannot wait to meet you. This is my dream which does not let me sleep. To be your good English wife!'
'What is …' Howard repeated.
'You see we say,' Misha explained, 'that you meet in a chat room and you talk there a long time, many months.' Misha's eyes twinkled at the cleverness of this. 'This chat room has no log, no records of messages, so it can be true, who knows.'
'But how does she know who I am?'
'We tell her, of course, when you agree,' Varya interposed.
'But …' The words of love again swelled in Howard's mind. *Darling Howard. I love you. Why I am smiling.* Howard, adjusting his glasses with both hands, was helpless.
'So now you write some back to her. I have some.' Misha reached into the file and pulled out new cards still in their plastic wrapping, some decorated with hearts, others with flowers or bottles of champagne and horseshoes. 'So then we have proof that you love each other.'

Howard tried to remember the photograph he had been shown and could retrieve curly brown hair, a big smile. But it was a girl, a definite girl. *Darling Howard.*

Varya said, 'Remember when she is here you don't have to be with her. Just married and that is all.' That was right, Howard told himself; it was just an arrangement.

Howard read another line. 'I look forward to when I can hold you and kiss you.' He thought of the empty house in Burnley, the nights sat smoking on the sofa hearing the terrible music from the man next door, his lonely shouts. The hours he'd spent wishing for a person. And Howard's mother shrunk to a piece of furniture upstairs. *And kiss you . . .*

'So you can write one now?' Misha asked. 'I get a pen. And later on you can propose.'

Varya put her hand on the back of Howard's. 'I can't believe it we find a so kind person. But I always like you.'

Blushing so hard he could feel his cheeks vibrate, Howard said, 'You polished my face.'

'No, no,' she laughed, 'we Russian, not Polish.'

'No, no, you polished.' Howard circled his hand in front of his face. 'You polished. You get me?'

'No, I don't . . .'

Misha returned with a handful of pens, picked up a card and bit into the wrapping. Spitting cellophane, he spread it open and slid it over to Howard.

'Please, please. You write.' He bit off the cap of a pen and handed it over.

'Oh God, God. What do I say?'

'You can start it, "Dear Irina".'

'Oh yes.' Howard began forming letters with slow care. 'How do you spell Irina?' He looked up to find Varya and Misha smiling at him like proud parents. He took their over-lapping dictation of the name. 'Now what?'

'Whatever you want. That you love her.'

Howard moved the pen down a line, his heart thumping. 'What? Really?'

'Yes, just write it.'

Howard wrote, 'I love you,' and stared down at the words.

'Very much,' Varya added.

Howard wrote the words gratefully; they made the phrase less painfully bare. 'And I can't wait to see you?' he suggested.

'Nice,' Misha said.

'When?'

'When what?'

'When will I see her?'

'When she comes if we do all this the right way. So put, "I tell my friends about you," like that.'

Howard wrote, 'I've told my mother about you. She is extremely happy. She can't wait to meet her new daughter.'

'Wonderful. We do another.'

'How do I sign it?'

'"Thinking about you", and kisses.'

Howard wrote the words and placed a little log-pile of crosses under his name.

'Okay. What now?'

'Another one. You want drink?'

'No, please.' Howard nibbled his way through the plastic of another card. This time he started writing without instruction.

Dear Irina,
I hope you are well. My job is okay only it's tiring, specially
in my arms.
The pay is okay so maybe we can find a flat together.
I love you very much. I can't wait to meet you.
Howard xx.

July 1st

Left alone in the beautiful calm bronze light of the room, where the sound of flutes accompanied the sound of trickling water, Barbara stripped down to her underpants and lay face down on the white leather table. The girl had not yet returned to do it, so Barbara broke her own breathing hole in the tissue spread over the hollow headrest that framed her face. The girl entered, quietly shut the door, and in silence draped Barbara with four warm, heavy towels. Barbara heard the girl's clogs on the floor, then the uncapping of bottles of oil. Wafted first was geranium to banish tension. The girl's hands made slick sounds together. She removed the towel that covered Barbara's shoulders then pressed warm, small, strong, oiled hands down onto her spine, anointing a line down her vertebrae then rising again to spread fragrant wings of oil across her shoulders. 'Oh,' said Barbara in a deep voice. 'Feels good, doesn't it. Lots of tension there.' The girl's voice recalled to Barbara her name.

'Yes, Catriona, there certainly is.'

'Any reason?' the girl asked. Barbara remembered the girl's cheaply dyed hair and high bosom inside her white tunic and her political theories, a weird tangle of oil conspiracies and extra terrestrials that she would slowly work through as you lay powerless under her hands. She decided to use her first name again in the authoritative way that Les had taught her.

'Catriona, this is too lovely to speak.'

'Of course,' the girl agreed. 'I understand.' She pushed skilled thumbs into the meat of Barbara's back.

Like chatting at the dentist, Barbara thought: not the easiest thing in the world. Your mouth full of wadding and tiny blades and noisy suction. 'So, how are you, Mrs Dawson-Smith?' There would be too much to talk about and it would not be understood.

Competition time was just over a week away! It was always such an effort explaining Saul and what he did. Only at the competitions did you meet other parents with similar passions and goals. And there Les would be too competitive to want to talk to them. Quite friendly some of them seemed, easing their nerves with supportive chat, but Les held himself (and Barbara) apart. The distance he maintained between them was intended to be that between winners and losers.

And Howard. Him still to think about, that big bear with his hidden sweets, his Catholic junk, his phone calls to Varya and Saul's poodlish devotion. How that man could look glamorous or heroic to anyone was beyond her, but that's how Saul seemed to view him. At least after the competition he would soon be gone.

The competition! Saul wouldn't be returning to school after the weekend to give him a week-long run-up. Les would take the time off as well. The house would be full again. Saul, suffering Saul – all over soon, sleep soon, no more nightmares. Maybe he could be given a massage. Oh, she'd like to clean him like linen, iron his creases out and fold him fresh and white again into his bed. Then see him sleep – those long-lashed eyes lightly closed, his hair clean, his lips parted to breathe. And then wake up knowing he had won!

Catriona folded the top of the towel that covered her midriff under the elastic of Barbara's knickers and lowered them sufficiently to reveal all of the small of her back and the rise of her buttocks. Her warm hands worked in the strained hollows around the base of her spine and swept down onto her bottom. Barbara wondered how much the girl could tell with her knowledgeable hands about her body. Whether she could know anything by touch, feeling how she lay or the quality of her skin. Barbara had this thought as a prelude to telling herself the news again. She had refrained long enough, holding her thoughts on other, lesser things, other people. Could Catriona feel the hidden glimmer in her flesh, the deep change? Barbara told herself again in a mental whisper, *No one must know.* She smiled through the hole in her tissue, smiled sightlessly down into nothing, at the floor, smiled so fiercely and uncontrollably that she felt the muscles of her face lift her head a quarter of an inch higher on the pillow.

Barbara was no longer alone. Deep inside, under her heart, there was someone else. She felt sure already that it was a girl. At least that was how she thought of it, as a girl who would join her in her world of men.

It was of course strictly against the rules. That had been agreed long ago. Les did not want another. Partly because he could not be bothered with the expense but partly, Barbara suspected, because he did not want to face the possibility of a child less perfect than Saul. But, but, if she acted ignorant long enough, if she let her grow and grow, or even sooner announce it in the euphoria after Saul's victory, then all would be agreed.

When could it have been, wonderful thing? Only that afternoon Les had come home from work early and found her in the bedroom and treated her again for a short while as his wife. Didn't matter, didn't matter when. Whenever it was, it was. Her mind skipped and sang.

Barbara was no longer alone.

July 2nd to 8th

After the meeting in Varya's flat, Howard and Misha communicated almost every day. Perhaps Misha knew that this was necessary. Certainly out of the Russian man's invigorating company, fear gnawed at Howard and ate away at the decision he had made, even though the melodies of love talk for the first time ever now played through Howard's head and undid him every time. Howard was richly confused: perplexed, moved, flattered, frightened and full of good intent. But when Misha appeared everything seemed very obvious and safe and even exciting. Misha made special trips to see Howard in his lunch breaks. Slinking away from his workmates to meet this loud, unusual friend who carried a file of love letters and embraced him when they met, Howard felt specially chosen and glad.

Misha even bought Howard's food a few times. He himself drank prodigious amounts of coffee when it was still too hot for Howard's mouth. The volume of Misha's voice reassured Howard that there was nothing to hide. And he was so affectionate, such a real friend. He asked Howard many questions about his past. Howard answered with a well edited but sincere account and Misha learned of his long loneliness in the house where his mother had died in the miserable north of England. Howard hadn't realised how lonely he had been until he spoke about it. He felt inside himself a fracturing like ice breaking up in the heat of Misha's presence. Even Andy had not been so good a friend. In return, Misha told him all about life in miserable Russia, where all the factories and mines were closed, just like Glasgow, and about the food you ate in Russia, and his brother who traded cars.

One time, at Misha and Varya's flat, with kindly Yelena there as well, Howard had actually spoken to Irina. He had tried to wave away the opportunity when offered the phone, but Misha had held it to his ear. Howard hid his eyes as he accepted the warm receiver. A higher-pitched voice than he had expected asked, 'Hello?' And the voice was so close, it was like her mouth was by his ear. Irina, that was, who for official reasons wrote him letters telling him she loved him and that she wanted to be his wife.

'Hello?'

'Hello.'

'You are Howard?'

'Yes, aha, I am.'

'Thank you to marrying me.'

'Uch, that's okay. I don't have a wife, so . . .'

Irina laughed, the noise blatting on the line with a tight echo as though the two of them were standing in a shower cubicle together.

'That's good,' she said. 'So I will be it.'

'What?'

'So I will be it. Your wife.'

'That's right.'

'See you soon, I hope.'

'Okay.'

And Misha took the phone back and spoke to Irina in rapid Russian.

That night Howard sat in his room and wrote her another letter, but this one came racing out, full of melody, and hard and quick as birdsong. It was like no writing he'd ever done before, so fluent and expressive it felt like he was speaking – his hand sped across the page. He couldn't restrain himself or deny any of the words that wanted to be written so halfway through he knew that he could never send it to her. But he couldn't throw it away either. The page, contoured with the pressure of his hand and with all those words on it, seemed like a live thing. He could hear it singing in his head. So he folded it up carefully, put it in an envelope, and hid it in his anorak pocket. It would be another secret to keep. He smiled at his mother standing there as he buttoned the pocket.

Later, lying and thinking of all this, he heard Saul whimpering and struggling inside another nightmare, the flat tones of his mother talking him out of it. Saul barely seemed to sleep at all at the moment with the competition a dwindling number of days away. It was so different to Fergus, of course, but Saul kept bringing that all back. The two boys seemed to know each other in Howard's mind. Fergus appeared every morning when Howard looked into Saul's bloodshot eyes. And that led him back to the train tracks, the wet stones. And the hundreds of nights after in Ridgemont, listening to other boys' nightmares. It was like a nightmare factory, that place. Howard felt so desperate for Saul, and for himself: it hurt to be pulled out of soft, circling thoughts of his new love and to be thrown back into the awful past.

But what could Howard do about it? Saul wasn't his lad. He couldn't wrap him in a blanket and cancel the competition. He couldn't even say anything useful. Saul was doomed to go through whatever it was this bloody competition put him through. Howard shouldn't even have been there. He'd spent as long as could hiding in Burnley until his hiding place had been clubbed open. He'd been extracted by these people and what was he now? Confused, useless, ridiculous and, in all sorts of ways, far too involved.

Three days before the world memory championships, Misha took Howard to see a lawyer. It had been explained to him why this was necessary and how long it would last but Howard still dreaded it. But meeting Misha again had its usual salutary effect and being freed from work in the afternoon was a small holiday, with bright daylight, passing people. Misha had bought a bag of salted cashews and fed himself and Howard as they walked. On the way they aligned their stories once more. They had met as the result of the wonderful coincidence that Irina already had friends and a strong support network in London.

In Hackney Howard entered an office of yellowish corridors, of doors panelled with glass the colour of pond ice and water coolers with drab shapes of wet at their feet. Misha spoke to a woman behind a high desk and led Howard into a waiting room full of suffering foreigners. There were Indian men sitting, neatly combed, holding wads of forms. Unshaven East Europeans hung forward, elbows on their jogging knees, and spoke quietly to each other without turning their heads. A pair of South American men, low in their seats, with smooth clay faces, remained impressively silent. There were several African women in brilliant floral dresses and flip-flops and a round-faced African baby lying on the floor screaming. Its tired mother rubbed its belly with her foot but the baby still screamed and screamed. The noise brought out the latent panic in Howard, who shivered and stalled until Misha arranged him in a seat. The atmosphere of need and long waiting was desperate. Locked inside their languages, all of these people were pleading to be allowed a life. On a table Howard saw magazines of worn and crazed pages which no one was reading. Only Misha's mood could not be dampened. He must have been through it all before. He brought water to Howard in a paper cone and continued munching cashews. It was a terrible enough place to be but Howard quite soon came to feel at home, recognising his own life there: outside the real, normal world being processed by the authorities, subject, problematic.

Howard watched people disappear through a door when called by a tired man in a suit. They prepared themselves for a second, touching hair, ties, clutching their papers. They emerged long minutes later looking no happier with new papers in their hands, trying to prolong their moment with this man, beseeching him, smiling and smiling and shaking hands. But their time was up. He called the next one in.

Eventually Howard's turn came. Misha winked good luck. On a reflex, Howard touched the unsent letter in his pocket. The man summoned him in, shook his hand, and quickly resumed the seat behind his desk. The wall behind him was shelved to the ceiling and full of box files. Howard couldn't imagine the effort that went into reading all that or the number of lives they contained. On the desk Howard noticed a photograph, presumably of the man's wife, looking exhausted, her hair particularly, which was flat to her head, but very happy, holding in her wrist-tagged arms an insensible newborn, mauve-faced with pursed lips and puffy eyes. The lawyer sat down, spread out a form, clicked a pen, and glanced up at Howard. The glance was very brief, almost as though he was as nervous as Howard or was forcing himself to look at something he didn't want to see. 'Mister Howard MacNamee,' he said slowly.

'That's me,' Howard admitted, and looked down at his nails. When he looked up again the lawyer was taking a bite out of a sandwich. Where had the sandwich come from? It seemed to have materialised from nowhere. Howard checked around for the source while the lawyer stared down at the form, his full cheeks bobbing. One of the desk drawers was open. So in the second that Howard had been looking away, the lawyer had pulled open the drawer, grabbed the sandwich and started to bite. He must have done it at incredible speed. Braced and formal as he was for this interview, Howard found this untoward and very distracting. Howard said absently 'Aha' when the lawyer swallowed and said, 'And you are engaged to Miss Irina Galitsina?' The lawyer took another bite. What was in the sandwich? That was another question. Some kind of brown meat, beef maybe. Or maybe it was sliced-up sausages.

Howard continued to answer the lawyer, thinking all the time about the sandwich, until the lawyer looked up and said,

'Okay, Mr MacNamee. I need you to answer the following question honestly. Do you love Irina?'

Howard went to say 'Yes' and in doing so found that he was so full of emotion, drowning in his love for her, that his voice wouldn't come. He shook his head, trying to focus, and stammered, eventually, 'Ay, I do.' And in that moment Howard knew that he was insane, an embarrassment, that he'd never be a normal person. All he had to do to save this girl was tell a few official lies and suddenly he was almost weeping for the amount of love he felt for her. He was useless. How could Misha think that Howard was a solid enough person to do this job?

He answered the ensuing questions mechanically, flushing with rage at himself. The lawyer shook his hand a second time, gave him some forms, and sent him outside.

Misha stood up to meet him. 'I cannae do this,' Howard told him. 'I'm not ... I can't.'

'Why not? There is problem?'

'No, no problem. But I can't. I just ... please.'

'But why?'

Misha was angry and wanted to have the argument right there. 'Why not? Why not you can't?'

'Please, can I go home?'

'But why? Why you can't?'

'Please.'

The baby was still on the floor, still crying, but Howard didn't realise it was the baby when he felt something tug at his trouser leg. He kicked and the baby spun on the bare tiles. See! He couldn't stop himself hurting people. The mother, a massive woman, flew out of her seat shouting. Howard didn't know what to do. Automatically he stopped and picked up the wailing baby, which hung on his hands and kicked in fury. Misha was asking, 'What are you doing?' Howard offered the baby to the woman but she kept on shouting and pointing. Howard offered it to Misha, who said, 'What's this? I don't want this.' Almost crying, Howard just put the baby back on the floor, laying it on its back because its legs buckled and wouldn't stand up. The mother bent to the child. Howard fled from the building.

That night, as Howard bumped down through his worries towards sleep, his bedroom door opened quietly and barefoot Saul walked in. 'I'm not asleep,' he whispered. 'I'm not having a nightmare.'

Howard rolled his head on his pillow to check his clock. 'Wee man, it's eleven thirty-seven. You *should* be asleep.'

'I'm up all night. Nobody knows. Anyway, you should be asleep too.'

'I cannae. I'm worried. Too much going on in my head and I cannae even remember it like you.'

Saul nodded in solidarity. 'What worries?' he asked.

'Doesnae matter. Different ones. Grown-up ones. Anyway, are you still here?'

'I'm worried too,' Saul confided and crept over to Howard's bed. He perched on the edge. Howard shuffled his body across to give Saul room to sit. He reached for his glasses before deciding he didn't need them and left the boy blurred. Saul meanwhile looked at the huge pink cylinder of Howard's upper arm. He saw unimaginable strength. What could Howard be worried about? 'Did you tell your mother about your worries?'

Howard blinked. 'Aha.' He blinked again and rubbed his eyes with thumb and forefinger hard enough to make a juicy sound.

'Do you think I could talk to her about mine?'

'What? No. Don't be stupid, Saul.'

'I'm not being stupid. Don't call me stupid. Why not? Please.'

'No. No way. Look, even if you did speak to her, one, she doesn't answer you back and two, what does she know about memory competitions and all your sorts of worries?'

Saul sniffed hard three times, clenched his hands into fists and tilted his head back as if to keep tears from rolling out. 'I ... just ... wanted ... to ...' he panted. Quite vividly in Saul's stricken face flashed Fergus's, white with pain, panicking Howard. But this wasn't his fault; Howard wasn't doing this.

'Oh Christ, Sauly-boy. Take it easy, there. I'm sorry. What do you need to speak to my mother for anyways? You've your own mother.'

Saul looked scathingly, narrowing his eyes.

'And I'm right here,' Howard went on.

'And what do you know about memory competitions?' Saul asked. For two hours that evening he had sat and failed to memorise a binary sequence. There was something about binary numbers, the endless, featureless string of ones and zeros, that he found hard to cope with. He knew what to do, to decode the number, break it up, break into it, but the visual blankness did something to his mind, refused it purchase, and his intelligence would slide away. Two hours of the sensation of failure building to a final admission to Simon with tears streaming down his stupid face.

'I don't know anything about them,' Howard admitted. 'But you do. You've done loads of them. You're good at them. I've seen you in the photos with the prizes.'

'Don't say that! Don't say that!'

'Sshh! Saul, wheesht yourself. We'll get caught.'

'How big *is* your hand? Show me.' Saul picked up Howard's hand by the wrist and pressed his hand against it, palm to palm.

Howard smiled. 'Tiny boy,' he said, and curled his fingers down over Saul's. Saul resisted, wrestling hands for a moment before giving up.

'I'm too tired,' he said. 'I'm so tired. I'm bloody, bloody tired.'

'Mind your language there, son.'

'I'm so tired. I feel sick. I wish ... I wish ... I want to ...'

Losing his way, he stopped. 'Anyway, I'm off school from now on. All the time memory.' He tapped his temples with crooked fingers and chanted, 'In it goes, in it goes, in it goes.'

'Saul, what did I say? Quiet there.'

'I don't want to be!'

Howard put his hand on Saul's hot, small shoulder. 'Take a hold of yourself there, wee man.'

Saul's mouth folded in. He looked down now and didn't resist the tears. 'Make it go away, Howard. Make it finish. Ask your mother to make it be finished.'

July 8th

Howard was in the warehouse, handing down chairs from a lorry, the day before the competition, when he saw Misha walk in through the door. Howard very nearly failed to catch hold of the chair Lester was handing him and had to resort to stopping it from falling with his forehead.

'Misha, go away, I cannae talk to you right now. And you shouldn't just walk in here.' The sudden appearance angered Howard, who was trying to keep things together, trying to hide. Now a door had been kicked in: Misha was there.

Misha spread his long arms and raised his voice. 'But I must speak with you, Howard. We need you. What happened? And you don't answer phone message.'

There had been a phone message? But Barbara must have heard it and not told him or maybe would tell him tonight when he got back. They would know. Everything was coming apart, falling together.

'What happened? I . . . I'm not the man you want.'

'Yes, you are. I want you. We want you. Varya is saying every day.'

'No, she isn't. Don't say that.'

'We must talk now. You come now. I buy food.'

'I can't.'

'You come.'

'Please, pal. I'm kind of busy right now.'

Ron tapped Howard on the shoulder. 'Do you want to take your girlfriend outside. Health and bloody safety for starters.'

'Oh ay, if I can.'

'It's not like you're doing much anyway.'

Howard stood down and walked with Misha out into the street. 'Misha, I can't explain.'

'Yes, you can of course.'

'No, I cannae. And wee Saul's going nuts. Please go.'

'Saul? This small boy they have? Anyway, I'm not going.'

Les walked terrifyingly past them, just as Howard had uttered his son's name. He climbed into his car without looking round and swerved out into the traffic.

'I am not going,' Misha repeated.

'Misha.'

'You want me to go, push me away.'

'Misha, for Christ's sake. I'm at work.'

'Push me away. Push me,' Misha said simply as though it were the most reasonable demand in the world.

'Fine,' Howard said. 'All right, if you want me to.' Howard placed his two hands on Misha's chest. Misha tried to look unperturbed. And Howard pushed. Misha walked up the road backwards with small, accelerating steps as Howard vented his rage along his arms, shoving with all his weight so that big Misha's eyes widened in fear as he stumbled back.

'Now would you leave me alone.'

Howard woke once to hear Saul being argued out of another nightmare. He lay and listened to the voices and the wind in the garden before falling asleep to dream that Fergus-Saul lay on stones trembling like a starving dog, grey-fleshed, dirty, barely alive. Howard staggered towards him over the crash of stones he dislodged and bent down to help. Saul-Fergus's face looked up and said in a whisper, *Why did you do this?* Howard, weeping, told him, *I never meant to. I never. I never.*

At breakfast, Saul was given two cards to open, one from his grandmother with a horseshoe on the front and one from his parents, who stood behind him as he read it. Inside, the card said, 'Always our Number 1', a message Saul visibly flinched at before receiving hugs and loud, rhetorical kisses on the top of his head. Barbara instructed Howard to dress as smartly as possible and to comb his hair. 'We can't have you letting the side down.' Howard was to this end lent a comb which he wetted and worked through his hair, scraping his bald spot as he stood in the bathroom in the same outfit he'd worn for Mrs Dawson's funeral. He descended to find Les alone in the kitchen, a mug of black coffee and his car keys on the table in front of him. He sat with his shoulders hunched, his hands clasped between his knees, his chin an inch or two from his mug. He did not look round. Howard stood very still, hardly breathing, remembering his dream. The dream had been long. Had started all the way back at the little scrap fire and went through all the running, the fear of the other boys, then stumbling out onto the tracks and what happened. All of it. The spitty rain hitting Howard while the world went wrong. Barbara entered in a smart navy dress and jewellery that gave her a clean and respectable ready-for-church look. She said grandly, 'May I present to you the future junior world memory champion,' and began applauding. Saul faltered in through the doorway, his eyes downcast. He wore a suit and shirt and red bow tie. His hair was parted down the middle into two thick pages. His skin was today so pale its colour was a vaporous blue. His suit made his limbs look tight and awkwardly connected. He glanced up directly into Howard's eyes. The eyes looked shockingly out of Howard's dream and he almost apologised again to Saul as if they were still there together.

'Can you win this one?' Les asked his son.

Saul nodded. 'I think so.'

'Course you can!' Les cried encouragingly. 'Let's just go there and do it! Right, then, let's hit the road.'

London, real London, red bus London, jerked past the car windows in cramped bursts of speed between traffic lights and jams. Les muttered imprecations at the other drivers and Saul held the diagonal of his seat belt out away from his neck. This was the first time they had all been in the car together since the long drive down to London. Howard usually liked being driven, liked being encased, protected and carried. The world running past like film. But this drive was an awkward, angular descent towards he knew not what kind of torment. It reminded him of the drive in the back of the van to Ridgemont with two other offenders. Saul certainly looked as if he were being carried towards his doom. Howard distracted himself with the views.

A shape through the window was as familiar as a person. Eventually it was recognised by Howard as Big Ben. Howard was reminded then of all the things in London, the famous places, Buckingham Palace and suchlike, that he'd completely forgotten were there at all. London for him had meant only the Underground and work, a dirty yellow-grey world walled with the meat of strangers' faces. The only other place he knew was Varya's rough estate. Howard confused himself by thinking that it was almost like there were two different words, 'London' and 'London', and he'd only seen one of them. The car swept now by a large, gated park with statues and trees and green royal distance.

Les held the steering wheel lightly with his fingertips and prepared to launch his son like a missile against the world. Saul looked so finished, so finely tempered in his competition clothes. To Les he seemed the prototype for an unstoppably successful human being. He recalled the first time he'd seen his son memorise the sequence of two shuffled packs of cards, the astonishment of these genius powers in his child. He'd wanted to frame the moment, to have it somehow to show to everybody, to carry it around with him in his wallet like a licence that entitled him to the respect of all parents, of all people everywhere.

Barbara held her breath, her poise. Barbara wanted Saul to win as much as her husband did. Possibly more, if that were possible. She needed it. She needed the champagne atmosphere, the new freedom, the laughter and illimitable optimism for her news to be accepted.

Les considered their enemies, the children who could rob Saul of the title, the children who could, by virtue of their winning, render him a loser. They were out there like unexploded mines. He could almost feel their approach to the hotel, each of them moving through London, moving towards him.

Parking was tense. When they had finally wedged the car into a spot, Barbara placed a calming hand on the back of Les's head but Les, too tense to be touched by Barbara, snapped his head forward. He sighed, pinched the bridge of his nose, and unlocked the doors. They walked then, grouped in their formal attire, through the weekend crowds. Most of them seemed to be tourists – Howard could hear languages. The shops were grand. Everything was grand. The buildings were tall, pillared, with angels on some of them and ladies holding urns. High above their cornices was sky, sky of a beautiful, televisual blue with white clouds in it. Down below again were tourist stands selling policemen's helmets and flags and T-shirts and post-cards of Lady Diana and a peculiar one of a woman's breasts painted with mouse faces. There were proper red buses sailing in the traffic and tourist buses with open tops and amplified voices of guides going past. Thus Howard learned that he was in the fashionable Regency area of Piccadilly. Les's dark head surged through the holiday crowd in front of Howard. Barbara swayed loyally beside him. Howard felt Saul reach up and hold his hand.

They arrived at the hotel, which was like something from a film. There were steps up into it and a man in a uniform beside a revolving door. He tipped his top hat as they took turns passing through a segment of the door and found themselves in a large reception of carpet and polished wood with carefully deployed seating areas, dried flowers standing on tables in bursts of light. An A-board welcomed them to the seventh annual world memory championships. Badged people with clipboards and smiles vocalised the welcome. The Dawson-Smiths' names were checked off the list by a woman with lipstick smeared on her teeth and a vivaciously swinging pony-tail. Howard's name was added to the list as a family member of a competitor. They were each given a competitor's information pack and individual laminated security passes to pin to their clothes, although Barbara preferred just to hold hers and save her jacket. Saul was wished good luck by this efficient and professionally charming woman. She instructed them to follow the signs.

Fellow competitors walked the same corridors. Howard stared eagerly at them. This was the first time he'd seen anyone else involved in this desperately important world aside from Saul and Simon. They were mostly men and varied in style but were not obviously impressive in any way. Some looked bleak, unaccountably ashamed of themselves and scared; they walked with heads bowed, close to the walls, their lunches in carrier bags. Several were brisk, carrying briefcases. A pair of short women walked together arm in arm, with matching pale spiral crowns in curly black hair. But it was for the other junior competitors that Les and Saul were most intensely vigilant. Saul glimpsed Vikram Chandrasinghe rounding a corner ahead of them and suffered a heartbeat so strong it unsteadied his step. Barbara called after his father to say hello and wish him luck, but Mr Chandrasinghe only turned and glared. Saul needed the toilet already. Barbara greeted an unfamiliar parent with the intense, empty warmth of a presidential first lady. Les scowled. The competition room astonished Howard. An empty ballroom complete with pillars, mirrors, gilding and chandeliers, it looked like something from a film with royal people in it. And you could have walked past the hotel without the first idea. All these pockets in the city, he reflected, like Varya's pocket of Russian people. A mirror showed Howard himself, mouth open, his hair already defying its combing. Banners proclaimed the championship, others just carried its logo, a brain like a bunchy cauliflower next to a thumping exclamation mark. Gold chairs with red-cushioned seats awaited the audience. The same chairs at single desks covered a stage much larger than the audience area. A large television screen hung on the back wall presently showing the championship title scrolling past while the brain from the logo rotated between animated jumps. On one side of the stage stood a spotlit lectern. The excitement of simultaneous voices in a large chamber filled Howard's stomach with flight. He looked around and saw a lot of foreign people in the crowd, Indians, orientals, tall, suited Africans. It was an extravagant kind of foreignness that suited the place well and did give the competition glamour; it reminded him of the crowd in the casino in a James Bond film. Not like the crowd in the lawyer's office that seemed to have been there forever, all close to rage or tears. Like Irina must be right now in Russia, in her freezing, dead town.

Les marshalled them quickly into their seats, then sat twisting from side to side looking at the people impatiently as if to disapprove them into their places so that things could get under way. Howard leaned down and said into Saul's pearly, well-scrubbed ear, 'This is a bit too grand for me, is this.' Saul shook his head, far from able to think of anything to say. 'Hey?' said Howard, 'Hey?' putting his hand on the boy's back, his one hand as wide as Saul's shoulder blades.

Quiet thudding of a microphone. The room now full. More thudding. The room reduced to a prickling silence of expectation. Applause as an official appeared at the lectern, a man with a black bar code of hair across his baldness and curves of shadow between nose and mouth that flexed violently in the light cast by the lectern's lamp.

'Ladies and gentlemen, mnemonists and fans, members of the press and public, welcome to the seventh annual World Memory Championships.'

A pelting storm of applause now as the audience vented its excitement. Saul's small hands blurred together and Howard thought he saw him possibly smile. After all, like Les had said, Saul had been in many competitions. He was probably always this tense before things started and now would come alive.

The applause thickened as the compère announced, 'And now please welcome the founder of this event, the best-selling author, media personality, corporate trainer, businesswoman, musician – I could go on but I think we're most of us fairly familiar with her long list of achievements, achievements that are summed up in a name. Please welcome to the stage Betty Zorin.'

From a side door strode onto the stage a middle-aged woman wearing a blue skirt and jacket, a roll neck and a necklace of amber pebbles. Her hair formed a high, starched, honey-coloured helmet around her head. Her face was round, bright-eyed, with apples in her cheeks. She chuckled with pleasure at her reception an inch or two too close to the microphone and produced a breathy blast through the speakers. She waved a hand to quieten the applause and camera flashes spasmed in response.

'Thank you, thank you,' she began. Her accent was glamorously American. Another amplified blast of nasal breath. She began again, her voice a notch or two lower and now that of a professional speaker: 'Ladies and gentlemen, mental athletes and friends, good afternoon and welcome indeed to the World Memory Championships and what an exciting event this should be.' There was a short relapse of applause which did not seem to please her and was soon gone. 'I am expecting records to crumble over the next two days as once again the best trained, most powerful synaptic stars in the world push back the frontiers of what has for too long been thought the limit of possibility for the human mind.' This time apparently she wanted applause and waited while a smattering spread through the crowd and she could again wave it into silence. She touched her lips with prayerful hands then leaned again to the microphone. Her timing was immaculate and she spoke into a silence at its most focused hush of interest. 'So for the next two days we are not merely partaking in the increasing popularity of a new sport, or enjoying *tricks*,' she mocked the word facially as she said it, 'performed by people akin to cranks and conjurors. I'm no snake oil saleswoman. I am employed by some of the world's major corporations because I bring results, results which prove my theories, *our* theories, of what we are capable of. We are redefining human achievement. We are redefining genius. We are proving that genius capabilities are available to us all. Each of our neuronal gladiators tells humanity that this too is in your power. We should dare to be more. Dare to explore your capabilities.' She looked up, open-faced, to express the simple wisdom of her theory. 'Because genius is a state of mind. Who knows how many Mozarts or Leonardos lie dormant among us, sitting listlessly in front of the television. It's a waste that really irks me.' This, for some reason, got a laugh and, pleased at that, she smiled before resuming her flight. 'I picture all that glittering ore of mental power out there and so few of us willing to refine it into gold. So this championship stands as a beacon. It says, "There is so much more to discover and become." It says, "Arise, humanity." She concluded smiling and calm, wagging a knowing finger, ' "And dare to be as magnificent as you are." '

Drenching applause, fluttering white light of camera flashes and cheers.

The compère returned to the lectern also applauding, hands held high in front of him, his head cocked to one side in gratitude and wonderment. 'Well,' he said, catching his breath, 'we're ready to start. Our first event will be binary numbers. Competitors from all categories will take part simultaneously. Our stewards will sort out the differential timings. There is behind me to your left a preparation room for competitors and their accompanying assistants. Through that door there to your right is a lounge where we will be selling merchandise as well as I think the complete back catalogue of Betty's books, including the latest, *Remembering To Succeed*. So, let the games begin!'

The games began with a wave of blue-suited officials breaking over the stage to gather the competitors to their seats. There was much milling and nervous, quiet talk as people jockeyed into position. Saul was led by Les to the stage and handed over to the same woman who had greeted them in the vestibule. Howard had instructed Saul, 'Go to it champ,' when he had got out of his seat to let them pass. Saul offered a brave smile before his face was smooshed by a sincere, two-second kiss on the cheek from his mother. Now on the stage he sat straightening his bow tie and setting out two sharpened pencils in front of him. Les stood in the aisle and closely surveyed the scene, glowing with warm contempt for the competitors. It was a secret source of strength for him that he lacked respect for these people, these cranks and obsessives. They didn't realise that this would be only one of Saul's achievements, one brilliant in his crown. He received a comradely slap on the shoulder which made him jump and turn angrily to confront its giver. Simon Clifford's mildly smiling face was met with a staccato, 'Did you have to do that?'

'I'm sorry. Tense times, no doubt,' he apologised in his relaxed Canadian tones. 'But we must own the stress and use its little engine, not the other way around. Hello, Howard.'

'Hello.'

'Well,' Simon sighed, 'I'd better get up there.'

'You're a mental ath— You're taking part?' Howard asked.

'Yes, indeedy.'

'Uch well, good luck. Hope you win.'

'Oh, I won't win,' he said, apparently not displeased. 'My limits are easily exceeded by some of my fellow competitors. David Blacket there, for example, or our own Eddie Moss. No, I will lose, although probably quite comfortably. Somewhere in the middle of the pack.'

'Oh.'

'No worries.' Simon moseyed forward to get on with his failure.

'And what about Saul?' Howard called after him.

'Oh, Saul can win. Just as long as he doesn't try to,' Simon called back.

The compère smoothed the lines of hair on his scalp, bulked the knot of his tie, and delivered himself of the rules. Thirty minutes to memorise, sixty to recall. Above his head the screen rippled with strings of ones and zeros. Howard did not know what binary numbers were and guessed they might be to do with sticking other numbers together. Six sheets of seven hundred and fifty digits were handed to each competitor. Betty Zorin returned to the stage. The screen image changed to the face of a stopwatch. Betty Zorin leaned towards the microphone. 'Synapses set . . .?' she whispered dramatically. 'Then go!' There was a short sizzle of applause before an anticlimactic silence, the intense, dull, rustle-and-cough-edged silence of an examination room. After ten very long minutes of watching the competitors – some jogging their feet and mouthing, others absolutely still with head in hands, one with arms folded staring wrathfully at the page, Vikram Chandrasinghe sitting stiff-spined with his fingers splayed on the desk, his dark, carved, aquiline head absolutely still – Les, whose lips were pressed together in a stumpy beak and whose eyes were clotted in his head, whispered, 'I can't take this,' and got up to join those who had already retreated into the merchandising lounge. Barbara and Howard followed.

An hour later, midway through the recall period when Saul should have been listing all his strikes and ciphers on the specially formatted competition paper, Howard walked into a large and beautiful marble toilet to find the boy standing alone. His crying face was limpidly reflected in two walls of mirrors. His tears shone everywhere. The trickling water, the heaped white towels, the boy in his bow tie, the subtle lighting, the picturesquely isolated emotion felt unreal. Howard spoke to test that it was actually happening. Saul hid his eyes with his hands. His hands glistened where tears had seeped through his fingers. Howard hurried towards him, accompanied by flying angelic reflections of himself. 'Saul,' he said, 'Saul.' The boy's mouth opened, a bright red cave, startlingly vivid in this most visual room. He had wet, trembling lips, his tongue rose and fell to say without noise, 'No, no.' Howard held Saul by the shoulders and Saul's head rolled. This was horrible.

Howard shook him, 'Pull yoursel' together, wee man,' he implored.

Saul shook his head. The last hour had been agony. It had started with him holding his throbbing temples and staring down at the lines of ones and zeros, thousand of switches flipping off and on in interpretable sequence, and all he had to do was start translating them into base-ten numbers that could then be affixed with the appropriate images from the matrix and hold them, hold them, before translating them back. He'd felt spit that wanted to roll from his lower lip onto the page and sucked it back. His brain would not start. He knew that inside his head was a calm machine, a thing of right angles and certain action, but it wouldn't start up. He couldn't get into it. He was outside the brain that was inside him, stranded among his weak personal thoughts that he feared were really himself, the true Saul. He saw this condition abstractly; it resembled a film of something alive seen through a microscope: weak, pullulating, curving filaments of stupid thoughts (worms!) the colour of orangey blood, they pushed up against the bright square of his trained brain. He'd let some spit patter down, magnifying numbers, blurring them, wrinkling the page. 'I can't, I can't,' he sobbed.

'Course you can, Saul. You do this all the time.'

'I can't, I can't.'

'Why? What?'

'It's not going in,' Saul shouted. 'It's just not. I want to go. I know it can do but it won't.'

'Just let it,' Howard pleaded. 'Simon said you just need to relax.'

'I can't relax.' Saul's body was tight and almost weightless in Howard's hands. 'I'm going to lose,' he sobbed. 'Dad's going to kill me.'

'You can do it. Simon says.' Howard was inspired. 'Think of that. Think Simon says, like the game. Simon says wash your face.'

'Howard, I ...'

'Please,' Howard begged, 'oh, please, please, please. Simon says wash your face. Simon says wash your face.'

Howard literally ran into Les in the competition lounge, where he was inspecting a table of books for sale, most of which he already owned. He was vaguely noting the development of Betty Zorin's face in her author photographs from nineteen-seventies black and white in which her centre-parted hair draped her round head and large glasses released to view only the very tip of her nose, to the more recent photographs in which her hair had inflated to a thing of voluminous authority, her glasses had disappeared, and her well-lit eyes twinkled with a mature compound of maternal encouragement, wealth, intelligence and frankly saucy flirtatiousness. Les tossed down *Unlimited Thinking* and asked Howard what the hell the panic was.

'Nothing at all,' Howard lied. 'I was just going to the toilet.'

'Well, it's in the precise opposite direction,' Les informed him.

On the way out, Simon caught hold of Les's shoulder. He looked exhausted but very awake, like an athlete after a race; he was holding a carrier bag, his lips distorting as he ate half a red pepper. 'Don't worry about it,' he said. 'It's not over.' He crunched the vegetable and spoke so that red fragments could be seen turning in his mouth like clothes in a washing machine. 'And I'm right. Saul can still do fine, can win even, just not by trying.' Saul did not look up as his tutor spoke. Barbara pulled her gold chain out so that it bit into the flesh of the back of her neck. Howard didn't breathe.

Les said nothing. He couldn't have been sure enough that his voice wouldn't have broken with emotion. Holding Saul's shoulder, he led the way and steered him out of the building.

*

Saul had not done well in any of the three events of the first day and when the scoreboard had scrolled down the junior section results, past Vikram Chandrasinghe's long, smug, impregnable name, it took a while to reach Saul's. The Dawson-Smiths drove home in a silence the like of which Howard had never known before. His head throbbed with the afterfright of the scene in the bathroom and he couldn't tell because Saul had sworn him to secrecy. Howard wished with great fervour that closing his eyes and opening them again could transport him elsewhere. When Howard did close his eyes he kicked a baby on the floor, staggered over Fergus's body, felt Misha grab him by the wrist, saw Irina weeping. With the competition falling apart, Howard became aware that all the other disasters he'd been hoping would go away were now just the other side of tomorrow. Eventually Les tried to speak, his voice calm and insinuatingly reasonable. 'Saul, all you need to do is relax and forget that this even is a competition,' he said. 'You have to act as if failure is impossible or irrelevant.' But each word and the tone in which it was uttered made failure more and more real to all of them. Saul found it numbing, terminal, utterly destroying. Howard saw that Barbara's eyes were large with tears, but didn't know that she was losing hope for her unborn daughter, then turned to see more tears roll silently down Saul's already sore face. He remembered with a sharp physical memory from his time at Ridgemont the sensation of salty tears burning against cracked, painful skin. Sudden anger made him want to punch through the sun roof of the car. All their crying faces made him furious. 'Good God!' he wanted to cry. 'So Saul can't remember some stupid bendary numbers, so what!' But he knew there was no 'so what' about it. This was the most important thing in all of their lives. Saul could break apart in the attempt and still they'd keep going. He saw Saul's loneliness and felt it deep inside him, emptying him out, returning him to his own lonely time as a boy, far from anyone. Alone.

Howard hid upstairs when the real arguments broke out at home. He wound his mother's rosary around his hand and sat on the floor at his mother's feet and immediately thought of what he should do.

The idea was strong, very strong, frightening, and Howard tried to shake it away. But it wouldn't go. It solved everything, every situation. It made up for everything; everything that had befallen Howard and Fergus, Saul could be saved from now, lifted clean out of. The thought sent Howard swimming with sensations of lightness. He remembered singing his mother's name at the door of the afterlife and the unbearable bliss of forgiveness. Well, maybe that was close. Maybe that had been instruction. Misha told him he could save Irina. He wasn't doing that any more because of how weak and broken open just the thought of it made him but he could still save Saul. That was a different kind of thing. He could do it. He could make up for all he'd done. Howard was heroic after all; Misha had told him so. The idea stayed with him all through the bitter evening of uneaten food, slammed doors and more tears. Under each crashing wave of Howard's worries, the idea remained like a rock. It was still there in the morning when Saul emerged with red, swollen face for the second day of the competition. When Saul started to twitch and talk to himself in the car, the idea was there. It shone. It was right. It was the best idea Howard had ever had. He would do it.

PART 3

Elsewhere, How Howard Met the
Whole Wide World

July 10th

The boy walked down the corridor carrying the square key to the red door to deliver a red apple to the short dark queen but each time he arrived at the door there was a dog, an irrelevant dog, of changeable species, stupid and fierce with wet fur at the hinge of its jaws, barking and barking for no reason. Saul had to start his narrative all over again and each time the sequence of cards failed him at this early point, forcing him back to start over and come again to the jagged brink. Even a card sequence wouldn't go in! Always his strongest event and he couldn't do it; it wouldn't happen ...

Saul looked up with desperate eyes at the screens, at the caricatured brain of the logo, which seemed so calm and round and smug, so happy in itself, and thought that he wanted to be a line drawing. The word *Thunk!* sounded in his head. Again at the stab of failure when the dog appeared, *Thunk! Thunk!* In their aching sockets his eyes twitched and the whole world and all its contestants tightly shimmied. He put a hand to his forehead to hold himself still. *Thunk!* Vikram Chandrasinghe was seated two desks ahead on the right hand side. With his fine hands resting in front of him on the wooden square of his desk, he seemed quite content. On his left hand Saul could see the four rings he was rumoured to use as part of his technique: silver ring, silver ring with red stone, gold ring, silver ring with blue stone. At one national competition Saul's dad had once unsuccessfully tried to persuade the judges to make Vikram take his rings off as they were distracting to other competitors. That had been one of the most embarrassing events ever in his life – his father getting angrier and angrier, his face red as a beetroot, almost like real sparks flying out of his mouth, and all the other parents staring. Saul noticed that he was thinking about other things and panic jerked inside. He had to crush his eyes shut to swallow down the acrid sick that had jumped into the back of his mouth. When he opened his eyes he almost let out a little cry. Howard was crouched right in front of his desk. In the middle of Howard's looming, murmuring, bovine face were his TV-shaped glasses; Saul could see his own face reflected and was alarmed to maked out that his lips were moving, apparently with words.

'Saul, can you hear me?'

Saul nodded, trying to listen to what his own mouth was saying.

'Saul, I want you to get up and follow me. Okay, son?'

Again Saul nodded.

'But you have to not say anything to anyone. Don't look at anyone. This is very important. Can you do that?'

Saul looked at him with cloudy eyes.

'Can you do that? Can you do that? Quick, Saul, say yes.' Howard looked over his shoulder. Doing this with an audience behind him! People were looking. Talking.

Saul opened and closed his lips. His head wavered forwards.

'Are you all right getting up? Come on then.'

Saul rose unsteadily, and put his hand in the small of Howard's back as he followed him. He felt eyes against him in the room, like living things, like fish, cold and gelid, but he followed still, walking as straight as he could with legs that were landing at odd angles. If he could have just climbed under one of those gold chairs and gone to sleep.

Howard's shape pushed forward and on out through the doors and into the corridor. Saul looked down and watched the diamond pattern of the carpet change to a fleur-de-lis pattern in the main vestibule. Nausea washed up inside him. Just before they reached the revolving door a voice stopped them. The voice, repeating something, came around them until it was stood in front: one of the competition stewards, a young man in a short-sleeved white shirt and blue tie. He repeated, with authoritative concern, 'Where are you going? Is everything all right?'

Howard tried to look in the man's eyes as he answered but they were frighteningly focused, observant, and Howard remembered that his own face should be unseen. He looked down at the crown of Saul's head.

'We're just going outside for some air. He doesnae feel so well.' Saul's weight pulled at Howard's arm. The boy was almost falling.

'Really? Is that right? Are you the boy's guardian?'

'Aha, I am. I'm his friend. I'm with him. I'm with the boy.'

'He is,' Saul mumbled.

'So, can I get you any kind of assistance? A glass of water?'

'We just need to get outside. Just please. If we can.'

The man didn't like the whining urgency in Howard's voice. He squatted down in front of Saul to check. Saul's face reared back in alarm. He took Saul's hand and started stroking it.

'Are you all right? Are you feeling unwell?'

Saul gave the best possible answer — Howard almost applauded — he stared at the man's hand interfering with his own, his eyes rolled and he vomited onto the man's cleanly laundered shoulder.

'Oh fuck,' the steward said, standing up. 'Fucking oh. Oh, this is . . .' He fought now with his own retches.

'I'm sorry about that,' Howard said. 'We'll just go outside.'

He pulled Saul so closely that they ended up in the same quadrant of the revolving doors. Saul's heels were chased by the glass behind him. He shuffled and bumped into Howard as they turned. They were outside. Howard's shirt was sweated through. He'd almost given up, almost decided against it. 'Well done, wee man. Jesus, thank you. Great sick.'

The street was very light and fast, full of streaming colours and faces. Saul shielded his eyes and asked Howard's stomach, 'Where are Mum and Dad?'

Howard rubbed Saul's shining lips with the sleeve of his anorak. 'They're in the lounge, having a cup of tea.'

Saul's curiosity was calmed by that respectable piece of information and he didn't want to know anything else; if he said nothing, perhaps Howard wouldn't notice that they had walked out of the competition. The thought that that was indeed what they had done produced the strangest sensation in Saul's body. He felt himself lifting, pouring like a liquid up towards the sky. To steady himself, to stop himself falling up, he looked down at the ground and saw that one of his shoelaces was undone, lying in a loose S-shape across a crack between the paving stones. Howard caught him as he tipped forward. So Howard knew that he had been right, that the boy had been about to collapse. But right outside the hotel with people surely about to come running was not the best place for this to happen. Howard held Saul tight against his leg, hoping that he would seem just tired or affectionate, and walked as quickly as he could, looking for somewhere to hide.

In scented darkness Saul awoke. Smell of what? Dust, flowers, smoke. He found himself sitting on a wooden bench, alone, at his feet a square – what was it? – cushion embroidered with a cross and a bird with a twig in its mouth. There was empty space to either side of him, a calm sense of empty height above. He saw that his shoelace was untied and remembered things. He lifted his head quickly to see where he was and saw Howard's unmistakable silhouette against a fluttering radiance of candle flames. The word 'church' formed like a bubble in his mind and he heard his own quiet voice say it. Howard was rocking back and forth in front of the candles, his hands in nervous flight – touching his bald spot, pulling his shirt, adjusting his glasses, scratching his burn. He was praying possibly. Anyway he was there and Saul felt cool relief. Clearly

Howard was looking after him. With renewed appetite, Saul looked around him to see only one other person, an old lady very low in her seat, just shoulders and brown hat like a mushroom growing in the darkness. Saul looked at the various saints standing on their pillars with holy downward or heavenward gazes, one holding a stick and a miniature church. He looked at the coloured glass and the people he couldn't quite make out, and finally at a nailed Jesus with thickly painted flesh, long toes, curled hands and thick blood pouring out in beaded strings. Saul didn't like looking at that. He slid along his bench and walked quickly over to Howard. The big man jumped when he touched his arm. Howard placed a hand over his left breast and panted.

'Hello, Howard.'

Saul's voice was frighteningly loud in the ecclesiastical silence. Howard shushed him by patting his own lips with a strict forefinger. His glasses swam with reflected flames. Saul looked down at the flagstones.

'It's okay, wee man. Don't fret. Everything is going to be okay.'

Howard pensively moved his glasses up his nose. His leg trembled then his mouth opened with a faint damp popping noise. 'Just wait here, wee man. I've had an idea.' He hurried away to where the old lady was hunched in prayer amid the dark carved pews. Saul rearranged his dress, straightening his bow tie, plucking at his underpants where they'd caught between his buttocks. He cleaned the corners of his eyes with his fingertips, rubbing too hard the delicate, itchy skin.

Howard returned grinning, his glasses at an angle, as though he'd given the old lady a big kiss. 'It's all right,' he said. 'I know where it is now. Let's go.'

There was an open door at the other end of the church, a rectangle of buzzing light and colour set into a wall of shadow. People flashed across it. Saul's scalp tightened as he walked towards it, as the door grew larger, and he flinched down into himself when they finally passed through and the deep water of the world closed over him. It was too much, too loud. He grasped Howard's hand and looked only down at his own feet in his polished shoes swinging alternately forward over the paving stones. As they neared steps down to an Underground station a newspaper vendor seated behind his desk of headlines shouted suddenly and Saul cried out. Howard scooped Saul up to carry him, Saul's knees resting against Howard's soft belly as they descended.

By the clunking ticket machines, Howard grabbed and dropped change from his anorak pocket, grovelling to collect what he could as it rolled away, while Saul was instructed to face the wall. He bought two tickets with coins that needed to be squeezed sideways into the slot then thrust nervous Saul through the snapping barriers.

On the train, Howard sat hunched, his hands a visor at his forehead to conceal his face. Saul gripped the armrests of his bouncing seat as the carriage clattered and roared through darkness. He felt light and mad, ready to laugh.

Howard led him out of a dreary, cream-tiled station into unknown, expensive streets. Calm white houses stood together behind strict black railings. Icy cars gleamed at the kerb. Saul saw many top-of-the-range models – rare sightings out on the road. He ran his hand along a railing for the trill against his palm, then bounced his palm on the low spikes. He remembered bouncing two jumping fingers from freezer to freezer in the supermarket when he was very little. His fingers had been a horse. Saul felt a sudden furious urge to touch everything he could see, particularly when they turned a corner towards a park with huge oaks in sumptuous summer leafage. He wanted to bite them. Among other strolling people they strolled along a crunchy sand path – Saul twisting his shoes with each step to get the best gritty squinch under his soles – towards now a gateway and curved sign which Saul immediately recognised from years before. They were going to London Zoo.

Howard again scooped money from his pocket to buy tickets, mumbling and avoiding the gaze of the the lady behind the glass whose voice emerged from a speaker to his right. The effort to avoid identifying contact didn't work: she made him repeat himself several times, finally instructing him to put his mouth by the microphone before he spoke. He spent a good minute in conversation with the lady, who eventually slid out to him one adult and one child ticket while suggesting he shouldn't try for a job on the radio.

They passed through the turnstile and blinked at the scene. Children and parents, pushchairs with balloons tied to them. In the background a chewing camel with a dull coat like a worn bath mat. There was a queue of children where Howard saw something that might help him recover: at the head of the queue a man deftly twirled pink candy floss onto sticks. Howard stood in line, bought two of the impaled clouds and handed one to Saul, who thanked him politely and started nibbling at the wispy edges. This was the first time Saul had eaten candy floss and he was dismayed by how the voluminous stuff immediately shrank to a grainy scrap of sugar in his mouth. Howard ate his with inappropriate appetite for such a silly food, holding it sideways and biting great gouts. He wiped his mouth with the back of his hand and smiled at Saul. 'This is fun, isn't it?'

'Better than being at the competition,' Saul agreed, although the words uttered made him feel sick.

'Oh yes, yes. Let's go and look at some animals.'

With his damp, deflossed stick, Howard conducted them forward, making a sort of fencer's lunge which embarrassed Saul and provoked a worried look from a woman wheeling a buggy from which hung a baby in an attitude of utmost sleep, folded exactly in half over its harness.

'Let's go and find the monkeys, I mean if that's all right with you, wee man?'

'Fine. Maybe there'll be room for you. Do you want to

finish this?' Saul offered his half-eaten treat and Howard took it from him, continuing without comment to eat.

Saul was light-headed in the sunshine. Where had the walls gone, the room, the people, all the things to do?

Most of the animals in the primates section seemed quiet and tired, sitting dejectedly in corners of their enclosures like exhausted grown-ups while little children banged on the glass. Howard still found them funny, though. 'Look at that one,' he chuckled to Saul, pointing out a chimp with a wrinkled leather face and glazed, plum-coloured eyes, 'just sitting there like all *bluh*.'

Saul drifted away and found himself in front of an orang-utan. From the forests of Borneo and Sumatra, his brain reminded him. He looked at the large plates of its face, its pale pursed lips and vacant eyes – no, not vacant; he realised with a shock that it was looking back at him. Its orange fur was long and loose. Bits of dry leaves were stuck in the fringes of its arms. Its short legs poked straight out under its pot belly and its large hands lay still, palms up on the ground. For no reason at all, Saul's brain started up and a two-hundred-and-eight-card sequence poured through – queen hearts, queen spades, three clubs, seven diamonds, four clubs, six clubs, five diamonds, nine spades, on and on, so quickly that Saul had to hold his head while it happened, trying to remember if this was a sequence he'd learned or one that his mind was just inventing. The orang-utan on the other side of the glass seemed very heavy, very far away and very real. Slowly, Saul managed to lift up his hand and rest it on the glass, then shouted, 'Howard.'

The amplified voice of a zoo keeper invited children to touch the snake and find out for themselves whether it was really slimy or not. The children squealed and giggled, doing small violences to each other, gripping and shoving, until one little boy stepped out, one hand holding the front of his shorts, the other feeling forward to make contact with the thick snake draped around the zoo keeper's neck.

'They're not slimy, they're dry. Everyone knows that,' Saul commented, sipping at the can of Coke Howard had prescribed after his second collapse. They sat together in the shade of a tree and watched the crowd. A bright, tiny plane howled overhead.

'How's the drink?' Howard asked.

'Nice.' Saul was never allowed the non-diet version and the sugar did indeed have an energising effect.

Howard still held the two sticks from his candy floss, one in each hand like a drummer. 'How do you know snakes are dry? Have you touched one?'

'No.' Saul tutted. 'Just everyone knows that.' An alarm went off in the pocket of his jacket and he stood upright in fright, dropping his drink. Howard stooped to pick up the can as it sobbed dark foam onto the ground. 'It's my phone,' Saul yelped, producing the object. He begged, 'What do I do? What do I do?'

'Who is it? Who?'

Saul looked at the flashing face. 'Who do you think? It's Mum and Dad,' he bleated.

'Sshh.' Howard flapped his hands and sticks. 'People are looking.'

'What do I do, though, what do I do?'

'Do you want to go back.'

'No, no, no, no, no.'

'And can you switch it off?'

Saul nodded, finding the button with a circling finger. 'It'll go to voicemail,' he said.

'Jesus.'

'I can erase the message. I don't have to listen to it.'

'Jesus.'

'Howard, where are we going to go now?'

'I don't know,' he answered honestly. 'Oh, no. I've an idea. I've got some friends.'

'Some friends,' Saul repeated, his eyes filling with tears. 'Let's go there then.'

It was rush hour when they got back on the train. Howard couldn't work out if that was good or bad, whether more people would see them or they'd become invisible in the crowd. Certainly Saul almost disappeared, crushed between commuters, when he wasn't being pressed embarrassingly hard into Howard's belly. Saul himself shut his eyes and just floated or fell – yes, it was falling, falling far, falling through the smelly air, falling through London, out of his life and down. He just let go of everything and let himself drop. Howard would catch him; he had twice already.

A beggar with a cardboard sign sat as expressionless and disconsolate as one of the zoo mammals, his face the colour of the cardboard, in the shroud of a sleeping bag. Saul hurried round to the other side of Howard to avoid contact with the man, who then, terrifyingly, spoke. 'I won't bite you, bow-tie boy.'

Saul tried desperately to convince himself that he was talking to someone else whilst simultaneously deciding that this was the worst, dirtiest place he'd ever been. Howard led him past loitering people, drug dealers probably, men with knives or guns in their pockets. Saul kept ducking around to hide behind Howard as they walked. Above the buildings the sky was livid with pink and gold cloud. Looking up, Saul was grabbed by the shoulder to stop him stepping in front of a car. 'Don't worry,' Howard said to Saul's wild face, 'our friends are just around the corner.'

Saul held Howard's hand and kept walking until a block of flats had closed over them and they stood in the dented metal interior of a lift. Howard held the top of the boy's head in one outspread hand and Saul straightened his tie, preparing to meet new people.

A door was opened, to Saul's surprise, by Varya, their former cleaner who had been fired for stealing. She looked just as startled to see him although she kissed Howard on both cheeks.

'You come back,' she said.

'I did.'

A large man came out to see what was happening. Recognising Howard, he charged forward frighteningly. 'You want me to push you? You want me to push you?' Howard's eyelids fluttered as he shrank away but the big man's face broke up in a smile as he grabbed Howard in a loud, back-slapping hug. Varya meanwhile wanted to know why Saul was there.

'It's okay, Varya, it's okay. We've run away. That's all. Everything's fine.'

Varya shouted other new and obvious questions at Howard while the large man threw back his head and laughed.

Another lady, small and plump, emerged from a further room and joined them. Saul had never heard so few people make so much noise in a small space. It was almost enjoyable, a little festival of panic. Through the doorway he could see a tiny, frightening, black-haired old man perched on a sofa looking with terror at the commotion. That decided him to silence them; raising both arms straight up above his head he screamed 'Quiet' and everyone was immediately quiet. Concerned faces stared down. In the silence he asked quite simply, 'Can I go to the toilet, please?' Varya replied, 'Yes, of course,' and led him away.

Misha led Howard into the kitchen, poured him a drink, and asked, 'You are complete mad man, no?'

In no mood to be questioned, Howard tipped his vodka into the sink, refilled his glass with tap water and answered, 'No. Can you help me?'

'Help you?' Misha's eyebrows were raised so far they almost

formed exclamation marks with his disbelieving blue eyes. 'Help you do what?'

Howard was impatient. He dropped his shoulders and shouted, 'Run away.'

'You are hungry?' Yelena asked.

'No,' Howard barked. 'Yes,' he corrected himself. 'Look,' he went on to Misha, 'we have to, the boy was almost ... I had to save him.'

'But where you go? How long? You should already be saving Irina.'

'Just a few days. Until it dies down.'

'You're a mad man. You can't do it.'

Saul reimposed silence by entering the room. 'Can I sit down?' he asked. Yelena pulled Misha off his chair and Saul sat. 'I don't feel very good,' he said, his stomach light and aching after being emptied in the bathroom. He closed his eyes and laid his head on his forearms.

'This is not good,' Misha warned. 'This is not good.'

'You need courage in life,' Howard reminded him. 'That's what you said. You said it.'

'No, but Howard ...'

'No,' Howard argued like a child. 'You said it.'

After dinner, Saul was encouraged to take a shower, which he did behind a loud plastic curtain printed with smiling frogs. He had to dry himself with a thin towel that smelt of a grown man, then get dressed back into his underwear and a huge T-shirt that the large man, Misha, had lent him. There was a bed prepared to go to after that in a room with a plate of home-made biscuits. He lay down and ate them, all of them, feeling lonely and thinking about how high up he was in this block of flats and wondering whether or not to listen to the messages on his phone. It wasn't until he woke up at an unidentified dark grey hour in the middle of the night that he did. Quite calmly he listened to his mother tearfully begging him to call, her voice urgent against a blurred background of public noise. He might have done had the next message not been his father ordering him to call. His mother was next. She reassured him that missing the competition was nothing to worry about. Another message was addressed directly to Howard; informed him that the police had been contacted and they were to return immediately if he wanted to avoid serious repercussions, and if anything were to happen to Saul … Les's voice broke off. Saul went to the toilet again, passing urine quietly against the ceramic side of the pan. He looked at his white, wavering face in the mirror and returned to bed. He felt cold and furiously hungry. There were voices in the kitchen. It took him long minutes to fall back asleep.

'But you cannot. It's ridiculous.' Misha plunged his fingers out of sight in his curly hair and sat back. He removed them again to strike the edge of the table. 'Ridiculous.'

Varya leaned forward, arms crossed under her bosom. She tilted her head and spoke quietly, intimately, knowing that Howard would respond to her. 'Hyoward, where are you going to go? You still have not give one answer.'

'I don't know. Just away.'

'Ridiculous,' Misha derided.

Varya put her hand on Howard's large hand. Howard wished she wouldn't touch him. She didn't know how powerful it was, how it affected him all through. Because you can't touch a person unless you're going to live up to that touch, to answer for it. 'Please. For Irina,' she said softly, 'you don't go.'

Howard hung his head. The two of them were so sure and they surrounded him. He wasn't given room to make a choice. 'Okay, we don't go.'

There was something different about Howard. Saul's confusion at waking up in this strange bed was total, so total that it took him a moment to identify the nagging oddness at the centre of his field of vision: Howard's hair was black and there was a line across the top of his forehead the colour of gravy. Beneath that, his eyebrows were still orange. Confusion was Saul's reaction, then laughter, which seemed to upset Howard.

'It's because we're running away,' he explained, grimacing, touching his stained hair.

'You could just wear a T-shirt that says RUNNING AWAY.'

'Aw, give it a chance though, wee man. It might work.'

'I'm hungry. What time is it?'

Howard checked his watch. 'Six oh three. Maybe we can take something before we go. Quick, get dressed.' He slapped the mound of Saul's legs under the duvet.

'Where're we going to go?'

'Aha.' Howard raised a mysterious finger. 'Just a little place I know.'

In the toilet, Saul saw the materials of Howard's transformation: an empty bottle and brown splotches on the sink, the floor, the shower curtain printed with frogs.

'Who gave the dye to you?' he asked in the kitchen.

'No one,' Howard whispered back, apparently pleased with his cunning. 'I did it when they were asleep. I think it belongs to the old man.'

The fridge produced a fine quick breakfast of white bread, margarine and strawberry jam. Howard slapped sandwiches together. They started eating them as they crept out of the front door.

Howard searched slowly through the newspaper for news of himself while through the train window tall grey buildings diminished to low red ones, diminished to empty fields. He held the paper up so that Saul wouldn't see the topless girls or any headline about themselves he might find. There was nothing, although it took Howard a long, unhappy time to establish that, searching even through the sports pages – in case there was a report on the memory championships. Folding the paper and setting it on the empty seat beside him, he looked at Saul, who appeared very small and neat in his jacket and dicky bow, with sky-blue shadows under his eyes, gazing out of the window at the flowing scene, only half-filling his seat. Howard felt strange, tired and panicky as a flock of sparrows scattering away from dangers he couldn't confront. He rested his head back against the top of his seat and wondered how much children's coats cost because they'd run away without Saul's. Good thing it was summer. Another train travelling in the opposite direction slammed past and Howard half-opened his eyes to see Saul gasp and close his. Then there were quiet fields again with blurring hedgerows and the occasional lonely clump of trees or road angling into the landscape. The carriage was warm, the noise rhythmical. Howard started drifting off with little pauses as he corrected his mouth hanging open or the heavy nodding of his head. He fell asleep strangely persuaded that Saul was getting up and going somewhere. When this thought had worked its way through to the centre of his mind, Howard forced himself entirely awake and found that Saul had indeed gone, and realised that he'd failed to explain to Saul that on the train it was best, if possible, not to be seen by anyone at all. He lurched up into difficulties with the luggage rack and the table gripping his knees, wondering if everything had not already been lost.

Howard fought his way along the tilting floor of the carriage, planting large, emphatic, unsteady feet as he gripped the seat backs and pulled himself along. He found the sign in the toilet door set at ENGAGED. Leaning his head close, he knocked on the door, saying, 'Saul, Saul, wee man, are you in there? Saul. Saul.' He knocked more forcefully. Standing between the carriages was uncomfortable. Loud air blew in from the open windows. The floors of the two carriages joined with an overlap that bucked, pivoting apart and together, suggesting violent, foot-crushing machinery beneath. 'Saul, Saul, please, just tell me are you in there?' The latch snapped across, the plastic door opened inward so that Howard had to grab the frame to stop himself falling in. An angry smartly dressed woman thrust past him, leaving behind her smell.

'Are you insane?' she demanded. Her nose was sharp, her mouth so tense and angry it looked pale and post-operatively numb. 'If you're that bloody desperate there's another loo just there.' She jabbed her finger past Howard's quaking bulk at a second door.

'I'm sorry, miss. I didn't ... I thought—'

'Whatever.' She raised a rejecting hand, the fingers so flattened they were bent backwards, and struck back into the carriage.

The latch slid across on the second toilet door. Howard held with one sweaty hand the breast beneath which his heart kicked. Saul emerged, his face pale and smiling and innocent, his hair wetted neat.

'Saul,' Howard gasped. 'Saul, you cannae, you cannae just disappear.'

'You were asleep,' Saul said reasonably. 'I didn't disappear, I just went to the toilet.'

'No, I, well that's okay then. But you must tell me when you go off somewheres.'

'You were asleep,' Saul repeated.

Howard, calming slowly, apologised. 'I'm sorry, wee man.

It's just, what we're doing,' he whispered, 'we have to be careful. Let's go and sit down.'

Saul led the way, taking nervous small steps along the canting aisle, his hands raised to grab the top of a seat if he needed to. They settled back either side of their table. Howard felt easier with Saul opposite him, safe in their separate area. Outside their dusty window flashed fields of yellow rape, lonely buildings.

Saul folded his arms and watched a pylon slowly turn its back on him as the train passed. Howard kept trained on Saul a tired smile of encouragement.

'Where are we?' Saul asked.

'I don't know,' Howard admitted. 'In the middle somewhere. We're heading north.'

'I know that. South-east to north-west.'

'I suppose. Clever laddie.' Howard winced when Saul looked at him – the compliment had somehow, after leaving Howard's mouth, become an allusion to the competition. They both had the thought and kept it to themselves.

The train rocked, counting bars of silence.

Howard's mind, on currents of fatigue, sank and rose and sank again. He could feel his mouth wanting to fall open. The seat was made of warm carpet.

Saul's voice pulled him back. 'I'm bored.'

Howard grunted, pushing sleep from his face with a rough hand. 'Bored, is it?'

'Yes. Aren't you bored?'

'Got a bit too much to think about to be honest with you there, Saul.'

Saul maintained the argument of his gaze.

'So read the paper, then,' Howard offered.

Saul picked up from the seat next to him the tabloid, which was puffy and misaligned after Howard's investigations. 'Thank you,' Saul said with a courteous nod Howard was confused by and took to be in part humorous.

Saul sat quietly back in his chair flushing hotly as he realised what forbidden thing he had in his possession. He held the paper upright so that Howard wouldn't see and opened with a trembling hand the first page. Smiled up at him Sandy, eighteen, from St Albans, who wore nothing but blue bikini briefs. With her hands placed stiffly on her hips, she smiled and pointed her bosoms at Saul, who studied with an excited fascination that had in it a strong element of dread their shiny forms topped with puckered, detailed nipples.

'Not that page,' whispered Howard, and Saul, ready to cry with embarrassment, quickly turned.

'I was reading it,' Saul croaked. He tried to read other things as he calmed down but the articles were too short, over before they'd started, and full of ugly, shouting slang. It wasn't how newspapers were supposed to be at all. 'It's boring,' he said and put it down.

'Are you hungry, then?' Howard asked.

'Not yet.' Saul spread the wings of his bow tie with the fingers of one hand. 'Do you recognise where we are yet?'

'Can't say I do, pal. Not yet.'

'A kestrel!' Saul shouted, standing up. 'There.'

Howard cringed into his shoulders. 'Sshh. Saul, please. Sit down. We cannae draw attention to oursel's. You cannot leap up shouting.'

'But did you see it? It was hunting right over the verge. Hovering. They do that to hunt. *Falco tinnunculus*.'

'Saul, please just sit down for me now.'

Saul collapsed back into his chair and folded his arms with rhetorical tightness. Tears grew on his eyes.

'Saul,' Howard cajoled. 'I'm not telling you off, really. I wish I'd seen that bird, I really do. But you have to understand we maybe ought to be a little bit careful, running away and all.'

'You took me away,' Saul corrected.

Howard's face was stricken. 'Saul. It's for you.'

'Oh, I want to go away as well,' Saul reassured him.

'Good, good. Jesus.' Howard smeared the sweat from his forehead with a feeble hand.

'There's no need to worry about it,' Saul went on. 'It's a good idea. I don't want to go back.'

'The reason I took you,' Howard made himself clear, 'was because you were looking in big trouble, ill-wise. I was scared ... I didn't want you ... I wanted to save you.'

'That's right.' Saul smiled brilliantly. 'Don't worry about it. Running away is great. It's great.'

And it was. Saul had never known such wild freedom. He felt almost savagely awake: the racing train striking away from home, the noise it made, the daytime liberty, no school, no work, not any limit that he could see. 'We're going back to where you used to live?' he asked.

'Ay,' Howard confirmed.

Saul was feeling chatty, excitable and interested in his friend's life. If they were buddies on the run together he really ought to get to know Howard a bit better. 'And how long did you live there?'

'A wee while,' Howard answered, then seeing the look of continued curiosity on Saul's face, went on: 'Since I was a teenager.'

'And before that you lived in Scotland.'

'Aha. In Glasgow.'

'So why did you move?' For a moment, shadows of telegraph posts flipped across Saul's face then left it bright and unavoidable again.

'Why did we move?' Howard remembered the day of the journey, the day of his release. He stepped out, carrying a bin bag of clothes now too small for him, to meet his mother under a soft Celtic rain. She had the suitcases ready and kissed his cheek with a hard, fervent, mistimed movement. His mother seemed to have shrunk because whenever they met for her visits she was always already seated at a table when he was led in with the others, so he hadn't had the comparison of their heights for years. Howard kept swallowing, one swallow after another. His mother asked him why he was doing it. He replied honestly that he didn't know. The realisation of his freedom was a slow fire eating his brain. All the walls had gone. Swallowing seemed to help keep him calm. At the end of the road was the dual carriageway and a bus towards their new life in England. 'We wanted to start again fresh somewhere.'

'Who? Your family?'

'My ma and me.'

'Not your father?'

'No, Saul. Not my father.'

'But why did you want to start fresh? What was stale?' Saul smiled.

'Saul, do you have to ask all these questions?'

'I'm just interested. I think we should get to know each other more.'

'I see.' Howard looked out of the window. 'But not right now. Oh God, a lady's coming with a trolley. Pretend to be asleep and hide your face the other way.'

Saul turned his face into the warm carpet of the seat, more questions tingling in his mind.

The girl arrived quickly, Howard having chosen a carriage with very few people in it. She pushed her trolley bent over, head hanging, like a miner pushing a load of coal. 'Crispsnacksdrinks,' she called. 'Teacoffee, crispsnacksdrinks.'

Howard had intended to let her go past but the large-size packets of crisps shone so invitingly in the colours of their flavours that he thought it might be worth the risk and halted her with a hoist of the chin and a plunge of his hand into his pocket. The girl's blonde hair, tied up in a tight band, emerged like a whale's spout from the top of her head and recorded the growth of undyed brown hair beneath. She looked angrily at Howard for having stopped her. 'Crispsnacksdrinks,' she said again spitefully.

'Can I have two of the barbecued beef, please, and a Coke.'

'We need water,' Saul whispered.

'Can I help you?' She turned to Saul.

'That's all right. He's asleep,' Howard intercepted. 'Can I have some water as well please.' She thumped a bottle of mineral water onto the table.

'Don't you have any tap water?'

She looked derisively at Howard. 'Not without a tap, I don't.' She produced a can of Coke and tossed two pillow-sized brown bags of crisps down, accepted money in a schoolgirlishly ink-stained hand, and shoved her trolley on. Over her shoulder – actually through her armpit – she said, 'Nice dye job.'

'Saul, what did I tell you about attracting attention,' Howard whispered urgently when she'd gone, pulling open the first bag of crisps. 'The police might be after us.'

'You were the one who stopped her,' Saul objected. 'Anyway, they are after us. My mother says so. I've got twenty-eight messages now. Do you want to see?'

'No, no, no. What do we do?' Howard stopped with a stack of crisps on its way to his mouth.

'We could text them and say that we're okay.'

'We could.'

'Shall we do that?'

'But don't . . . Aren't there satellites . . . can't they tell where we are?'

'But they wouldn't know. I mean we're on a train; we're moving.'

Howard looked with wonder at the bright little knife of intelligence sitting opposite him. He fed himself crisps, considering. 'Okay,' he concluded, 'just a quick text to say you're happy and safe.'

'Do I say I'm with you?'

Howard rolled a mash of meaty potato across his tongue looking at the green world flowing past. 'Okay,' he said, and exhaled, letting his belly sink on his lap.

Saul worked a moment with rapid thumbs, announced, 'Done.'

Howard opened the second bag. 'Twenty-five messages?' he asked.

'Twenty-eight.' Saul screwed up his face with the effort of cracking open the bottle of water. 'Bad, isn't it?'

'Bad in a way. Good that they're worried about you.'

'Not about you, though.' Saul laughed before his phone sounded its shrill alarm.

'Don't answer it,' Howard begged.

Saul picked it up and gestured throwing it through the window. He would have loved to have done it, to have sent it through exploding glass, brilliant splinters and crystals, out into the long grass of a field that was nowhere near anything. Instead he set it carefully back on the table and waited for it to fall silent. When it did so, Saul looked up at Howard jogged by the train and took a sip of water. The phone beeped for a message. Howard sucked his salty fingers one by one. He grimaced then as he worked impacted crisps from his back teeth with an arching tongue. The phone beeped again, a different sound, a single chirp. 'She's sent a text as well,' Saul said. 'It says, "Thank god exclamation mark call immediately we want you back dad has gone looking for you." Do you want to see?'

Howard shook his head, watching Saul for his reaction. Saul meanwhile was busy at the keypad again. 'There,' he said, 'I've deleted it. And all the others. Where do you think Dad has gone?'

Howard's mouth fell open, a beefy cavern, as he tried to squeeze his mind together to think. Eventually he asked, 'You deleted all of them?'

'Yes.' Elbows together on the table, Saul held his hands in front of his face and opened and shut his fingers to peep through.

'But they said something about the police maybe we should know?'

'Not really. Just that they're after us. I remember them all. All that happens is that Mum gets more and more worried and starts crying and begs a lot and says that they've contacted the police and they hope you're not hurting me.'

'Oh God, oh God, oh God, oh God.'

'But I've just told them that you're not, so don't worry.'

'Aha, aha.' Howard nodded, dragging his hand across his half-brown forehead.

'Stop staring, Howard. You look barmy.'

'I feel a bit barmy.'

'Well, we are barmy to do this. Mad. Mad.' Saul stood up and shouted, 'Mad! Ma-ad! Let the lions out! Let the monkeys out! Mad!' until Howard hauled him back down into his seat.

With Howard's mixed blessing, Saul ceremoniously dropped the phone into a bin when they arrived in Burnley. They both looked at it lying among the cans and wrappers. Howard hesitated; it was a tool, and expensive. Saul protested as Howard plunged his hand into the rubbish and pulled it out, but Howard answered that maybe they could sell it, an idea that was renegade and attractive enough to silence the boy. 'Also,' Howard went on, 'I need to make a call just now.'

Clouds the colour of corrugated iron gave a low roof to the world. They were reflected in the windscreens of the car park and caused Howard to wonder if his newly blackened hair would survive a downpour. He leaned against a van and smoked and asked Saul to stop explaining to him the precise physical effect that cigarettes have on human lungs. He was tired. He had repeatedly the sensation of fast gliding motion suddenly ceased that left him unsteady in the middle of a place. He and the boy had been travelling all day and his stillness as he leaned, breathing grey clouds of his own, had a churning in it, like an eddy pool in which he'd turn before catching the current again. He was agitated. Everything was incomplete and unsafe, but it was too much to think about, so he didn't. A few drops scattered down from above, landing as dark spots on the tarmac and as surprised little splats onto autoglass. Howard twiddled wet hairs between thumb and forefinger where his head had been hit. The grey traces he found on his fingerprints afterwards he decided were there already and not the dye melting loose.

Into the car park emerged Howard's old fridge in the shape of Hassan looking rectangular in a T-shirt and tracksuit jacket. Howard ducked, grabbing Saul's arm to pull him down with him. Saul whispered 'What?' to Howard, who raised a silencing finger to his lips and somehow managed to almost burn his cheek with his cigarette. He listened to Hassan clunk into his car, start the engine, rev it three times, each time to a higher pitch, then spurt forwards and corner sharply onto the road. When his engine had died into the distance Howard explained that he was just a person it was definitely better to avoid.

'How long do we have to wait here for?' Saul complained.

'Not long.'

'Can I get up now?'

'Yes.' Howard thought of a distraction. 'Hey, why don't you go and balance on one of those.' Howard pointed to a line of concrete posts with loops of chain between them.

Saul, having nothing better to do and happy to follow clear, simple instructions on this peculiar day, walked off obediently to balance on a bollard from where he saw an acned teenager, open-mouthed and squinting at the light, his hunched shoulders thin and sharp inside his polo shirt, called to by Howard, who frantically waved his arms above his head. Leaning to watch them meet and shake hands in the lee of the van, Saul tilted too far, lost his footing, and fell hard onto his left side. There he discovered that he lacked the energy to get up again and lay there waiting, watching the clouds slide slowly up out of the side of the tarmac. Bouncing in front of them, on the great wall of the world, Howard and his friend came running to help. Just fall down and they come.

Howard knelt by Saul, who looked, dressed in his suit, with his short, straight, narrow legs, lying there with an unprotesting calm that was almost inanimate, like a dropped marionette. His sideways face was uncanny as his eyes rolled up and his lips moved. 'I'm fine, Howard,' Saul reassured him, his voice seeming suddenly very high and posh and southern to Howard in the company of Andy. 'I just hit my head a little bit. I'll get up presently.'

Andy, leaning over holding his knees, stood behind Howard. 'Who's your friend, Howard?' he asked.

Howard, panting from the short sprint, nevertheless properly introduced the prone boy. 'Andy, this is Saul. Saul's going to get up now, aren't you, wee man?'

'Just a moment, please.'

'No, Saul. Please, get up now.' Saul must get up. Saul could not lie there ruined. This boy could not lie there ruined.

'Okay, okay.'

Saul took Howard's hand and Howard lifted him with one movement onto his feet.

'What's going on, Howard?' Andy asked, holding himself against the cold. Howard held his face with his hands, fingertips under his glasses pressing his eyes.

'We're having an adventure,' Saul piped.

'You what?' Andy asked, his face set in his unfortunate questioning snarl.

'Howard, tell him,' Saul instructed.

'Aha. It's a long story maybe. You see, we've run away … a little bit. Saul was in big trouble. I mean, it really is a long story.'

Andy's eyes narrowed with apprehension to the point of disappearance – it was his teeth that stared. His confusion wasn't eased at all when Saul suddenly screamed, 'Get down! Get down!' and grabbed him by the wrist. He also grabbed Howard, who bent forwards and asked what the problem was. 'It's my dad.' Saul was ready to cry with fear. Howard heard a car approaching and was quickly on his knees.

'What the fuck . . .?' was Andy's incomplete question when Howard pulled his other arm so hard that he had no choice but to get on the ground.

'Under the van,' Howard instructed. The chassis had enough clearance, just, to allow Howard to flop and wriggle underneath, undulating forward on his belly until he was entirely hidden. Saul shuffled in behind his feet and Andy now was next to him. A very comfortable space, Howard found it – recalling corners of the sofa, the toilet, safe hiding places – or at least it would have been if the suffocating rabbit of his heart hadn't been trapped under him.

They listened to the car grind to a standstill somewhere front and left of where they lay, then the wiry wrench of the handbrake.

'What the fuck is going on?' Andy hissed.

'Sshh.' Howard tried to raise a finger to his lips but his arm got stuck on the way. 'Saul, was it definitely him?'

'Definitely, definitely.'

'Did you tell anyone I called you?' Howard asked Andy's pained face, which he found nose to nose with his own when he turned.

'No, not nobody.'

'I'm going to get out to look,' Saul announced.

'No, please.' Howard tried to throw his voice commandingly over his shoulder and back beyond his feet but Saul was already wriggling back through the valance of daylight.

'But if he's gone in,' Saul reasoned, 'we can all get out and run away.'

A moment later his upside-down face appeared in front of Howard's, making the large man jump, a thick pulse through his body which squeezed him between tarmac and van. 'Dad's inside,' Saul whispered. 'Let's go.'

Andy edged out and Howard followed, rowing forward with frantic, useless haste. Andy helped him through the final stage, dragging him out by his arms.

'I'll be really interested to find out what the fuck's going on,' Andy said.

'Can we go, please,' said Saul.

'Jesus, yes.' Howard started off on unsteady legs.

'We'd better run,' Saul said. He turned to Andy. 'And there's no need to use swear words. There are enough words in the English language ...' But Andy didn't hear the rest of the sentence because Saul was already sprinting away.

'So. if you want to disguise yourselves I'm thinking maybe Saul here shouldn't keep on wearing his bow tie.'

Andy sat cross-legged on his bed, advising his friend. The room was small and pungent with spray deodorant and dirty clothes. Serenely indulgent of this were the girls on the posters showing the lower fraction of their buttocks under short skirts or lying brownly on beaches looking as though they were made from something glossy and hard that was better than flesh – looking like cars.

Howard gestured for Saul to unfasten his tie which turned out to be a clip-on. Saul tucked the stiff bow into his pocket.

'So you had been told?' Howard checked again.

'Like I said. Morning staff meeting. Cocky up on his hind legs. Police matter. Former employee Howard MacNamee, abduction, whatever.'

Saul sat on the carpet with his back pressed against the stiff pleats of the radiator, enjoying the heat through his jacket, the small circle of hot water burn on the back of his head, so scalding it ran cold. He sat and listened to the questions tilting back and forth between Howard and his friend, observing Andy's angry skin, the jewelled scabs, the crust and swelling that Andy patrolled unconsciously with his fingertips while he spoke.

'This is not good,' Andy moaned. 'This is no bloody good. And that stupid hair. You stick out like a sore thumb. Can it not be washed off? Oh fuck, why did you come and find me at all?'

Howard apologised. 'I'm sorry, pal, I just thought you're my friend and everything ...'

'Jesus Christ, I hardly know you.'

Howard whispered. 'You gave me your phone number and everything.'

'Well, how was I to know you'd turn up as an escaped convict. The pair of you – Bonnie and bloody Clyde, Michael Jackson and Bubbles.'

'I'm sorry, pal. I'm really sorry. We don't have to stay. We'll get going.' Howard tried to rock himself upright off the bed.

'Wait up, you fat fool. It's just, what the fuck do I know? I don't know you, not really. I mean you seem like a nice guy. I mean I do like you, you're a laugh. But you could actually be up to anything, and if I'm caught up in it ...'

'I'm not. I explained already.'

'He's not,' Saul confirmed. 'He's helping me.'

'And you were visiting that old lady in secret for ages – that's weird. Little bit psycho.'

'What old lady?' Saul asked.

'Mrs Dawson,' Andy snapped, then remembered. 'Your gran.'

'Oh yes, I'd forgotten that,' Saul said slowly, burning his head, holding it against the radiator, thinking. 'But they were friends.'

'In a way ...'

A knock at the door shocked them all into silence.

Andy's voice emerged peevishly high-pitched from his frightened throat. 'Who is it?'

'Who d'you think?' came the answer, and the door was

opened by a fourteen-year-old girl the smell of whose hairspray entered as palpably as she did, wafting from a petrified cascade of dark red hair. Her lips were glossed, her eyes underlined, her midriff was pale and bare. That she had learned much from television was obvious just from the way she was standing. 'Who're your friends?' she demanded.

'Go away.'

'I'll not. Who are they? What's going on?'

'Just shut that door. Kelly, come on.'

'I'll call Mam.'

'Just shut the fuckin' door. Jesus.'

Howard sweated into his anorak and held his face averted.

'But what's going on?'

'They're just mates of mine.'

'What, an old bloke and a little boy?'

'From the gym. Please. Anyway, he's not that old.'

Kelly stepped in and shut the door behind her. With daytime TV gestures she emphasised her point, making tweezers of her fingers and rocking her head sideways. 'Obviously Mam doesn't know they're here.'

'They'll not be long. Kelly, get out now before I skin you.'

Kelly's mouth fell open in outrage. 'You owe me three squidillions.'

'Do I buggery. Since when?'

'Yahuh!' She blinked slowly, rocking her head again. 'Since you took it from me last Tuesday for the machines.'

'Oh, Jesus Christ.' Andy stamped to his feet and dug into his trouser pocket before filling her hand with change.

'Thanks, bro. That's more'n you owe me, probably.'

'You can keep it all if you keep quiet about these two.'

Howard, still refusing to turn round, felt his back gripped by the teenager's appraisal. 'My lips are sealed,' she cooed, miming zipping them shut, locking them at one end, then nonsensically opening them again to swallow the key.

The door burst once more and a little boy spun in with an

action figure in his hand. He made shooting noises with his mouth as he massacred the folks inside, falling silent when he saw that there were strange faces among the dead.

Howard did turn round now in fear and his eyes momentarily met the girl's.

'Oh Jesus, Tom,' Andy complained, 'get out now or I'll wallop you.' He got up from his bed and physically pushed both siblings from the room, guiding Tom out with his foot. He shut the door and pressed against it with his forehead for emphasis. Still with his nose to the wood, he said, 'Take me with you. At least fuckin' invite me to go with you. I mean you could have invited me.'

Howard laughed then realised Andy was serious. 'What?' He looked at Saul but Saul strangely was highly amused, suppressing laughter by forcing it down the tight funnel of his nose. 'We don't even know where we're going,' Howard discouraged.

'Well, I'm not doing anything *here*. I'm not doing owt. And you've got me involved already so I might as well do *something*.'

'No, no, no,' Howard reasoned. 'I mean you could get into trouble.'

'Which I'm already in trouble for helping you as it is.'

'No, no, you're not in trouble. Only if someone finds out.'

'And they probably will. *You* might tell 'em.'

'I won't. Why would I?' Appalled at this new complexity, Howard shook his head. That he might betray Andy.

'No, but how could you not? So you see I'm already in trouble. This has all happened, so I might as well come with you.'

Howard kept shaking his large, stained head, waiting for the perfect excuse to appear inside it. He didn't want Andy to come. It wasn't right. It wasn't what he'd foreseen, which was himself and the boy alone, free, beyond their power, laughing, unscathed. 'No, no, no . . . you're best here.'

'But why?' Andy seemed really angry. 'Oh, fuck it. Like I

said, I don't know you. I could get into serious shit. There's no reason for me to trust you. I don't know you.'

'You do know me, you're—'

With apparitional swiftness and silence, Saul surged upright, stilling the voices around him. 'Has it occurred to anyone,' he asked, 'that my dad could be here any minute?'

'Oh, God. I'd actually forgotten about him,' Howard lamented.

'Why would he come here?' Andy challenged.

'Because,' Saul calmly explained, 'you're known as Howard's friend and we know that he was just in the gym looking for me and asking questions, probably. Right? Or the police at least, if not my dad.'

'Fine then.' Andy clapped his hands. 'Let's go before he gets here.'

Howard shook his head. 'I've said, Andy, pal, really, I don't think it's wise.'

'Why don't you come into my office for a moment?'

'What? Andy, don't be weird.'

'Come over here a minute.' Andy beckoned him over while Saul tutted, was stared at by Andy, and sat back down.

Howard stepped over junk to where Andy stood. Andy pulled open a drawer.

'See that,' Andy whispered. He lifted up a wad of T-shirts to reveal, lying neatly at the bottom, some banknotes. 'I've been saving.'

'How much?'

'Couple of hundred.'

'What for?'

'To go somewhere. To get away.'

'It'll not get you far. Unless you mean one way, and then there's to live on.' Howard placed a hand on Andy's shoulder, patted him. 'I don't think it's a good idea. Three people. It's harder to hide than two people. And we've got to go.'

'Oh, please?'

'No.'

Andy held his gaze. Howard stared back patiently. 'Fine,' Andy snapped. 'There are some trainers I want, anyway. I'll get them. I'll stay here in my new trainers, maybe get some other stuff as well, and you can run around with the police after you.'

Howard patted him again, but was shrugged off. 'Thanks, Andy,' he said. 'In a little while, maybe we'll go somewhere together.'

Andy nodded sulkily. 'That'd be good. Still gonna get those trainers, though.'

Automatic doors jerked apart with what seemed like apologetic swiftness just before Howard would have walked unthinkingly into the glass. Saul, carrying the bag of pasties, drinks and crisps, entered the hotel behind Howard and was struck by its familiar smell – perhaps of a particular air freshener – which was the smell of the strange few days when Saul had experienced the adult privacy of his own hotel room, and his father was very quiet and ugly and inside himself, and he went to see his grandmother be cremated.

Howard approached the desk, his scalp gripping his skull as though it could hide his dark, mad hair. A girl in a blue jacket sat turned towards a sniggering male behind her, a chubby, pretty boy with a large gold initial ring on one little finger and spiked hair that looked like vinyl it was so carefully gelled. He was repeating a catchphrase from a TV comedy. 'It took me hours to get it all off.' The girl laughed. He improvised: 'I've still got half of it up me left side.' They were both giggling, the boy mostly at the sight of the girl, who was almost helpless. Howard started smiling. Always in these situations he wanted to join in with the laughter, people laughing in itself was funny and so friendly. Saul tugged his sleeve, though, and Howard cleared his throat so that the girl turned, her mouth held stiffly to freeze the laugh, her cheeks red, her wet eyes downcast. Her gold name tag read FIONA WALKER. The boy behind her made a noise to speak again but she silenced him with a desperate noise of her own, a kind of moaning sigh, and he smiled, fiddling his soft lips shut with his fingers.

'Good evening, sir. How can I help you?' Halfway through the greeting her voice found its professional camber.

'I want a room,' Howard mumbled.

'A double room?' she asked raising eyebrows plucked to single lines across orange brows. 'Or two singles?'

'A double room.'

'Certainly, sir. What's the name, please?'

'Fergus Mathieson,' Howard answered. Saul looked at him.

'And the boy?'

'Jasper. Mathieson.'

'Very good, sir. Would you like to pay by credit card?'

'No, no. Cash please.'

Her eyebrows flexed as Howard pulled from his pockets and piled on the desk crumpled ten- and twenty-pound notes. Her comic friend looked curiously at this also, Saul noticed.

Fiona Walker, however, accepted payment without comment, provided change, then began a rattling speech about facilities and when breakfast was served. 'Now.' She produced a sheet of paper and laid it on the desk, half-standing to guide Howard through it with the tip of her pen. Howard remembered the pretty nurse and her biro, and then with a shock that she was not even far away. 'This is a customer feedback form so we can monitor your satisfaction et cetera and please feel free to put any comments you might have on it; it's just to make sure we're all singing to the same hymn sheet, et cetera. We hope you enjoy your stay and, ah, yep, that's everything, I think.'

Crumbs from Howard's pasty sprinkled his bed cover. Sat on the dressing-table stool eating his own oniony pasty, the plastic wrapping crinkling against his nose as he took small bites,

Saul watched Howard with disgust. The Scotsman looked huge and not especially clean, and wouldn't those crumbs get into his bed and make him itchy all night? Howard lifted his can of Tango to his mouth and tilted it to drink. Saul could hear the bubbly stuff glugging into his whale's mouth.

'So you came down to England just with your mother?' Saul asked.

Howard tipped his head forward and burped, his eyes thick in their sockets. 'Ay,' he said.

'Why was that?' Saul took a bite. 'I mean, where was your father?'

Howard looked at Saul perched on his little chair, his feet only just touching the carpet. 'My parents broke up, you know how it is.'

'But why?' Saul went on. 'Why didn't they stay together?'

Howard tasted eggy bread in his mouth, the saddest, most delicious, most awful taste in the world. He saw his father, uncontainable, unstoppable even by himself, approach his mother in two awkwardly overlong strides. His arm goes back. His mother, matter-of-factly, as if this is just something happening, an ordinary thing, like a bus going past or a shop closing, without crying out, doubles over and falls to the floor. Howard, hiding under the window, has already had his and has nothing to do now but count how many times he kicks. One. Two. Three. Four. Five. Six. A pause; his father is tiring. Seven. He leaves with a crash, a great sucking commotion of sound through the front door, and the two of them are left on the carpet, far apart. His mother will be ashamed and does not look at him, so he leaves her there resting. He goes to the bathroom and looks at his bruises, then walks around the flat righting furniture, sweeping up anything that has been smashed. Eventually his mother gets up, still in silence, smoothes her clothes, then hobbles into the kitchen to make them both eggy bread, Howard doesn't know why. She just always does this, whether they've already had supper or not.

They sit together in damaged silence and eat the rich bread thickly sprinkled with crunchy white sugar.

'Well, why?' Saul asked again.

'They didn't get on.'

'Well, that doesn't tell me very much. What are all your secrets?' He repeated Andy's words: 'I mean, what do I really know about you in the end?'

'I don't have any secrets, wee man. My parents did not get on. Do you have any secrets?'

'What did your father do?'

'He was a welder. He worked on ships, in Glasgow. Shipyards. Amazing, huge steel ships I remember from when I was a kid.' His father, gloved and masked, hanging on the ship's side, sparks showering below his feet, a blaze in his hand, a man trying to cram a star into a cupboard. 'Amazing place. I'll take you maybe.' That was an idea. 'And then they weren't building ships so much any more . . .'

'Why not?'

'I don't know. So he was unemployed. Things were tough. He got all . . . cross about it. Tough man.'

'I know what you mean. My dad's tough on me.'

Howard lifted his chin, absorbing the comparison. 'Mm. He is. In a way.'

Saul detected doubt in Howard's slow response. 'He is.'

'My dad beat me,' Howard said competitively. 'Bruises. All over me. For years.'

Saul looked at Howard for a long moment. Howard suspected he'd startled the boy into a rush of appalled sympathy. He wouldn't have minded that. Instead Saul answered, 'Maybe mine's worse because it's all in my head where nobody can see it.'

'There is that,' Howard conceded. 'There is that.'

Scrunching his eyes shut, Saul opened his own can of drink at arm's length.

'Otherwise why did you rescue me?' he asked, sipping.

'You've got a point, sunshine.'

They ate in silence for a while, opening packets, munching, cars droning round the roundabout outside.

'Do you think Andy will tell anyone?'

'Nah.' Howard inserted a mini pork pie and, smiling, chewed.

'Even if the police go round and ask him?'

'Especially if they do. He's not a grass. You can tell. And he could get into trouble himself don't forget.'

'But what if they interrogate him for hours? Or his sister or his brother tell them?'

Doubt passed through Howard; it flushed sweat through his skin. 'Okay, so, then we'd be arrested quite soon.'

'You'll get arrested,' Saul corrected him. 'I'll just be rescued again. Of course I'll tell them to release you.'

'You better, wee man.'

Saul was animated again. Maybe it was the sugar in his drink. He crushed the empty can with both hands – a feat of macho destruction he'd never be allowed at home – and threw it into the bin. Standing, then balancing on the dressing table, he had a new thought. 'Hey, if my dad is up here looking for us, which we know he is, maybe he would stay here. I mean maybe not if he can't find us. But if he did wouldn't he come back to this hotel as well, like we did? I mean had you thought about that?' Saul was almost laughing with excitement.

Howard stood up himself. 'No, wee man. To be perfectly honest I hadn't really thought about that at all.'

'He could be here right now,' Saul squealed.

'Oh God, but how would we know? I mean, he could be sitting there at breakfast in the morning. Or he could be just on the other side of that wall listening and calling the police.'

'Don't, Dad, don't!'

'Saul, shut up for Christ's sakes.'

Saul laughed.

'Saul, you better take this seriously. If you're my pal on this adventure use your cleverness powers.'

'Cleverness powers?' Saul sighed. 'You could check in the car park. If his car's here then he's here.'

'Oh Jesus, I don't want to go outside the room. I mean he could be ... maybe he's down there right now.'

'Do you want me to go?'

'No, no, no, no, no.'

'I could. I could sneak down.'

'No, no. What about your phone? Are there any messages?'

'Loads,' Saul smiled, 'but I deleted them all without listening to them.'

Howard paced to the blank, unmotherly wardrobe, head-butted the door and set the hangers jangling.

'Maybe,' Saul stood on the stool to make his point, 'we should just run away again now.'

'And go where?'

'Just outside. Like soldiers. It's not that cold. Into a field or something.'

'Don't be mad.'

'But if we stay here people can find us. If we're out there then we're nowhere and nobody knows.'

Howard headbutted the wardrobe.

When cars passed, the hedge behind them hollowed with light, grey shadows swerved under their feet, the hedge in front swelled towards them, the grass stood straight and frightened. Saul was quicker over the uneven ground than heavy Howard, whose ankles burned with sprain and who worried that Saul was too visible, even two fields away from the hotel, the little imp, dressed for warmth in a stolen bathrobe. In front of him he dipped and shuddered like the palest white flame and Howard followed. Howard wore his own robe under his anorak. The robes were a standard size, of course, and Saul's trailed royally behind him.

They needed to find somewhere soon, a tree, a corner, somewhere they could hide. If he turned, Howard could still see the hotel, a lit box, safe and habitable, beside its insomniac companions, the roundabout and street lamps and signs. Ahead Saul had stopped and was evidently waiting for Howard to catch up. When, wheezing fugitive, Howard made it there, Saul said brightly, 'Look, we can get over here.' Saul's enjoyment seemed tremendous. It was he who had insisted that they carry on, even after the car park had been checked, and Howard had followed, chased away by voices from the bar. The looming hedge now proved to be a stone wall which knocked and clucked as Saul scrambled over it. Howard, not being one for climbing, tried to just swing a leg over it but found that the ground was much lower on the other side. He ground his buttocks on the stones, lay back to lift over his other leg and fell sideways onto grass. Standing up he walked to Saul feeling the ground become abruptly smooth and hard. It was disconcertingly artificial after the rough tormenting ground of the field which had left his legs quaking.

'We're on a little road,' Saul explained.

'So I see.' Howard put his hand on the boy's towelling shoulder, securing him in the dark.

'Not see, exactly. Do you know where we are?'

'I haven't the faintest, sunshine.'

'I thought you lived round here?'

'I did, but not in a field in the dark.'

'Oh, really? I thought that's where you did live – in a field in the dark.'

'I could throw you over that wall,' Howard offered.

'Haya!' Saul cried and chopped Howard's wrist so that his hand flew from Saul's shoulder.

'Jesus, don't do that.' In the dark, unmoored, Howard felt himself rocking as in water.

'Sorry,' Saul whispered and the quietness of his voice gathered the night around them. They were silent a moment.

Many stars grew into Howard's field of vision. 'Well,' Saul said very quietly, both of them alert, 'we can't stay on this road for long. We might as well just go straight over into the next field.'

Saul's face flared and vanished, flared again, as he played with Howard's lighter. Under the tree with the long flame dancing and Saul's peaceful face staring into the light, it looked like a nativity scene as Howard blundered back from his piss and sat down again, feeling his way down the trunk to his quite comfortable seat between two roots.

'Don't waste the gas,' he cautioned. 'Who knows when we might need it. Oh, but hang about one second. He fished a cigarette from his anorak pocket and leaned forward to light it.

'Have you always smoked?'

'Ay. Ever since I was born. But I started with a pipe, of course.'

A laugh spluttered out of Saul. Howard pursued, delighted. He loved seeing Saul laugh. 'One of those big, curly, Arab jobbies. That was my favourite back then.'

'No, really. When did you start?' Saul let the lighter go out. His laughing face remained as a webby image on the darkness.

'Uch, usual time. A teenager.'

'What, in school?'

'No, not school.' Howard panicked. 'Oh no, actually, yes, it was school. Behind the bike sheds kind of thing.'

'How did you get them?'

'Doesnae matter. As long as you know never to do it yourself.'

'I'm not an idiot.'

'Well, good then.' Howard's cigarette glowed as he took a drag.

Saul's face flashed and disappeared.

'Gimme that.' Howard reappropriated the lighter, its metal

parts hot enough to burn his hand. Above them leaves lifted in the night wind. Branches were solidified darkness. Stars could be seen through them.

'So, who were Jasper and, what was the other one, Fergal?'

'What?'

'The names you gave at the hotel.'

'So they were going to be us.'

'No, but who were they?'

'Just lads I knew, you know. At school.' Jasper. The very name, with its strangeness and rasping confidence, was for Howard the very limit of the imaginable strength and daring in a boy, unfrightened even by the new school. Howard when he remembered him thought, of course, of the evening that ended with them all on the train tracks. The early part with Kev and Little Iain and Michael and the scrappy fire they made behind the flats. He saw Jasper's tattered sandshoes whisking through the nervous tops of the flames as he leapt then landed with a loud double report. Then later with the sirens, the convulsive lights. 'You're full of questions tonight, aren't you, wee man? Why don't I ask you some for a change?'

'It's cold.'

'No, come on.'

'It's too cold.'

'It is a bit cold.'

Through the leaves above them the wind made lonely sea sounds.

'It'll get worse,' Howard said. 'Through the night. We should lie close together for the warmth.'

Saul shuffled an inch or two closer.

'It'll have to be closer than that, wee man. We should lie down and maybe try to get some sleep.'

'One us should stay awake to keep guard.'

'It's all right. We'll wake up at dawn when it's light. Nobody's sleeping for very long.'

'What if we wake up and there's a bull in the field?'

'Well, you'll just have to ride him home. Come on now, lie down.'

Saul felt his way between the roots to somewhere he could be flat. Afterwards, Howard joined him, feeling the boy's body with his hand to know how he lay then fitting in behind him, lying with him tucked into his front. He laid an arm across the towelling of his gown and secured the crown of Saul's head under his chin. It was indeed warm. Howard felt unbearable love for the gentle, frightened boy and his quietly breathing body. It was lovely to hold him. Howard closed his eyes. The word Irina sounded in his mind.

'Now go to sleep,' he whispered.

'I'll try,' Saul promised. Howard felt the boy ebb away after clenches of fear, beautiful jerks of his muscles. He felt himself fading also as he lay and listened to the leaves.

July 12th

Horse. A horse. A brown horse in the dawn light bowed to the grass, its forelegs spread like the legs of a tripod, its long face sunk into the blue vapour that stirred with the movement of its feeding. Behind the strong shape of the horse the pale sky was water and blood. The only sounds, apart from a distant road, were the fibrous cropping of the horse and a single bird going mental in the tree, bubbles and swoops and skirls of song. Gently Howard shook Saul's shoulder, whispering to him to keep quiet.

Saul pushed himself up on his hands, moaning. 'What time is it?' he asked.

'Just gone five thirty,' Howard whispered.

'My God.' Saul rubbed his face. 'We did it. We slept outside. I mean I knew you *could* do it, but I never thought—'

'Sshh. Just look at the horse.'

'What?'

Saul turned and saw and fell silent.

The horse seemed to look at them or rather hold them in its field of vision. Its eye a dark convexity between stiff lashes; its jaw ground herbs.

'Roan,' Saul said eventually.

'What?'

'All the horse colours have different names to normal colours. That light brown is roan.'

'I cannae believe it was here all night and we never knew.'

'It would've been asleep, standing up, dead still in the dark.'

The horse shook its head, blew its lips, and ambled forward a couple of paces, lifting soft hooves through the glimmering wet. It swished its tail, raised its head and gazed again – Saul pictured how they must appear to it, a ragged heap of humans at the foot of the tree – and dropped its head back again to feeding.

'It's a beautiful animal,' Howard said.

'Yes.' After a long moment of attention, Saul whispered, 'What are we going to do now?'

'I know somewhere we can go,' Howard whispered, 'but it's too early yet. Why don't we just sit and watch for a bit.'

'We could,' Saul agreed. 'That bird's so loud it's amazing.'

Barbara woke up for the third day of her ordeal at five having woken up twice already. This time she got out of bed, weak, sour-mouthed, already thinking, and wrapped the long planes of her body in her dressing gown. Les was already up and about, clattering in the kitchen. He'd returned in the night, popped up to tell her he'd found nothing, and hadn't gone to bed. Instead he'd sat in an armchair with the phone in his hand. His small, unshaven face looked mouldy with fear, fruit starting to rot. It crumpled in at the sight of his wife. He did not like discussing the situation with Barbara. Perhaps he preferred to think that they understood each other without talking – the situation, after all, was bitterly simple – so they sat side by side and had parallel conversations with Jean, the officer assigned to them. Jean was a sweet girl. Her full name was, ludicrously, Jean Harlowe. Solid features, cockney accent, lovely clear skin, she would shut off the crashing static of her radio and explain precisely where they were in the operation. Which was where? Which was nowhere. CCTV footage which lost them in the Underground system on the first night was still being examined. There were no definite reports of sightings. The entire police network now knew who they were and was apparently looking but so far nothing. A precise grid had been laid over a void.

And Saul was out there, her boy.

Her own boy out there, somewhere.

In a ditch.

In a café.

In a room.

Fast asleep.

Wide awake.

Frightened.

Laughing.

By the sea.

In a sleeping bag.

Memorising his exact location.

Calling for help in the dawn.

Riding on Howard's back.

Asleep near dangerous electric wires.

In a house with drugs.

In a room with men.

With men about to do something.

Tied to a chair.

In a car.

A bus.

A train.

A plane.

In a cottage.

Playing with a dog.

About to tell someone in a park.

And he was with Howard. Howard was a great deal to think about. He had seemed such a gentle idiot, so nervous. Well, it turned out he had a criminal record from years ago, from when he was himself near enough Saul's age, and it was for hurting a boy. Fact. Les seemed sure that he was a pervert, a murderer, any kind of demon who had deceived them and stolen their son. But Barbara, despite the knowledge of his crime, could not entirely believe it. Not only would believing it have destroyed her, she just actually didn't believe it. It was strange but inside the nauseous, billowing turmoil of panic,

Barbara was somehow calm. She just felt that Howard was good. Les had not, for example, considered the possibility that maybe their clever son had persuaded that big lug to run away with him.

Deep inside, where Saul's new sister was starting, Barbara was for no good reason calm.

There was no other calm, none outside. Barbara had demanded that her mother come round during the days just to keep her from tying up the phone line. She should move in – why not? – Barbara's house was a free house. Anyone could move in, take what they wanted, plunder her life. They received endless useless phone calls from friends and business acquaintances. Even a brief visit from Ted Holland, who was currently in the country, and a sympathetic phone call from Betty Zorin, who clearly did not relish the publicity.

Les was feverish, muttery. Barbara panicked with him. Three days was too long for this strange adventure to go on. She yearned into the future to forgiving stupid little Saul when he came back through that front door.

Alf angled his feet into his slippers – Theresa groaned as the bed rocked free of his weight – and shuffled over to the window to see what the hell was going on, who the hell was ringing his buzzer at this time. In the street below he saw leaning towards his door Howard's head switching from side to side, unmistakably his head only with black hair and his bald spot dyed the colour of brown sauce. Beside him was a small boy standing calm and still. Exactly as the police had said.

'What's going on?' Theresa murmured in Portuguese from under the heaped white bedclothes.

'Nothing at all,' Alf answered before opening the window and calling down, 'Okay, shut up now, I'm coming down.'

Sure that action was imminent, Alf quickly dressed, pulling on trousers and shirt, smearing his hair flat across his baldness.

'If nothing is going on, then why are you so busy and

shouting?' Theresa asked, her lips moving like a fish's, puckered out from her sleeping face.

'It's a delivery,' Alf explained. 'I don't know why these madmen come so early.'

He dashed down and opened the front door. Into the empty shop came Howard apologising and the small boy attached to Howard's left hand, blinking and saying nothing.

Alf spoke over Howard's words. 'You know the police have already been here asking about you. Of course I say them you are too stupid to do anything wrong.'

'When were they here?'

'Yesterday. One of them. It's a policeman I know, local one, John, they send him here to ask about you. He had a battered sausage as well. He always have one. I say you moved away, I don't hear from you, all what's true.'

'They were just after us the now. We escaped.' The small boy nodded in solemn confirmation.

'Where from?' Alf demanded. 'Where are you?'

'We were in that hotel, you know it maybe, by the big road.' Howard shook his head. 'I don't know what you call the road, on the W42 route. Anyways, we was there the one night. Well, not all the night. It's a long story.'

Alf turned to Saul. 'We, we, we. And you, you are the stolen boy?'

Saul shifted on his feet and tightened his grip on Howard's hand. 'I'm not stolen,' he corrected. 'We're having respite together.'

'Respite?' Alf said, appalled, wagging a finger in Howard's face. 'What is "respite"?'

Howard shrugged and looked down at Saul for the answer.

'It means a rest,' Saul educated them.

Howard rushed to agree. 'Ay, that's all it is. We're no doing anything bad. It's a rest. We's just getting away. Saul was getting really ill; he collapsed nearly . . .'

'I did collapse. Twice.'

'Yes, he did. Twice.' Howard stopped when he heard the soft thudding of footfalls overhead. 'Who's that?'

'It's Theresa. Who you think it is? I tell her to stay up there,' Alf assured them.

'Can we go somewhere?' Saul asked. 'Can we not be seen? It's really, really important.' Alf beat down the boy's fears with outspread hands and spoke to Howard: 'I go tell her it's nothing and we can go for a drive.'

'Aw, great. You're such a pal,' Howard enthused as Alf disappeared into the dark living area. Howard rubbed sweat from his lips and forehead and adjusted his glasses. With Alf out of the room, Saul let go of his hand. Howard gestured at the stainless steel equipment and the lucid jars of pickles of the empty chip shop. 'I worked here,' he boasted. 'It's where I burnt my arm. Your fellow's name is Alf, by the way.' Saul looked around with genuine fascination. He would have loved to have gone behind the counter to have a look or up to the photographs of boxers and meals, but Alf returned and hurried them out of the front door again.

'We got to be quick so no one sees you.' Alf chivvied them ahead of him around the corner to where his car was parked. 'I told Theresa I got to go somewhere.' He unlocked the driver's door.

'Where did you say you were going?' Howard asked.

'I don't know. I don't think of that,' Alf admitted before disappearing down into the car. He lunged across inside and lifted the locks for Howard and Saul. When they were all seated, Alf looked back over his shoulder towards Saul and said, 'You do up your seat belt, please. I don't want a dead stolen boy all over my car. I am Alf, by the way. I do not know your name.' He stretched his right hand back as far as he could; Saul had to sit forward to shake it. Alf looked very strange to Saul with his lashless eyes and comb-over of hair still bent by his pillow. 'I'm Saul,' he said. 'How do you do?'

Alf squeezed his hand with painful sincerity. 'I am very

well, thank you, Saul. It is nice to see that you too are well. I'm sure everything is going to be fine.'

Saul had a thought. 'You're not going to take us to the police, are you?'

Alf tutted. 'No, no, no. We just go away somewhere we can talk.' He turned and started the engine, a sound of grinding friction rising to a scream then breaking into a rich choking. 'How's your arm, fat man?' he asked Howard as he pulled away from the kerb.

'Uch, fine. No worries there at all.'

Saul struggled to connect his seat belt into its lock as Alf's small car grunted forward, lurching in speed for every change of gear. Finally he felt its secure click and sat back, hooking his hand into the handle above the window to stop himself sliding about. The car was old and perforated with dusty windows and a round rear end; it let in whistling air although everything seemed to be shut. There weren't many controls on the dashboard. The button was missing from Saul's window handle leaving a plastic bar with an exposed metal end which confused him; it was, apart from its dilapidation, the first manual window control Saul had ever seen. A crucified Jesus hung from the rear-view mirror and, with Alf's jerky driving, swung back and forth so hard it almost somersaulted.

'That's my road.' Howard tapped on his window. 'Alf, can we go down it to show Saul? Aw, but what if there's a stake-out?'

'What stake-out? You don't even live there any more.' Alf pounced on the brake and turned fast enough to make Saul remember in a rush centrifugal force and its concomitant g-force effect.

Howard directed Alf to his old house. The tyres came to a squidgy stop in front of number thirty-five and Howard stared. It looked exactly the same but for an addition made by the new tenant: a flaccid St George's flag hanging from the upstairs window. Howard looked at the boring, boxy face of his former home and tried to ignite something in himself by saying to Saul, 'This is where I used to live.' Saul nodded silently in the back. 'My ma lived here with me.' Nothing. He couldn't start anything from its cover. And then out of nowhere he saw his mother back from church, fumbling for her keys in her bag. And then she was gone through the door and he heard its familiar closure, the chain swinging against the painted wood.

He worked his mother clearly into his thoughts as Alf drove them away and out towards the fields. He remembered her during a supervised visit, on the other side of a grey table with her gift of a cake on it, always the same fruitcake he never had butter for, saying, 'So we'll go to England after, just our own two souls together. Plenty of work down there. It'll be brand new and just fine for us.' Why she chose Burnley he'd never know, she liked the misery maybe.

You had to hold on it, tight, even though it was gone, even though it went like water into sand, like people did.

Saul watched the landscape of large bare hills flushing deep green in the sun, shadows of clouds moving like animals over them. It reminded him of the scrolling, schematic landscape of a flight simulation game on his computer. In some of the fields, divided by thick, lichen-splotched stone walls, were sheep, marked with aerosol patches of blue and red.

'Do vandals do that, you know, hooligans?'

'Do what?'

'Spray the sheep like that?'

'No, no, wee man. It's the farmers, so they know whose is whose.'

Saul filed away the explanation, another thing that Howard had taught him.

'Vandals.' Alf laughed. 'And the police say you a genius boy.' He pulled into a rutted hollow in front of a gate and stopped the car.

Howard reached into his pocket for his packet of cigarettes, offered Alf the open end, was refused with a lift of Alf's upper lip towards his nose, and lit one himself.

'So, open the bloody window,' Alf reprimanded. 'You smoke the boy like a ham.' Howard was quick to do as he was told, blowing the rest of his exhalation towards the fields and uselessly trying to scoop smoke out, but the mobile air returned most of his fumes into the car, where Saul watched with pleasure their relaxing scrolls and dissipating eddies.

They sat.

From a single grey cloud overhead came a short attack of rain against the windscreen. It left bright remnants that shook in the wind.

'So,' Alf's voice was slow, cogitative, 'you run away. Okay, great. You make a big action.' He gripped the steering wheel at the end of his straight arms as if bracing himself against it, and let go. 'You make a big action. Run away. Police run after you.'

'It was for the boy's good. I saved him. He said so.'

Alf shrugged. 'Fine, good, you save him from this what was it?'

'A memory competition,' Howard said, finding that the phrase did not on its own convey the horror from which Saul needed to be rescued.

'Memory competition? Like what memorising ...'

Saul explained: 'Cards. Base-ten numbers. Binary numbers. Names and faces. A poem. Various things.'

Alf looked at Saul over his shoulder with uncertain comprehension. He shrugged again. 'Okay you save him from a memory competition. But you've got to think what you are going to do now you've gone.'

Ah, Howard thought, not relishing the difficult question. 'Oh,' he said.

'Yes, yes, yes, yes, yes, yes,' Alf muttered.

Saul looked out at the shining grass, and up at the few clouds with their burning edges. A scrambled trilling came from a point high overhead. Saul pressed against the glass to look up. 'I think that's a skylark,' he said, his eyes hurting with light. The two heavy-bodied men in the front seats didn't seem interested. They sat with their hands in their laps and thought.

'I ran away once,' Alf said. 'Like you.' He turned in his seat. 'I was older than you, Saul, little bit, and I ran away.' He turned back to continue more comfortably his story. 'I had a competition also to do, a fight, big one, for my region, the amateur boys boxing. And I know this boy I am going to fight. I have watch him fight other boys. I sat by the ring and have blood splash onto my face, a horrible thing. I remember they had to stop this fight. The boy's name was Nando, Fernando, who I had to fight. Anyway they stop it after he knock down his opponent, who gets up and feels what you call them pins and needles in his neck and then he is sick right on the canvas. This is a very bad sign. He turned out okay, but this is very close, and Jesus God I don't want to fight Nando. I don't want to see what my insides look like all over the floor. Nando was so strong and so crazy, when he was beating a person he looked like he want to bite them as well. Just wanted to kill you. And this is boys' amateur boxing, this isn't professional. This is about scoring points, Queensberry Rules, gentleman art, but if you get in the ring with Nando Caiero it's a different story. He kill anything you put in the ring with him – lions, little girls, horses, I don't know. And he was taller than me also, longer arms so I know I'm not even going to get near him. I will be mince meat. But I got to do it for the tournament.'

Saul listened with great interest to this very relevant confession, picturing the serenely talented Vikram Chandrasinghe as his own bloodthirsty opponent.

Alf's voice took on a pleading tone. 'I don't want him to smash up my beautiful face for the ladies. So what can I do? One day before this big fight, I ran away. First thing take some food, ham and cheese – this is very early in the morning. I get bread from the baker on my way out, saying him it is for my mother, I've come because she is ill today. I walk out of the village, bit bigger than a village, small town place that was my home, and up the road, walking, walking, nobody stop me, all very easy, and into the fields, and I am a free man.'

Howard tossed his cigarette end out of the window and wound it shut. In the sealed quiet of the car, blustered upon from outside, Alf's voice was, apart from Howard's whistling nasal breath, the only sound. It was rich, worn, authoritative. Saul sat fascinated.

'I walk all day till I have gone a good few villages away. There is land which I know is from my uncle, a few miles from my mother's family place, and he has a stone barn for the sheep in the winter but this is summer so the sheep are outside so I can hide in the barn and stay there.'

'Ha.'

'What?'

'Oh no, it's just funny – we slept in a field last night.'

'You did?'

'Aha. After the hotel.'

Alf turned to Saul. 'You did this?'

'Yes, we did.'

'Oh, that's very nice for the boy, to sleep in a field. Anyway, where am I? You confuse me.'

'Sheep,' Saul prompted him.

'Yes, yes, the sheep. The sheep do not have much looking after this time of year. The lambs is all finished. Sometimes my uncle will come but they are like these ones.' Alf pointed out of the window to the white shapes of sheep in a green field. 'Just okay wandering about eating grass they can find. I stayed there,' Alf narrowed his eyes as if at the remembered glare of the sun, 'three days. Long, long hours. There is a well I can get water so that is okay but I have to be careful with the food. I see my uncle one time bringing extra food to the sheep and, fine, I hide and he goes away. I am alone there. Really

236

alone. Really quiet, you know. So what do I do? I shadow-box for hours. Stupid but it's true. And then I just lie there.' Alf gripped the steering wheel again. 'And sheep! I used to like sheep, you know, nice animals, strong legs, nice, but after three days of just them and no persons ... They don't have nice eyes. Their pupils are not round, they are rectangular with bits that come out further like a letter I. You look at them, they look back at you, they look past you. It's all the same. You don't even know if they see you.'

Alf folded his hands in his lap and paused. He looked straight ahead to where the gate was tied at one side with frayed blue nylon rope, but his gaze was inward. Wind flickered over the car. The silence was long. Eventually Saul piped up, 'What happened next then, if you don't mind me asking?' Alf's hands flew apart as if he had been woken. He shifted his buttocks back in his seat and started again.

'On the fourth day I wake up. I have been sleeping outside this time. I got to know the stars very good in this few days. I woke up. A line of men is coming across the field, spaced out, looking for me, or my body. Sometimes they call my name. On the left side I can see my father. I didn't run away. I just sat up and watched them coming. It was a strange feeling. Like yes I had died and these were the people afterwards. I don't know. And so they find me and they celebrate and my father hugs me then beats the shit out of me and I go home again. They rearrange the fight for later and I got this.' Alf pointed to his waxy, flattened nose. 'Absolute waste of time.'

'But you could have stayed away,' Howard protested. 'You could have carried on, gone somewhere else.'

Alf considered this. 'Where?' he asked. 'I could have gone to a monastery.' He laughed. 'I could have become a monk. And you, are you going to become a monk? You have the right hair for it.'

'No,' Howard answered as though the question were serious.

'But you got to do something now. What are you going to do?'

Howard surprised himself with an answer. 'I wannae go to Scotland.'

'With Saul?'

'Of course. Just for a wee bit.'

'But you get on a train all the police will catch you.'

'So maybe you could drive us?'

'Me?' Alf pointed to his chest. 'I need to get arrested? You are such a big idiot.' Alf clipped Howard on the back of his head with the flat of his hand.

'Don't hit him!' Saul shouted.

Howard rubbed his brown bald spot, not especially upset. 'Aw, come on, Alf,' he said. 'It's just up the road. You can drop us and come back in time to open the shop.'

'You know the way?' Alf asked.

'It's just straight up, isn't it? Aw, come on.'

'I can't, I can't do this. I'm not a mad man.'

'Please, can you?' Saul implored. 'We just need respite.'

Alf double-took on that still unfamiliar word. He shook his head. 'You are asking me. You, the boy, you say you are well because if not, if he is hurting you – be quiet, Howard – you tell me and I kill him and we call the police.'

'Alf, how could you think—'

'Shut up. I'm not talking to you, I'm talking to him.'

'He's not hurting me. I promise.'

Again Alf grabbed the steering wheel of his car and shook. The others watched as he went through this spasm of personal violence for quite a long time. Eventually he quietened down.

'But if anyone stop us,' Alf warned, 'I'm saying you threatened poor old man Alf and made me do it.'

Jean Harlowe leaned forward, her clean palms pressed together between her knees, her chunks of black shoes pointing towards each other, and spoke quietly to Barbara. A television plea, she explained, was often very effective at producing results. They connect with the public who then come forward in great numbers. There is no more powerful tool for us than a strong media campaign. You remember the case of … Barbara watched her abandon that sentence because, she suspected, the most famous little girls had all been found dead. It can be traumatic, obviously, facing press questions, but we'll be there to help you through. It was absolutely what Jean would advise doing at this juncture.

Barbara looked up from Jean's shoes but avoided her searching eyes. She had unruly hair, Jean Harlowe, dense and dry. Escaping from clips at her temples were scribbles of hair that caught the light. It made Jean quite endearing, the way she exceeded her uniform in this way, like a hard-working, messy schoolgirl. Barbara smiled at the comparison and held on to that, the hair – right now she could only work from whatever came into focus. Jean was a nice woman; she would agree. 'What about Les?' she whispered.

'Les has already agreed.'

Les was behind them somewhere, moving. Barbara needed him at that moment, to pull him in and catch hold of him. He moved behind her like cloud in cloud.

'Darling!' she shouted, dropping her head and looking sidelong. 'Darling!'

Jean hurried away to find him. Presently his face was in front of hers. His eyes were not crying but they were red and sweated tears. Both of his hands were turning a mug of coffee. 'It's got to be a good idea,' he said.

'He's all right,' Barbara said. 'I know he's all right.'

His head was so familiar, everything around her was so familiar, and yet it functioned so strangely, in such a jolting, dreamlike way. 'We should do this appeal, absolutely one hundred per cent.'

'Oh, yes,' Barbara said. It was obvious. Hadn't she agreed already?

Les nodded stiffly once, drank from his mug, squeezed her shoulder and walked away. She needed to talk to him. Still she hadn't told him.

Jean Harlowe bent down to speak to her. 'So, we'll set that up for you, then?'

Barbara nodded. She would send her voice out there, into the airwaves, and call him back. Saul. Out there. Call him back.

Saul couldn't stay awake, even with the wind howling through small holes in the sides of Alf's car and the screams of more powerful engines overtaking. But he couldn't stay asleep either. Thoughts chased in his mind. Packs of cards swelled and shuffled and disintegrated (those faces – familiar as family to him – queen's chin, the king's beard, the jack's curtains of hair), binary numbers streamed past his eyes too quickly to be read, let alone learnt. In one strange flash he saw his parents locked in the kitchen together both trying to get out by different doors. His father was talking. But it was Alf's voice which passed from his thoughts into the air inside the car.

'Look at him,' he was saying to Howard. 'All asleep. He is a beautiful one. Tired boy, all this escaping around. He is a good child, you can see it.'

Saul kept his eyes shut so as not to stop them talking. How strange it was that they called him a child when he had never felt himself to be one. Of course he had been and there were things he remembered that were definitely childish, like the famous time when aged four he'd embarrassed his mother by asking a woman in a shop why she had a moustache, and the other time when he was even smaller and he'd played at hiding his mother's keys in a teapot and they hadn't been able to leave the house. His mother had searched everywhere until she thought to ask him where they were, at which point he led her to the cupboard, opened the lid of the pot and showed her what he'd done. But even then he'd felt perfectly adult. He was a person, that was all, just one that was not as old as they were.

Howard did turn and look at Saul. He saw the blue veins under his right temple, the bulky, unwashed hair. His mouth was open in sleep. At their rims his lips were silvery and dry but they were dark and wet by the glimmering teeth. His legs in his creased trousers hung limp and useless as a paraplegic's. In his lap his fingers lay crimped around some object in his dreams. Such cargo! Almost frightening: a whole small person, breathing, dreaming, alive.

He turned back. 'He's a good wee laddie. You're no wrong there.'

'Kids are good,' Alf generalised. 'I would have enjoyed to be a father.'

'Why aren't you?' Howard asked automatically, then raised his hands. 'I'm sorry, Alf, I . . .'

'It is not possible,' Alf replied, calmly staring at the road. 'For me and Theresa.'

'Uch, I'm sorry.' Howard looked at Alf's blunt profile a moment. 'It was the same for my ma. After me, I mean. And she was a long while getting me. Waste of time that was.'

'Oh?' Alf checked Howard's face. 'It's hard. Not good. Not nice.'

'It was bad for me ma, you know, us being Catholics and all that.'

'Well, it is the same for us.'

'So it is.'

'Theresa, she misses them. She imagines them. One time she told me this, she actually have them in her mind. Two boys and a girl. She really, you know, thought what they would be.'

Howard saw it clearly: the sad dark space behind the chip shop, Theresa at her prayers, the invisible children running around. 'I'm sorry about that,' he offered.

'So what can you do?' Alf said, suddenly very loudly. 'That is life, your one – you live it. Okay. Fine.'

'I suppose you're right,' Howard agreed, although slowly, as though it were in some way possible to live a different one.

Alf heard the doubt. 'What? It's true. Whatever you do it's your life, your one to live. That's God's plan.'

Howard tucked his chin into his neck. The seat belt was cutting into the side of his right breast. He said, 'But if he forgives you, you can change and start again and all that.'

Saul decided to simulate waking up now: he stretched his fists out, curved his back and yawned loudly.

'You wake up now,' Alf called over his shoulder. 'You have a good sleep?'

Howard interjected as Saul's friend and protector, 'Are you all right there, wee man?'

'I'm fine,' Saul said, 'but what about the car?'

'What about it?'

'That noise.'

'What noise?'

'The high one – there – you must be able to hear it. It's been making it for ages.'

'It's fine.' Alf turned down his mouth in deprecation. 'This car just makes different noises. It's like an animal.'

Saul didn't think the car was anything like an animal, even an unspecified one that made different noises. He knew that it was mechanical and all the parts he could see were old and more or less broken so he wasn't surprised when that noise – a whining suction, something escaping, or trapped and chafing – after an hour or so became much louder, and Alf's short legs punched down on the pedals with less and less effect, and the car coasted to a standstill on the hard shoulder.

Saul stood with Howard while Alf leaned over the engine trying to wave a gap in the smoke that would let him see down to the problem. Howard was panicking. Alf was angry, repeating the word 'fuck' over and over like a crow's one note.

Saul himself was scared. This was not a good place for them to be in, marooned in plain sight with the whole world driving past.

'I can't fix it,' Alf despaired. 'I don't even know what I'm looking at.' A truck roared past making him squint. 'Something's not working.'

'We could get a repair man,' Howard shouted.

'I don't have a number.'

'We could walk and find one of those emergency phones.'

'But then they'll find us,' Saul warned. 'They'll get Alf's registration number. The police will have put out a message.'

'Oh, Jesus, Jesus, Jesus, fuck.' Howard held his stiff, boot-polish black hair and paced.

'But what can we do?' Alf shouted. 'We can't stay here. I knew I shouldn't go with you. I will go to jail now for helping a stupid man. And look at this – everyone can see us. You two get back in the car.'

'No,' Saul said.

'Don't argue with me, Einstein boy. Just get in the bloody car.'

'No, no. I've got an idea.'

'You know how to fix cars as well?'

'Howard and me – and I – could hitchhike to carry on. Then you can get help on your own and be safe. You can use my phone to call a repair man before we go.'

Alf's eyes searched the ground as he thought about it for a moment, his comb-over streaming up from his head. 'Howard,' he called, 'what do you think about this one?'

Howard, still pacing, didn't hear, heard only the blasting traffic and the doom in his mind. It took Saul grabbing his elbow to bring him back into the conversation.

'What?' he asked, his face all red blubber and woe.

'You have to come with me,' Saul instructed, seeing no point in a debate and already handing Alf his phone. 'We're going to hitchhike so Alf can go home without having to go to jail.'

'I don't like this,' Howard moaned. 'I really don't like this.'

It took Alf several calls to get what he needed, shouting information with his middle finger plugged into his exposed ear. 'One is coming,' he said finally, handing back the phone.

'Quick now.' Saul pulled Howard's arm and they started walking up the motorway to some point out of sight of Alf and the smoking carcass of his car.

Howard didn't even have the wherewithal to shake Alf's hand but his eyes rolled back after him like a frightened cow's, and Alf shouted though his hands, 'Good luck,' his voice faint against the noise of the motorway, his shreds of hair blown about by the wind.

The minutes were strange as a vision during which Howard followed Saul along the side of the motorway, to their left the bright, stiff grass on the steep bank, to the right the wide road of monstrous traffic banging past, and Saul in front, silent and steady in the roaring air, a spirit leading him on. It was the negative of the night's vision of him in the white robe against the black, star-fretted sky, the same photograph with the colours flipped.

When they were out of sight of the car Saul stopped, Howard caught up with him, and the hallucination ended.

'We should have a sign,' Saul said. 'That's what hitchhikers have.'

'I know,' Howard said. 'Just got to do the old thumbs-up thing.'

They stood beside each other, their left thumbs, little fish hooks, trying to catch someone's help.

Quite quickly Howard couldn't bear it. It was a disaster. They were supposed to be hiding, on the run, and here they were in the middle of the day, still hours away from Scotland, desperately trying to *attract* attention. And people were looking. Howard felt the cold grease of people's stares slide over him from every car that passed, each safe, disdainful box hurtling past having made its judgement. Normal people were in them, decent people encased in proper lives, and he, with all his sins and madness, was on the side of the road. He thought of all the immigrants in the lawyer's office, all begging to be let in. And Misha. How he could have done with Misha's adventurous help right now.

Howard shut his eyes to make it all easier to bear but found himself too scared at the noise, the sudden shoves of hot, dirty wind from the passing trucks. Instead, he narrowed his eyes until he'd reduced everything to a yellow-grey haze with flashing beads of colour. His arm began to droop; it couldn't take the exertion, and his scar didn't like the sun. Saul had his own technique: whenever a vehicle approached that he really wanted to stop he stuck his arm up higher, like a pupil desperate to answer the question.

The noise of cars became a rhythm, a heartbeat, and the dream descended again on unfocused Howard. This would never end. Or this was the end. They were dead. They called for mercy. They were lost.

And then it ended. A long vehicle switched on its hazards, a hand waving inside the cabin, and shuddered to a halt fifty yards beyond them. Waiting, it spluttered and shook.

'This is it.' Saul tugged Howard's arm. 'Come on.' He crunched away on his dusty competition shoes towards the unknown owner of the hand and Howard followed.

'Let me go first,' Howard insisted when they got there, his heart shaking all through his body. He climbed onto the step, his throat drying, his glasses sweating down his nose, and poked his head through the window. A man in yellow glasses smiled at him. 'Hello,' Howard croaked.

'Hi,' the man said, nodding with most of his upper body as though rocking to music. Howard heard an accent in the monosyllable.

'Can you give us a lift?' Howard asked.

'Yeah, yeah. That's why I'm stopping. Where are you going?'

'Scotland? Glasgow?'

'Cool. I too am going to Scotland.'

Howard looked down at the curious Saul. 'He says he can give us a lift.'

'Well, go on then.'

Howard worked out how to hang back and open the door without sweeping himself down into the dust, then climbed onto a chunky leather seat, reaching his arm down to pull Saul up onto the step.

The man in yellow glasses smiled at them both when Saul had pulled the heavy door shut behind him. The cab smelt strongly of chemical pine and previous coffee. Saul enjoyed seats that were huge and amazingly comfortable and he had never been so thrillingly high off the tarmac before. Being in the cab was different to being in a car. You felt superior and completely in charge of the road. He looked down at the scudding traffic.

'Hi,' the driver said. 'My name is Max. Let's go to Scotland.'

'Oh, God,' Howard said.

Max looked quizzically at Howard.

'We're Jasper and Fergus,' Saul said, peering round his bulky friend. 'Pleased to meet you.'

'Oh, God,' Howard said again as those names pierced him and he remembered again where he was going.

'Pleased to meet you, too,' answered Max, ignoring Howard's moans and pursuing with Saul the authorised, Berlitz version of the conversation.

'Jasper has a bit of a headache,' Saul explained, 'but he's fine really.'

Max nodded; a smile glazed the front of his face in a way that indicated either comprehension or not. He turned the huge steering wheel and edged back onto the road.

Saul studied him with interest. Max wore a check shirt opened to reveal a talisman, vaguely ancient-looking, tribal, on a leather thong. His hair was faded brown, kinky, and looked like something that had gone through the washing machine too many times and now didn't quite fit his head. His yellow glasses (Saul thought they must be scientifically better for looking at roads) cast a Day-Glo parallelogram onto his cheek, a thick wad of flesh stippled with beard. The interior of the cab was amazing, all leather and black and wood polished to reveal its smoky swirls. There were stickers from all different countries across the dashboard and one Saul could see of a naked girl in a top hat. The adult world of travel again seemed marvellous to the boy – the best of all lives, on your own, nobody telling you what to do, free to look at naked girls. No rules at all.

'Okay, I put the radio on?' Max asked.

'Absolutely, pal,' Howard answered.

'Yes, please,' Saul said. Way below him on the left the blurred road skimmed behind.

What came on when Max pressed the button was a news bulletin, the kind that has an almost American voice giving lumps of information in time to drumbeats and electronic chords. When the voice said, 'A plea will be put out later today by the parents of a boy who disappeared from the World Memory Championships on Saturday. The prodigy was last seen—' Saul started speaking in a loud robotic voice over the broadcast.

'It's a beautiful view,' he began. 'I'm so pleased I'm going to Scotland. I hear wonderful things.'

Howard joined in, his face wet with fear staring into Saul's. 'That's right. It's a lovely place, a lovely place, and very interesting.'

'Full of history,' Saul said.

'Yes, full of fascinating history.'

'An amazing history of wars and broils.'

Max glanced across at them. He nodded his upper body again with enthusiasm and seemed ready to join in the conversation himself. The opportunity arose when the news report ended and both Howard and Saul fell suddenly silent, panting.

'You like Scotland?' Max asked.

'Uch, yes,' Howard said. 'Best place in the world.'

'I don't know about that one.' Max smiled, hoping to raise a debate. 'It's a good place.'

'Where are you from?' Howard asked.

Max drew a spiral in the air with his forefinger. 'Zzzzp. I go all over.'

Saul flushed at the thought.

'But where are you from originally?'

'It's not important, my friend.'

'Are you German? I mean, I'm not prejudiced. The war was a long time ago.'

'I don't care about that,' Max said, pushing his glasses back up his nose with his middle finger, just like Howard. 'It doesn't matter. Here we are driving along. I just met you. You just met me. What's the problem? We don't need so many questions. Just one man, one man. That's better, I think.'

'I see what you're saying, pal.'

'I agree,' said Saul, looking around Howard to see Max turn to him and smile.

'It's better,' Max repeated with the tone of uttering something self-evident, one hand raised.

The road markings sped towards them, the small cars glinted below. Glasgow was getting closer.

Barbara sat beside her husband, who had to his right Detective Inspector Peter Coombs. To Barbara's left was Jean. So there were four of them seated at the table with the microphones, which for some reason made Barbara imagine giving the sports results. Behind them were screens with the Metropolitan Police symbol on it and a helpline number. In front of them were about twenty-five journalists seated and standing. There were snapping newspaper cameras and television cameras that were unblinking. Barbara felt their steady vacuum pulling at her like they were pulling her clothes from her body or her hands from her face. Constable Jean Harlowe had persuaded Barbara to do this so that a plea would be ready for broadcast on the evening news. Jean had told her not to underestimate the effect that hearing the voices of the parents directly had on people. The effect on Howard might be shattering, or at least could make him think again, get some perspective. Barbara, looking at the glassy pink shapes of her nails in her lap which looked old and strange, remnants from a former life, had nodded in agreement.

The cameras had finished their first convulsions now; they twitched with an occasional flash until Barbara picked up her head to look at them and stirred a small frenzy. The television reporters were distinguishable partly because of their almost familiar faces but also because they wore smart outfits. The cameramen, photographers, boom operators and print journalists seemed to Barbara to be almost disrespectfully casually dressed.

Inspector Peter Coombs addressed the room with weary urgency. He presented clear information about what had occurred, the age and appearance of people involved, the sighting last night in a hotel near Burnley. You could hear the facts becoming bullet points on journalists' pads. Howard MacNamee was not thought to be a dangerous man. His motivations were unknown. Likewise it was not known if he posed a threat to the boy's safety. However, he did have a criminal record as a juvenile for a very serious assault on another boy. Detective Inspector Peter Coombs then explained that Mr and Mrs Dawson-Smith wished to make a personal plea for the safe return of their son.

With trembling hands holding pages dimpled by his sweaty fingertips, Les read out the statement that he had composed. Barbara looked down at her lap. Les also looked down so that the cameras mostly had a shot of his clammy forehead and the flattened V of his hairline, like a child's drawing of a seagull.

The frustration in the room was fairly palpable and discharged itself in a barrage of flashes when Les looked up like a tearful child to get Peter Coombs's nod of approval. *For what, though?* Les thought after. His son was dead. Barbara didn't know this yet – her terror was not nearly complete – but Les knew that they were just waiting to recover the body from some God-forsaken garage or wood. Barbara didn't know what men were, what they could do, and did, what was in their thoughts. So how would she know that Saul was dead, that Howard, large and gentle Howard, inside was a killer? Les dropped his head, ground his sweaty palms together and waited to leave.

The journalists wanted more, however, and Barbara felt many gazes pushing at her. A female journalist in the front row whose face was familiar and the bumping rhythm of whose name arrived in Barbara's head when she started to speak ('This is Meredith Davies …') asked Barbara directly what she in particular would say to Saul and Mr MacNamee if they were watching right now. Barbara looked up with a shaking face and falling tears into a storm of white light.

'I … I …' She just wanted him back, wanted her children, her life was so strange. 'I … I … I … I … would just say come home. I know you wouldn't do anything bad, Howard. So just come home. I can't … I can't bear this.'

'And what would you say to Saul if you could?' The questioner was one of the print journalists. He was a thick-necked, handsome young man in a rugby shirt.

'I would say, "Saul …"' It was saying his name that did it. The name dragged terror and longing right out of her chest and through her mouth. She hung her head and wept while, far on the other side of herself, she felt a hand patting her back. She recovered finally to say, ' "Just come home. There'll be no more competitions. Anything you like. Just come home."'

There was an appreciative hush at this photogenic grief,

broken when another journalist asked, 'So you think the competition is the reason?'

Peter Coombs leaned to a microphone and told the room that that would be all.

Afterwards, Jean squeezed her arm and handed from her seemingly infinite supply more tissues. She had done well. This could really be the key.

A siren wailed. For them? A police car striped like a venomous animal overtook them and signalled for them to pull in. Max said, 'What the ...' and slapped his steering wheel. Howard felt a fear too large to be really felt; it was much larger than he was. He leaned back in his seat. His bones were water. Alf had been caught. Theresa had probably called the police. Alf had told them the plan and now here they were. Although maybe ... if they hadn't been seen ...

'Shouldn't you go out to talk to them?' Howard suggested.

'No. I'm fine. If they want me, they come and get me.'

So that was that. Howard couldn't find the voice to beg.

Over a period of years a policeman emerged from the passenger seat of the car and walked towards them. Howard watched the swing of each official step until the policeman was out of sight below them. He reappeared suddenly at Max's window.

'Don't bother getting down,' he said. He eyed Howard and Saul. 'I just want to take a quick look in the back, sir, if you wouldn't mind obliging.' He disappeared and slapped the door twice.

Max cursed in an unknown language and got out.

Saul and Howard were left alone in the cab. Saul, unhelpfully, was giggling. 'I don't believe it,' he whispered. 'I don't believe he didn't recognise us.'

'Sshh,' Howard scolded, staring at his knees.

Behind them, the back of the lorry rattled open. Each

second cut into Howard, the fine hand on his watch flinching slowly round.

Max returned to the cab. The policeman appeared again at the window but before he could say anything a voice crashed out of the radio on his lapel. He reacted as though it were an emergency, his face scowling, his eyes skyward, as he concentrated. *This is it,* thought Howard, *this is it, this is it.* The policeman raised a finger at them then said, 'Oh, shit.' He vanished and reappeared running away towards his car. The siren went on and the car sped off.

Howard was confused. Why wasn't he being seized? The car continued speeding away, was already almost, was, out of sight.

'Stupid pigs, you call them,' summarised Max.

Saul was giggling again and then openly laughing. The laugh was infectious. Howard cracked up.

Max also started laughing. He thought he'd said something funny. 'What?' he asked. 'Is that not how you say it?'

Max, it transpired, had a great passion for fishing and delivered a long speech of broken poetry about rivers, the silence under trees, the solitude. He spoke about different kinds of rods and mimed casting with a supple wrist. Saul asked questions and Max kept on talking, clearly relishing the company he had. He found things funny as he went along and would erupt unpredictably, his neck buckling as he released a grinding, gurgling sound which reminded Saul of the waste disposal in the sink at home. And when he laughed, Saul's own mouth opened in delight. He was learning so much, so much real stuff about the world from this man from nowhere who knew about currents and fish and drove around Europe for a living.

Howard observed the conversation, watched Saul leaning forward past his belly to talk to Max, and wondered. He tried to think things through – the situation demanded thought – but could achieve no useful sequence. Ideas were balled up in his head. Why go to Glasgow? They had to go somewhere, to run so as not to get caught. Any minute they might be caught. Howard expected sirens. He looked up once to check that a blatter of helicopter noise wasn't the police chasing him down. But why Glasgow? It was somewhere, one of the two or three places he knew. To find his father? Why? He had Saul to show him, the boy intact. He could prove him wrong. And it was time. Howard was twenty-eight now. It had been sixteen years. What harm could he do to him now? And it needed doing. Howard had in fact grown sick of hiding. *Fuck it all*, he thought, *fuck it all*. He sank towards the city, his heart lifting with fear. Wiping the sweat from his forehead, he tuned back into the conversation. They were on to politics now.

'So the Conservatives are actually *bad?*' Saul asked.

'Okay,' Jean Harlowe held Barbara's wrist, 'we do have some news. Officers have picked up a known associate of Mr Mac-Namee on a motorway. His name is,' she checked her notebook, 'Alfonso Continho.'

Barbara didn't like that one bit, the frightening foreignness of the name. Did he traffic children? She pictured someone dark and unshaven and capable of anything. Someone muscular and relentless in a vest. She pictured Carlos the Jackal.

'He ran the chip shop where Mr MacNamee worked. He had been visited by Mr MacNamee, who was with Saul who, he said, was absolutely fine. Now, he said that they said they were going to hitchhike to Scotland. He let them go then had a big crisis of conscience or what have you and decided to chase them but then his car broke down. His wife had reported him missing already, although it seems he didn't know that. He's still being questioned.'

By Barbara's shoulder, quaking with joy at learning that his son was still alive, Les's head said, 'We're getting closer, Howard. We're coming after you, don't you worry.'

Barbara wondered from which film he'd learned to talk

like that. But for herself she couldn't talk like anything. Jean Harlowe squeezed her wrist and finally she blinked.

Scotland? What was in Scotland? Barbara had been there only once with school as a teenager. She remembered horrible hikes and midges and wet heather and cold lakes enamelled with cloud. She set her small son down in that empty place. And next to him she saw the large, grey, indeterminate shape of Howard MacNamee.

They crossed the dark Clyde and the city rose around them. Howard felt locked in between serrations of tall buildings. But then again, because it was familiar from childhood but unseen since, a city in his mind, it seemed fragile and unreal – cardboard scenery he could have poked his finger through. Max set them down by the station. He himself was heading east; Glasgow it turned out had been a detour to prolong the conversation. Saul hopped down from the cab followed by Howard's more awkward descent: he tried to come down facing out and had to slide, his arms bending up behind him as he held on to the ledge. The step caught under his bum and pitched him down onto his feet. Max blasted farewell with his terrifyingly loud horn and pulled away.

Howard was there. Home. Back in that time. It came towards him in waves and flowed away. He was at its stricken centre.

Best to walk, to keep moving. But which way?

Saul stood waiting for the answer. 'This way,' Howard said. He walked at random. Or maybe not. He might have been remembering where he was going but didn't know. Unsafely, he was drawn towards movement and numbers and went in amongst the people.

They did look familiar. Red-headed girls and square tough women with shopping bags. And the accent. His own voice he heard after years, his mother's voice. His father's. Which reminded him: anyone might have been in the crowd, anyone from way back, Fergus or Michael or his dad. The crowd was alive with threat and had his early life swirling like poison within it. Only, famous as he was, nobody seemed to notice him. No one was looking at them at all. It made Howard want to tug on sleeves and demand, 'Don't you know who I am? Don't you know what we're doing here?' Why wasn't importance visible in the world? Anyway it wasn't, and the day carried on as though nothing were happening. On closer inspection the crowd seemed younger than Howard had expected, and well-dressed, happy. Glasgow didn't seem to resemble the frowning brown mothers' city he remembered. And when had all this pedestrianisation happened? There were new shops, shopping centres. There was a gloss of advertising and money which made it look more or less like everywhere else. He'd imagined an absolute difference of some kind, some kind of awful ceremony to take place on his return. But here were the same shops and brand names, the same posters that were up on the Underground in London. Maybe nothing was like it had been; nobody would recognise him; nothing would happen.

Ah but no. Right there was a shop he remembered: Frasers. Walking alongside his mother in the fierce, sea-scented January wind through cloggy street snow towards the sales. Inside the store, entering through the overhead heaters' curtain of warmth, in that sparkling, musical interior, still with the Christmas decorations up, his mother became extra-serious, cynical of what rubbish they'd allowed into the sale, but Howard knew that inside she was wild with fantasy. The sales were a delirium so intense for her that she could only cope by putting on the demeanour of an angry Scots rationalist. He should have scattered her ashes in the haberdashery department.

Frasers ... which meant ... they were on Sauchiehall Street. Such a warm day as well and the air seemed clean. The breeze, although strong, was soft. Howard had become used to dirty London air so laden with sharp grit that a gust felt like having cutlery thrown at you. But Glasgow as he remembered it had been filthy. Still, this was in town. It was always smarter there. When he found his way back to Govan, then he'd see.

'Security check.' Saul grabbed his arm, making him jump. 'I think we should look at the news, find out what's going on.'

'Ah, okay,' Howard said, adjusting his glasses and refocusing on the boy, which was hard because behind Saul floated tinkling bubbles. Howard traced them back to their source, a Chinese man squatting on his heels in front of a small cloth covered with plastic toys, dogs that yapped and flipped, and in his hand a plastic gun that pumped out mechanical music and soap bubbles.

Saul again commandeered Howard's attention. 'Howard! We can go in here and look at the papers.'

'Ah, yes.' Howard looked up at the sign above the newsagent's. 'That's a good idea.'

'I know it is. Wake up.' Saul took hold of Howard's hand and dragged him inside. There was a report on them in both of the papers they looked at before they fled. MEMORY BOY STOLEN. CHILD GENIUS ABDUCTED. They didn't seem to know where Howard and Saul were but there were three photographs reproduced: the photograph from Les's desk of Saul smiling in suit and cummerbund, a CCTV image of Howard taken it seemed in an Underground station, and a weird portrait photograph of Howard in jumper and tie with his eyes shut. The CCTV image made Howard look very sleazy, mouth ajar, restless, misshapen; having the date and time in the frame made him unambiguously criminal. Saul read the caption under the photograph of Howard in jumper and tie which explained why it looked so odd: Howard's school photograph had been aged forward on a computer. The simulated years had produced a red-headed man with a hefty, turgid face adorned with crow's feet, a mealy mouth and a frowning plastic forehead. The child had turned into a madman. Saul found the picture almost funny. Howard hissed at him to be quiet. For himself he didn't know what he thought. He thought of the people now working on him, trying to find him, all those strangers who now knew his name and were telling everybody in the world, showing everybody what he looked like. Howard Howard Howard Howard. The criminal child who grew up no better, famous for the second time in this town. If they just wouldn't catch him for a little bit longer then he would have the chance to make it right. And anyway was saving Saul really a crime? They knew fuck all.

'Are you buying any of those papers, pal?'

Howard spiralled out of view under a protective hand. Saul answered for him with bizarre cunning. 'No. Have you got any ping-pong balls?'

'No. Can't say as we have.'

'We'll go somewhere else then. Thank you.'

Barbara stood at the sink washing cups by hand. She hadn't washed crockery by hand for years and didn't need to now; she found herself doing it, saw her skin reddening under hot water, steam rising into sunlight. Then out of the window she saw her husband alone in the garden, walking vaguely, drifting sideways. When he put both hands to the sides of his head she turned off the taps and went out to join him.

She rocked a little at the change of air, narrowed her eyes against the large light. Her hands were still wet. She smeared her palms against her trousers then, in a quick gesture repeated many times a day, she ran her right hand down the front of her stomach, defining the safe limit of her daughter's world.

'Darling,' she said. 'Les.'

'Yeah,' he said, turning. 'I'm fine, I'm fine.' There were tiny lightning forks of blood vessels in the whites of his eyes. 'Just getting, you know, air.'

'I know.'

'You know,' he tried a bitter laugh, showing his teeth, shaking his head, 'the garden doesn't even look that good.'

Barbara knew what he was talking about. In their state of emergency they were deeply married; with the exception of Barbara's secret, their minds circled the same few things. 'We didn't hire him as a gardener though, at first. There were different reasons. Complicated.'

'No.' Les also answered her thought directly. 'Don't say it was to do with my mother.'

'Wasn't it?'

'It was a favour. Services rendered. Obvious thing to do.'

'Pretty big favour.'

'Look, don't think for a second that I blame myself for any of this.' Les had raised a finger which trembled. Barbara saw him as though collected through a lens. His fingertip made an apex, behind it his fierce eyes, the tense muscles of his mouth, then all of him flowing down to the black slippers in the green grass. Barbara raised a hand to her throat. This fierce little man still didn't know what she had to tell him. 'There's only one person I blame for this and that's Howard. Howard.' He dropped his hand and turned away.

Where he looked, beneath a tree the image of Howard congealed, standing there with a broom in his hand, gross, sly, stupid, full of design. A murderer, a big-armed killer who he had invited in. Who by now had surely killed his son.

'It's not about blame though, is it?' Barbara said. 'It doesn't matter. It's no help.' She placed a hand on Les's shoulder. He flinched then relaxed slightly under the pressure.

'Maybe. Whatever. Fuck.' He turned and dipped his head down so that his forehead touched her collarbone. She stroked the top of his head. 'You're right,' he said and Barbara felt the words formed against her skin.

'Shall we go back in?' she asked. 'They might have something to tell us.'

Les knew what they would have to tell them soon enough.

He looked at the ground as he walked back but in the corners of his vision Howard's shade disintegrated and reappeared, blood-spattered and smiling.

'But mentally I'm already packed. I've written lists. My mind's going over the same things I have to do for the journey, over and over every day. I can't believe this is happening.'

'It is. I'm sorry. It is happening.'

'My grandmother weeps every time she looks at me now anyway. If I told her this!'

'So, don't tell her.'

'How did this happen? I mean, what kind of a man did you pick out for me that he kidnaps a child? It's a pederast you chose?'

'It's not kidnap. He doesn't want ransom.' Misha, standing next to Varya made imploring gestures with his hands, clutching lumps of air. Varya tried to wave him away as she continued. 'Irina, calm down, please. It's not that bad. They've only been gone a couple of days. And they'll come back. It shows he is a dynamic person, anyway.'

'You're out of your mind. What do they put in the food over there? I don't need a dynamic kidnapper. I need a normal person.'

'He's trying to help the boy probably. I saw that boy being cooked by those parents. It's a good thing.'

'I can't believe you're telling me this is a good thing. A good thing? Why am I arguing about this? This is all so clear. It's obvious. It's obviously completely fucked up.'

'Give me the phone.' Misha pulled the receiver from Varya's hand before she'd finished passing it. 'Listen,' he said, 'everything will be fine.'

'But the process is under way. I can't start again with someone else. How would that look?'

'What did I say?'

'What *did* you say?'

'What did I say?'

'What *did* you say? Misha, what the fuck is going on?'

'I said everything is going to be fine. He'll come back. I'll sort him out. It will be fine.'

'Optimist doesn't even begin to describe you. Just because we *want* this.'

'We'll get what we want. It will happen.'

'How the hell does Varya put up with you?'

'It will happen.'

'And if he's arrested? If he goes to jail?'

'Then we'll have another discussion.'

'My grandmother should hear this because then she'd know her granddaughter is staying in this fucking country.'

'How many times do I have to tell you? We can bring her over here with you. It can be arranged.'

'Every time she looks at me she weeps. It's driving me nuts.'

'So what are they?' Saul asked, eyes narrowed against the wind that came off the river.

Howard remembered the winter version of that wind, not this puffing summer version as the sunlight found its way through clouds to light up the water, but loud, numbing, Glaswegian wind. His father would come home with purple hands and the wind still in the furrows of his jacket, little pockets of freezing air you could find there hours later.

'Tell you the truth, wee man, I've not a clue.'

They had walked to where the shops had petered out in a succession of Indian restaurants and then on to where the cars started getting smarter and large trees lined the streets. Signs had led them away from this down to the river. Now they stood on the north bank of the Clyde. Looking left they could see new apartment buildings with blue steel balconies and dark glass, buildings that resembled machines. Looking right, Howard knew where he was and felt the fear, the invitation;

they could see the empty docks, the motionless cranes, the gull-encircled silence.

But directly opposite them it seemed that aliens had landed. In a cleared space of grass and gravel, a giant silver balloon had fallen softly on its side. There was beside it a silver tower with a pod on top like something from Flash Gordon. Another silver building was of overlapping segments, a huge animal's shell. 'Whatever it is, it wasnae here when I left.'

'Can we go and see?' Saul asked. His fringe sprayed up from his clear forehead. The wind roughened the water, quickening the patches of broken light.

'Well, we could,' Howard said slowly. It had not been part of the plan – whatever the plan was – and Howard had other things to attend to. There, on the other side of the river it was all amassed, somewhere in the dingy, red-brick streets and those flats, the flats he could see right now, looming up against the slump of background hills, somewhere in there would come a reckoning. Or not. The wind hissed through his glasses.

'Come on,' Saul tried again, 'just to see what it is.'

'We could do,' Howard said before hurrying to catch up with Saul, who was already on his way to the bridge.

Howard followed him onto the footbridge. Slightly springy under his tread, it curved like an arrow's flight to the other bank where there was a sign.

'It's a science centre,' Howard said.

'I know,' said smirking Saul. 'There was a signpost ages ago. Can we go in?'

'Ach, Saul, please.'

'What?'

'Just wait a minute, please. To think.'

'*Je pense, tu penses, il pense* ...'

'Saul, wheesht, boy!' Howard held one arm of his glasses and looked at the ground. A beetle was passing in front of his shoes.

Saul insisted. 'Please. Please can we. Where else are we going to go?'

'To buggery.'

'Unv, you swore. Right, I'm going right inside now to tell someone.'

'What?'

'I am.'

'Saul.' The boy was acting strangely. Howard didn't know what it was but something sort of sideways was happening, straying out of control. 'This way,' Howard announced, and started walking.

'Where, though?'

'I don't know. We'll see. An adventure.'

'I can't hear you,' Saul complained. The wind destroyed Howard's mumbled words.

'Come on!' he shouted over his shoulder as he tramped. The rapid air skated over his bald spot.

'But where?'

Howard thought that the best thing was not to answer. He walked. The silver buildings revolved slowly behind him as he walked into waste ground full of stiff, airy grasses, scrappy weeds and odd flowers.

Saul caught up with him. 'But we're walking right past it,' he complained.

'Aha. That's right.'

'You're mean.'

'Saul, we cannae go into there. It'll be all security cameras everywhere. Anyway, look, keep up.'

'You keep up,' Saul said. 'Fatty,' he added quietly.

'Finally he starts on my physique. You're a bit late there, wee man. I've heard that all for the last twenty-five years.'

'I'm sorry.'

'No, no. Try some more. There are some good ones. Lard-arse. Butterball. Hippo. Pig. Porky. Porky-pig. Jelly. Jumbo. Greedyguts. Fat boy. Fat pig. Fat bastard. Fat fuck ... '

All the names came to him as they walked out of the open space and onto a street, one of the streets. The name-callers had lived here and away in back where the flats were. He was telling them he was home. Then fear hit him and Howard turned irrelevantly east, away from where he knew he must go.

Even so it was looking like home and to walk a swift line into it felt like performing surgery on himself. He'd seen it on telly: one clean stroke with a scalpel and the chest falls open, a prim-lipped wound and wet red convulsing stuff inside. His burnt arm prickled. At any moment he might see anyone at all. He felt light with dread and the feeling got worse. Suddenly he realised why – he realised that if he turned up this particular street, which without thinking he did, he would see, he did see, the school.

Flaring red bricks, large smudged windows with things taped to them inside, a tarmacked playground with flaking lines painted on it, benches, a water fountain, a couple of goals. It wasn't the same size as in his memory, of course, which now warped and dragged to fit itself to the real place. Over there were those big cylinder bins, the ones you could climb into that reeked with the runny brown liqueur of old rubbish skulking in the bottom. And there were those rails you could hold against your hips, lift your legs, and somersault around. He'd only been there when he was still physically small, relatively speaking – puberty had hit later, in Ridgemont, the last place it should ever have to happen to anyone, where ... Howard became aware of Saul's voice asking questions. Without listening to what they were he answered, 'I was at school here for a wee while.'

A mixed school. Primary school had been Catholic only, safe and demented with prayer and violent nuns. But this school was not and that meant trouble, although probably the trouble would have been about something else if it weren't for that. New kids were always smacked around at any school, especially fat ones. Toilets were a place of especial terror. Pelted with soaked toilet paper, shoved forward onto the urinal as you peed, gobbed on, laughed at, your shoes peed on, your head smacked into the tiles, the occasional bogwashing, being accused of smells, slapped.

Jasper they didn't touch for some reason. Inviolate and strong, they left him alone. Michael got some attention for being a Catholic, but not nearly as bad. The older boys, Douggie and Fergus – Fergus still whole and fierce – Alasdair and Paul paid particular attention to outsize Howard so that Howard couldn't remember whether the bruise was theirs or from his father when he went into that room right there for his medical.

Howard stood in his underpants waiting for the lady to check him. He kept his arms carefully folded. Under the fluorescent light he was as white as lard and soft, his belly round, his knees dimpled recesses in the thickness of his legs. The lady chewed gum as she jotted things onto a form. She said, 'Will you stand under the measure,' without looking up, indicating with the capped end of her pen where she meant, a wooden contraption by the door. With his arms still folded, hands cupping the small purses of his chest, he stood where he was told and waited. Then she was upon him, breathing quick minty breaths disturbingly onto his naked skin and adjusting the arm of the device so that it descended and gently touched the top of his hair. 'Have to get it down through that brush of yours.' She smiled and lowered it minutely, ticklishly, until it made contact with the top of his skull. 'Well, you're tall enough,' she told him, 'but we've to weigh you and you look a bit too fond of the buttered foods.' Her hair was a heavy bob with many dry grey strands in it, pinned back by her glasses. 'On you hop.' Howard stepped onto the scales' cold rubber mat, which felt both gritty and slimy under his feet. She flicked small weights back and forth until the scales balanced. Her expression was disapproving. Briefly she stopped

chewing and swallowed her spit, then her jaws started bouncing again and he could hear the wad of elastic wetness
between her molars. 'Nine stone four. That's no good at all for
your height. You know what you need, Sonny Jim?' Howard
shook his head. 'Plenty of oats and running about. You live in
the flats, don't you?' Howard nodded then realised what she
meant. 'I go out, though,' he told her. 'Well, go out more. And
use the stairs. And what are you holding yourself like that for?
It isnae cold in here.' Howard kept careful hold as he shrugged.
A thick eyebrow rose above the frames of her glasses. Howard
looked past her head at the red tree of the human vascular
system as depicted on a laminated poster. 'You'll have to let
yourself go now, laddie. I've to take your boompity-boom.'
Without moving her feet she let herself fall towards her desk,
landed on her hands, and collected that very enviable object,
a stethoscope, before pushing herself upright again with a
groan. Howard stepped off the scales and waited fearfully,
feeling hot and moist where his thighs met. He watched her
plug in the headphones and approach him with the metal
circle on its flex. The moment was on him. She looked at him
with both eyebrows above her frames. He dropped his hands
and revealed on his left pap a large bruise: an active-looking
purple centre, a muddy green outline and a surrounding stain
of urinous yellow. She swatted her headphones from her ears.
'That's a nice old knock. How did you get it?'

Howard delivered the prepared lie, the phrase that he had
been chanting in his head all the while. 'Playing football.'

She nodded. 'Well, it's nothing to be embarrassed about.
It'll be gone in a week or so.'

Howard nodded. A hot rain of relief poured down inside
him. He had got away with it.

She refitted the earpieces and pressed the cold metal of
the stethoscope directly onto the bruise. The sensation was
tingling and deep. The strange woman's head was inches from
his chest. He could look down and see flakes of white skin

near her parting. He wanted to pee. And he had got away with it! He had got away with it and she was so close to it listening to his heart underneath it and nobody knew and so he realised that he had to carry on, that he had to leave this room and go back to it all. Nothing was going to happen. Nobody knew.

'Is this where you hurt that boy?' Saul asked.

'Wha . . . 'Howard's head drained of blood.

'That boy. You maimed him. It said in the paper.' He quoted from memory, using his affectless voice of recall: '"Howard MacNamee served two years in Ridgemont young offenders' institution near Glasgow for the maiming of a boy on a railway track. However, he has not offended since and the police are uncertain as to whether or not he poses a threat to Saul Dawson-Smith or other members of the public."'

'It said . . . wha . . .'

Howard had not actually read to the ends of the articles about him when he was in the newsagent's. He'd been too busy surfing his fear and looking at the pictures, and besides he never really enjoyed reading and had made no exception even for these crucial paragraphs. He had been negligent, as ever, in charge of his own life.

'Your criminal record.' Saul's face was a sharp flint in the middle of Howard's throbbing vision. It needed answering. This was all too much. Right there, right in front of the school.

'It was an accident,' he whimpered. 'I never meant . . . It was an accident. I . . . he . . . was older than me.' Howard didn't know how he could have forgotten that Saul didn't know about that when he was reading the article. Why could he never control anything? He remembered the chaos of the actual moment. Fergus grabbing at him and himself falling towards the tracks and doing the only thing he could – grabbing a stone and raising it and bringing it down with all his force and leaving a red triangular dent in Fergus's forehead from which slow blood pours. Howard saw the blood turn

Fergus's eyebrow to red velvet. Then they were at each other, knees and foreheads knocking, blood smeared about, the train screaming closer and the final blur in which it happened. It was the first time Howard had seen it all in his mind for ages. And then earlier, the three boys appearing in the distance, their bodies insectile, beady and staring in the damp air. Then seeing them set off to chase him. But that didn't explain it; the event was much larger and included the months that led to the tracks, Howard hammered and hammered by them, by his father, by day after day through which they came at him, until finally he couldn't not react.

'You're not going to maim me, are you?'

'Jesus Christ, no.' Howard was angry at Saul, that he was capable of the thought. 'I was just a wee boy. He was older than I was. I'll explain it, I can explain it.'

'I didn't want to go to the science centre,' Saul said.

'What?'

'I was thinking about telling somebody.'

'Aw come on, Jesus. Saul, it's me. You know I wouldnae hurt you.'

'That's what I thought. But why didn't you tell me?'

'What would I say?'

'You could have just told me. You're my friend, remember. And it might have been important information, don't you think?'

'Saul, please.' Howard found himself crouching until he was almost on his knees.

Saul looked into his huge trembling face and really did see only a desperate innocence.

'What happened?'

'I'll tell you. Soon. Not here, though. Please. I am your friend.'

Saul felt now almost embarrassed by the declaration that he'd wrung from this old, helpless, slack-faced man. 'Good,' he said. 'Fine. Let's just carry on then.'

'Really? Oh, thank you, Sauly-boy. Oh, thank you.' Howard removed his glasses to wipe his face with his anorak sleeve.

'It's all right, really.'

'So, why didn't you just use your phone?' Howard asked, reassembling himself.

'Oh. I don't know.'

'Aha!' Howard pointed down at Saul. 'You didn't think of that one, did you?'

'No. No, I didn't.'

'Silly, silly.'

'Yes. Maybe I'm catching being an idiot from you.'

They walked and walked, describing fretful parallelograms through the streets as Howard refused any serious direction. They didn't speak. Together they ignored the futility of the exercise and kept on marching; fatigue was a solid result that would answer for a point or product. It might also drain the flashing colour from Howard's thoughts. He muttered and shook his head at memories of that dusk. Little Stephen had been there right at the beginning by the dirty fire with a *Star Wars* figure that Michael had wanted to have a go with. Jasper leapt again and again through that fire in Howard's mind. Then when Fergus and friends had started coming after them, they'd run under the flats and away, and Howard hadn't been able to, not fast enough anyway. He'd tried, but running was never for him like it was for other people, a forward flight. His weight banged his feet straight up and down on the tarmac and his knees hurt. They had chased him. He hadn't looked for trouble.

Eventually, with damp socks and aching legs, they returned to the river's breathing width and cold green smell.

'Why are we going back across?'

'Are you no hungry?'

It was getting late. Light had begun to drain massively into the far west of the river. Its waters were violet and black. Saul wanted to stop and look down, to look at the gulls glowing white, at the yellow boat with the bulldozer's jaw on its front, but Howard hurried them on, away. He wanted to get away from the south side right now.

Sitar music tingled around his ears. Out of the wind and rapid, slurring streets, his skin tingled. Damp, heaped, he came slowly to himself on a seat the sides of which he overspread like something melting.

For safety's sake, even though it was only six o'clock and they were the only customers in the place, Howard faced the wall and saw therefore only Saul and the wallpaper pattern that grew out of the sides of his head. Saul saw the mound of Howard, his exhausted face wearing an encouraging smile that kept fading back into expressionlessness, and behind him empty tables and chairs, bright glasses, cutlery, mitred napkins and a dark, lurking waiter.

'God, I'm hungry,' Howard said. 'Are you hungry? Have you chosen what you want?'

Saul looked again at his menu.

'And these are all different types of curry, you say?'

'Aha. There are starters as well. Do you want starters?'

Saul held his head with dignity as he considered. He was in an adult restaurant, which was a rare treat, and he would behave appropriately.

'But what exactly is in curry?' he asked in a whisper.

'Oh, you know, meat, chicken, whatever, and curry, just curry. Sauce.'

'Is it spicy? I mean, I know Indian cuisine is noted for its spices.'

'Aha. Or not always. Do you not like spicy food?'

'No, I do.' Saul would be grown-up in his choices also.

'So do I. Give me something to just blast me out of the water.'

Saul fell again to silent study of the menu. Howard felt awful, suffering mudslides of tiredness inside, of stirred emotion. He needed food and turned in his seat to summon the waiter, who arrived on swift, sneakered feet. As he inclined solicitously towards his big customer, his wide face smooth and smiling, Saul saw that his spiked hair showed lines of pale scalp as if under a searchlight, paler than the skin of his hands and face.

'Poppadoms, please,' Howard said.

'What are they?' Saul hissed.

'Big crisps, with sauce. And a chicken biriani. Saul? Jasper, rather?'

Saul looked up in fear, cornered by the attention. 'You choose, please. No, no,' he interrupted himself, 'I'll have the same.'

'And to drink, sir?' The waiter once more smilingly dipped towards Howard.

'Oh, crumbs, a beer, please, a pint.' With the words out, Howard felt a clutch of panic and the urge to retrieve them. Drinking in his father's city, and him maybe as close as anything! But Howard's thirst was deep. 'And an Irn-Bru for the laddie.'

Saul watched the waiter recede through the empty restaurant and disappear through metal kitchen doors. 'What's that drink you ordered?'

'It's Scottish. You'll like it.'

'This is like being on holiday, isn't it?'

'Ay, it is,' Howard agreed, recalling Blackpool: his mother at a loss in her leisure, not knowing what to do, just walking around from place to place, allowing Howard a trickle of small change for the arcades, taking her time in the tea shops, sipping her tea, bright-eyed, unburdened, quiet. An endless week.

The waiter returned with drinks and bubbly poppadoms wider than the plate they balanced on. He jogged away again towards the noises of the kitchen and returned once more with chutneys.

Howard lifted his beer, considered it, said 'Cheers' to his small companion, and took a long, relieving pull. Every cell of his body seemed to get an immediate share, for they all relaxed in thanks. Saul, watching him very closely, said, 'Can I have a taste?' 'No,' Howard answered and broke the poppadoms into shards with a swipe of his hand.

'This tastes like bubblegum,' Saul said of his own drink with surprise. 'And it's orange.'

'That's right. Nice, though.'

Howard got to work with the mango chutney and ate.

Saul tried the same combination, his face pensive as he chewed, but he made a manful effort to like it and carried on. He made similar endeavours when his biriani arrived, taking at first small forkfuls from the perimeter of his heaped rice and wet curry while Howard breathed loudly through his nose and ate his passionately with a spoon.

Afterwards, Howard sat back and smoked, the blue curls rising from him as from the peaceful fire now banked down inside his gut. Saul kept nibbling and wanted to talk. His tone was of partaking in nonchalant restaurant conversation but his questions were starting to get urgent.

'So you moved down to England just with your mother?'

'That's right. I said that already.'

'Because your parents didn't get on.'

'That's right.'

'So where's your father now?'

Howard straightened his back. 'He's here. I mean, I think he's hereabouts, in Glasgow.'

'And is that why we've come here, then, to see him?'

Howard drank the last lacy remnant of his lager, deciding. 'That's right,' he confirmed in a voice he kept confident and level. 'Tomorrow, I'm thinking. Tomorrow.'

'But you don't know where he is exactly?'

'Not exactly, no.'

'He might be anywhere.'

'That's right.'

'Not in Glasgow even.'

'Aha.'

'Oh, we'll find him,' Saul said breezily. 'Look how far we've got already. I can't really believe it. Although obviously I know how we did it when I think about it.'

'I cannae believe it either. I can't believe I actually did it.'

'Do you think my parents will split up?'

'What?' Somehow, sitting up in his surprise, Howard found a way to burn the palm of his hand with his cigarette. He rubbed his hand hard on the tablecloth.

'I said do you think my parents will split up?'

'Well, no.' That was the point of them, surely? If Les and Barbara were anything, they were people who didn't split up. They were not like Howard's parents, or even anything in his world. They were serious and sober and so connected they weren't even quite two people. They were Les-and-Barbara. They stood there in Howard's mind not moving.

'I don't know,' Saul said, looking out of the window. 'Do you think they like each other? I mean really? My dad is very strict.'

Howard looked again at the picture of them in his mind, Maybe they did look quite hard and separate in his mind. But they did fit together. Their house was a machine. Their lives worked; things got done. There was no shouting, no sobbing, no blood ever. So what could be wrong?

'I think they're fine,' Howard comforted; 'they're just, you know, clever, busy people. They've got lots on their plates.'

'My mum should get a job.' This idea, which Saul would not have dared to utter at home, had struck him a few months ago as a brilliant solution. It would end that inactive solitude his mother had, the too-thoughtful silence which was scary with things she wasn't saying. 'She'll lose her marbles in that house on her own. And it'll be worse now I've failed and run away. They'll be so unhappy.' Saul held his forehead. 'But I needed to,' he reasoned to himself, lips trembling whitely. 'I needed to.'

'That's right,' Howard rushed to agree. 'You were in a bad way big time. We had to go.'

'But when we go back what's it going to be like?'

'When you go back, I cannae go with you. They'll bloody well arrest me.'

Saul looked at Howard, wiped his face with his sleeve. 'I'll ask them not to.' He sighed a long shaky breath. 'I'm tired,' he said. 'I want to go to bed.'

'Fine, let's go and find somewhere.'

'People are coming in now as well.' It was true. The first diners had arrived, a pair of short, square women with matching blonde hair that fitted their heads like floral swimming caps. Howard checked that he knew neither of them and averted his gaze. He paid the waiter quickly at the door with too many notes.

The receptionist wore a security badge on her lapel which showed her face uplifted and smiling inside a blonde bob but her real face was tired under dark, fringed hair. It spasmed suddenly with a corporate expression of welcome at the man in front of Howard in the queue then emptied instantly, like throwing something out of a bucket. Howard thought she must have been tired because of the conference. Behind Howard and Saul were suited businessmen. The entire lobby was full of businessmen drinking beer or coffee, with outspread papers or mattly glowing laptops, or standing alone talking into their mobile phones. Howard of course wanted fast service so as to be out of that crowd as soon as possible; they were exactly the sort of men who read papers and knew what was in the news.

She lifted her face finally to Howard and didn't even attempt to smile. He had never had the air of someone important or even acceptable, and he didn't expect anything else. Right now, the only point was to be quick. Her face looked trodden on by the day and Howard was scared of her eyes so he addressed himself to the genial blonde she had once been.

'I'd like a double room,' Howard said.

She looked at Saul. 'Are you two ...'

'We're brothers.'

'Brothers?'

'Aha.'

'You don't look very alike.'

'Can we have an en suite bathroom?' Saul said.

'We wouldn't look alike,' Howard explained. 'Different families.'

She flinched as she took in their almost simultaneous sentences, but fatigue stopped her from trying to untangle them. Her laminated blonde self at least seemed quite happy with the situation.

Finally she said, 'What's the name, please?'

'Michael Doyle,' Howard said.

'Really? I knew a Michael Doyle.'

Howard became animated. 'Really. And he's still alive; he hasn't passed away at all?' Howard heard the businessman behind them snigger.

Another hotel room with too many thoughts to contain in its plain small shell, the tight dead space with beds, mirror, TV, an empty wardrobe.

Saul took off his shoes and jacket and disappeared into the bathroom. His stomach had remained sensitive since even before the competition and his biriani now produced sharp liquid pains high in his abdomen.

Howard took off his anorak and hung it over the back of the chair; he didn't want to touch the wardrobe. In the scoop of his hood he saw something caught. He inspected. It was grass, a whiskery braid of seeds, the heavy head of a wild grass. It took Howard some moments to work out where it had come

274

from, tracing himself back through the day, restaurant to river to school to shops to Max and the truck to Alf and the car, Alf's flat, the field. The field and the horse. It was mind-blowing that that had been the same day. And that the horse was still there maybe. Howard sat down on the bed still holding the grass head, light and tacky, in his palm. Old-fashioned it looked, like something from the Bible. Was there a Bible illustration he was remembering? It placed in his mind the word 'harvest'.

Saul returned from the bathroom, his face wet and grey.

'Wee man, you remember the horsey this morning?'

'I'm very tired,' Saul said frowning, holding the top of his head. Then, as if he'd remembered what he needed to do next, he removed his shirt and trousers. 'I don't feel well.' He got into bed and held the covers under his chin with his fist.

'Oh no, what's wrong?'

'No, it's nothing bad, I'm just tired. My tummy's a bit upset.'

'Do you want me to get a doctor?'

Saul opened his eyes narrowly. 'Do you really think that's a good idea?'

Howard flexed the grass head in his hand. 'No,' he admitted. 'But I could go to the chemist for you, though.'

'No, I'm fine. I'm just tired. Just let me go to sleep.'

'Are you still thinking about your parents?'

'Howard, I just want to go to sleep,' Saul said in a crying voice. 'I don't want to think about my parents. I'm too tired to think about anybody, any bloody body. Just let me sleep.'

'Ay, sorry, wee man. I'll be quiet. Here, I'll pull the curtains.'

Howard induced twilight by drawing nubbly grey curtains that felt coarse and dead, curtains for government offices. Weren't they the same ones there had been in that lawyer's office where he'd failed Irina with his love for her. He sat back down on his bed and thought about how much he wanted a cigarette; there were still three or four in his packet.

He needed Saul to fall asleep.

He fell back on his own bed and looked at the ceiling tiles.

Marauding out of his mind's disorder came all the unsorted thoughts. They came as images mostly. His computer-aged face in the paper, turgid-fleshed, uncanny, a monster child. The three blocks of flats grouped in the distance from which a low, frightening sound seemed to come, a resonance he could feel in his chest. They would be there tomorrow waiting for him. The horse standing in the field. Les. Barbara. Les and Barbara. Saul calmly considering them splitting apart. Barbara sobbing. Misha. Irina. Irina. Her voice on the phone. Had Andy told anyone? Had Alf? His father. His father's red stubble. His father terrible to contain.

Howard got up and went to the bathroom.

Howard sat on the toilet to pee. He was too tired to try and aim in the cramped, mirrored space of the bathroom. Air conditioning had whirred as soon as he'd turned on the light, loud enough, it seemed, to wake Saul. Heart-sodden, Howard unwrapped a new bar of soap as he sat, unpicking a sealing sticker and spreading the crimped paper. He sniffed the white object a moment then threw it as hard as he possibly could into the little resounding bin.

When he came back into the room he heard the long, light notes of Saul's breathing and knew that the boy was asleep. So Howard was alone.

He rubbed his hands and pretended that he was glad and now could relax. He put the little plastic kettle on to boil and found that it made a terrible roar, spewing masses of steam, so that Howard felt like he was locked in the room with a maniac. When it finished he was so relieved, the relief was such a solid occurrence inside him that it seemed to have been the whole point and replaced the idea of making a drink which he now forgot to do.

He picked up the remote control for the television, made ready with the volume down button, and switched it on. It barked the word 'refugees' until he squeezed it silent. News.

He watched it with the sound switched off. He watched it until his own image appeared, the CCTV one. He wondered for a moment where he was going so hurried and suspicious. He watched until Les and Barbara appeared seated at a desk with policemen. He didn't dare switch up the volume. He watched Barbara in close-up weeping behind the silent glass.

He turned. Saul was still asleep.

Howard switched off the television with both hands and stood by the wardrobe, his forehead against it.

He was falling.

He looked at Saul to keep himself still. Saul was still there, still breathing, his light body coated with blankets. Whole. No one was hurt. Saul had been rescued; he lay on no stones with no blood kicking out.

Howard had a fantasy that had never left him of apologising to Fergus, pleading with him, his knees plunged into the sharp trackside stones, rain spitting on his neck. He pleads and pleads, exerting all of himself, pouring himself out in a pure beseeching stream, and Fergus forgives him.

Forgives him.

When dead, Howard had been forgiven. He had floated in bodiless whiteness above the bed and seen his mother floating also and had sung with wonderful heat of love and heavenly tears in his eyes her name. And he had known that he was through, forgiven.

This room was too small. He walked again into the bathroom, took off his glasses and washed his face. He hung blurred and dripping in the mirror opposite. He could smell his body odour rising from his squeezed, overlapping flesh. Maybe he'd wash his entire body. Thinking about it, he left the bathroom.

The room was so small he could feel other people pressing at its walls. There was a picture on one of them. He went over and looked at the picture. A small cottage with a ravel of smoke from its chimney, set under a glowing lilac mountain.

In the foreground orange sheep were tended by a rudimentary farmer in a smock, himself gently smoking through a pipe.

Howard sat down and rested his head on his forearms, his belly on his lap. He jerked and twitched a short way into sleep but found it awkward getting air into the crushed tubes of his throat. He sat up. The blood flowed out of his head, leaving it cold.

He should see his father. But why? Because it was time for payback? To show him Saul?

Because where else was he going?

July 13th

The thought stood perpendicular in his mind like a block of flats and then was erased by the brilliance of the next. To find out where someone lives you look them up in a phone book! He picked up the room key, kissed Saul's sleeping face and fled downstairs.

Down how many flights of stairs? He didn't know. He didn't remember even which floor his room was on. He knew very little – the stairs underneath him existed as a rippled chute. He ran down them so fast it was mostly falling. He only remembered when he reached the bottom that he'd run right past the lift.

The foyer was deserted apart from one tired businessman in an armchair who seemed asleep with a briefcase on his knees. What time was it? He couldn't have been upstairs for that long. He searched the wall for a clock, then his own wrist. It was just after midnight. He looked disbelievingly at the grey numbers of his watch and felt his head again run cold, his heart belatedly flummoxed by the stairs. His knees proclaimed their existence with an ache.

A phone book. A public phone. He searched, rocking backwards and forwards a few paces before choosing a direction. There was a sign. Back towards the stairs. Under a plastic hood placidly waited a phone. Under the phone were phone books. He tore into the top one, turning chunks of pages at a time. Donald MacNamee. Donald MacNamee. Donald Mac-Namee. And there it was finally, his own father's name, as plain as plain in the mesh of other innocent names and numbers. Donald MacNamee, his address and number available to anyone who picked up the book. For years it must have been there, unknown to him. Howard started tearing out the page as quietly as he could – there was no way he'd remember it in the morning. Howard heard a voice behind him.

'Hello, there. I was hoping I'd see you again this evening.'

'What?' Howard turned, guiltily stuffing the stolen page into his pocket as though it were the worst of his crimes.

The man's eyes were quick, glinting. 'Don't worry about that. I'm not interested in that.' It was the businessman from the armchair.

He stepped closer, close enough for Howard to smell on his breath a recent tuna sandwich. 'I've been waiting for you.'

'What? Who are you?'

The businessman sniggered. 'I'm surprised I am seeing you, actually. I know you have better things to be doing, but we live in hope. You're the fellow with the little "brother".' He clawed the air with inverted commas. 'I was behind you in the queue.'

'I don't know what you're talking about. I'm going to bed.'

'You improvised that rubbish about being brothers. Well, well. Whatever works, I always think. It made me laugh, I have to say.'

'I don't know what you're talking about, pal. I'm going to bed.' Howard walked away quickly now into the foyer but the man followed him. And grabbed his arm.

'You do know what I'm talking about. You know exactly what I'm talking about. Slow down a second, please. And I'm not being unfriendly. All I'm asking is a little time with him myself.'

'What the fuck're you talking about?'

'I have money. I have lots of money. And I wouldn't hurt him.'

'Are you ... are you ...?'

The man's face said that he was. 'It's not an unreasonable

request. I mean, you wouldn't want others to know what you're already up to, would you?'

'If … if …'

The man laughed in Howard's purpling face. He lifted his chin and shouted: 'Wake up! Wake up, hotel! Help! Help! A monster!'

Blood buckled in Howard's temples and the strength of a bomb went down his arms. Howard grabbed at the man's throat, getting hold of skin and lapel.

'Don't …' The man's eyes were terrified. 'I was joking. I thought … It was just a request. As a fellow—'

Howard grabbed him with his other hand, both now around the man's throat.

'I … will call … police,' the man said, thick-tongued, lightly holding Howard's wrist.

'You will not, you fuck,' Howard said quietly. 'Because I have done nothing to that boy, who's my friend by the way, and if the police start on investigating *you* they're gonnee find some filth, eh?'

The man's eyes grew fat; his lips writhed to form words he could give no sound.

Not since Ridgemont had Howard used his strength like this, for safety and control, and it returned to him now as a skill long mastered. He felt cleanly focused and quite calm inside the moment's emergency. Certainly everything was clear. His arms were straight lines, his thumbs strong. He had his father's address. He knew where he was going. He had Saul in his care.

'Now listen, pal. In a second I'm gonnee let go of you and you're gonnee go away nice and quiet. And if you make any trouble, you wee fucking perv, I will come after you and hurt you. Y'understand?'

The businessman was trying to pry his fingers under Howard's hand. Howard rocked him from side to side by his throat. 'Y'understand?'

Howard felt the man's muscles move for a nod. He let go.

The man fell to his knees holding his crushed neck, making rasping, glottal, choking sounds.

'You're all right,' Howard told him. 'Just get up.'

The man managed to get up onto one knee, staring up, still choking, as though proposing to Howard in dolphin language.

'You're all right,' Howard repeated and helped him up. 'Just go to your room and keep quiet and don't come out until ten o'clock in the morning. You're lucky you didn't get worse, you fucking perv.' Howard tried to remain calm as the angering thoughts came home. What this man was, what he'd said, what he thought. 'Now fuck off before I get angry.'

The man nodded, breathing almost regularly, and walked to the lift.

Howard watched him go. His fingers felt strained. He pushed his glasses back up his sweaty nose and set off up the stairs to get Saul. Evidently it was time to leave. Saul who this man would have ... who thought that Howard was, had ... and wasn't that what the police thought, the newspapers, everyone? It made him want to cry that the world had him so mistaken. And not for the first time. The word 'monster' chased him as he yanked his way up the bannister, taking the stairs two at a time.

Howard cleaned himself in the bathroom as best he could then rushed to wake Saul, who was hard to rouse. Howard had to resort to picking him up out of bed and setting him down on his collapsing legs. Doing so, Howard found himself supporting him with one hand momentarily on his buttocks, bare where his pants had ridden up. Nausea washed through him. That anyone could think ... that the whole world thought! And here he was with the nearly naked boy – that he loved, he would admit it – in his arms. He wanted him safely dressed as quickly as possible. 'Saul, Saul, Saul, Saul,' he said into his ear. 'We have to go. This is an emergency, big time.'

Howard dropped him onto his bed and fetched his clothes. Saul came to as Howard was dressing him. 'Tired,' he said.

'Uch, I know. But we've no choice.'

Saul made crying noises, rolling his head. 'What's happening? Where am I?'

'Stop acting, wee man, and move. Come on, Sauly-boy. We'll away. Now.'

'All right, all right.' Saul wiped his mouth and fell past Howard to put on his shoes. 'Is it the police?' he asked.

'It could be. But not yet. Quick.'

They bundled out of the room into the silence of the corridor. Howard fled for the stairs, pulling Saul with him, who held him back, reaching for the lift button as they went past. They ran downstairs together. Saul whined, 'Why are we running? I'm tired. Why do we have to go anywhere?'

'Look, we have to keep moving, wee man,' Howard answered as they started across the foyer. 'We're on the run. So we have to run.'

'Why are we on the run? I don't want to run. What have you done? Is it because you are a criminal. You are!'

'Saul, for fuck's sake!' Howard grabbed Saul by the collar of his jacket and dragged him out through the automatic doors. Cold air made him shiver. His fingers twisted painfully as Saul struggled against his grip.

'Saul, calm down. I'm no going to hurt you. Be quiet right now.'

'Help!' Saul cried. 'Help!'

Howard shook him. 'Shut up. Shut up, you little fuck. I said I'm no going to hurt you. There was a man in there that wanted to hurt you. This man did. So I fought him and now we've got to go.'

'What are you talking about!' Tears, yellow in the street light, shone on Saul's face.

'That man in there was a pervert. He wanted ... he wanted to rape you. He asked me if he could.'

'What are you talking about? I'm not a lady. You can't rape me.'

'Yes, he could. He could have abused you. He bloody well thought *I* was abusing you. He wanted to hurt you. He thought that's what I was doing.' Howard, fighting his own confusion, grabbed Saul in a hug, capturing his sharp arms awkwardly inside his own. 'Please, Saul, please. We've got to get away.'

'What did you do to him?'

'It was just, you know, karate. Very simple. He'll be fine in a minute. Please. This way.' Howard stood up, firmly took Saul's hand and started walking, he didn't know in which direction. Towards the centre maybe. Behind him was the pervert choking in his room, maybe calling the police already, their own abandoned room, the television in which Barbara had silently sobbed for her son. In his pocket was his father's address. In his hand, the distraught, frightened boy he was saving. Right now that boy asked him to walk more slowly.

'I'm sorry, wee man, I'm sorry, I'm sorry.' Howard apologised for everything else as well. He felt a few drops of rain hitting his head. One struck the left lens of his glasses, melting a streak of night. Howard would have liked a deluge, crashing waters to wipe out the city, a long and punishing rain. That he could be thought a paedophile! Nausea swamped him again, his biriani in his stomach. And this was what the whole world thought. His distress knew no limits. Oh come, rain, fall, rain, fall and fall.

The rain remained light, barely noticeable. Like the rain with Fergus. Howard was a criminal, was useless and appalling; the police were after him, but the disaster was too large to get worked up about – it was quite beyond him. As long as he thought about no particular aspect of the situation but held it all in his mind as one single explosion, then there was nothing he could do and nothing he could worry about. He just kept on walking with Saul by his side.

The false calm created by the clumped, indistinct mass of

his thoughts didn't last. Saul had questions that needed specific answers. Saul asking, 'So you know karate, then?' was enough to dislodge him back into that particular chaos, the man's eyes, vascular and distended, as he writhed beyond breath. 'Ay, I do,' Howard mumbled in answer. 'Just enough to get out of scrapes.'

They were walking past dark shops now, their own wavering orange-grey reflections accompanying them in the vitrines. So they must have been heading for the centre.

A door opened between two shops and twenty or so people flooded out onto the street, laughing and whooping. Thudding music was cut off when the door swung shut behind them. Howard considered turning on his heels but it was too late, he was already among the people.

One of them stopped just in front of his face and cheered. 'Waaay!' he cried, raising both arms. His hair was sweaty. Some of his friends cheered as well. A ring of girls held each other and tried to dance in step, raising their legs alternately and staggering. The boy in front of Howard grinned broadly. 'Oh what a beautiful morning!' he sang.

Saul wound himself closer into Howard's side.

'You got a ciggy?' the young man asked Howard, who looked only for a route through the crowd.

'Oh, ay.' Howard reached into his pocket and proffered the open end of the pack. The man took two, tucking one behind his ear, one in his mouth, and winked.

'I know you!' Another man staggered towards them. 'I know you, frae the telly. Fuck me.' He was caught in a net of girls' arms and surrounded by laughter. Howard and Saul ran.

'Waay!' the crowd cheered. 'Waay!' And buried in their noise was the man's voice saying, 'I'm sure I seen him. Jesus fuck, who is he again?'

Two taxis sleeked towards the group, their headlights casting horror-movie shadows of Howard and Saul as they ran, all knees and flailing arms. Howard yanked Saul around a corner into a narrow street.

They turned left and headed back on themselves, away from the middle of town, parallel to the clubbers. The right-angled geometry of it was unsensed by Howard, who walked hollowed out with adrenalin along pavements that billowed under him, masts of orange street lamps swaying overhead, the wind mercifully chilling some of the sweat off his face. Almost recognised, and there was the pervert probably describing him into his phone right now.

Howard looked down to check that Saul was still attached to his hand. He was, his eyes half-closed as he stumbled forwards. See, everything was all right. The man in the hotel had been a pervert – Howard should actually have dispatched him to hell. He regretted that he hadn't.

'Slow down, slow down,' Saul moaned. Howard realised that with these thoughts he'd been gaining speed. 'Why don't we stop here?' Saul asked. 'We could rest here.' They were standing by a bus shelter, a three-sided cabin with a bench underneath a huge shivering oak tree.

'Okay,' Howard agreed. 'Good idea.'

The bench didn't seem to have been made for prolonged sitting, nor for a bum of Howard's size. It was a tilted plastic plank which poured Howard's weight down through his aching knees. Saul rested his head against Howard's shoulder and the big man put an arm around him. Saul quickly seemed to be asleep again. Stranded in the effort to hold himself up, Howard blinked, listened to the wind riffling the tree, and took the moment to release a fart which seemed to have corners and came out sideways. Opposite him were homes with dark windows and cars outside, windows behind which people slept, normal people, real people, the others. For a while there he'd been turning into one of them what with his decent job and thinking about getting a flat and his Russian situation. Not any more, though. He was right back outside where he'd always been. But then again other rescuers were lonely. Superman, for example, could have no real friends.

Howard heard footsteps.

He continued to hear footsteps. They didn't click like a woman's shoes. A man was coming.

Was he hidden enough – could he just sit it out?

No, he knew what to do. He placed a hand over poor Saul's mouth and shook him awake. He picked him up, released his mouth (Saul had understood) and took up a position pressed against the end wall of the shelter. In silence they waited until the footsteps reached them and a figure appeared. A man. Just a man walking. He didn't stop. When he was ten yards away Howard and Saul slid around the shelter wall until they were on the other side, again out of sight. When the steps were gone and the only sound was again the wind in the tree, they sat back down on the painful bench.

Again Saul fell asleep and this time Howard joined him part way, nodding and nodding. He was woken by someone he hadn't had the cunning to avoid who stood right there, a man with a trolley and a broom saying indistinctly, 'You cannae stay here.' Howard flinched awake. 'What?' he asked.

'You cannae stay here. I have to clean this one now.' The man's words were wet and mumbled. He sounded just like . . . He had the same repaired hare lip. It was, Howard saw. It was Billy.

'Oh my God,' Howard said to himself. Was he dreaming? He shook his head the way television had taught him to dispel illusions. But the figure didn't change. It was him. Billy didn't seem to be recognising him. There was a long stare between them. Billy's eyes in the darkness were only half visible but Howard felt them swivelling away from his face. Billy didn't like to look at you straight. He looked at your throat when he talked to you, very specifically at your throat, which was unnerving even though it was obviously only because he was too scared to look you in the eye. He'd always been out of it.

When Howard arrived at Ridgemont Billy had just made himself famous by accepting a dare to eat the cube of bleach out of a urinal. He'd done it, crunching it and swallowing it down, puking only hours later, having held it down growling, shaking, sweating, staring furiously ahead and sitting as still as he could. So this was where he'd ended up.

'Billy, is it you?' Howard asked, full of an affection he certainly hadn't felt all those years ago when Billy was just another nutter to be avoided.

Billy shied his head, mumbling.

'Billy, I said is it you?'

'I've got to clean here,' Billy said. Billy's eyes were opaque, downcast, black as felt. If he recognised Howard he was refusing to mention it and felt none of the big man's warmth at reunion. So he was still just surviving, trying to go unhurt.

'You're all right there, pal. We'll move on.'

'Move on,' Billy mumbled. 'Got to clean it up.'

Howard took the now woken Saul quietly away, trying to shake wakefulness into his cold, delirious head. Of all the people to bump into again strange that it should be Billy. Howard hadn't thought of him for years, or even really known him. At least Billy would be too out of it to tell anyone. Howard and Saul carried on away from town and turned up right again where they had found themselves by a park.

'Nobody goes into a park at night,' Saul sensibly commented.

'Good thinking,' Howard said. 'I'll give you a leg up.'

With some struggle Saul was delivered over the railings, jumping onto grass. His landing looked painful and mistimed. He hit the ground like a sack full of tools and took a moment before he got back onto his feet.

Howard then thought to consider his own position on the street side of the fence. There was no way he could pull himself up by his arms so they jogged along together like forbidden lovers with the railings blurring between them until Howard found a green electricity box he could use as a step. He got one foot up on the railings and flung himself over the top, landing on the cold, greasy grass more or less on his face, giving a stout, ringing blow to his forehead. But when he pushed himself back up onto his feet he found that they were now in and safe with a railing behind them and an entire empty park in which to hide. Saul seemed happy too. He spread out his arms like two drooping wings as they walked through the green and black darkness by small blustery bushes and creaking trees. There was even a river, black and smooth in the night, darkly flowing, because rivers do not know night or day and flow constantly, every moment towards the sea. This was something that Saul had never properly realised before. It arrived as another small revelation along his journey. Max the lorry driver would already have known it, he reflected. Probably he even fished at night.

Together they found a stone shelter of similar design to the bus stop but with deeper, more sincere wooden benches, and together they resumed their bus shelter posture, leaning together for warmth and security, and together they fell asleep.

Saul woke up in darkness because of a sound. Not Howard's snoring, which was quite constant, even pleasant, warm and furrowed like corduroy, but a different sound, a slithering, a shifting. Saul opened his eyes and saw in the darkness the dark shape of a man sitting on the floor, leaning against a wall of the shelter. Saul tried to pretend he hadn't woken up, keeping as still as he could. He could always wake Howard if he needed to; meanwhile it was probably safest not to show any sign of life. The dark shape had hinges he could identify as elbows and knees. The man was doing something. There was a splutter of light from a cigarette lighter and before he could close his eyes Saul saw a thin, yellow face with bits of beard and purple lips. Through his eyelids, Saul could see that the light was gone. He opened his eyes a fraction. The man had one trouser leg rolled up. With the quiet concentration of an engraver at work, the man injected himself near the ankle. It became very difficult for Saul's breath to counterfeit sleep as his heart raced in terror. Drowning inside himself, Saul now assumed he would have to wake Howard when the man went berserk on drugs. But the man hardly did anything. He tossed the needle away into the grass, leaned his head back against the bricks, and let out a long sigh through his teeth. He twitched a couple of times but that was it. Saul watched for a few minutes, but still the man did nothing, so he closed his eyes and pretended to be asleep. His breathing slowed with his heart rate. Howard kept snoring. Saul fell back to sleep.

He woke once more in thick, grey dawn light and the man was gone. Relieved, his heavy eyelids rolled down and again he fell asleep.

A voice said to Howard, 'Are you a religious man? Are you? I am. Very religious. Very religious.'

Howard opened his eyes and his brain was flooded with the wet white light of dawn. In the middle of this light was a face from which the voice issued, a bearded face, red and cracked like a smashed brick. Grass shuddered into view behind the face. The man's breath was a gusting alcoholic vapour as he spoke. 'I'm a religious man,' he continued, 'not Catholic or Proddy or anything. I'm a Quaker. And do yous know what that means?' He gestured with the forefinger of a hand wrapped around a can of cider. 'It means that one is silent for ages and ages, then I say what I fucking well think. I say the truth, you ken?'

Howard did not know what to say. Saul was still asleep against him. He said, 'Who are you?'

'Nice one. Nice question. Here I am.' He spread his hands. 'If you want a name is what you're after you can say John. I'm John.'

John swigged from his can. He swallowed and burped through his teeth. 'I know who yous two are,' he said. 'I read all the papers when I'm settling down. So I know who yous two are. You're him that's run away and the genius boy. You're taking care of him, then?'

'That's not who we are, you drunk fuck. I don't know who you're even thinking of. We're ... This is my nephew, Saul ... omon.'

'Solomon. Oh, Jeese. Whatever you say, pal. I bet wee Solomon's all sore from the bumfucks, eh? That's why he's sleeping, maybe. Shall I wake him up and ask him?' John stretched a chicken's-foot hand towards Saul's knee.

'You touch him and I'll pull the fucking head off of you! You ken?'

Saul moaned at the sudden noise.

'Eh, I'll ask him,' John threatened.

'That's it.' Howard let go of Saul and surged forwards with his arms out towards John.

The tramp slithered onto his back and pleaded. 'A joke, a wee joke. Don't. Stop. Come awn. I'll shout for the police.'

'What's going on?' Saul was awake now.

'Nothing,' Howard barked. 'Just a tramp bothering us. Wants some money.'

'Ay, that's all,' John said. 'Just a wee bit of money, for a bru. I'll be quiet.'

Howard studied John's battered head wavering against the sweet greenness of the grass. Visions, one at a time, and you spoke to them as they came. One day it would make sense. Meanwhile you just did what you had to do.

'You've got some change, haven't you? He'll go away after that,' Saul prompted. Howard scooped all of the change he had out of his anorak pocket and handed it over.

'Uch, that's very kind,' John said, 'very kind.'

'It's not kind. You threatened me,' Howard objected.

'There's no need to get aggressive, son. I was just asking for the price of a bru. Between friends.'

'You threatened to call the police.'

'Fuck off. Hey, what do you call a Russian prostitute?'

'Not in front of my boy. Are the gates open?'

'No, but you could get out. Getonyerbackyoubitch,' John said and laughed, wheezing out through broken teeth.

'That's an old one. Are the gates open?' Howard repeated.

'Don't call the police,' Saul begged. 'Nothing's wrong.'

'In an hour. Maintenance only. But you can slip through. Has Solomon got any money for me?'

'Fuck off.'

'Aw, it's just a favour.'

'Fuck off.'

John stood up and raised an orator's arm, taking a deep breath before shouting, 'You fuck off! This is my chamber, Mr Criminal! So you just go yoursel', giving orders to me. That's what I say to yous.'

Howard led Saul away. 'Don't worry about him,' he said. 'Just drunk. They all get like that.'

'Mr Criminal,' Saul moaned. 'Everyone says you're a criminal.'

'He's drunk. How does he even know what he's saying?'

Saul's tired legs stumbled and he suddenly fell onto his hands and knees on the damp grass, still as a table. 'Come on,' Howard said, but Saul stayed down.

'Ow,' he said quietly.

'You're all right.' Howard lifted him with a hand under one shoulder. Saul stood a moment, dark circles on his knees, swaying, recovering the energy to carry on.

'That hurt.'

'You're fine. Toughie.'

'Toffee?'

'Toffee? Toughie. Don't be stupid, come on. Aw, Jees, though, look.' Howard pointed towards the path, the gate and the maintenance vehicles on the way. 'How do we get out now? I'm not going over the fence. People'll see.'

'Just walk past them,' Saul said, his voice flat, uninterested.

'We can't.'

'I will.' Saul started walking. Howard followed. Eventually, as they passed, Howard could see through the white sky reflected in the windscreens and found there was no one in them. Somewhere away behind was the fritter and buzz of vegetation being mechanically stripped.

Howard took hold of the heavy, cold gate, pulled it open, and out they went.

The city had hardly woken. Occasionally trucks grunted past, but they were alone on the pavement, as though let loose in an empty house. The stone quietly rung with their steps. Heavy-limbed, speechless, they pushed through the blurred, early air.

They passed a business building of some kind: upswept blue glass, with a large vent in one side pumping out warm, second-hand air. They walked through the hot noise then Saul went back. 'Let's stay a minute,' he shouted. 'I'm cold.' So Howard joined him.

'You've got something in your eye,' Howard said, pointing at a blot of mucus stuck in Saul's lashes.

'Where?' Saul said, hunched and squinting. Where his hair was blown open, his scalp showed like the centre of a flower.

Howard pointed again. Saul wiped at the bridge of his nose but didn't retrieve the thing.

'Here.' Howard went in to get it himself, pressing his finger into the warm, trembling corner of Saul's eye and scooping out the mess.

'You're too rough,' Saul said and Howard wiped his finger down his coat.

Howard couldn't hear him in the noise of the vent. 'What?'

Saul took hold of his sleeve and pulled him into the adjacent quiet.

'You're too rough.'

'I got it out,' Howard replied, one side of his face now dry and tight from the blasting vent.

'Mr Criminal.'

'You what?'

'And you never finished telling me what happened, about the boy you maimed.'

Howard took a step, to be further from the roaring behind him. 'Yes, I did. I told you.'

The expression on Saul's face was weary, cynical, even spiteful. 'I did tell you.'

'No, you didn't.'

'Okay, hang on. I said it was an accident, didn't I?'

'What kind of an accident?'

Telling Saul this time, Howard suffered no real remembering, which made it easier. In fact, he delivered his statement watching Saul's reaction, adjusting it as he went. 'I was bullied. Okay, so, that was going on. You know, a lot. And I had enough in the end ...'

'What kind of bullying?'

'The normal. Names. I was always fat, so, you know. And kicking and punching. Hiding my stuff. Other things. And I had enough in the end and fought back and that was when the accident happened.'

Saul nodded.

'There were four of them. Then just one. We were on train tracks. Didn't I tell you this bit? Anyway, he was on me and I hit him and he fell and got hurt ... under a train.'

'Did he die? Oh no,' Saul corrected himself. 'He was maimed.'

'Ay. He was hurt properly badly, right enough. His hand.' Howard held up his own hand in useless clarification. 'And I got, you know ...' Saul's face showed that he definitely didn't know. '... sent away.'

'To prison?'

'Yep. Remand. Young offenders. You know, youth prison.'

'What was that like? Wasn't it horrible?'

Howard laughed and then for a while couldn't stop, carried away by the comedy of it, too weak to resist: this polite boy looking up at him with a dirty, sincere, innocent face, asking in his proper accent if Ridgemont was 'horrible'.

'What? What did I say?'

'Yes,' Howard answered, sobering. 'Yes, it was horrible. Really, totally horrible. You'll never know.'

'Maybe I will,' Saul said with a sting of pride.

'No, please God you won't. You haven't done anything wrong, anyway.' Surely the boy would never know: impossible that a child like this would end up in a place like Ridgemont, seeing the things that Howard had seen.

'Yes, I have. I've run away. But anyway, how did you survive?'

Howard shrugged. 'Dunno. Didn't die, I suppose. That's the main thing, isn't it, for surviving. You hungry?' He ruffled Saul's hair, or tried to; unwashed, it was a little greasy.

'Don't do that,' Saul complained.

'I'm hungry,' Howard went on. 'There's bound to be a café open with no one in it and all the sausages waiting for us. Come on. And then we're on a visit.'

Three hours later, awake with much coffee, with sweet breakfast meats turning to one gnarl of gristle inside him, his face and hands approximately clean from the café toilet although his trousers and shirt smelt acridly human, Howard stood outside what he thought was his father's front door waiting for the surge of courage that would carry his hand to the bell.

Saul stood beside him, exhausted and irritable, tired at the prospect of meeting another stranger, particularly one Howard said was so horrible. He felt no real fear, though; he'd been through so much in the last few days and survived it all that he was starting to think that nothing could harm him, that he was invincible. Besides, one thing he had definitely learned was that you can always run away. 'So,' he said, 'go on, then.'

'Sshh,' Howard hissed. His world turned black and white and trembly for a moment as he adjusted his glasses with the hand holding the page from the telephone directory. The wind was strong. They were just across the road from the river and docks, the whole ruined place with its cold, shining water. Howard was relieved that he hadn't had to walk any further into Govan or out to the flats where his life had started. This was far enough.

The house Howard stood in front of was surprisingly decent. Only one floor, it was a bungalow, a red-brick thing set with others along a small curving road. The bricks were bright and unweathered; there was an ornamental circle of them around the doorway and textured glass in the door. The house number was of flashing silver numerals. The smartness of the place made Howard wonder if the Donald MacNamee he'd found in the phone book was the right one. There must be a dozen of them in Scotland.

It was the momentary doubt, the suspicion that he would find himself apologising and backing away from a stranger, awash with relief, that allowed Howard's hand to float up and press the bell.

Nothing. Saul looked at Howard. Howard pressed the bell again. Was it too early? He pressed the bell again.

There was a noise inside, a voice, not a word just a voice, a groan, and footfalls.

Through the textured glass Howard saw a man growing larger, watery and indistinct, a pink head and a blue body. As though preparing for a formal photograph, Howard placed his hand on Saul's shoulder.

The door opened and Howard's eyes fixed on the man's face. It was him. His face had narrowed and hardened and some of his bulk was gone. Howard sensed rather than saw this; his eyes were fixed on the face. Donald MacNamee's blue dressing gown could have been whelming seawater far below for all Howard knew. What else was different? The hair. There was much less and it had faded to a yellow-grey although the chin was still rusty with red stubble. There were broken blood vessels in his cheeks, little red fibres that wormed through the flesh. Was he drunk? Howard couldn't smell anything. Did he recognise who'd come knocking?

'What happened to your hair?' Don asked.

'Wha?' Howard kept forgetting his cunning black hair. He held Saul for support, shocked by his father's voice.

He held him too hard and Saul twisted under his hand and cried out, 'Ow!'

'You're no hurting him, are ye?' Don asked.

Howard answered him in a fury, much louder than he'd intended. 'No way! I am not at all! Not at all!'

'He isn't,' Saul corroborated.

'All right, all right.' Don had winced and stepped back at the force of Howard's reply. Eye level, Howard realised; for the first time in his life he was eye level with his father. Howard could just hit him if he wanted to, just lay him out flat. Why didn't he?

Howard felt a disturbance at ankle height, a soft pushing which he now connected with his father's stumble. He looked down and saw streaked brown fur, then a cat's neat face looking up at him. The mouth opened and it mewed. Saul bent down and stroked its head.

'Don't let him run out,' Don said to Saul, and Howard knew that he wanted to prevent any direct contact between Don and Saul. He also saw in that moment a gap in Don's mouth, a missing tooth. 'I'm going inside,' Don said, pushing the cat in with his foot. 'Come if you want.' Don turned and retreated up the hallway. The slab of his back was so familiar it felt cold in Howard's mind. He stepped into the house, where Saul already was, rummaging in the cat's fur. Fear rose out of him, turned in a nauseous slow swirl and collapsed back. He closed the door. Saul looked up and whispered, 'Does he speak English?'

'What?' Howard was too distracted for a joke. 'Oh, the accent. It is a wee bit thick.'

They walked in, down a wallpapered hall, and found Don

in his small kitchen. It was new, bare, and dirty with stacked plates, glasses everywhere, and pebbles of cat food around a plastic bowl.

'Would yous like a drink, tea or whatnot?'

Howard saw bottles around a dustbin. 'Drinking yoursel' then?' His father blinked.

Howard saw a bread knife on the table. His mind thrilled along its edge for a moment. He saw himself plunge it in, scarlet blood fountaining from his father's chest. He blinked.

'I don't want anything,' Saul said. 'May I sit down?'

'What? Oh, ay, ay,' Don answered. '*Mia casa.*'

Saul squeaked out a chair and sat at the table with the knife, newspapers, a loaded ashtray and a box of Coco Pops.

'Why don't you and me leave the lad alone, go for a wee talk maybe?' Howard suggested.

'Oh fine. No drink?'

'Not for me.'

'Okay then. Through here.'

Howard watched his father walk on ahead and noticed that the shoulders looked soft, like the strength had gone out of them. A man living alone, drinking.

Saul was relieved when they'd gone, taking their weird mood with them. He opened a paper to read. Too tired to be excited by the girls he opened one of the ones about horses.

The room Don lead Howard to was also compact and squalid but this bungalow was so new and orderly that the squalor lay as a thin film over its hard decency.

'How d'you get this place?' Howard asked.

'Council. No bad, eh? Sit down.'

Don sat on a wooden-framed sofa with large green cushions, leaving Howard an armchair of the same design beside a loud television. Don leaned back, his bare feet nearest to his son, and started to roll a cigarette, gathering papers and tobacco from the cushion beside him. Howard said nothing and watched the sixty-year-old's careful preparations, the slight frown as he flattened hairy tobacco into a paper, rolled it, licked, plugged it into his mouth and lit it with a plastic lighter held sideways. He looked like an invalid. The desire to thump him seemed gross; it was obviously far too late. The urgency in Howard's chest was ebbing away.

'Do you mind if I turn the telly off?' he asked.

Don nodded, drawing deeply on his cigarette. Howard leaned across and silenced the daytime programme; its bright peach studio disappeared.

'I saw you on there,' Don told him. He raised a loose fist. 'Go on, sonny-boy!' His laugh afterwards was like a window swinging open in a storm, loud air from his decrepit lungs and the gap in his teeth – a missing incisor – clearly visible. How could Howard confront his father if he wasn't the same? 'The police havenae caught up with you then?'

Howard shook his head. Any minute now, though, he thought, they'd be coming through that door. So what did he want to say?

It was Don who started talking. 'I was telling ... there's a man comes here, pal of mine, he's ... We sit and have a few brus, his name's George. Anyways, I was telling him about you on the news and all that and he had a few suggestions, you ken, about what might be going on and I said,' Don rose up in his seat, '"No way, not my boy, he's no like that." And the laddie seems okay. So what are you running away for anyway?'

'Ah.' Howard thought for a moment, coming out of the trance of watching his father talk. 'We had to get away. He was collapsing and stuff. It sounds stupid now you say it but, you know, it was very stressful. I needed to get him away. From London.'

'Oh, ay.' Maybe 'from London' had made sense to Don. Howard couldn't tell what of that had entered his brain. The hand that held his cigarette was smooth and mauve, the swollen, cracked, shiny hand of an alcoholic.

'London,' Don echoed. 'The police said you were there.'

'The police have been here?'

'Oh ay. I didn't tell them anything, though. Didn't know anything.'

'When was this?'

'Couple of days ago. Dinnae fret. I didn't tell them anything. Didn't know. And I wouldn't. So, anyway, what can I do for you?'

He was chirpy, this wasted father, as though short on visitors and, more to the point, Howard thought, as though with no recollection of how they'd parted, of how many times he'd planted those fists on his wife and the son sitting in front of him. Howard sat there for a moment as forcefully as he could, gripping his knees, staring into the old man, challenging him, *I'm here, I'm here,* but Don hardly seemed aware. Maybe the drink had burned it all away and he no longer knew. Maybe he didn't think there was anything wrong with it in the first place. But you can't – you can't hit a woman and not know. His wife had left him. His wife! Howard's heart gripped at his blood. Did he even know that? His throat clogged as he tried to speak. Repeating the word 'Ma' he fought his voice back into place.

'What's that?' Don took a sip, quite daintily but long, from a can of lager he had by his feet.

'Ma,' Howard said. 'You know, Ma …'

'I know.' Don shook his head. 'She's dead. The police told me.' He took another long sip; Howard could hear the beer running into his mouth. 'I'm sorry, son. Really, I am.'

Howard held his hands over his mouth to keep it all in. He confused Don by standing up a moment then sitting down again. Don shook his head and muttered something.

Howard waited till the crisis of emotion had drained out of him, leaving his head dizzy and cold. Glassily he watched his father, the man he'd raced up the country to see only to find he wasn't there. There was no sign of matching emotion in him; he seemed hollowed out. The man was an empty socket where his father had been. Even talking of his ex-wife's death there was nothing. Howard realised that only he would carry it around, only he was in possession of it. More than ever he'd make a sanctuary of his memories. But here in this room, nothing. None of Howard's life was there. No Fergus, Alf, his mother, Mrs Dawson, Misha, Irina. Only Saul in the next room. Tired and weak inside his anorak, Howard stood up again to go out to his small friend.

'Where're you going?'

'Water, kitchen. To see the boy.'

'Oh, ay. Would you put the telly on on your way out?'

Les sat beside Barbara in front of the breakfast news. He had had the foresight to put down his mug of coffee – he didn't want to be holding boiling liquid when they appeared – and now had his left arm around the hard, trembling shell of Barbara's back as she wept with herself on the screen. Les chewed his lips and willed the broadcast out into the deepest reaches of the world, pushing it with his mind into criminal flats, into the minds of strangers who didn't yet realise what they vitally knew. Then they were finished and it hadn't been nearly long enough. Les could feel people ignoring, feel their crying faces sink through the air as to the bottom of an ocean.

What could be worse than this? Les ran his hand across Barbara's shoulders as they shook and his own eyes watered. You live a life calmly and productively, all the time expecting grief, expecting the terrible events you know you'll have to live through, but for it to be this. So much worse, so much stranger than could have been imagined. It made his father's death seem . . . and the thought of the turmoil around his bankruptcy almost made Les laugh. He laid his head back on the sofa, looked up at the pale blue ceiling, and radiated his will out through every pore in his body. If only he could be wrong. If only it wasn't already over. If only it would end, so terrible it must cry out to the world and get an answer. It must.

Saul sat at the small square, littered table with the paper open in front of him, his eyes closed but his lips mumbling. The cat crunched a bit of food in the side of its mouth.

'Saul.' Howard spoke his name and gently touched the top of his head. The large eyes opened.

'It's easy memorising the names of horses because their names are all so different.'

'Are you okay, wee man?'

'Fine. Maybe my brain likes memorising things again.'

'Maybe.'

'I wonder who won the competition. Somebody must have won it.'

'I suppose.'

'Are we going now? It's not very nice here.'

Poor Saul. It had all been about rescuing him until Howard had become distracted by his own adventure, dragging the boy around. 'Aha, yes. I think we will.'

'The police might arrive.'

'You never know.'

'Bang the door down.'

His own sense of destination now expired, Howard asked Saul, 'Where would you like to go?'

'Back to London.'

'Really?'

'I don't mean—' Saul corrected himself, hiding his desire for home: 'I mean, we could go back to your friends, couldn't we? To Varya's?'

'Oh yes, Misha.' Of course. Misha was bound to have some ideas. He always had plenty. Saul was typically clever to think of it. 'Saul, can I borrow your phone off you?'

'Of course.' Saul stretched out his aching legs to reach into his pocket. 'There you are.'

Howard received the phone, warmed to Saul's temperature. 'I'll just be out back here.' He nodded towards the back door. 'Just shout if you need me.'

'I'll shout.'

At the door Howard felt the cat's body flow across his ankle. He steered it back with a foot, resisting its light, determined head, and let himself out.

Clear air. Scrappy blue distances through broken cloud. There were a few square yards of concrete and weeds grown right through it, shivering over their shadows. He breathed out and in, and dialled.

'Hello, hello? Misha?'

'Oh my God, Howard? Is you?' Misha's voice, as usual, was loud. Howard pulled the receiver a little away from his ear.

'Misha, everything's fine, sort of; no one's hurt or anything—'

'Howard, shut up. Where are you?'

Howard hunched forward, touching his bald spot. 'We're away right now. Not far really. Please, Misha, I—'

'Howard.' Misha's voice was deep as he took control. 'Howard, I told you go home when you come here. Stop to run away. And look now what is happening. Policemen. Newspapers.'

'It's all right, Misha. I know it looks bad.'

'Looks bad! You in papers. Is he killer? Is he molestator? Where are you? You must come back now. We still need you for helping Irina. She can't start now with new person. So you come back and beg not guilty and come back. Oh my God, Saul! Why am I not ask about Saul?'

'He's fine, he's fine. You know I'm no like that. I wouldn't hurt him. He's precious.'

'I know? What do I know, choosing madman to help? Where are you?'

'Misha.'

'What?'

'Would it be okay if we came back to your place?'

'No.'

'But, Misha—'

'First go back to his poor crying parents on the television on your knees and beg and if you don't go to prison you carry on to help me and Irina and Varya.'

'Maybe I can,' Howard murmured; he was quite capable of begging. But helping Irina? Hadn't this whole pointless disaster only finally proved what a useless failure he was? There was Saul sitting inside and neither of them with anywhere to go, no ideas. 'Misha, I'm sorry. I'm sorry, I don't think—'

'Wait just one minute. One minute. I have good idea. I have your number on my phone? Yes. Wait. I get Irina to call you. One minute.'

Howard's heart, what was left of it, leapt up in his chest, a burning streak. 'No, no, please.'

'She call you in one minute. Just wait.'

'Misha!' The phone was silent The small yard resumed Howard as he remembered where he was. He turned to check on Saul. Through cloud-images on the window, he could be seen learning racehorses. The cat was still by the door. It looked up at Howard, who turned again, pushed his glasses up his nose and touched his bald spot once more. The weeds shook, up to their waists in concrete. A rag of memory flapped in the image. Where was it? It was the space out by the bins behind Falcon's gym, the weeds that grew around the drain. Places always looked like each other. The phone came alive in his hand. Howard braced himself for the next moment in his life; with a press of his thumb he allowed it to arrive.

'Hello? Hello?'

Howard heard her voice. 'Hello. Is Howard? Is Irina.'

'Is me. Yes.' She had a beautiful voice. He pressed the phone against his ear, squeezing it into him to get all the benefit before he never spoke to her again.

'Howard?'

'Yes.'

'Misha he said me to call you. The little boy, he is well?'

'Yes, he is.' There was a warm furred silence that surrounded her voice, a dark, electrical silence of humming wires. Howard saw it clearly in his mind, saw the line that connected them across many miles.

'That's good. So you can go back and everything be okay.' There was a faint pop on the line, a rush of air.

'Are you smoking?' Howard asked.

'Yes. I am smoking cigarette. Are you?'

'Yes.' Howard lied to match her. To make it more real, he plunged his hand into his pocket to feel his cigarette packet; his hand skated over the unsent letter. 'I didn't know you smoked.'

'Yes, of course. Is bad for you, I know.'

'Terrible. That's why not so many people are doing it any more. Just you and me.'

'Howard—'

He interrupted her. 'I liked your letters, by the way. I'm really sorry, really I am, that I can't help you out.'

'Don't be stupid man. I like your letters too. When Misha read them to me.'

'Oh.' Howard held the frame of his glasses with trembling fingers. 'Did you?'

'I like the one you sent about the garden. You still want to work in gardens?'

'Yes. No. I mean, I don't know if I can ...'

'Because of this?'

'Ay.'

'Maybe prison garden.' She laughed.

Howard did too. 'In my stripy jim-jams,' he added.

'What? Look, Howard, if you make everything okay. Everyone is safe so no one goes to prison. Everything will be like before and you be my husband.'

'I can't,' Howard insisted. He reached into his pocket, this time to take out his cigarettes. Again he felt the letter. 'I can't.'

'Of course. Is easy.'

'No, I can't.'

'Why not?'

'I'm not right. It's not right. I'm not the right person.'

'What are you talking about?' Irina's beautiful voice was strong; it sounded in the centre of Howard's brain. 'What reason have you got? None. So.'

What reason had he got? Howard held the unsent letter in his fingers, the letter that proved him mad, and thought, *What the hell*. He was too tired, too far gone, for evasion. 'You want to know why not?'

'Yes.'

'You want to know why not?'

'I said you yes.'

'Because I'm no good and mixed up. Irina, darling, I wrote you a letter I never sent you. You want to hear it? You want to know?'

'Maybe. Maybe is better I know.'

'Okay, hen. One second.' Howard held the phone in his teeth as he pulled out and unfolded the letter, his words still there, just as he'd written them. 'You still there? I didn't bite through the line?'

'What are you talking? I'm still here, Howard.'

'Good. This is what I wrote.' He read quickly through the opening formalities: '"Dear Irina I hope this letter finds you well in good health and that you are looking forward to coming over as much as I am."' He slowed. '"I think about you all the time at the moment. Although we have sent a lot of letters and cards to each other I still don't feel I really know you. I remember what Misha has told me about you work,"' he corrected his grammar, '"about you working at the post office and live with your brothers and grandmother and I remember your photograph in the stripy dress and voice on the telephone

but it's not the same as actually meeting someone in the flesh."
Are you still there?'

'I am listening. Please, you carry on.'

'Okay. "Do you have parents at all or are you like me? I do
have a father alive but I don't see him and don't want to because
of too much water under the bridge. I want to tell you about
myself because marriage is a big step. I'm tall but I'm not dark
or handsome but I am a stranger!" That's a joke, by the way.'

'Okay.'

'Probably I didn't say it right. "I'm used to being on my own
in a way, at least not with people my own age, just my mother,
and I like being left in peace, so my current situation in
London is a bit different. They are a nice family but I am
worried about the wee" – small, that means small – "boy who
works so hard and has nightmares. But I'm wandering off the
subject."' When writing the letter, it had felt as though he'd
wandered off the subject for some time. It was a surprise to
find that it had only been for a couple of seconds. '"So, I've
kept mostly to myself and I don't mind it although if you can't
sleep it's bad all night with the rain on the roof and just you
in the house and thinking about old things. I've just decided
I'm not" – this is what I wrote – "I've just decided I'm not
going to post this to you so I'll carry on regardless. And now
I'm thinking about you all the time and thinking yes I'd really
like to be your husband even if you don't really want me to be
and even if I keep it a secret all to myself I think I'll love you
whatever and look after you and work hard to have a home
for you to live in after you've been poor. I think about you all
the time and the whole thing is so unbelievable really that it
could be me that I get all breathless, more than usual" – I'm
fat and I smoke – "and I'm bursting to tell someone, to tell
you, but I can't. It's a relief to tell you now even if you'll never
know. There are other things you'll never know and that makes
me think we'll never get married or know each other. But I
dream that we will live together and eventually you'll love me

as much as I love you because I'm devoted and reliable and I'll live a normal life like everyone else and won't feel ashamed all the time. I know this letter doesn't make sense but that's why I'm not sending it. I love you so much, Howard." Well,' he breathed, his hand shaking, 'I've sent it now.'

'What you mean?'

'I told it you. I told you what's in it. You got the letter.'

'Howard?'

'Yes. What?' he snapped. He resented her slow, serene voice as he waited for it to end this moment by making his misery final.

'Howard, I don't understand what is problem.'

'Aw, come on. I just told you.'

'What?'

'Don't you understand what I just told you?'

'No.'

'I just told you that I love you and I think about you all the time even when I'm just supposed to be signing forms for you. All those cards, Irina, I actually meant them.'

'And? That's not problem.'

'Oh, for God's sake. I actually want to be your husband.'

'But that's what I need. I mean we not couple. I not have sex you—'

'Oh Jesus Christ, please, I never meant—'

'But I need husband. If you like me that's not such a big problem.'

'What? What are you saying?'

'You think I want not to come because you are man with big feelings?'

'Please, please.' Howard held his hand against the side of his head. Between the phone and his damp palm his head seemed to have grown light and unstable, a balloon, an eggshell. 'I can't ... and the police'll be here any second. My da's in there getting fucked in front of Richard and Judy, Saul's in a zone of his own—'

'I don't understand what you are saying. Why aren't you listening to me?'

'Look at me. Looked at how I've fucked this all up.'

'Not yet. You go back.'

'Back to prison. Listen, are you really still saying you want to carry on after what I've told you?'

'That was the plan from Misha. Of course we carry on.'

A smile gripped Howard's face; he fought it down. 'I'm a wee bit confused right now,' he said slowly and clearly. 'Can I call you back?'

'Of course.'

'Good.'

'Howard?'

'Yes?'

'Really is all right. You go home.'

'Good bye.'

'Good bye.'

For a moment Howard listened to the silence after she'd hung up, not the warm, black silence of connection, but a silence that was flat and close, a wall. Alone again, with that wild new possibility, if that's what it was, if he could believe it, he had to make the next move. And that before the police arrived. He stepped again through the back door.

Saul looked up. 'Are you ready to go now?'

'Ay.' Howard giggled. 'I don't know what I'm ready to do.'

'So you'll go and tell your dad we're going.'

'Or we could just slip out.'

'Whatever you want.'

'But what do you want to do?'

Saul was exasperated. 'He's your father.'

'Maybe. What's left of him. Better say something, I suppose.'

Donald MacNamee took up a small portion of his sofa, his head rocking slightly as he watched the screen. He looked up at his son only when Howard stood in the way of the picture.

'I can't see,' he said.

'We're going now,' Howard said.

'What?'

'I'm switching it off for a minute.' The TV voices plunged into silence. 'We're going now.' Howard indicated over his shoulder Saul standing in the doorway, one foot on top of the other.

'Oh, ay. Keeping ahead.'

'That's the one.' What to say next? Howard didn't know and he didn't care. Irina filled his mind. His father was old news. Again he heard beer bubbling from the can into his mouth.

His father breathed after. 'I haven't any money, anything. Nothing to steal.'

'There's the telly.'

'Don't take that, come on.'

'I'm not going to take it.'

'Good. Okay then. You all right?'

'Mostly. Oh.' Howard had a thought and rolled up his sleeve. 'See that. That's a scar I got where I got burned.'

Don leaned forward, wobbly-headed, over Howard's wound. 'Looks bad.'

'It was hospital. And that's skin they took from ... other parts of my body.'

'It's amazing what they can do, so it is.'

Howard held on to the fence with both hands, his fingers oddly grouped in the diamonds of wire, the wind whining minutely through the links, pushing at his hair and curling in ticklishly round his glasses. He lowered eyelids that felt worn to a fineness and hot. In the reddish darkness he held himself steady with the fence. His body was light and empty, shut. He swayed on his feet, starting to fall, and opened his eyes to settle the world back into place.

Saul beside him spoke. 'So that was your dad.'

'Yep.'

'He's quite scary.'

'You're telling me.'

'What's wrong with him, then?'

'Drink. And, I don't know, things going against him. But drink.'

'My dad drinks sometimes.'

'Not really, Saul. Not instead of breakfast.'

'No. I suppose not.'

'No. He doesn't. Believe me, you'd know.'

'No. When was the last time you visited?'

'Never. Last saw him years ago.'

'Oh.' Saul also took hold of the wire, threading his small fingers through. 'Will you see him again?'

'Probably not.'

With his mouth open, Saul leaned back, holding himself upright with the fence. 'Why do you think there's barbed wire on top?'

'Stop people getting in. It's dangerous, maybe. Or vandals.'

'It's so big.'

'Ay, well. The ships were huge. Big as anything. Bigger than the pyramids.' Howard quoted what they used to say.

Ten yards in front of them was a pile of broken bricks the size of a house, and stretching behind it the docks with the idle water sleeping in its alleys, the old timber slides and stone steps, derelict machining sheds, a stack of gates, weeds and stone walkways.

'You could get anything here,' Howard said. 'It was like a wee town. Booze, fruit and veg from allotments. Ciggies. Clothes. Anything.'

'Was that the workers selling things to each other?'

'Ay, it was. I saw the queen here once.'

'Don't make things up.'

'I'm no making anything up. She came to launch a ship – you know, when they smash a bottle against the side. I was only wee. I just remember everyone there, all the men and wives in their clothes, everyone, and this woman making a speech through a microphone in this funny English voice, haw-hee-haw-hee-haw, and prayers and everything, blessings, one Catholic and one Proddy, and the launch was the best bit. It was amazing. The ship is huge just huge so it has to go into the river sideways. It goes down a slide, like a whole block of flats just sliding away, and pushes up a huge smooth wave that you watch going across. And then after my mother held me up to see the queen's car go past.' Actually it was his father who had held him up, and through the glass of the spotless black car he'd seen the queen in a round yellow hat smiling – large-toothed, her mouth curved like a bay window – and holding up a motionless hand in a kind of incessant wave, too posh to move it. 'You'll remember that now all your life,' his mother had said after, adjusting her own hat. '"The day I saw the queen."'

Two gulls went overhead calling at each other, loud, big birds. They planed down to the surface of the water, settled, argued, cranked away up.

Howard's thighs really itched from his dirty trousers. A shower wouldn't be good enough. A water cannon might get him clean.

So that was his father. A real man in a real house. And now, after years, it was over. Awful the way things had to happen, one after the other and no way back or across, his father sitting there like something he'd shaken from a box: just how it fell out. 'Would you have worked here?' Saul asked.

'No chance.'

'Really?'

'No. It was all over when I was a kid.'

'Even if you could have?'

'I'd have done something else.'

'Even if you couldn't?'

'Saul.'

'What?'

'Don't confuse me. I'm tired.'

'*You're* tired.'

'Sauly-boy, you'll ask your parents not to put me away, will you?'

'Of course. I'll say it was all my idea and they'll say, "Well, Howard wasn't clever enough to come up with it on his own, so . . ."'

'Cheeky bugger.'

'Look at those big iron rings. Is that where they tied the ships?'

'Maybe. I don't really know. That might not stop your parents, though.'

'No.'

'You have to try, though. You can stop them. They'll be that pleased to see you. You've got to do it, Saul, or I'm in big trouble.'

'I'll try. Of course I'll try.'

'Why don't you get started and call your ma now and tell her you're on your way?'

'How on my way?'

'We'll call the police. They'll take you home. I'll hide. We'll work out a lie about where I am.'

'But I don't want to go without you.'

'But I can't go with you, can I?'

Saul looked up at Howard, at the big, shabby, familiar face, creased with concern, dark against the sky. He really wanted the big man with him.

Howard saw that useless wish in the boy's silent face. 'Can I?' he repeated.

'I don't know.' Saul looked down. 'No.'

Howard, looking back through the links, shook the fence, making short waves across it, like slapping his belly. He didn't want to feel the loss of Saul, the startling, small friend slowly pulled from his side. Neither of them wanted to be alone again. Howard's fingers, crowded on each other, were starting to feel rubbery and dead. He let go and turned back to Saul.

'At least you won't forget any of this.'

'I wouldn't forget it even if I was normal,' Saul answered.

'Neither would I.' Howard pushed his glasses up his nose. 'Go on, then. Call them. Don't be scared. Just remember to ask them not to arrest me. Ask your mother.' Mercy from Barbara seemed a more likely prospect than from Les.

'I'm not scared,' Saul protested, simplifying whatever cocktail of immunity, bravado and dread he did feel. 'They'll be so happy to have me back.'

'Exactly. So call them and it will all be fine.'

'We can always not go back if it isn't.'

'But it will be. They're not like my dad, are they?'

'I don't know. No. Your dad seemed a bit ...'

'Drunk. Now, are you trying to avoid something, eh? Weren't you about to call your folks?'

'Okay, okay, I'm doing it.' Saul pulled out the phone, was quick with his thumbs on the keypad.

Hoping his terror wasn't obvious, Howard turned again to look through the fence at the wind-scuffed water.

Barbara answered. Howard heard her high, tiny ecstasy inside the machine. 'I'm fine, everything's fine,' Saul said into the noise. After a while, her voice slowed and Saul could speak into silence. 'Promise me you won't sue Howard. Promise me. He's been very nice to me.' Howard couldn't hear if he'd got the right response before the voice in the phone deepened. 'It doesn't matter where we are. We're fine. Howard looked after me.' Howard ran his tongue over dry teeth. Saul touched his sleeve. 'He wants to talk to you.'

'No, no, no,' Howard said, receiving the phone into his hand.

'It's all all right,' Saul insisted, which was true for himself. He felt massively relieved by the conversation. He may have failed, have declared himself a failure, and that would be the case forever, and he may have done the worst thing he'd ever done, but it seemed he'd scared his parents into gratitude and passivity. They were just so happy that he was alive.

Howard lifted the hot phone to his ear, holding the fence for support.

'Howard? Howard?'

'Yes,' he whispered.

'Howard, you phenomenal piece of shit, you filthy fucking criminal, I'm going to put you through the grinder for what you've put us through, I'm going to—'

Howard handed the phone back to Saul.

'I'm not coming back if you don't promise—'

Les's voice spattered out of the phone.

'If you don't promise,' Saul repeated. Howard swatted a tear from his nose. 'Yes, yes. I'll call the police now. That's what I said.' Saul's tone was impatient. 'Yes. I said that. I'll be back in the afternoon probably.' His voice quietened. 'Yes, you too. Bye. Bye.' He ended the call. 'It'll be fine. He did promise.'

'Did he?' Howard wiped warm water from his cheeks.

'Yes, he did.'

'Tell him I didn't want them to worry. I made you text them. That was me. I did it … You collapsed, remember. *They* weren't going to help you.'

'He promised. I made him.'

Howard removed his glasses, rubbed his eye sockets with his cuff, put them back on. 'I never meant to—'

'What are you talking about?' Saul was almost angry. He didn't want more confusion after three days of it. Everything was now settled. 'You saved me. I already said that.'

Light! Unbelievable. And air! Rushing in. His voice. Had she known it was him when the phone started ringing? She had. But then she'd felt it was him several times before, only this time it was true. Her son, alive, on his way home. But now it was true! She had heard his voice. The news flew her through the house on weightless feet out into the garden – only the real sky was large enough to hold her. After a minute Les followed. And then his prickly little face was against hers, his arms around her so tightly she could feel his muscles trembling with the strain. The moment was long; it revolved in the air. She felt tears on her cheek, heard more apologies. As though just singing to herself she let it out, told Les her news. His arms tightened again. She didn't know whether he'd truly understood or not. Again she crooned it to herself and it was out there, a kernel of brightness in the greater light, a star at daybreak.

Les kissed her cheek again and again. There. He was there. Everything was right. His son was not dead. From a thousand alleys and apartments of his imagination his mutilated, dead son rose to his feet and started home, his wounds closing, his skin again white. And there was a new child. Could that be right? A new child! He started to choke with the physical confusion of joy. He kissed his wife again and went inside to wash his face.

Barbara stood in the garden and clapped, actually applauded the world, enjoying the stinging contact of her hands together and the exuberant noise travelling into the air. There was a commotion inside. Les must have told Jean. She was running out to congratulate Barbara.

Saul was coming home. Under her heart his sister grew.

Saul was gone. Saul was gone and it was over. Parting had been so difficult that they had both pretended it wasn't really happening, that it was just one element of the plan – when Saul met the police he was to say that Howard had taken a train to Newcastle hours earlier – as though when it was accomplished they would meet up again and carry on. Only when the moment finally came and Howard had to turn and walk from that street corner had he bent down quickly and kissed the side of the boy's face, his lips feeling large and wet against Saul's delicate jawbone. Saul wiped it with his hand, didn't say anything, but squeezed Howard's wrist and turned himself to allow Howard to walk away. Howard could still feel the tingling bracelet of pressure where Saul had held him. No doubt that little boy was the best friend Howard had ever had or would have and Howard missed him a great deal, regretting again that the flight had become Howard's adventure. They should have done more things like going to the zoo, albeit they couldn't because of the police.

Where were the police? Only minutes ago he'd heard the siren of the car that came for Saul. Maybe Saul, weak under their questions, had failed to convince them of the story. Or the man in the hotel had called. Or they were about to pop in on his father. Surely he had to start running. But still he stood alone, unharmed, unseen, returned unwisely to the docks.

Looking out over the bricks and derelict water, Howard fully comprehended that it was all gone, that he was alone. Solitude permeated him slowly, a slow wave that lifted and slightly separated the objects of his confusion. It didn't exactly calm him but it left him entirely at the centre of his situation and not needing words. That was a relief – not needing to talk. Words were so bulky and often sliding in the wrong directions. Not since being with his mother in Burnley had he been completely alone, able to think.

And the first thing he thought of was Irina, her voice in the purring blackness of telecommunication telling him that his letter wasn't demented, that it was allowed, that he could love her, that it didn't matter. He'd be doing it on his own: she had no such feelings. But that was okay. Just to be in a house with someone else and allowed to love her, having dinner after their days at their jobs, or watching television. Would they be in the same house together? He would suggest it as the most sensible thing for legal reasons. The thought of it all staggered him and again he held on to the fence as on to the side of the turning world. If little Les didn't have him sent to prison, it could all happen. Had all his running, all his stupid life up till then, been towards that? What a thought! The thought was so loud in his head that it took him a moment to realise that the other sound was that of a police car pulling up behind him and even then he could have turned and thrown open his arms to embrace them.

PART 4

London, How Irina Met Misha

December 17th

Irina's drink vibrated on her pull-out plastic tray. She took it up again and sipped, allowing a moment for the bubbles – salty, almost painful – to swarm on her tongue and the roof of her mouth. She turned her head and swallowed, looking out of her thick oval of window at the incredible blue and brilliant white cobbles of cloud beneath. Always summer this side of the clouds, even in winter. The water wasn't really helping her headache but sipping was soothingly rhythmical and ordinary. Her headache wasn't really even a proper headache, caused as it was by Irina straining her attention as far as she could into her future, pushing forward in the moment, vexing it to disclose more, and now her vision was glassy, her eye muscles ached, and a small pain had formed just behind her forehead. Now, in the sky, with nothing she could do for a couple of hours, she should be able to relax, to relent back into herself and breathe a little, travelling effortlessly through the sky, but still her shoulders were tight, her hands restless, her eyes hungry. She sipped her water again. She felt she was sipping too quickly, like a bird at a puddle, a little hysterically. She tried to leave a little longer before the next sip but sipped again.

Maybe it was unspent emotion that made her feel so wired. She hadn't wept at the bus station. Her relatives' faces had been wet with emotion, their voices like cellos as they moaned at her departure – all except Yuri, of course, the brother who remained mocking and calm, hopeless himself and never expecting to leave. She had hidden her dry, heated face in her grandmother's neck and moaned back, impatient for the next moment when they'd be gone, she could step onto the bus for the airport, and her new life would start.

The man beside her breathed heavily through fur-lined nostrils. His short fingers held open a novel about Alexander the Great. He wore a striped white and burgundy shirt, a brown tie and a thick bracelet-type watch. Irina tried to distract herself by wondering about him. He had a black leather briefcase with snapping combination latches held upright between his feet. She thought of her own luggage riding in the hold beneath. Just one heavy suitcase with her underwear in the same multiples needed for a holiday. The only thing obviously different about what she carried was the envelope of photos and file of documents, birth certificate, medical records, school certificates. She'd checked them off a list Misha had dictated. Just a little while longer, a matter of minutes, and she'd be seeing Misha again. She would collect her baggage from the place he'd described, walk out through passport control – nothing to worry about; you arrive as a tourist and then apply – and out again through the gates to see Misha and the others waiting to greet her. How long would it take to spot them? That depended on how many people were waiting, people's friends and families with smiles breaking out as the wave of recognition hit, taxi drivers with signs. Maybe Misha would have made a sign. It was the kind of thing he would do, exuberant and artistic. Probably he would have decorated it with flourishes of his art, streaks and flashes of coloured pen. She sipped her water again, finishing it, panicking slightly at just how excited she would be at that moment, how desperate she would be to see everything, everything, everything as they started out through London.

Oh yes, the man next to her. He was probably a businessman who had already moved there. Now, after a visit to his parents, he was returning to his wife and child. Maybe there'd been a death in the family. But he seemed very calm and content. Maybe he was calm because he was English. But no, what was she thinking? He looked so Russian and, stupid, the book he was reading was in Russian. Russian isn't French; people don't speak it unless they have to.

Which reminded her, she must ask Misha and Varya to speak to her in English, otherwise she'd never learn. That was a conversational moment she had envisioned and replayed many times: with Varya and Misha against an unimaginable London background, Irina laughs, throwing her head back a little, saying, 'Otherwise I'll never learn.' All these loops of tape playing in her head, foolish little wishes and expectations.

Eventually the plane declined from its sparkling height, conforming to the order of events, slowly bumping back down into the weather as the seat belt sign came on. Irina didn't need it; her belt was already buckled. Then the whole window was grey and rapid and then again the vapour thinned and Irina could look down and see outlying dull green and red roofs packed together, curving round roads, wider roads, motorways and smaller roads, and buildings, huge numbers of buildings ... and was this it? Was this London? It might be although it didn't really look like a city. She couldn't see any tall buildings. What did it look like? She didn't know. She just looked, through rain now hitting the windows.

And then, in the correct sequence, the plane landed, banging its rear wheels down before slowly levering down the front end and roaring to a stop.

And then she was waiting at the baggage carousel, watching the motion of its overlapping black plastic slats, suddenly very tired. But a hard wakefulness stiffened her as her passport was checked and stamped. And real excitement resumed as she walked out of the gates to meet Misha and Varya, maybe Yelena.

She didn't find the expectant crowd that she had perhaps pasted in from news reports of rock stars arriving at airports and which would have matched the intensity of her mood. The barrier was sparsely populated and Misha had made no sign and it wasn't Varya with him; it was, she assumed, Howard, it must be, the one part of this whole thing she'd tried to block, and moreover she'd actually asked Misha to keep his role as small as possible, his presence infrequent. The man was clearly insane. Her eyes stayed on the tall, fat man even while Misha crushed the air out of her in a hug. 'You brought the lunatic,' she said to Misha. 'Don't worry, don't worry,' he assured her. 'He's under control.' Howard was larger than she'd imagined, his hair a peculiar, chemical red-brown. He stood, hesitating, seemingly fearful and shy but intensely there, as though he was holding back things he wanted to say. He spoke little, though, and was polite, she assumed; his quiet voice was not quite comprehensible. She understood, of course, when he offered her a cigarette and Irina, breaking her resolution to give up as soon as she arrived in Britain, accepted. Misha was talking, of their route home, and not to expect much of the flat, of Varya, and she tuned in and out, looking around at the bright shops and quick people. They started to walk out to catch a bus and Howard took up her case. She couldn't help noticing, as they stepped out through sliding doors into a bitter, damp wind, that Howard, wearing only a shirt and no jumper or coat, didn't seem to feel the cold, like a true Russian.

The Truth about These Strange Times

READING GROUP NOTES

IN BRIEF

Howard had the urge to slap Mr Cox's bald head. It wasn't because he was being told off, it was for the fun of the almighty thwacking sound that one of Howard's meaty palms could produce. Instead, Howard tried to look contrite – he really needed the job after all. He didn't cut the kind of dash that was required at the Burnley fitness centre, and both Howard and Mr Cox knew this. Howard only collected the towels, but his considerable bulk, combined with his unkempt appearance and not entirely clean uniform, wasn't sending out the right message apparently. His timekeeping didn't help either. Howard seemed destined for the chop.

Mrs Dawson seemed to like Howard. He stopped for a chat each time he met the nice old lady in the corridor; but there was something different about her today. What was it? She had no trousers on! Should he say something? But before Howard could marshal his embarrassed thoughts, Mrs Dawson collapsed down the wall and landed in a heap at his feet. The ambulance men wanted Howard to go with

Mrs Dawson to the hospital, though Howard wasn't at all sure about this new centre-of-attention stuff.

The telephone call bringing the news to Les could not have been more unwelcome. Years go by, now she's seriously ill. Just weeks to go to the World Memory Championships; all the training his ten-year-old son Saul still needed, and now this.

It was easier for Howard to tell the hospital he was a relative. It meant he could go and sit with her as often as he liked. It just wasn't the same at home now. His mother had been gradually fading from the house since her death. Now he only really felt her presence when he looked into her wardrobe – that was where he chose to talk to her anyway. Somehow Mrs Dawson was a little like his mother.

♤ ◇ ♧ ♡

Job-wise, though, Howard had sort of fallen on his feet. After the inevitable further appearance before Mr Cox, and the expected marching orders, Howard had explained his precarious position to the local chip-shop owner, and been promptly offered a job!

The close proximity to chips didn't make up for the lower salary however – keeping the bailiffs at bay seemed ever more unlikely.

Then Mrs Dawson died. Howard was back with her at the time after recovering from an unfortunate hot-fat incident. And that was when Howard met Saul. Les was grateful for the care Howard showed his mother, and guilty for the lack of care he had shown, so they all ended up in Les's car giving Howard a lift. Les, his wife Barbara and Saul needed to find a hotel, so Howard directed them to the only one he knew. While Les and Barbara checked in, Howard and Saul played the quiz game in the bar, and an unlikely friendship was born.

And so a sequence of events begins that will take Howard to the London home of his new friends. Howard will garden, inform on a fellow worker, and become involved with Eastern Europeans. But perhaps most importantly of all, Howard will see the effect of the approaching championships on his new friend, and decide on a course of action to save Saul, which will surely doom Howard in the process . . .

ABOUT THE AUTHOR

Adam Foulds is thirty-one years old and lives in South London. He read English at St Catherine's, Oxford, has a Creative Writing MA from UEA and received the Harper-Wood fellowship from St John's College, Cambridge. He is currently working as a warehouse assistant to support his writing and has begun work on his second novel. His poetry, praised by Christopher Reid and Craig Raine, has appeared in magazines such as *Arete*, *Stand* and *Quadrant*. His first poetry volume, a single long poem set during the Mau Mau uprising in Kenya entitled *The Broken Word*, was published in April 2008. *The Truth About These Strange Times* is his first novel.

FOR DISCUSSION

- 'He took the world as it came.' Does Howard change? If he does, what makes him?

- 'The world abrades your finesse away.' What does the author think of the world?

- 'Howard really missed telly. Without it, he couldn't switch off.' Is this a good or bad thing for Howard?

- 'In a good mood, Les had no worries at all.' What does this tell us about Les?

- Who is inside and who is outside?

- 'Was there no one out there who wasn't against him?' Is everyone against Howard?

- What do Saul and Howard have in common?

- What role does the author give to mothers in the novel?

- 'Howard had always liked armour.' Why is Howard vulnerable?

- 'Why wasn't importance visible in the world?' It is, isn't it, sometimes?

- 'So that was his father. A real man in a real house.' Do the characters in the novel see and imagine each other accurately?

SUGGESTED FURTHER READING

Gifted by Nikita Lalwani

Careless by Deborah Robertson

The Outcast by Sadie Jones

According to Ruth by Jane Feaver

Broken by Daniel Clay